HUNTERS OF DUNE

THE DUNE SERIES

BY FRANK HERBERT

Dune
Dune Messiah
Children of Dune
God Emperor of Dune
Heretics of Dune
Chapterhouse: Dune

BY FRANK HERBERT, BRIAN HERBERT, AND KEVIN J. ANDERSON

The Road to Dune (includes original short novel *Spice Planet*)

BY BRIAN HERBERT AND KEVIN J. ANDERSON

Dune: House Atreides
Dune: House Harkonnen
Dune: House Corrino

Dune: The Butlerian Jihad
Dune: The Machine Crusade
Dune: The Battle of Corrin

Hunters of Dune
Sandworms of Dune (forthcoming)
Paul of Dune (forthcoming)

BY BRIAN HERBERT

Dreamer of Dune
(biography of Frank Herbert)

HUNTERS OF DUNE

Brian Herbert &
Kevin J. Anderson

Based on an outline by Frank Herbert

HODDER &
STOUGHTON

First published in Great Britain in 2006 by Hodder & Stoughton
A division of Hodder Headline

The right of Brian Herbert and Kevin J. Anderson to be identified as
the Authors of the Work has been asserted by them in accordance
with the Copyright, Designs and Patents Act 1988.

A Hodder & Stoughton Book

1

A CIP catalogue record for this title is available from the British Library

Hardback ISBN-10 0 340 83747 0
Hardback ISBN-13 9 780 340 83847 4
Trade paperback ISBN-10 0 340 83748 9
Trade paperback ISBN-13 9 780 340 83748 1

Printed and bound by Mackays of Chatham Ltd, Chatham, Kent

Hodder Headline's policy is to use papers that are natural,
renewable and recyclable products and made from wood grown in
sustainable forests. The logging and manufacturing processes are expected
to conform to the environmental regulations of the country of origin.

Hodder & Stoughton Ltd
A division of Hodder Headline
338 Euston Road
London NW1 3BH

To Tom Doherty

Whose support and enthusiasm for the Dune universe—and for us as authors—has been unflagging. A dedicated publisher and perceptive businessman, Tom is a longtime Dune fan and was a good friend to Frank Herbert.

ACKNOWLEDGMENTS

As with all of our previous Dune novels, we have depended on the efforts of a great many people to make the manuscript as good as possible. We would like to thank Pat LoBrutto, Tom Doherty, and Paul Stevens at Tor Books; Carolyn Caughey at Hodder & Stoughton; Catherine Sidor, Louis Moesta, and Diane Jones at WordFire, Inc. Byron Merritt and Mike Anderson put in a great deal of work on the dunenovels.com Web site. Alex Paskie offered in-depth advice on Jewish philosophy and traditions, and Dr. Attila Torkos worked very hard on fact-checking and consistency.

In addition, we have had many supporters of the new Dune novels, including John Silbersack, Robert Gottlieb, and Claire Roberts at Trident Media Group; Richard Rubinstein, Mike Messina, John Harrison, and Emily Austin-Bruns at New Amsterdam Entertainment; Penny and Ron Merritt, David Merritt, Julie Herbert, Robert Merritt, Kimberly Herbert, Margaux Herbert, and Theresa Shackelford at Herbert Properties LLC.

And as always, these books would not exist without the unending help and support from our wives, Janet Herbert and Rebecca Moesta Anderson, or the original genius of Frank Herbert.

AUTHORS' NOTE

We wish Frank Herbert could have been here to write this book.

After the publication of *Heretics of Dune* (1984) and *Chapterhouse: Dune* (1985), he had much more in mind for the story, a fantastic grand climax to the epic Dune Chronicles. Anyone who has read *Chapterhouse* knows the excruciating cliffhanger ending.

The last novel Frank Herbert wrote, *Man of Two Worlds*, was a collaboration with Brian, and the two of them discussed working on future Dune books together, particularly the story of the Butlerian Jihad. However, with the beautiful dedication and coda that Frank wrote at the end of *Chapterhouse*, a loving tribute to his wife, Beverly, Brian originally thought that the Dune Chronicles should end there. As he explained in *Dreamer of Dune*, the biography of Frank Herbert, his parents had been a writing team, and they were gone. So Brian left the series untouched for many years.

In 1997, more than a decade after the death of his father, Brian began to discuss with Kevin J. Anderson the possibility of completing the project, of writing the fabled *Dune 7*. But apparently Frank Herbert had left no notes, and we thought we would have to do the project based solely on our own imaginations. After further discussions, we realized that a great deal of preliminary work needed to be completed before we could tackle *Dune 7*—not just laying groundwork for the story itself, but also reintroducing the book-buying audience and a whole new generation of readers to the incredible, highly imaginative Dune universe.

More than twenty years have passed since the publication of *Chapterhouse: Dune*. While many readers loved the original classic *Dune* or even the first three books in the series, a significant portion of the audience had not continued all the way through to that last book. We needed to reawaken interest and get those readers prepared.

We decided to write a trilogy of prequels first—the Prelude series of *House Atreides, House Harkonnen,* and *House Corrino.* When we began to dig through all of Frank Herbert's stored papers in preparation for writing *House Atreides,* Brian was surprised to learn of two safe-deposit boxes that his father had taken out before his death. Inside the boxes, Brian and an estate attorney discovered a dot-matrix printout and two old-style computer disks labeled "Dune 7 Outline" and "Dune 7 Notes"—pages describing exactly where the creator of Dune had intended to take his story.

Reading this material, we saw instantly that *Dune 7* would be a magnificent culmination of the series, tying together the history and the characters we all knew in an exciting plot with many twists, turns, and surprises. In storage we also discovered additional notes and papers describing characters and their histories, pages of unused epigraphs, and outlines for other works.

Now that we had a road map in front of us, we plunged into the Prelude to Dune trilogy, which followed the stories of Duke Leto and Lady Jessica, the evil Baron Harkonnen, and the planetologist Pardot Kynes. After that trilogy, we wrote the Legends of Dune—*The Butlerian Jihad, The Machine Crusade,* and *The Battle of Corrin*—which introduced the seminal conflicts and events that form the foundations of the whole Dune universe.

Indisputably, Frank Herbert was a genius. *Dune* is the best-selling and most beloved science fiction novel of all time. From the beginning of our monumental task, we realized that it would not only be impossible, but also foolish, to attempt to imitate Frank Herbert's writing style. Both of us were strongly influenced by his writing, and some fans have remarked on certain similarities in style. However, we consciously chose to write these books to capture the feel and scope of *Dune,* using aspects of Frank Herbert's style, but with our own pacing and syntax.

We are pleased to report that since the publication of *House Atreides,* the sales of Frank Herbert's original Dune Chronicles have gone up dramatically. Two six-hour TV miniseries starring William Hurt and Susan Sarandon—*Frank Herbert's Dune* and *Frank Herbert's Children of*

Dune—have been broadcast to large audiences and wide acclaim (as well as winning Emmy Awards). They are two of the three most-watched shows in the history of the Sci-Fi Channel.

At last, after more than nine years of preparation, we feel the time is right for *Dune 7*. Upon poring over Frank Herbert's outline and notes, we realized that the breadth and scope of the story would have resulted in a novel of more than 1,300 pages. For this reason, the story is being presented in two volumes, *Hunters of Dune* and the forthcoming *Sandworms of Dune*.

Much more of the epic remains to be written, and we intend to create additional exciting novels, telling other parts of the grand, brilliant tale that Frank Herbert laid out. The saga of Dune is far from over!

—Brian Herbert and Kevin J. Anderson, April 2006

Following the 3,500-year reign of the Tyrant Leto II, an empire was left to fend for itself. During the Famine Times and the subsequent Scattering, the remnants of the human race cast themselves far into the wilderness of space. They fled to unknown realms where they sought riches and safety, to no avail. For fifteen hundred years these survivors and their descendants endured terrible hardships, a whole reorganization of humanity.

Stripped of its energy and resources, the ancient government of the Old Empire fell away. New power groups took root and grew strong, but never again would humans allow themselves to depend upon a monolithic leader or a key, finite substance. Single points of failure.

Some say the Scattering was Leto II's Golden Path, a crucible in which to strengthen the human race forever, to teach us a lesson we could not forget. But how could one man—even a man-god who was partially a sandworm—willingly inflict such suffering upon his children? Now that descendants of the Lost Ones are returning from the Scattering, we can only imagine the true horrors our brothers and sisters faced out there.

—Guild Bank Records, Gammu Branch

Even the most learned of us cannot imagine the scope of the Scattering. As a historian, I am dismayed to think of all the knowledge that has been lost forever, the accurate records of triumphs and tragedies. Entire civilizations rose and fell while out there those who remained in the Old Empire sat in complacency.

New weapons and technologies were spawned by the hardships of the Famine Times. What enemies did we inadvertently create? What religions, distortions, and social processes did the Tyrant set in motion? We can never know, and I fear that this ignorance will come back to haunt us.

—SISTER TAMALANE, Chapterhouse Archives

Our own estranged brothers, those Lost Tleilaxu who vanished in the turmoil of the Scattering, have come back to us. But they are changed in fundamental ways. They bring an improved strain of Face Dancers with them, asserting that they designed these shape-shifters themselves. My analysis of the Lost Tleilaxu, however, indicates that they are clearly inferior to us. They cannot even create spice from axlotl tanks, but they claim to have developed superior Face Dancers? How can that be?

And the Honored Matres. They make overtures of alliance, yet their actions show only brutality and the enslavement of conquered peoples. They have destroyed Rakis! How can we have faith in them, or in the Lost Tleilaxu?

—MASTER SCYTALE,
sealed notes found in burned lab on Tleilax

Duncan Idaho and Sheeana have stolen our no-ship and flown off to points unknown. They took with them many heretical Sisters, even the ghola of our Bashar Miles Teg. With our newly forged alliance, I am tempted to command all Bene Gesserits and Honored Matres to turn their attention to recapturing this ship and its valuable passengers.

But I will not. Who can find a no-ship out in the vast universe? More importantly, we can never forget that a far more dangerous Enemy is coming for us.

—Emergency message from
MURBELLA, REVEREND MOTHER SUPERIOR
AND GREAT HONORED MATRE

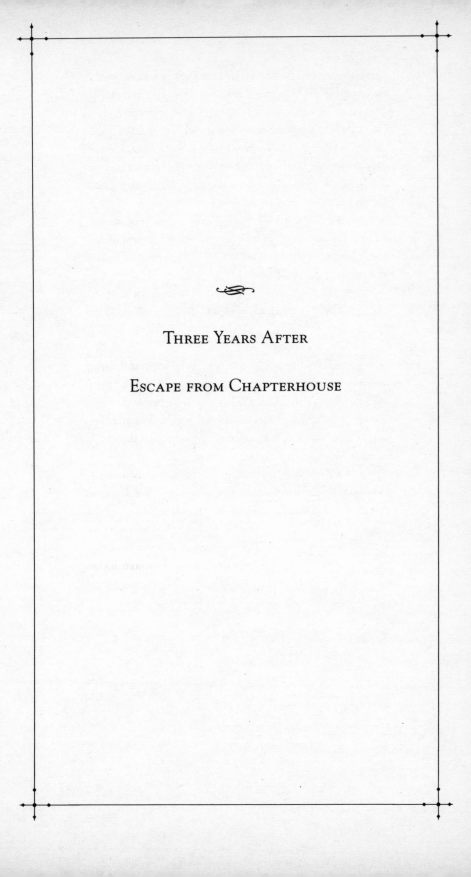

THREE YEARS AFTER

ESCAPE FROM CHAPTERHOUSE

Memory is a weapon sharp enough to inflict deep wounds.
—The Mentat's Lament

On the day he died, Rakis—the planet commonly known as Dune—died with him.

Dune. Lost forever!

In the archives chamber of the fleeing no-ship *Ithaca*, the ghola of Miles Teg reviewed the desert world's final moments. Melange-scented steam wafted from a stimulant beverage at his left elbow, but the thirteen-year-old ignored it, descending instead into deep Mentat focus. These historical records and holo-images held great fascination for him.

This was where and how his original body had been killed. How an entire world had been murdered. Rakis . . . the legendary desert planet, now no more than a charred ball.

Projected above a flat table, the archival images showed Honored Matre war vessels gathering above the mottled tan globe. The immense, undetectable no-ships—like the stolen one on which Teg and his fellow refugees now lived—wielded firepower superior to anything the Bene Gesserit had ever employed. Traditional atomics were little more than a pinprick by comparison.

Those new weapons must have been developed out in the Scattering. Teg pursued a Mentat projection. Human ingenuity born out of desperation? Or was it something else entirely?

In the floating image, the bristling ships opened fire, unleashing incineration waves with devices the Bene Gesserit had since named "Obliterators." The bombardment had continued until the planet was devoid of life. The sandy dunes were turned to black glass; even Rakis's atmosphere caught fire. Giant worms and sprawling cities, people and sand plankton, everything annihilated. Nothing could have survived down there, not even him.

Now, nearly fourteen years later and in a vastly changed universe, the gangly teenager adjusted the study chair to a more comfortable height. *Reviewing the circumstances of my own death. Again.*

By strict definition, Teg was a clone rather than a ghola grown of cells gathered from a dead body, though the latter was the word most people used to describe him. Inside his young flesh lived an old man, a veteran of numerous campaigns for the Bene Gesserit; he could not remember the last few moments of his life, but these records left little doubt.

The senseless annihilation of Dune demonstrated the true ruthlessness of the Honored Matres. *Whores,* the Sisterhood called them. And with good reason.

Nudging the intuitive finger controls, he called up the images yet again. It felt odd to be an outside observer, knowing that he himself had been down there fighting and dying when these images were recorded. . . .

Teg heard a sound at the door of the archives and saw Sheeana watching him from the corridor. Her face was lean and angular, her skin brown from a Rakian heritage. The unruly umber hair flashed with streaks of copper from a childhood spent under the desert sun. Her eyes were the total blue of lifelong melange consumption, as well as the Spice Agony that had turned her into a Reverend Mother. The youngest ever to survive, Teg had been told.

Sheeana's generous lips held an elusive smile. "Studying battles again, Miles? It's a bad thing for a military commander to be so predictable."

"I have a great many of them to review," Teg answered in his cracking young man's voice. "The Bashar accomplished a great deal in three hundred standard years, before I died."

When Sheeana recognized the projected record, her expression fell into a troubled mask. Teg had been watching those images of Rakis to the point of obsession, ever since they fled into this bizarre and uncharted universe.

"Any word from Duncan yet?" he asked, trying to divert her attention. "He was attempting a new navigation algorithm to get us away from—"

"We know exactly where we are." Sheeana lifted her chin in an unconscious gesture she had come to use more and more often since becoming the leader of this group of refugees. "We are *lost*."

Teg automatically intercepted the criticism of Duncan Idaho. It had been their intent to prevent anyone—the Honored Matres, the corrupted Bene Gesserit order, or the mysterious Enemy—from finding the ship. "At least we're safe."

Sheeana did not seem convinced. "So many unknowns trouble me, where are we, who is chasing us . . ." Her voice trailed off, and then she said, "I will leave you to your studies. We are about to have another meeting to discuss our situation."

He perked up. "Has anything changed?"

"No, Miles. And I expect the same arguments over and over again." She shrugged. "The other Sisters seem to insist on it." With a quiet rustle of robes, she exited the archives chamber, leaving him with the humming silence of the great invisible ship.

Back to Rakis. Back to my death . . . and the events leading up to it. Teg rewound the recordings, gathering old reports and perspectives, and watched them yet again, traveling farther backward in time.

Now that his memories had been awakened, he knew what he had done up to his death. He did not need these records to see how the old Bashar Teg had gotten into such a predicament on Rakis, how he himself had provoked it. Back then, he and his loyal men—veterans of his many famous military campaigns—had stolen a no-ship on Gammu, a planet that history had once called Giedi Prime, homeworld of the evil but long-exterminated House Harkonnen.

Years earlier, Teg had been brought in to guard the young ghola of Duncan Idaho, after eleven previous Duncan gholas had been assassinated. The old Bashar succeeded in keeping the twelfth alive until adulthood and finally restored Duncan's memories, then helped him escape from Gammu. When one of the Honored Matres, Murbella, tried to sexually enslave Duncan, he instead trapped *her* with unsuspected abilities wired into him by his Tleilaxu creators. It turned out that Duncan was a living weapon specifically designed to thwart the Honored Matres. No wonder the enraged whores were so desperate to find and kill him.

After slaughtering hundreds of Honored Matres and their minions, the old Bashar hid among men who had sworn their lives to protect him. No great general had commanded such loyalty since Paul Muad'Dib, perhaps not even since the fanatical days of the Butlerian Jihad. Amidst drinks, food, and misty-eyed nostalgia, the Bashar had explained that he needed them to steal a no-ship for him. Though the task seemed impossible, the veterans never questioned a thing.

Ensconced in the archives now, young Miles reviewed surveillance records from Gammu's spaceport security, images taken from tall Guild Bank buildings in the city. Each step of the assault made perfect sense to him, even as he studied the records many years later. *It was the only way to succeed, and we accomplished it. . . .*

After flying to Rakis, Teg and his men had found Reverend Mother Odrade and Sheeana riding a giant old worm to meet the no-ship out in the great desert. Time was short. The vengeful Honored Matres would be coming, apoplectic because the Bashar had made fools of them on Gammu. On Rakis, he and his surviving men departed the no-ship with armored vehicles and extra weapons. Time for one last, but vital, engagement.

Before the Bashar led his loyal soldiers out to face the whores, Odrade casually but expertly scratched the skin of his leathery neck, not-so-subtly collecting cell samples. Both Teg and the Reverend Mother understood it was the Sisterhood's last chance to preserve one of the greatest military minds since the Scattering. They realized he was about to die. Miles Teg's final battle.

By the time the Bashar and his men clashed with Honored Matres on the ground, other groups of the whores were swiftly taking over the Rakian population centers. They slew the Bene Gesserit Sisters who remained behind in Keen. They killed the Tleilaxu Masters and the Priests of the Divided God.

The battle was already lost, but Teg and his troops hurled themselves against the enemy defenses with unparalleled violence. Since Honored Matre hubris would not allow them to accept such humiliation, the whores retaliated against the whole world, destroying everything and everyone there. Including him.

In the meantime, the old Bashar's fighters had created a diversion so the no-ship could escape, carrying Odrade, the Duncan ghola, and Sheeana, who had tempted the ancient sandworm into the vessel's cavernous cargo hold. Soon after the ship flew to safety, Rakis was destroyed—and that worm became the last of its kind.

That had been Teg's first life. His real memories ended there.

WATCHING IMAGES OF the final bombardment now, Miles Teg wondered at what point his original body had been obliterated. Did it really matter? Now that he was alive again, he had a second chance.

Using the cells Odrade had taken from his neck, the Sisterhood grew a copy of their Bashar and triggered his genetic memories. The Bene Gesserit knew they would require his tactical genius in the war with the Honored Matres. And the boy Teg had indeed led the Sisterhood to its victory on Gammu and Junction. He had done everything they asked of him.

Later, he and Duncan, along with Sheeana and her dissidents, had stolen the no-ship yet again and fled from Chapterhouse, unable to bear what Murbella was allowing to happen to the Bene Gesserit. Better than anyone else, the escapees understood about the mysterious Enemy that continued to hunt for them, no matter how lost the no-ship might be. . . .

Weary with facts and forced memories, Teg switched off the records, stretched his thin arms, and left the archives sector. He would spend several hours in vigorous physical training, then work on his weapons skills.

Though he lived in the body of a thirteen-year-old, it was his job to remain ready for everything, and never lower his guard.

Why ask a man who is already lost to lead you? Why then are you surprised if he leads you nowhere?

—DUNCAN IDAHO,
A Thousand Lives

They were adrift. They were safe. They were lost.

An unidentifiable ship in an unidentifiable universe.

Alone on the navigation bridge, as he often was, Duncan Idaho knew that powerful enemies were still after them. Threats within threats within threats. The no-ship wandered the frigid void, far from any recorded human exploration. A different universe entirely. He couldn't decide whether they were hiding or trapped. He wouldn't have known how to get back to a familiar star system, even if he'd wanted to.

According to the bridge's independent chronometers, they had been in this strange, distorted otherwhere for years . . . though who could say how time flowed in another universe? The laws of physics and the landscape of the galaxy might be completely altered here.

Abruptly, as if his concerns had been laced with prescience, he noticed the main instrument panel blinking erratically, while the stabilizing engines surged up and down. Though he couldn't see anything more unusual than the now-familiar twistings of gases and distorted energy ripples, the no-ship had encountered what he'd come to think of as a "rough patch." How could they encounter turbulence in space when nothing was *there?*

The ship shook in a whiplash of strange gravity, jarred by a spray of high-energy particles. When Duncan switched off the automatic piloting systems and altered course, the situation worsened. Barely perceptible flashes of orange light appeared in front of the vessel, like a faint, flickering fire. He felt the deck shudder, as if he had rammed into some obstacle, but he could see nothing. Nothing at all! It should have been an empty vacuum, giving them no sensation of movement or turbulence. Strange universe.

Duncan corrected course until the instruments and engines smoothed out, and the flashes disappeared. If the danger grew any worse, he might be forced to attempt yet another risky foldspace jump. Upon leaving Chapterhouse, he had flown the no-ship without guidance, having purged all navigation systems and coordinate files, using nothing but his intuition and rudimentary prescience. Each time he activated the Holtzman engines, Duncan gambled with the whole ship, and the lives of the 150 refugees aboard. He wouldn't do it unless he had to.

Three years ago, he'd had no choice. Duncan had lifted the great craft from its landing field—not escaping per se, but stealing the entire prison where the Sisterhood had put him. And simply flying away wasn't sufficient. In his attuned mind, he had seen the trap closing around them. The Outside Enemy observers, in their bizarrely innocuous guises of an old man and an old woman, had a net they could cast across vast distances to entangle the no-ship. He'd seen the sparkling multicolored mesh begin to contract, and the strange old couple smiling with victory. They had thought he and the no-ship were in their grasp.

His fingers a blur, his concentration sharp as a diamond chip, Duncan had made the Holtzman engines do things that not even a Guild Navigator would ask of them. As the Enemy's invisible web ensnared the no-ship, Duncan had flung them away, flying the enormous vessel so deeply into the folds of space that he tore the fabric of the universe itself and slid beyond. His ancient Swordmaster training had come to his aid. *Like a slow blade slipping through an otherwise impenetrable body shield.*

And the no-ship had found itself somewhere else entirely. But he had remained vigilant, not allowing himself to breathe a sigh of relief. In this incomprehensible universe, what might be next?

Now he studied external images transmitted from sensors extended beyond the no-field. The view outside had not changed: twisted veils of nebula gas, inside-out streamers that would never condense into stars. Was this a young universe, not yet finished coalescing, or a universe so unspeakably ancient that all suns had burned out and been reduced to molecular ash?

The group of misfit refugees desperately wanted to get back to normal . . . or at the very least to somewhere *else*. Over such a long time, their fear and anxiety had faded first to confusion, then to restlessness and malaise. They wanted more than simply being lost and unharmed. Either they looked to Duncan Idaho with hope, or they blamed him for their plight.

The ship contained a hodgepodge of humanity's factions (or did Sheeana and her Bene Gesserit Sisters view them all as mere "specimens?"). The assortment included a sprinkling of orthodox Bene Gesserits—acolytes, proctors, Reverend Mothers, even male workers— along with Duncan himself and the young Miles Teg ghola. Also aboard were a Rabbi and his group of Jews who had been rescued from an attempted Honored Matre pogrom on Gammu; one surviving Tleilaxu Master; and four animalistic Futars—monstrous human-feline hybrids created out in the Scattering and enslaved by the whores. In addition, the great hold was home to seven small sandworms.

Truly, we are a strange mixture. A ship of fools.

A year after escaping from Chapterhouse and becoming mired in this distorted and incomprehensible universe, Sheeana and her Bene Gesserit followers had joined Duncan in a christening ceremony. In light of the no-ship's endless wanderings, the name *Ithaca* seemed appropriate.

Ithaca, a small island in ancient Greece, had been the home of Odysseus, who had spent ten years wandering after the end of the Trojan War, trying to find his way back home. Similarly, Duncan and his companions needed a place to call home, a safe haven. These people were on their own great odyssey, and without so much as a map or a star chart, Duncan was as lost as age-old Odysseus.

No one realized how much Duncan longed to go back to Chapter-house. Heartstrings linked him to Murbella, his love, his slave, and his master. Breaking free of her had been the single most difficult and painful endeavor he could remember in his multiple lifetimes. He doubted he would ever entirely recover from her. *Murbella* . . .

Yet Duncan Idaho had always placed duty above personal feelings. Regardless of the heartache, he assumed responsibility for keeping the no-ship and its passengers safe, even in a skewed universe.

At odd times, stray combinations of odors reminded him of Murbella's distinctive scent. Organic esters that drifted through the no-ship's processed air would strike his olfactory receptors, triggering memories from their eleven years together. Murbella's perspiration, her dark amber hair, the particular taste of her lips, and the seawater scent of their "sexual collisions." Their passionate, codependent encounters had been both intimate and violent for years, with neither of them strong enough to break free.

I must not confuse mutual addiction with love. The pain was at least as sharp and unendurable as the debilitating agony of drug withdrawal. Hour by hour as the no-ship flew through the void, Duncan drew farther from her.

He leaned back and opened his unique senses, reaching out, always wary that someone might find the no-ship. The danger in letting himself do this passive sentry duty was that he occasionally descended into muddled woolgathering about Murbella. To get around the problem, Duncan compartmentalized his Mentat mind. If a portion of it drifted, another portion was always alert, always on the lookout for danger.

In their years together, he and Murbella had produced four daughters. The oldest two—twins—would be nearly grown now. But from the moment the Agony had transformed his Murbella into a true Bene Gesserit, she had been lost to him. Because an Honored Matre had never before completed training—actually, *retraining*—to become a Bene Gesserit Reverend Mother, the Sisterhood had been exceptionally pleased with her. Duncan's shattered heart had been, and still was, merely collateral damage.

In his mind's eye, Murbella's lovely countenance haunted him. His Mentat abilities—both a skill and a curse—allowed him to call up every detail of her features: her oval face and wide brow, the hard green eyes that reminded him of jade, the willowy body that could fight and make love with equal prowess. Then he remembered that her green eyes had become blue after the spice Agony. Not the same person . . .

His thoughts wandered, and Murbella's features shifted in his mind. Like an afterimage burned onto his retinas, another woman began to take shape, and he was startled. This was an outside presence, a mind immeasurably superior to his own, searching for him, wrapping gentle strands around the *Ithaca*.

Duncan Idaho, a voice called, soothing and feminine.

He felt a rush of emotions, as well as an awareness of danger. Why hadn't his Mentat sentry system seen this coming? His compartmentalized mind snapped into full survival mode. He jumped toward the Holtzman controls, intending once again to fling the no-ship far away, without guidance.

The voice tried to intercede. *Duncan Idaho, do not flee. I am not your enemy.*

The old man and woman had made similar assurances. Though he had no idea who they were, Duncan did comprehend that *they* were the real danger. But this new muliebral presence, this vast intellect, had touched him from outside of the strange, unidentified universe that the no-ship currently inhabited. He struggled to get away but could not escape the voice.

I am the Oracle of Time.

In several of his lives, Duncan had heard of the Oracle—the guiding force of the Spacing Guild. Benevolent and all-seeing, the Oracle of Time was said to be a shepherding presence that had watched over the Guild since its formation fifteen thousand years ago. Duncan had always considered it an odd manifestation of religion among the hyperacute Navigators.

"The Oracle is a myth." His fingers hovered over the touchpads of the command console.

I am many things. He was surprised when the voice did not contradict his accusation. *Many seek you. You will be found here.*

"I trust in my own abilities." Duncan powered up the foldspace engines. From her external point of view, he hoped the Oracle wouldn't notice what he was doing. He would take the no-ship some-where else, fleeing again. How many different powers were hunting them?

The future demands your presence. You have a role to play in Kralizec.

Kralizec . . . typhoon struggle . . . the long-foretold battle at the end of the universe that would forever change the shape of the future.

"Another myth," Duncan said, even as he activated the foldspace jump without warning the other passengers. He couldn't risk staying here. The no-ship lurched, then plunged once more into the unknown.

He heard the voice fading as the ship escaped the Oracle's clutches, but she did not seem dismayed. *Here*, the distant voice said, *I will guide you.* The intruding voice faded, ripping away like shreds of cotton.

The *Ithaca* careened through foldspace and, after an interminably brief instant, tumbled out again.

Stars shone all around the ship. Real stars. Duncan studied the sen-sors, checked the navigation grid, and saw the sparkles of suns and nebulae. Normal space again. Without further verification he knew that they had fallen back into their own universe. He couldn't decide whether to rejoice or cry out in despair.

Duncan no longer sensed the Oracle of Time, nor could he detect any of the likely searchers—the mysterious Enemy and the unified Sisterhood—though they must still be out there. They would not have given up, not even after three years.

The no-ship continued to run.

The strongest and most altruistic leader, even if his office is dependent on the support of the masses, must look first to the dictates of his heart, never allowing his decisions to be swayed by popular opinion. It is only through courage and strength of character that a true and memorable legacy is ever attained.

—from "Collected Sayings of Muad'Dib" by the
PRINCESS IRULAN

Like a dragon empress surveying her subjects, Murbella sat on a high throne in the large receiving hall of the Bene Gesserit Keep. Early morning sunlight poured through the tall stained-glass windows, splashing colors around the chamber.

Chapterhouse was the center of a most peculiar civil war. Reverend Mothers and Honored Matres came together with all the finesse of colliding spacecraft. Murbella—following Odrade's grand plan—allowed them no other option. Chapterhouse was home to both groups now.

Each faction hated Murbella for the changes she had imposed, and neither had the strength to defy her. Through their union, the conflicting philosophies and societies of the Honored Matres and the Bene Gesserits merged like horrific Siamese twins. The very concept was appalling to many of them. The potential for reigniting bloodshed always hung in the air, and the forced alliance teetered on the edge of failure.

That was a gamble some in the Sisterhood had not been willing to accept. "Survival at the cost of destroying ourselves is no survival at all," Sheeana had said just before she and Duncan took the no-ship and flew away. "Voting with their feet," as the old saying went. *Oh, Duncan!* Was it possible that Mother Superior Odrade had not guessed what Sheeana planned to do?

Of course I knew, said the voice of Odrade from Other Memory. *Sheeana hid it from me for a long time, but in the end I knew.*

"And you chose not to warn me of it?" Murbella often sparred aloud with the voice of her predecessor, one of the many ancestral inner voices she could access since becoming a Reverend Mother.

I chose to warn no one. Sheeana made her decisions for her own reasons.

"And now we must both live with the consequences."

From her throne, Murbella watched the guards lead in a female prisoner. Another disciplinary matter for her to handle. Another *example* she must make. Though such demonstrations appalled the Bene Gesserits, the Honored Matres appreciated their value.

This situation was more important than others, so Murbella would handle it personally. She smoothed her shimmering black-and-gold robe across her lap. Unlike the Bene Gesserits, who understood their places and required no ostentatious symbols of rank, Honored Matres demanded gaudy signs of status, like extravagant thrones or chairdogs, ornate capes in vivid colors. Thus, the self-proclaimed Mother Commander was forced to sit on an imposing throne encrusted with soostones and firegems.

Enough to purchase a major planet, she thought, *if there were any I wanted to buy.*

Murbella had come to hate the trappings of office, but she knew the necessity. Women in the different costumes of the two orders attended her constantly, alert for any sign of weakness in her. Though they underwent training in the ways of the Sisterhood, Honored Matres clung to their traditional garments, serpent-scribed capes and scarves, and formfitting leotard bodysuits. By contrast, the Bene Gesserits shunned bright colors and covered themselves with dark, loose robes. The disparity was as clear as that between gaudy peacocks and camouflaged bush wrens.

The prisoner, an Honored Matre named Annine, had short blond hair and wore a canary yellow leotard with a flamboyant cape of sapphire plazsilk moire. Electronic restraints kept her arms folded across her midsection, as if she wore an invisible straitjacket; a nerve-deadening gag muzzled her mouth. Annine struggled ineffectively against the restraints, and her attempts to speak came out as unintelligible grunts.

Guards positioned the rebellious woman at the foot of the steps below the throne. Murbella focused on the wild eyes that screamed defiance at her. "I no longer wish to hear what you have to say, Annine. You have already said too much."

This woman had criticized the Mother Commander's leadership once too often, holding her own meetings and railing against the merging of Honored Matres and Bene Gesserits. Some of Annine's followers had even disappeared from the main city and established their own base in the uninhabited northern territories. Murbella could not allow such a provocation to pass unchallenged.

The way Annine had handled her dissatisfaction—embarrassing Murbella and diminishing her authority and prestige from behind a cloak of cowardly anonymity—had been unforgivable. The Mother Commander knew Annine's type well enough. No negotiation, no compromise, no appeal for understanding would ever change her mind. The woman defined herself through her opposition.

A *waste of human raw material*. Murbella flashed an expression of disgust. If Annine had only turned her anger against a real enemy . . .

Women of both factions observed from either side of the great hall. The two groups were reluctant to mix, instead separating into "whores" on one side and "witches" on the other. *Like oil and water.*

In the years since forcing this unification, Murbella had come through numerous situations in which she might have been killed, but she eluded every trap, sliding, adapting, administering harsh punishments.

Her authority over these women was wholly legitimate: She was both Reverend Mother Superior, selected by Odrade, as well as Great Honored Matre by virtue of assassinating her predecessor. She had chosen the title of Mother Commander for herself to symbolize the integration of the two important ranks, and as time passed, she noticed that the women had all become rather protective of her. Murbella's lessons were having the desired effect, albeit slowly.

Following the seesaw battle on Junction, the only way for the embattled Sisterhood to survive the violence of the Honored Matres had been to let them *believe* they were victorious. In a philosophical turnabout, the captors actually became captives before they realized it; Bene Gesserit knowledge, training, and wiles subsumed their competitors' rigid beliefs. In most cases.

At a hand signal, the Mother Commander caused her guards to tighten Annine's restraints. The woman's face contorted in pain.

Murbella descended the polished steps, never taking her eyes off the captive. Reaching the floor, Murbella glared down at the shorter woman. It pleased her to see the eyes change, filling with fear instead of defiance as realization swept over her.

Honored Matres rarely bothered to hold back their emotions, choosing instead to exploit them. They found that a provocative feral expression, a clear indication of anger and danger, could make their victims prone to submission. In sharp contrast, Reverend Mothers considered emotions a weakness and controlled them rigidly.

"Over the years, I have met many challengers and killed them all," Murbella said. "I dueled with Honored Matres who did not acknowledge my rule. I stood up to Bene Gesserits who refused to accept what I am doing. How much more blood and time must I waste on this nonsense when we have a real Enemy hunting us?"

Without releasing Annine's restraints or loosening her gag, Murbella brought forth a gleaming dagger from her sash and thrust it into Annine's throat. No ceremony or dignity . . . no wasting of time.

The guards held the dying prisoner up as she twitched and thrashed and gurgled half words, then slumped over, her eyes glassy and dead. Annine hadn't even made a mess on the floor.

"Remove her." Murbella wiped the knife on the victim's plazsilk cape, then resumed her seat on the throne. "I have more important business to take care of."

Out in the galaxy, ruthless and untamed Honored Matres—still greatly outnumbering the Bene Gesserits—operated in independent cells, discrete groups. Many of those women refused to recognize the Mother Commander's authority and continued their original plan of slash and burn, destroy and run. Before they could face the real Enemy, Murbella would have to bring them into line. All of them.

Sensing that Odrade was once again available, Murbella said to her dead mentor in the silence of her mind, "I wish this sort of thing were not necessary."

Your way is more brutal than I'd prefer, but your challenges are great, and different from mine. I entrusted you with the task of the Sisterhood's survival. Now the work falls to you.

"You are dead and relegated to the role of observer."

Odrade-within chuckled. *I find that role to be far less stressful.*

Throughout the internal exchange, Murbella kept her face a placid mask, since so many in the receiving hall were watching her.

From beside the ornate throne, the aged and enormously fat Bellonda leaned over. "The Guildship has arrived. We are escorting their six-member delegation here with all due speed." Bell had been Odrade's foil and companion. The two had disagreed a great deal, especially about the Duncan Idaho project.

"I have decided to make them wait. No need to let them think we are anxious to see them." She knew what the Guild wanted. Spice. Always the same, spice.

Bellonda's chins folded together as she nodded. "Certainly. We can find endless formalities to observe, if you wish. Give the Guild a taste of their own bureaucracy."

Legend holds that a pearl of Leto II's awareness remains within each of the sandworms that arose from his divided body. The God Emperor himself said he would henceforth live in an endless dream. But what if he should waken? When he sees what we have done with ourselves, will the Tyrant laugh at us?

—PRIESTESS ARDATH,
the Cult of Sheeana on the planet Dan

Though the desert planet had been roasted clean of all life, the soul of Dune survived aboard the no-ship. Sheeana herself had seen to that.

She and her sober-faced aide Garimi stood at the viewing window above the *Ithaca*'s great hold. Garimi watched the shallow dunes stirring as the seven captive sandworms moved. "They have grown."

The worms were smaller than the behemoths Sheeana remembered from Rakis, but larger than any she had seen on the overly moist desert band of Chapterhouse. The environmental controls in this ship's vast hold were precise enough to provide a perfect simulated desert.

Sheeana shook her head, knowing that the creatures' primitive memories must recall swimming through an endless sea of dunes. "Our worms are crowded, restless. They have no place to go."

Just before the whores obliterated Rakis, Sheeana had rescued an ancient sandworm and transported it to Chapterhouse. Near death when it arrived, the mammoth creature broke down soon after it touched the fertile soil, and its skin fissioned into thousands of reproducing sandtrout that burrowed into the ground. Over the next fourteen years, those sandtrout began to transform the lush world into another arid wasteland, a new home for the worms. Finally, when conditions were right, the magnificent creatures rose again—small ones at first that over time would become larger and more powerful.

When Sheeana had decided to escape from Chapterhouse, she took some of the stunted sandworms with her.

Fascinated by movement in the sand, Garimi leaned closer to the plaz observation window. The dark-haired aide's expression was so serious it belonged on a woman decades older. Garimi was a workhorse, a true Bene Gesserit conservative who had the parochial tendency to see the world around her as straightforward, black-and-white. Though younger than Sheeana, she clung more to Bene Gesserit purity and was deeply offended by the idea of the hated Honored Matres joining the Sisterhood. Garimi had helped Sheeana develop the risky plan that allowed them to escape from the "corruption."

Looking at the restless worms, Garimi said, "Now that we are out of that other universe, when will Duncan find us a world? When will he decide we're safe?"

The *Ithaca* had been built to serve as a great city in space. Artificially lit sectors were designed as greenhouses for produce, while algae vats and recycling ponds provided less palatable food. Because it carried a relatively small number of passengers, the no-ship's supplies and scrubbing systems would provide edibles, air, and water for decades yet. The current population barely registered on the vessel's capacity.

Sheeana turned from the observation window. "I wasn't sure Duncan could ever return us to normal space, but now he's done so. Isn't that enough for now?"

"No! We must select a planet for our new Bene Gesserit headquarters, turn these worms loose, and convert it into another Rakis. We must begin reproducing, building a new core for the Sisterhood." She rested her hands on narrow hips. "We cannot keep wandering forever."

"Three years is hardly forever. You are starting to sound like the Rabbi."

The younger woman looked uncertain whether to take the comment as a joke or a rebuke. "The Rabbi likes to complain. I think it comforts him. I was simply looking to our future."

"We will have a future, Garimi. Do not worry."

The aide's face brightened, turned hopeful. "Are you speaking from prescience?"

"No, from my faith."

Day by day, Sheeana consumed more of their hoarded spice than most, a dose sufficient for her to map out vague and fog-shrouded paths ahead of them. During the time that the *Ithaca* had been lost in the void, she had seen nothing, but since the recent unexpected lurch back into normal space, she had felt different . . . better.

The largest sandworm rose up in the cargo hold, its open maw like the mouth of a cave. The other worms stirred like a writhing nest of snakes. Two more heads emerged, and a powder of sand cascaded down.

Garimi gasped in awe. "Look, they can sense you, even up here."

"And I sense them." Sheeana placed her palms against the plaz barrier, imagining that she could smell the melange on their breath even through the walls. Neither she nor the worms would be satisfied until they had a new desert on which to roam.

But Duncan insisted they keep running to stay one step ahead of the hunters. Not everyone agreed with his plan, such as it was. Many aboard the ship had never wanted to come along on this journey in the first place: the Rabbi and his refugee Jews, the Tleilaxu Scytale, and the four bestial Futars.

And what about the worms? she wondered. *What do they truly want?*

All seven worms had surfaced now, their eyeless heads questing back and forth. A troubled look crossed Garimi's hardened face. "Do you think the Tyrant is really in there? A pearl of awareness in an endless dream? Can he sense that you are special?"

"Because I am his hundred-times-removed great-grandniece? Perhaps. Certainly no one on Rakis expected a little girl from an isolated desert village to be able to command the great worms."

The corrupt priesthood on Rakis had seen Sheeana as a link to their Divided God. Later, the Bene Gesserit's Missionaria Protectiva created legends about Sheeana, shaping her into an earth mother, a holy virgin. As far as the population of the Old Empire knew, their revered Sheeana had perished along with Rakis. A religion had grown up around her supposed martyrdom, becoming yet another weapon for the Sisterhood to use. They were undoubtedly still exploiting her name and legend.

"All of us believe in you, Sheeana. That is why we came on this"— Garimi caught herself, as if on the verge of uttering a deprecatory word—"on this odyssey."

Below, the worms dove beneath the mounded sand, where they tested the boundaries of the hold. Sheeana watched them in their restless motion, wondering how much they understood of their strange situation.

If Leto II was indeed inside those creatures, he must be having troubled dreams.

Some like to live in complacency, hoping for stability without upset.
I much prefer to turn over rocks and see what scurries out.

— MOTHER SUPERIOR DARWIL ODRADE,
Observations on Honored Matre Motivations

Even after so many years, the *Ithaca* divulged its secrets like old bones rising to the surface of a battlefield after a drenching rain.

The old Bashar had stolen this great vessel from Gammu long ago; Duncan was held prisoner aboard it for over a decade on the Chapterhouse landing field, and they had been flying for three years now. But the *Ithaca's* immense size, and the small number of people aboard, made it impossible to explore all its mysteries, much less keep a diligent watch everywhere.

The vessel, a compact city over a kilometer in diameter, was more than a hundred decks high, with uncounted passageways and rooms. Although the main decks and compartments were equipped with surveillance imagers, it was beyond the Sisters' capacity to monitor the entire no-ship—especially since it had mysterious electronic dead zones where the imagers did not function. Perhaps the Honored Matres or the original builders of the vessel had installed blocking devices to preserve certain secrets. Numerous code-locked doors had remained unopened since the ship left Gammu. There were, literally, thousands of chambers that no one had entered or inventoried.

Nevertheless, Duncan did not expect to discover a long-sealed death chamber on one of the rarely visited decks.

The lift tube paused at one of the deep central levels. Although he had not requested this floor, the doors opened as the tube took itself out of service for a series of self-maintenance procedures, which the old ship performed automatically.

Duncan studied the deck in front of him, noted that it was cold and barren, dimly lit, unoccupied. The metal walls had been painted with no more than a white primer layer that didn't completely cover the rough-surfaced metal underneath. He'd known about these unfinished levels but had never felt a need to investigate them, because he assumed they were abandoned or never used.

However, the Honored Matres had owned this ship for years before Teg stole it from under their noses. Duncan should not have assumed anything.

He stepped out of the lift tube and wandered alone down a long corridor that continued for a surprising distance. Exploring unknown decks and chambers was like making a blind foldspace jump: He didn't know where he would end up. As he walked, he randomly opened chambers. Doors slid aside to reveal dim, empty rooms. From the dust and lack of furnishings, he guessed that no one had ever occupied them.

At the center of the deck level, a short corridor circled an enclosed section that had two doors, each marked "Machinery Room." The doors did not open at his touch. Curious, Duncan studied the locking mechanism; his own bioprint had been keyed into the ship's systems, supposedly granting him complete access. Using a master code, he overrode the door controls and forced open the seals.

When he stepped inside, he instantly detected a different quality to the darkness, an unpleasant long-faded odor in the air. The chamber was unlike any other he had seen aboard the ship, its walls a bright discordant red. The splash of violent color was jarring. Driving back his uneasiness, he spotted what looked like a patch of exposed metal on one wall. Duncan passed a hand over it, and abruptly the entire center section of the chamber began to slide and turn over with a groan.

As he stepped out of the way, ominous-looking devices came up from the floor, machines manufactured for the sole purpose of inflicting pain.

Honored Matre torture devices.

The lights in the dim chamber came up, as if in eager anticipation. To his right he saw an austere table and hard, flat chairs. Dirty dishes strewn on the table with what looked like the crusted, unfinished remains of a meal. The whores must have been interrupted while eating.

One machine in the array still held a human skeleton bound together with dry sinews, thorny wires, and the rags of a black robe. Female. The bones hung from the side of a large stylized vise; the victim's entire arm was still caught in the compression mechanism.

Touching long-dormant controls, Duncan opened the vise. With great care and respect, he removed the crumbling body from the harsh metal embrace and lowered it to the deck. Mostly mummified, she weighed little.

It was clearly a Bene Gesserit captive, perhaps a Reverend Mother from one of the Sisterhood planets the whores had destroyed. Duncan could tell that the unfortunate victim had not died quickly or easily. Looking at the withered iron-hard lips, he could almost hear the curses the woman must have whispered as the Honored Matres killed her.

Under the increased illumination from the glowpanels, Duncan continued to explore the large room and its labyrinth of odd machines. Near the door through which he had entered, he found a clearplaz bin, its grisly contents visible: four more female skeletons, all piled in disarray, as if thrown unceremoniously inside. Killed and discarded. All of them wore black robes.

No matter how much pain they had inflicted, the Honored Matres would not have gotten the information they demanded: the location of Chapterhouse and the key to Bene Gesserit bodily control, the ability of a Reverend Mother to manipulate her own internal chemistry. Frustrated and infuriated, the whores would have killed their Bene Gesserit prisoners one by one.

Duncan pondered his discovery in silence. Words did not seem adequate. Best to tell Sheeana about this terrible room. As a Reverend Mother, she would know what to do.

After executing the defiant Honored Matre, Murbella was in no hurry to meet the Guild delegation. She wanted to make sure all traces of the disturbance were cleaned up before any outsiders were allowed into the Keep's main chamber.

These little rebellions were like brushfires—as soon as she stamped one out, others flared up elsewhere. Until her rule was unchallenged on Chapterhouse, the Mother Commander could not turn her efforts to bringing the dissident Honored Matre cells on other planets into the New Sisterhood.

And she had to accomplish *that* before they could all stand against the unknown, oncoming Enemy that had driven Honored Matres from the fringes of the Scattering. To succeed against the ultimate threat, she would need the Spacing Guild, and they had already proved to be insufficiently motivated. She would change that.

Each step of the overall plan hummed past like connected cars on a maglev train.

Bellonda shuffled to the foot of the dais below Murbella's ornamented chair. She demonstrated a businesslike, efficient manner, with just the right amount of deference. "Mother Commander, the Guild delegation grows impatient—as you intended. I believe they are ripe for your meeting."

Murbella regarded the obese woman. Since Bene Gesserits were able to control the most minute nuances of their body chemistry, the fact that Bellonda let herself become so fat carried a message of its own. A sign of rebellion? Flaunting her lack of interest in being viewed as a sexual figure? Some might consider it a slap at the Honored Matres, who used more traditional methods to hone their bodies to wiry perfection. Murbella, though, suspected that Bellonda used her obesity to distract and lull any potential opponents: Assuming her to be slow and weak, they would underestimate her. But Murbella knew better.

"Bring me spice coffee. I must be at my sharpest. Those Guildsmen will no doubt attempt to manipulate me."

"Shall I send them in now?"

"My coffee first, then the Guild. And summon Doria as well. I want both of you beside me."

With a knowing smile, Bellonda lumbered away.

Preparing herself, Murbella sat forward in her great chair and squared her shoulders. Her hands gripped the hard and silky-smooth soostones on the throne's arms. After years of violence, all the men she had enslaved and the women she had killed, she knew how to look intimidating.

As soon as Murbella had her coffee, she nodded to Bellonda. The old Sister touched a communications stub in her ear, called for the Guild supplicants.

Doria hurried in, knowing she was late. The ambitious young woman, who currently served as the Mother Commander's key advisor from the Honored Matre faction, had risen in rank by killing close rivals while other Honored Matres wasted time on duels with competing Bene Gesserits. The whip-thin Doria had recognized the emerging patterns of power and decided she would rather be deputy to the victor than leader of the vanquished.

"Take your places on either side of me. Who is the formal represen-

tative? Did the Guild send someone of particular importance?" Murbella knew only that the Guild delegation had come to the New
Sisterhood, demanding—no, *begging for*—an audience with her.

Prior to the Battle of Junction, not even the Guild had known the
location of Chapterhouse. The Sisterhood kept their homeworld hidden behind a moat of no-ships, its coordinates in no Guild navigation
record. However, once the floodgates were opened and Honored
Matres had arrived in droves, the site of Chapterhouse was no longer a
closely held secret. Even so, few outsiders came directly to the Keep.

"Their highest human administrative official," Doria said in a hard,
flinty voice, "and a Navigator,"

"A Navigator?" Even Bellonda sounded surprised. "Here?"

Scowling at her counterpart, Doria continued. "I've received
reports from the docking center where the Guildship landed. He's an
Edric-class Navigator bearing the gene markers of an old bloodline."

Murbella's wide forehead creased. She sifted through direct knowledge as well as information that had surfaced from the chain of Other
Memories inside her head. "An Administrator and a Navigator?" She
allowed a cold smile. "The Guild must have an important message
indeed."

"Maybe it is no more than groveling, Mother Commander," Bellonda said. "The Guild is desperate for spice."

"And well they should be!" Doria snapped. She and Bellonda were
always at odds. Though their heated debates occasionally produced
interesting perspectives, at the moment Murbella found it juvenile.

"Enough, both of you. I will not allow the Guildsmen to see you
bickering. Such childish displays demonstrate weakness." Both advisors fell silent as if a gate had slammed shut across their mouths.

As the hall's great doors swung open, female attendants stepped
aside to allow the delegation of gray-robed men to enter. The newcomers' bodies were squat, the heads hairless, their faces slightly mal-
formed and *wrong*. The Guild did not breed with an eye to physical
perfection or attractiveness; they focused on maximizing the potential
of the human mind.

At their lead strode a tall, silver-robed man, whose bald head was as smooth as polished marble, except for a white braid that dangled from the base of his skull like a long electrical cord. The administrative official stopped to survey the room with milky eyes (though he did not seem to be blind), then stepped forward to clear a path for the bulky construction that followed.

Behind the Guildsmen levitated a great armored aquarium, a transparent distorted-bubble of a tank filled with orange spice gas. Heavy scrolled metalwork reached up like support ribs against the tank. Through the thick plaz, Murbella observed a misshapen form, no longer quite human, its limbs wasted and thin, as if the body was little more than a stem to support the expanded mind. The Navigator.

Murbella rose from her throne as a sign that she looked down upon this delegation, not as a gesture of respect. She wondered how many times such grand representatives had presented themselves before political leaders and emperors, browbeating them with the Spacing Guild's mighty monopoly on space travel. This time, though, she sensed a difference: The Navigator, the high Administrator, and five Guildsmen escorts came as cowed supplicants.

While the gray-robed escorts lowered their faces from her gaze, the braided representative put himself in front of the Navigator's tank and bowed before her. "I am Administrator Rentel Gorus. We represent the Spacing Guild."

"Obviously," Murbella said coolly.

As if afraid of being upstaged, the Navigator drifted to the curved front pane of his tank. His voice was distorted from speaker/translators in the metal support ribs. "Mother Superior of the Bene Gesserit . . . or do we address you as Great Honored Matre?"

Murbella knew that most Navigators were so isolated and obscure they could barely communicate with normal humans. With brains as folded as the fabric of space, they could not utter a comprehensible sentence and communed instead with their even more bizarre and exotic Oracle of Time. Some Navigators, however, clung to shreds of their genetic past, intentionally "stunting themselves" so they could act as liaisons with mere humans.

"You may address me as Mother Commander, provided you do so with respect. What is your name, Navigator?"

"I am Edrik. Many in my line have interacted with governments and individuals, dating back to the time of Emperor Muad'Dib." He swam closer to the walls of his tank, and she could see the otherworldly eyes set in his large misshapen head.

"I am less interested in history than in your present predicament," Murbella said, choosing to use the steel of the Honored Matres rather than the cool negotiating manner of the Bene Gesserits.

Administrator Gorus continued to bow, as if speaking to the floor at Murbella's feet. "With the destruction of Rakis, all of its sandworms died, and thus the desert planet produces no more spice. Compounding the problem, Honored Matres slew the old Tleilaxu Masters, so the secret of creating spice from axlotl tanks has been lost."

"Quite a quandary," Doria muttered with a bit of a sneer.

Murbella curled her own lips downward in a frown. She remained on her feet. "You state these things as if we did not know them."

The Navigator continued, amplifying his voice in order to drown out further words from Gorus. "In days past, melange was plentiful and we had numerous independent sources. Now, after little more than a decade, the Guild has only its own stockpiles remaining, and they are dwindling rapidly. It is becoming difficult to obtain spice even on the black market."

Murbella crossed her arms over her chest. On either side of her, Bellonda and Doria looked supremely satisfied. "But *we* can provide you with new spice. If we choose to do so. If you give us good reason."

Edrik drifted in his tank. The escort party of Guildsmen looked away.

The desert band girdling Chapterhouse was continuing to expand every year. Spice blows had occurred, and the stunted sandworms were growing larger, though they were only shadows of the monsters that once churned the dunes of Rakis. Decades ago, before the Honored Matres obliterated Dune, the Bene Gesserit order had gathered huge stockpiles of the then-plentiful spice. In contrast, the Spacing Guild— assuming the days of scarce melange were long over and the market was strong—did not make preparations for a possible shortage. Even the ancient trading conglomerate of CHOAM had been caught off guard.

Murbella stepped closer to the tank, focused on the Navigator.

Gorus folded his hands and said to her, "The reason we have come is therefore obvious . . . Mother Commander."

Murbella said, "My Sisters and I have good reason for cutting off your supplies."

Nonplussed, Edrik waved his webbed hands in the swirling mists. "Mother Commander, what have we done to invoke your displeasure?"

She lifted her thin eyebrows in scorn. "Your Guild knew that Honored Matres bore weapons from the Scattering that were capable of destroying entire planets. And you still transported the whores against us!"

"Honored Matres had their own ships from the Scattering. Their own technologies—" Gorus began.

"But they flew blind, did not know the landscape of the Old Empire until you guided them. The Guild showed them their targets, led them to vulnerable worlds. The Guild is complicit in the eradication of billions of lives—not just on Rakis itself, but on our library world of Lampadas and countless other planets. All the worlds of the Bene Tleilax have been crushed or conquered, while our own Sisters remain enslaved on Buzzell, harvesting soostones for rebel Honored Matres who will not bow to my rule." She laced her fingers together. "The Spacing Guild is at least partly responsible for those crimes, so you must make recompense."

"Without spice, space travel and all galactic commerce will be hobbled!" Alarm rang clearly in Administrator Gorus's voice.

"So? The Guild has previously flaunted its alliance with the Ixians by using primitive navigation machines. Use them instead of Navigators, if your supply of spice is inadequate." She waited to see if he would call her bluff.

"Inferior substitutes," Edrik insisted.

Bellonda added, "Ships in the Scattering flew without spice or Navigators."

"Countless numbers were lost," Edrik said.

Gorus was quick to change his voice to a conciliatory tone. "Mother Commander, the Ixian machines were mere fallback devices, to be used in emergencies only. We have never relied on them. All Guild ships must carry a functional Navigator."

"So, when you showed off these machines, it was all a sham to drive down the price of melange? To convince the Priests of the Divided God and the Tleilaxu that you didn't need what they were selling?" Her lips curled in disdain. During the years that Chapterhouse was hidden, even the Bene Gesserits had shunned Guildships. The Sisters held the location of their planet in their own minds. "And now that you do require spice, there is no one to sell it to you. No one but us."

Murbella had her own deceptions. The extravagant use of melange on Chapterhouse was mainly for show, a bluff. So far, the worms in the desert belt provided only a trickle of spice, but the Bene Gesserit kept the market open by freely selling melange from their copious stockpiles, implying that it came from the newborn worms in the arid belt. Eventually, the Chapterhouse desert would indeed be as rich in spice as the sands of Rakis, but for now the Sisterhood's ruse was necessary to increase the perception of power and limitless wealth.

And somewhere, eventually, there would be other planets producing melange. Before the long night of the Honored Matres, Mother Superior Odrade had dispersed groups of Sisters in unguided no-ships across uncharted space. They had carried sandtrout specimens and clear instructions on how to seed new desert worlds. Right now, there might already be more than a dozen alternative "Dunes" being created out there. "Remove the single point of failure," Odrade often said then, and afterward from Other Memory. The spice bottleneck would once again be gone, and fresh sources of melange would appear throughout the galaxy.

For now, though, the iron grip of monopoly was the New Sisterhood's.

Gorus bowed even more deeply, refusing to raise his milky eyes. "Mother Commander, we will pay whatever you wish."

"Then you shall pay with your suffering. Have you ever heard of a Bene Gesserit punishment?" She drew a long, cool breath of air. "Your request is denied. Navigator Edrik and Administrator Gorus, you may tell your Oracle of Time and your fellow Navigators that the Guild will have more spice when . . . and if . . . I decide you warrant it." She felt a warmth of satisfaction and guessed that it came from Odrade-within. When they were hungry enough, the Guild would be prepared to do exactly as she wished. It was all part of a great plan coming together.

Trembling, Gorus said, "Can your New Sisterhood survive without the Guild? We could bring a huge force of Heighliners and take the spice from you."

Murbella smiled to herself, knowing his threat had no teeth. "Accepting your ludicrous assertion for a moment, would you risk destroying the spice forever? We have installed explosives, cleverly rigged to annihilate the spice sands and flood them out with our water reserves if we detect even the slightest incursion from outside. The last sandworms would die."

"You're as bad as Paul Atreides," the Guildsman cried. "He made a similar threat against the Guild."

"I take that as a compliment." Murbella looked at the confused Navigator floating in his spice gas. The Administrator's bald head glistened with sweat.

Now she addressed the five gray-clothed Guildsmen escorts. "Raise your eyes to me. All of you!" The escorts turned their faces upward, revealing collective fear. Gorus snapped his head up as well, and the Navigator pressed his mutated face against the transparent plaz.

Although Murbella spoke to the Guild contingent, her words were also meant for the two factions of women who listened in the great hall. "Selfish fools, there is a greater danger coming—an Enemy that was powerful enough to drive the Honored Matres back from the Scattering. We all know this."

"We have all *heard* this, Mother Commander." The Administrator's voice dripped with skepticism. "We have seen no proof."

Her eyes flashed. "Oh, yes. They are coming, but the threat is so vast that no one—not the New Sisterhood, nor the Spacing Guild, nor CHOAM, nor even the Honored Matres—understand how to get out of the way. We have weakened ourselves and wasted our energies in meaningless struggles, while ignoring the true threat." She swirled her serpent-scribed robe. "If the Guild provides us with sufficient assistance in the coming battle, and with sufficient enthusiasm, perhaps I will reconsider opening our stockpiles to you. If we cannot stand against the relentless Enemy, then bickering over spice will be the least of our problems."

*Do the Masters truly control the strings—or can we use the strings
to ensnare the Masters?*

—TLEILAXU MASTER ALEF
(presumed to be a Face Dancer replica)

Face Dancer representatives came to a conference chamber aboard one of the Guildships used by the Lost Tleilaxu. The Face Dancers had been summoned by the breeding wizards from the Scattering to receive explicit new instructions.

Second-rank Uxtal attended the meeting as a note taker and observer; he did not intend to speak, since speaking would earn him a reprimand from his betters. He wasn't important enough to bear such a responsibility, especially with the equivalent of a Master present, one of those who called themselves Elders. But Uxtal was confident they would recognize his talent, sooner or later.

A faithful Tleilaxu, he was gray-skinned and diminutive, his features elfin, his flesh impregnated with metals and blockers to foil any scanners. No one could steal the secrets of genetics, the Language of God, from the Lost Tleilaxu.

Like an oversize elf, Elder Burah perched on his raised seat at the head of the table as Face Dancers began to arrive, one at a time. Eight of them—a sacred number to the Tleilaxu, which Uxtal had learned from studying ancient scriptures and deciphering secret gnostic meanings in the preserved words of the Prophet. Though Elder Burah had commanded the shape-shifters to appear, Uxtal had an uneasy feeling in their presence, one that he could not quite put into thoughts or words.

The Face Dancers looked like completely nondescript, average crewmen. Over the years, they had been planted aboard the Guildship, where they performed their duties quietly and efficiently; not even the Guild suspected that replacements had occurred. This new breed of Face Dancers had extensively infiltrated the remnants of the Old Empire; they could fool most tests, even one of the witches' Truthsayers. Burah and other Lost Tleilaxu leaders often snickered that they had achieved their victory while the Honored Matres and Bene Gesserits scrambled around preparing for some mysterious great Enemy. The real invasion was already well underway, and Uxtal was awed and impressed with what his people had accomplished. He was proud to be among them.

At Burah's command, the Face Dancers took their seats, deferring to one who seemed to be their spokesman (though Uxtal had thought that all of those creatures were identical, like drones in an insect hive). Watching them, scribbling notes, he wondered for the first time if Face Dancers might have their own secret organization, as the Tleilaxu leaders did. No, of course not. The shape-shifters were bred to be followers, not independent thinkers.

Uxtal paid close attention, remembering not to speak. Later, he would transcribe this meeting and disseminate the information to other Elders of the Lost Tleilaxu. His job was to serve as an assistant; if he performed well enough, he could rise through the ranks, eventually achieving the title of Elder among his people. Could there be a grander dream? To become one of the new Masters!

Elder Burah and the present kehl, or council, represented the Lost Tleilaxu race and their Great Belief. Besides Burah, only six Elders existed—a total of seven, while *eight* was the holy number. Though he would never speak it aloud, Uxtal felt they should appoint someone else soon, or even promote *him*, so that the prescribed numbers were in proper balance.

As he surveyed the Face Dancers, Burah's lips pressed together in a petulant frown. "I demand a report on your progress. What records have you salvaged from the destroyed Tleilaxu worlds? We barely know enough of their technology to continue with the sacred work. Our fallen stepbrothers knew much more than we have recovered. This is not acceptable."

The placid-looking "leader" of the Face Dancers smiled in his Guildsman's uniform. He addressed his shape-shifter comrades, as if he hadn't even heard Elder Burah speak. "I have received our next set of commands. Our primary instructions remain the same. We are to find the no-ship that escaped from Chapterhouse. The search must continue."

To Uxtal's surprise, the other Face Dancers turned away from Burah, focusing instead on their own spokesman. Flustered, the Elder pounded a small fist on the table. "An escaped no-ship? What do we care about a no-ship? Who are you—which one? I can never tell you apart, not even by scent."

The Face Dancer leader looked at Burah and seemed to consider whether or not to answer the question. "At the moment, I am called Khrone."

Sitting against the copper-plated wall, Uxtal flicked his gaze from the innocent-looking Face Dancers to Elder Burah. He couldn't grasp the undercurrents here, but he sensed a strange threat. So many things were just slightly beyond the edge of his comprehension.

"Your *priority*," Burah doggedly continued, "is to rediscover how to manufacture melange using axlotl tanks. From old knowledge we took with us into the Scattering, we know how to use the tanks to create gholas—but not to make spice, a technique that our stepbrothers developed during the Famine Times, long after our line of Tleilaxu departed."

When the Lost Tleilaxu returned from the Scattering, their stepbrothers had accepted them only hesitantly, allowing them back into the fold of their race as no more than second-class citizens. Uxtal didn't think it was fair. But he and his fellow outsiders, all of them prodigal sons according to the original Tleilaxu, accepted the deprecatory comments they received, remembering an important quote from the catechism of the Great Belief: "Only those who are truly lost can ever hope to find the truth. Trust not in your maps, but in the guidance of God."

As time passed, the returned Elders came to see that it was not *they* who were "lost," but the original Masters who had strayed from the Great Belief. Only the Lost Tleilaxu—forged in the rigors of the Scattering—had kept the veracity of God's commands, while the heretical ones wallowed in delusions. Eventually, the Lost Tleilaxu had realized that they would have to reeducate their misguided brothers, or remove them. Uxtal understood, having been told so many times, that the Lost Tleilaxu were far superior.

The original Masters were a suspicious lot, however, and they had never entirely trusted outsiders, not even outsiders of their own race. In this case, their problematic paranoia had not been misguided, for the Lost Tleilaxu were indeed in league with the Honored Matres. They used the terrible women as tools for reasserting the Great Belief upon their complacent stepbrothers. The whores had wiped out the original Tleilaxu worlds, eliminating every last original Master (a more extreme reaction than Uxtal had anticipated). Victory should have been simple enough to achieve.

During this meeting, however, Khrone and his fellows were not acting as expected. In the copper-walled chamber, Uxtal noticed subtle changes in their demeanor, and he saw the concern on Elder Burah's face.

"Our priorities are different from yours," Khrone said baldly.

Uxtal stifled a gasp. Burah was so displeased that his grayish expression turned a bruised purple. "Different priorities? How could any orders supersede mine, an Elder of the Tleilaxu?" He laughed with a sound like dull metal scraped across slate. "Oh, now I remember that silly story! Do you mean your mysterious old man and old woman who communicate with you from afar?"

"Yes," Khrone said. "According to their projections, the escaped no-ship holds something or someone supremely important to them. We must find it, capture it, and deliver it to them."

Uxtal found this all so incomprehensible that he had to speak up. "What old man and old woman?" No one ever told him the things he needed to know.

Burah glanced dismissively at his assistant. "Face Dancer delusions."

Khrone looked down at the Elder as if he were a maggot. "Their projections are infallible. Aboard that no-ship is, or will be, the necessary fulcrum to influence the battle at the end of the universe. That takes precedence over your need for a convenient source of spice."

"But . . . but how do they know this?" Uxtal asked, surprised that he was finding the nerve to speak. "Is it a prophecy?" He tried to imagine a numerical code that might apply, one buried in the sacred writings.

Burah snapped at him. "Prophecy, prescience, or some sort of bizarre mathematical projection—it does not matter!"

As Khrone stood, he seemed to grow taller. "On the contrary, *you* do not matter." He turned to his fellow Face Dancers while the Elder sat in speechless shock. "We must turn our minds and our efforts to discovering where that vessel has gone. We are everywhere, but it has been three years and the trail has grown cold."

The other seven shape-shifters nodded, speaking in a sort of rapid humming undertone that sounded like the buzz of insects. "We will find them."

"They cannot escape."

"The tachyon net extends far and it draws tighter."

"The no-ship will be found."

"I do not give you permission for this foolish search!" Burah shouted. Uxtal wanted to cheer for him. "You will heed my commands. I told you to scour the conquered Tleilaxu planets, investigate the laboratories of the fallen Masters, and learn their methods of creating spice with axlotl tanks. Not only do we require it for ourselves, but it is a priceless commodity that we can use to break the Bene Gesserit monopoly and claim the commercial power that is our due." He delivered this grand speech, as if expecting the Face Dancers to stand up and shout their approval.

"*No,*" Khrone said emphatically. "That is not our intention."

Uxtal remained aghast. He himself had never dreamed of challenging an Elder, and this was a mere Face Dancer! He shrank back against the copper wall, wishing he could melt into it. This wasn't the way things were supposed to happen.

Angry and confused, Burah twisted back and forth in his chair. "We created Face Dancers, and you will follow our orders." He sniffed and got to his feet. "Why am I even discussing this with you?"

In unison, as if they shared a single mind, the entire contingent of Face Dancers stood. From their positions around the table, they blocked Elder Burah's exit. He sat back down on his high seat, and now he seemed nervous.

"Are you certain you Lost Tleilaxu created us . . . or did you simply *find* us out in the Scattering? True, in the distant shadows of the past, a Tleilaxu Master was responsible for our seed stock. He made modifications and dispatched us to the ends of the universe shortly before the birth of Paul Muad'Dib. But we have evolved since then."

As if a veil had been lifted simultaneously from their faces, Khrone and his companions blurred and shifted. Their nondescript human expressions melted away, and the Face Dancers returned to their blank state, a bland yet unnervingly inhuman set of features: sunken black-button eyes, pug noses, slack mouths. Their skin was pale and malleable, their vestigial hair bristly and white. Using a genetic map, they could form their muscles and epidermis into any desired pattern to mimic humans.

"We no longer need to expend effort on continuing illusions," Khrone announced. "That deception has become a waste of time."

Uxtal and Elder Burah stared at them.

Khrone continued, "Long ago, the original Tleilaxu Masters produced the genesis of what we have become. You, Elder Burah, and your fellows are but faded copies, diluted memories of your race's former greatness. It offends us that you consider yourselves our masters."

Three of the Face Dancers moved toward the high seat of Elder Burah. One stepped behind him and one on either side, closing him in. With each passing moment, the Elder looked more afraid.

Uxtal felt as if he would faint. He barely dared to breathe and wanted to flee, but knew there were many more Face Dancers aboard the Guildship than these eight. He would never escape alive.

"Stop this! I command you!" Burah tried to stand up, but the two flanking Face Dancers held his slumped shoulders to keep him from leaving his elevated seat.

Khrone said, "No wonder the others call you Lost. You Masters from the Scattering have always been blind."

Behind him, a third Face Dancer reached forward with both hands to cover Burah's eyes. Using his forefingers, the Face Dancer squeezed, pressing like an iron vise into Burah's skull. The Elder screamed. His eyeballs burst; blood and fluid ran down his cheeks.

Khrone let out a mild, artificial-sounding laugh. "Maybe your Tleilaxu companions could create old-fashioned metal eyes for you. Or have you lost that technology as well?"

Burah's continuing screams were abruptly cut short as the Face Dancer snapped the man's head to one side, breaking his neck. Within moments, the shape-shifter had taken a deep imprint; his body shifted, shrank, and acquired the elfin features of the dead Elder. When the transition was complete, he flexed his small fingers and smiled down at the bloodied, identical body on the floor.

"Another one replaced," the Face Dancer said.

Another one? Uxtal froze, trying to keep from screaming, and wishing he could just become invisible.

Now the shape-shifters turned to face the assistant. Unable to do more than cringe, he held up his hands in complete surrender, though he doubted that would do any good. They would kill him and replace him. No one would ever know. A quiet moan escaped from his throat.

"We will no longer pretend that you are our masters," Khrone said to Uxtal.

The Face Dancers stepped away from Burah's body. The copy bent down and wiped his bloody fingers on the crumpled Elder's garment.

"However, for the overall plan we still need to use certain Tleilaxu procedures, and for that we will retain some of the original genetic stock—if you qualify." Khrone stepped very close to Uxtal and stared hard at him. "Do you understand the hierarchy here? Do you realize who is your true master?"

Uxtal managed no more than a hoarse gasp as he answered, "Y-yes, of course."

Three years of wandering in this ship! Our people certainly comprehend the incredible search for the Promised Land. We will endure as we have always endured. We will be patient as we have always been patient. Still, the doubting voice within me asks, "Does anyone know where we are going?"

THE RABBI,
speech to his followers aboard the no-ship

The Jewish passengers were given all the freedom they could desire aboard the giant vessel, but Sheeana knew that every prison had its bars, and every camp its fences.

The only Reverend Mother among the refugee Jews, a woman named Rebecca, sought out her boundaries, diligent and quietly curious. Sheeana had always found her to be intriguing, a wild Reverend Mother, a woman who had undergone the Agony without the benefit of Bene Gesserit training. The very idea amazed her, but other such anomalies had occurred throughout history. Sheeana often accompanied Rebecca on her contemplative walks, each of which was more a journey of the mind than an effort to reach any specific room or deck.

"Are we just going to wander in circles again?" the Rabbi complained, tagging along. A former Suk doctor, he always preferred to evaluate the point of any activity before engaging in it. "Why should I waste my time in futile pursuits when one can study the word of God?"

The Rabbi acted as if they were forcing him to walk along with them. To him, he had an obligation to study the Torah for the sake of study, but Sheeana knew that Jewish women were to study for the sake of knowing the practical application of Torah law. Rebecca had gone far beyond either.

"All of life is a journey. We are carried along at life's pace, whether we choose to run or sit still," Sheeana said.

He scowled and looked to Rebecca for support, but found none. "Don't quote your Bene Gesserit platitudes to me," he said. "Jewish mysticism is far more ancient than anything you witches have developed."

"Would you rather I quoted your Kabbalah? Many of the other lives within me studied the Kabbalah extensively, even though they were technically not allowed to do so. Jewish mysticism is quite fascinating."

The Rabbi seemed nonplussed, as if she had stolen something from him. He pushed his spectacles higher on his nose and walked closer to Rebecca, trying to shut out Sheeana.

Whenever the old man joined their conversations, the debate became a clash between Sheeana and the Rabbi. The old man insisted on a battleground of scholarship, rather than any direct wisdom Sheeana carried within her from her myriad Other Memories. It made her feel practically invisible. Regardless of her clout aboard the no-ship, the Rabbi did not consider Sheeana relevant to the concerns of his Jews, and Rebecca did well holding her own.

Now they passed down the curving corridors, descending from one deck to another with Rebecca leading the way. She had bound her long brown hair into a thick braid that was shot with so many threads of gray that it resembled driftwood. She wore her usual loose, drab robe.

The Rabbi walked close beside her, jockeying his position in a not-accidental attempt to shoulder Sheeana behind the two of them. Sheeana found it amusing.

The Rabbi never missed an opportunity to lecture Rebecca when her thoughts strayed from the narrow confines of what he considered proper behavior. He often browbeat Rebecca, reminding her that she was irretrievably tainted in his eyes because of what the Bene Gesserit had done to her. Regardless of the old man's scorn and concern, Sheeana knew that Rebecca would always have the Sisterhood's gratitude.

Ages ago, the secret Jews had made a pact with the Bene Gesserit for mutual protection. The Sisterhood had offered them sanctuary at times throughout history, hiding them, carrying them away from pogroms and prejudice after the violent tides of intolerance had once again swung against the children of Israel. In exchange, the Jews had been obligated to protect the Bene Gesserit Sisters from the Honored Matres.

When the ferocious whores had come to the Sisterhood's library world of Lampadas with the clear intention of destroying it, the Bene Gesserit had Shared their own memories. Millions of lives poured into thousands of minds, and those thousands distilled into hundreds, and those hundreds all Shared into one Reverend Mother, Lucilla, who escaped with that irreplaceable knowledge.

Fleeing to Gammu, Lucilla had begged sanctuary from the hidden Jews, but the Honored Matres came hunting after her. The only way to preserve the Lampadas horde in her mind had been to Share it with an unexpected recipient—the wild Reverend Mother Rebecca—and then to offer up herself as a sacrifice.

So, Rebecca had accepted all those desperate, clamoring thoughts into her brain, and preserved them even after the whores had killed Lucilla. She eventually delivered her priceless treasure to the Bene Gesserit, who accepted the rescued knowledge of Lampadas and distributed it widely among the women at Chapterhouse. Thus, the Jews had fulfilled their ancient obligations.

A debt is a debt, Sheeana thought. *Honor is honor. Truth is truth.*

But she knew Rebecca was forever changed by the experience. How could she not be, after living the lives of millions of Bene Gesserits— millions who thought differently, who experienced many astonishing things, who accepted behaviors and opinions that were anathema to the Rabbi? No wonder Sheeana and Rebecca frightened him, intimidated him. As for Rebecca, though she had Shared those memories with others, she still carried the kaleidoscope chains of life after life, traveling backward into myriad pasts. How could she be expected to shrug that aside and return to mere memorized knowledge? She had lost her innocence. Even the Rabbi must understand that.

The old man had been Rebecca's teacher and mentor. Before Lampadas, she might have debated with him, sharpening wit and intellect, but she would never have doubted him. Sheeana felt sorry for what the other woman had lost. Now, Rebecca must see the immense gaps in even the Rabbi's understanding. To discover that one's mentor knows little is a terrible thing. The old man's view of the universe encompassed only the barest tip of an iceberg. Rebecca had once confided to Sheeana that she missed her prior, innocent relationship with the old man, but it could never be regained.

The Rabbi wore a white skullcap on his balding head as he walked along beside Rebecca with a fit and energetic stride. His dusky ship clothes hung loosely on his small frame, but he refused to have them refitted or new garments manufactured. His gray beard had grown paler in recent years, contrasting with his leathery skin, but he was still extremely healthy.

Though the verbal sparring did not seem to bother Rebecca, Sheeana had learned not to press the Rabbi beyond a certain point in philosophical debates. Whenever he was about to lose an argument, the old man vehemently quoted some line from the Torah, whether or not he understood the meanings within meanings, and stalked away in feigned triumph.

The three of them wandered down deck after deck until they reached the no-ship's brig levels. This stolen vessel had been built by people from the Scattering and flown by Honored Matres, probably aided by the duplicitous Spacing Guild. Every large vessel—even from the days of sailing ships on the seas of near-forgotten Earth—contained secure cells for holding unruly people. The Rabbi appeared nervous when he noticed where Rebecca had led them.

Sheeana certainly knew what was kept in the brig: Futars. How often did Rebecca visit the creatures? Half-beasts. Sheeana wondered if the whores had used these brig cells as torture chambers, like in an ancient Bastille. Or had dangerous prisoners been kept aboard this vessel?

Dangerous. None could be more dangerous than these four Futars—beast-men created in the shadows of the Scattering, muscular hybrids as close to animals as they were to humans. They were born hunters with wiry hair, long fangs, and sharp claws, animals bred to track down and kill.

"Why do we go down here, daughter? What is it you seek from these . . . these inhuman things?"

"I always seek answers, Rabbi."

"An honorable pursuit," Sheeana said from behind them.

He spun to snap at her, "Some answers should never be learned."

"And some answers help protect us from the unknown," Rebecca said, but it was clear by her voice that she knew she would never convince him.

Rebecca and Sheeana stopped in front of the transparent wall of one of the holding chambers, though the Rabbi now hovered a step behind them. Sheeana always found herself intrigued and disgusted by the Futars. Even in their confinement, they maintained their muscular physiques, prowling and pacing. The beasts moved about aimlessly, separated by brig walls, circling from side wall to plaz doorway to back wall and then around again, testing and retesting boundaries.

Predators are optimists, Sheeana realized. *They have to be.* She could see their stored energy, their primitive needs. The Futars longed to lope through a forest again, to track down prey and sink claws and fangs into unresisting flesh.

During a battle on Gammu, the Jewish refugees had run to the Bene Gesserit forces demanding the protection accorded them by the old agreement. At the same time, four escaped Futars had come aboard, asking to be taken to "Handlers." Afterward, the predatory half-human creatures had been held on the no-ship until the Bene Gesserit could decide what to do with them. When the no-ship flew off into nowhere, Sheeana and Duncan took everyone with them.

Sensing the visitors, one of the Futars rushed to the plaz wall of his brig cell. He pressed against it, his wiry body hair bristling, his olive-green eyes alight with fire and interest. "You Handlers?" The Futar sniffed, but the plaz barrier was impenetrable. With obvious disappointment and disdain, he hunched his shoulders and slunk away. "You not Handlers."

"It smells down here, daughter." The Rabbi's voice wavered. "There must be something wrong with the recirculation vents." Sheeana could detect no difference in the air.

Rebecca looked sidelong at him, a challenging expression on her pinched face. "Why do you hate them so, Rabbi? They cannot help what they are." Was she referring to herself, too?

His answer was glib. "They are not God's creatures. Ki-layim. The Torah quite clearly prohibits mixing breeds. Two different animals are not even allowed to plow a field side by side on one bridle. These Futars are . . . wrong on many different levels." The Rabbi scowled. "As you should well know, daughter."

The four Futars continued their restless prowling. Rebecca could think of no way to help them. Somewhere out in the Scattering, the "Handlers" had bred Futars for the express purpose of hunting down and killing Honored Matres, who in turn had captured and broken a few Futars. The moment they saw a chance for freedom on Gammu, these animal-men had escaped.

"Why do you want the Handlers so badly?" Sheeana said to the Futar, not knowing if he would understand the question.

With a snakelike motion, the beast-man snapped his head up and came forward. "Need Handlers."

Leaning closer, Sheeana saw violence in his eyes, but she also detected intelligence mixed with longing. "Why do you need the Handlers? Are they your slave masters? Or is there more of a bond between you?"

"Need Handlers. Where are Handlers?"

The Rabbi shook his head, ignoring Sheeana again. "You see, daughter? Animals can't understand freedom. They comprehend nothing more than what has been bred and trained into them."

He clutched Rebecca's lean arm, pretending to hold onto her for strength as he pulled her from the prison cell. In his demeanor Sheeana could sense the old man's revulsion, like the heat of flames from a furnace.

"These hybrids are abominations," he said in a low voice, his tone a feral growling sound of his own.

Rebecca exchanged an instant, knowing glance with Sheeana before saying, "I have seen many worse abominations, Rabbi." This was something any Reverend Mother could understand.

As they turned from the brig, Sheeana was startled to see a flushed Garimi emerge from the lift and rush forward with Bene Gesserit grace and silence. Her face looked pale and disturbed. "Worse abominations? We have just found one. Something the whores left behind for us."

Sheeana felt a lump harden in her throat. "What is it?"

"An old torture chamber. Duncan discovered it. He asks you to come."

We lay this body of our Sister to rest, though her mind and memories will never be stilled. Even death cannot turn a Reverend Mother from her work.

— Bene Gesserit memorial ceremony

As a veteran battlefield commander, Bashar Miles Teg had attended more than his share of funerals. This ceremony, though, seemed eerily unfamiliar, acknowledging long-ago suffering the Bene Gesserit refused to forget.

Solemnly, the ship's entire company gathered on the main deck near one of the small cargo airlocks. Though the chamber was large, the 150 attendees crowded together along the walls for the observance. Sheeana, Garimi, and two other Reverend Mothers named Elyen and Calissa stood on a raised platform at the center of the room. Near the airlock door, wrapped in black, lay the five bodies extricated from the Honored Matre torture chamber.

Not far from Teg, Duncan stood next to Sheeana, leaving the navigation bridge empty for the duration of the funeral. Although he ostensibly served as the no-ship's captain, these Bene Gesserits would never let a mere man—even a ghola with a hundred lifetimes—have command over them.

Since emerging from the oddly distorted universe, Duncan had not engaged the Holtzman engines again, or selected a course. Without navigational guidance, each jump through foldspace carried considerable risk, so now the no-ship hung in empty space without coordinates. Although he could have mapped nearby star systems on the long-range projection and flagged possible planets to explore, Duncan let the ship drift, rudderless.

In their three years in the other universe, they had encountered no sign of the old man and woman, or of the gossamer web that Duncan insisted continued to search for them. Though Teg did not disbelieve the other man's fears of the mysterious hunters that only he could see, the young Bashar also wished for an end—or just a *point*—to their odyssey.

Garimi's lips sank into a deep frown as she stared at the mummified corpses. "See, we were right to leave Chapterhouse. Did we need any further proof that witches and whores do not mix?"

Sheeana raised her voice, addressing all of them. "For three years, we carried the bodies of our fallen Sisters without knowing they were here. In all that time, they have not been able to rest. These Reverend Mothers died without Sharing, without adding their lives to Other Memory. We can guess, but we cannot know, what agonies they endured before the whores killed them."

"We do know that they refused to reveal the information the whores tried to wrest from them," Garimi spoke up. "Chapterhouse remained intact and our private knowledge secure, until Murbella's unholy alliance."

Teg nodded to himself. When the Honored Matres had returned to the Old Empire, they had demanded the Bene Gesserit secret for manipulating a body's biochemistry, presumably so that they could shrug off any further epidemics such as the ones the Enemy had inflicted on them. The Sisters had all refused. And they died for it.

No one knew the origin of the Honored Matres. After the Famine Times, somewhere out in the farthest reaches of the Scattering, perhaps some wild Reverend Mothers had collided with remnants of Leto II's female Fish Speakers. Yet this blending could not have accounted for the seed of vengeful violence in their genetic makeup. The whores destroyed whole planets in their fury at being rebuffed by the Bene

Gesserit and then by the old Tleilaxu. Teg knew that there must have been many dead Reverend Mothers in many torture chambers over the past decade.

The old Bashar had his own experiences with Honored Matre interrogators and their appalling torture devices back on Gammu. Even a hardened military commander could not withstand the incredible agony of their T-probes, and he had been fundamentally changed by the experience, though not in a way those women had expected. . . .

In the ceremony, Sheeana named the five victims from identifications found with their robes, then closed her eyes and lowered her head, as did everyone in the chamber. This moment of silence was the Bene Gesserit equivalent of prayer, a time when each Sister pondered a private blessing for the departed souls who lay before them.

Then Sheeana and Garimi carried one of the black-wrapped bodies into the airlock chamber. Retreating from the small vault, they let Elyen and Calissa carry another dead woman into the airlock. Sheeana had refused to let Teg or Duncan help. "This reminder of the whores' vicious cruelty is our own burden." When all of the mummified corpses had been placed reverently inside the chamber, Sheeana sealed the outer door and cycled the systems.

Everyone remained hushed, listening to the whisper of draining air. Finally, the outer door opened and the five bodies floated out along with the wispy residue of atmosphere. Drifting without a home . . . like everyone aboard the *Ithaca*. Like satellites of the no-ship, the wrapped humans accompanied the wandering vessel for a time, then slowly increased their separation until, against the night of space, the black cadavers became invisible.

Duncan Idaho stared out the windowport in the direction of the dwindling shapes. Teg could tell that finding the bodies and the torture chamber had affected him. Suddenly, Duncan stiffened with alarm and pressed closer to the plaz, though the young Bashar could see nothing in the void but faraway stars.

Teg knew him better than anyone else aboard. "Duncan, what is—?"

"The net! Can't you see it?" He whirled. "The net cast by the old man and woman. They've found us again—and nobody's on the navigation bridge!" Shouldering aside Bene Gesserit women and the Rabbi's people, Duncan charged toward the door of the chamber. "I've got to activate the Holtzman engines and foldspace before the net closes in!"

Because of a special sensitivity—perhaps from gene markers that his Tleilaxu creators had secretly planted in his ghola body—only Duncan could see through the gauzy fabric of the universe. Now, after three years, the old couple's net had found the no-ship again.

Teg ran after him, but he knew the elevator would be far too slow. He also knew that in the chaos and sudden confusion he would be able to do something he otherwise feared to do. Rushing past the crowd of people who had come to see the burial in space and bypassing the lift tube, he ran to an empty corridor. There, out of view of too-curious eyes, Miles Teg *accelerated* himself.

No one here knew of his ability, though hints and rumors of impossible things the old Bashar had achieved might have raised some suspicions. During his torture by the Honored Matres, he had discovered the capacity to hypercharge his metabolism and move at incredible speeds. The mind-ripping agony of an Ixian T-probe had somehow released this unknown gift from within Teg's Atreides genes. When his body sped up, the universe seemed to slow down, and he could move with such speed that a simple tap was enough to kill his captors. In this manner he had slaughtered hundreds of Honored Matres and their minions inside one of their strongholds on Gammu. His new ghola body retained that ability.

Now he raced down the empty corridor, feeling the heat of his metabolism, the scrape of air past his face. He scrambled up the rungs of access ladders much faster than the lift tube could ever travel.

Teg didn't know how much longer he could keep his gift to himself, but knew he had to. In the past, because of a single fear, the Sisterhood had shown little tolerance for males with special abilities, and Teg was certain that the women had been responsible for killing a number of such "male abominations." Afraid of creating another Kwisatz Haderach, they threw away many potential advantages.

It reminded him of how human civilization had dispensed with all aspects of computerized technology following the Butlerian Jihad because of their hatred for evil thinking machines. He knew the old cliché "throwing the baby out with the bath water," and feared he would meet a similar fate, should the Sisterhood learn he was special.

Teg burst onto the navigation bridge and ran to the engine controls. He looked out through the broad observation plaz. Space seemed calm and peaceful. Even though he saw no sign of the deadly web closing in, he did not question Duncan's abilities.

His fingers a blur across the controls, Teg engaged the enormous Holtzman engines and picked a course at random, without Duncan and without a Navigator. What choice did he have? He only hoped that he didn't plunge the *Ithaca* into a star or wayward planet. As horrible as that possibility was, he thought it preferable to letting the old man and woman seize them.

Space folded, and the no-ship dropped away, appearing elsewhere, far from where the gossamer strands had tried to wrap around them, far from the drifting bodies of the five tortured Bene Gesserits.

Finally allowing himself to feel safe, Teg slowed himself down to normal time. Furnace-intensity body heat radiated from him, and perspiration poured from his scalp and down his face. He felt as if he had burned off a year of his life. Now the ravenous hunger slammed into him. Shuddering, Teg slumped back. Very soon, he would have to consume enough calories to make up for the huge quantity he had just expended, mainly carbohydrates with a restorative dose of melange.

The lift door opened and a frantic Duncan Idaho charged onto the navigation bridge. Seeing Teg at the controls, he stuttered to a halt and looked out the viewing plaz, astonished to see the new starfield.

"The net is gone." Panting, he turned his question-filled eyes toward Teg. "Miles, how did you get here? What happened?"

"I folded space—thanks to your warning. I ran to a different lift tube, which took me here immediately. It must have been faster than yours." He wiped perspiration off his forehead. When Duncan clearly remained skeptical of the explanation, the Bashar searched for a way to distract the other man. "Have we gotten away from the web?"

Duncan looked out at the emptiness around them. "This is bad, Miles. So soon after we popped back into normal space, the hunters have picked up our scent again."

Is there a more terrifying sensation than to stand on the brink and peer into the void of an empty future? Extinction not only of your life, but of all that has been accomplished by your forefathers? If we Tleilaxu plunge into the abyss of nothingness, does our race's long history signify anything at all?

TLEILAXU MASTER SCYTALE,
Wisdom for My Successor

After the funeral in space and the emergency with the unseen net, the last original Tleilaxu Master sat in his cell and contemplated his own mortality.

Scytale had been trapped aboard the no-ship for more than a decade before Sheeana and Duncan escaped from Chapterhouse. No longer was he simply a captive shielded from the hunting Honored Matres. The ship had been flung off into . . . he knew not where.

Of course, the whores swarming into Chapterhouse would surely have killed him as soon as they learned of his existence. Both he and Duncan Idaho were marked for death. At least out here, Scytale was safe from Murbella and her minions. But other threats abounded.

While back on Chapterhouse, he had been held in his inner chambers and prevented from seeing outside. Therefore, the witches could easily have modified the onboard diurnal cycles, creating some sort of insidious deception to throw off his bodily rhythms. They could have made him forget the holy days and misjudge the passage of time, though they paid lip service to the Tleilaxu Great Belief, claiming to share the sacred truths of the Islamiyat.

Scytale drew his thin legs up to his chest and wrapped his arms around his bony shins. It didn't matter. Though he was now allowed to move about in a large section of the huge ship, his incarceration had become an unendurable expanse of days and years, regardless of how it was cut up into smaller segments.

And the spaciousness of his austere quarters and confinement areas could not make him forget that he was still imprisoned. Scytale was permitted to leave this deck only under close supervision. After so much time, what did they think he might do? If the *Ithaca* was going to wander forever, they would eventually have to let down their barriers. Still, the Tleilaxu man preferred to remain apart from the other passengers.

No one had spoken with Scytale for a long time. *Dirty Tleilaxu!* He thought they were afraid of his taint . . . or maybe they simply enjoyed isolating him. No one would explain their plans to him, or tell him where this great ship was going.

The witch Sheeana knew he was holding something back. He couldn't lie to her—it did no good. At the beginning of this journey, the Tleilaxu Master had grudgingly revealed the method for making spice in axlotl tanks. With the ship's melange supplies obviously insufficient for the people aboard, he had offered a solution. That initial revelation—one of his most valuable bargaining chips—had been self-serving, since Scytale, too, feared spice withdrawal. He had bargained vigorously with Sheeana, finally agreeing on access to the library database and confinement in a much larger section of the no-ship as his reward.

Sheeana knew he had at least one other important secret, a piece of incredibly vital knowledge. The witch could sense it! But Scytale had never been driven to the extremes necessary to reveal what he carried. Not yet.

As far as he knew, he was the only surviving original Master. The Lost Ones had betrayed his people, aligning themselves with the Honored Matres who obliterated one sacred Tleilaxu world after another. As he had escaped from Tleilax, he had seen the ferocious whores launch their attack on holy Bandalong itself. Just thinking of it brought tears to his eyes.

By default, am I now the Mahai, the Master of Masters?

Scytale had escaped the rampaging Honored Matres and demanded sanctuary among the Bene Gesserit on Chapterhouse. Oh, they had kept him safe, but the witches had been unwilling to negotiate with him unless he gave up his sacred secrets. All of them! Initially the Sisterhood had wanted Tleilaxu axlotl tanks to create their own gholas, and he had been forced to reveal the information to them. Within a year after the destruction of Rakis, they grew a ghola of Bashar Miles Teg. Next, the Mother Superior had pressured him to explain how to use the tanks to manufacture melange, and Scytale refused, considering it too great a concession.

Unfortunately, he had hoarded his special knowledge too well, holding on to his advantage for too long. By the time he chose to reveal the workings of the axlotl tanks, the Bene Gesserits had already found their own solution. They had brought back small sandworms, and spice was sure to follow. He had been stupid to negotiate with them! To trust them! That bargaining chip had become useless until the passengers aboard the *Ithaca* had needed spice.

Of all the secrets Scytale had within him, only the largest one remained, and even his dire need had not been great enough to reveal it. Until now.

Everything had changed. Everything.

Scytale looked down at the untouched remnants of his meal. Powindah food, unclean outsider food. They tried to disguise it so that he would eat, yet he always suspected that their cooking contained impure substances. He had no choice, however. Would the Prophet prefer him to starve rather than eat unacceptable food . . . especially now, since he was the last great Master? Scytale alone carried the future of his once-great people, the intricate knowledge of the language of God. His survival was more vital than ever.

He paced the perimeter of his private chambers, measuring the boundaries of his confinement one tiny footstep at a time. The silence weighed heavily on him. He knew exactly what he had to do. He would offer the last scraps of his dignity and his hidden knowledge in the process; he had to gain as much advantage as he could.

There wasn't much time!

After a wave of dizziness passed, his stomach roiled, and he clutched his abdomen. Slumping back onto his cot, Scytale tried to drive away the pounding in his head and the twisting in his gut. He could feel the creeping death inside. The progressive bodily degeneration had taken root and was even now seeping through his body, winding through the tissues, the threads of muscle, the nerve fibers.

The Tleilaxu Masters never planned for an eventuality such as this. Scytale and the other Masters had survived numerous serial lifetimes. Their bodies died, but each time they were restored, their memories awakened in ghola after ghola after ghola. A new copy was always growing in a tank, ready for whenever it might be needed.

As genetic wizards, the great Tleilaxu created their own path from one physical body to the next. Their schemes had continued for so many millennia that the Masters let themselves become complacent. Proud and blind, they had not considered the depths into which Fate might hurl them.

Now the Tleilaxu worlds were overrun, the laboratories ransacked, all the gholas of the Masters destroyed. No reincarnation of Scytale waited in the wings. He had nowhere to turn.

And now he was dying.

In creating one ghola after another, the Tleilaxu Masters had wasted no effort on perfection, which they believed was arrogance in the eyes of God, since any human creation must be flawed. Thus, the Masters' gholas contained cumulative genetic mistakes, errors in repetition that eventually resulted in a shortened life span for each body.

Scytale and his fellow Masters had allowed themselves to believe the shortened life span of each incarnation was irrelevant, since they could simply be restored in a new, fresh body. What was the significance of an extra decade or two, so long as the chain of reawakened gholas remained unbroken?

Unfortunately, Scytale now faced the fatal flaw, *alone*. There were no gholas of himself and no available axlotl tanks that he could use to create one. But the witches could do it. . . .

He didn't know how much time he had left.

Closely attuned to his bodily processes, Scytale was tormented by his degeneration. If he was optimistic, he might have fifteen years remaining. Always before, Scytale had held onto the final secret hidden inside his body, refusing to offer it in trade. But now his last resistance was broken. As the sole remaining keeper of Tleilaxu secrets and memories, he could risk no further delay. Survival was more important than secrets.

He touched his chest, knowing that implanted beneath his skin was a hitherto-undetected nullentropy capsule, a tiny treasure trove of preserved cells that the Tleilaxu had collected for thousands upon thousands of years. Key figures from history were contained therein, obtained from secret scrapings of dead bodies: Tleilaxu Masters, Face Dancers—even Paul Muad'Dib, Duke Leto Atreides and Jessica, Chani, Stilgar, the Tyrant Leto II, Gurney Halleck, Thufir Hawat, and other legendary figures all the way back to Serena Butler and Xavier Harkonnen from the Butlerian Jihad.

The Sisterhood would be desperate to have this. Granting him complete freedom of the ship would be a minor concession compared to what he would demand as his true recompense. *My own ghola.* Continuation.

Scytale swallowed hard, felt the tendrils of death within him, and knew there could be no turning back. *Survival is more important than secrets,* he repeated to himself in the privacy of his mind.

He sent a signal to summon Sheeana. He would make the witches an offer that they could not afford to ignore.

*We carry our grail in our heads. Hold it gently and reverently if it
ever surfaces in your consciousness.*

—MOTHER SUPERIOR DARWI ODRADE

The air smelled of spice, harsh and unprocessed, the acrid odor of
the deadly Water of Life. The scent of fear and triumph, the
Agony which all potential Reverend Mothers must face.

Please, Murbella thought, *let my daughter survive this, as I did.* She
did not know to whom she was praying.

As Mother Commander, she had to show strength and confidence,
regardless of what she felt inside. But Rinya was one of the twins, a last
tenuous connection with Duncan. The tests had demonstrated that
she was qualified, talented, and, despite her young age, ready. Rinya
had always been the more aggressive of the twins, goal driven, reaching
for the impossible. She wanted to become a Reverend Mother as young
as Sheeana had been. Fourteen! Murbella both admired her daughter
for that drive, and feared for her.

In the background, she heard the deep-voiced Bene Gesserit Bellonda engaged in a vociferous argument with her Honored Matre
counterpart, Doria. A common occurrence. The pair were squabbling
in the corridor of the Chapterhouse Keep. "She is young, far too
young! Only a child—"

"A child?" Doria said. "She is the daughter of the Mother Commander and Duncan Idaho!"

"Yes, the genetics are strong, but it is still madness. We risk so much if we push her too soon. Give her another year."

"She is part Honored Matre. That alone should carry her through."

They all turned to watch as black-robed proctors brought Rinya from an anteroom, prepared for her ordeal. As Mother Commander and a Bene Gesserit, Murbella was not supposed to show favoritism or love toward her own daughters. In fact, most of the Sisterhood's children did not know the identity of their parents.

Rinya had been born only a few minutes before her sister Janess. The girl—a prodigy—was ambitious, impatient, and unquestionably talented, while her sister shared the same qualities but with just a hint more caution. Rinya always had to be first.

Murbella had watched her twin daughters excel at every challenge, and acceded to Rinya's request. If anyone had superior potential, this one did—or so Rinya had convinced herself.

The current time of crisis forced the New Sisterhood to take greater risks than usual, to chance losing daughters in order to gain much-needed Reverend Mothers. If Rinya failed at this, there would be no second chance for her. None. Murbella felt a knot in her chest.

Moving methodically, the proctors strapped Rinya's arms to a table to keep her from lashing out during the throes of the transition. One proctor gave an extra tug to the strap on her left wrist, making the girl wince and then flash a dark glare of displeasure—so like an Honored Matre! But Rinya uttered no complaint. Her lips moved faintly, and Murbella recognized the words, the age-old Litany Against Fear.

I must not fear . . .

Good! At least the girl was not so arrogant as to ignore the true weight and terror of what she was about to go through. Murbella remembered when she had faced the same test.

Glancing toward the door, where Bellonda and Doria had finally stopped bickering, she saw the other twin enter. Janess was named after a woman from long ago who had saved young Duncan Idaho from the Harkonnens. Duncan had told her that story one night after they'd made love, no doubt believing that Murbella would forget. He himself had never learned the names of any of their daughters: Rinya and Janess, Tanidia who was just beginning her acolyte training, and Gianne, only three years old, born just before Duncan had escaped.

Now Janess seemed reluctant to come all the way into the room, but she would not leave her sister alone during this ordeal. She brushed her curly black hair out of her face, revealing fearful eyes; she clearly didn't want to think about what could go wrong when Rinya consumed the deadly poison. Spice Agony. Even the words evoked mystery and terror.

Looking down at the table, Murbella saw her daughter mouth the Litany again: *Fear is the mind-killer . . .*

She didn't seem aware of Janess or any of the women in the room. The air had a close, heady scent of bitter cinnamon and possibilities. The Mother Commander could not interfere, did not even touch the girl's hand to comfort her. Rinya was strong and determined. This ritual was not about comfort, but about adaptation and survival. A fight against death.

Fear is the little-death that brings total obliteration . . .

Analyzing her emotions (how like a Bene Gesserit!) Murbella wondered whether she feared losing Rinya as a potential and valuable Reverend Mother for the Sisterhood, or as a person. Or was she more afraid of losing one of her few tangible reminders of her long-lost Duncan?

Rinya and Janess had been eleven when the no-ship disappeared with their father. The twins had been acolytes, dutifully undergoing strict Bene Gesserit training. In all those years before Duncan's departure, neither girl had been allowed to meet him.

Murbella's gaze met Janess's, and a flash of emotion passed between them like roiling smoke. She turned away, concentrating on the girl on the table, reassuring Rinya by her presence. The visible strain on her daughter's face fanned the flames of her own doubt.

Flushed, Bellonda entered the room, disturbing the solemn meditations. She glanced at the imperfectly hidden anxiety on Rinya's face, then up at Murbella. "Preparations are complete, Mother Commander."

Close behind her, Doria said, "We should get on with it."

Strapped down on the table, Rinya lifted her head against the restraints, turned her gaze from her twin sister to her mother, and then flashed Janess a reassuring smile. "I am ready. You will be too, my sister." She lay back, refocused, and continued mouthing the litany.

I will face my fear . . .

Saying nothing, Murbella went to stand by Janess, who was clearly in turmoil, barely restraining herself. Murbella gripped her forearm, but her daughter didn't flinch. What did she know? What doubts had the twins voiced to each other in their acolyte bungalows at night?

One of the proctors swung an oral syringe into position, then used her fingers to open Rinya's mouth. The young woman let her mouth fall slack as the proctor inserted the syringe.

Murbella wanted to shout at her daughter, telling her that she did not need to prove anything. Not until she was absolutely ready. But even if she'd had doubts, Rinya would never change her mind. She was stubborn, determined to go through with the process. And Murbella was forbidden to interfere. She was Mother Commander now, not a mere mother.

Caught up in her ordeal, Rinya closed her eyes in total acceptance. The line of her jaw was firm, defying anything to harm her. Murbella had seen that expression on Duncan's face many times.

Janess burst forward unexpectedly, no longer able to contain her misgivings. "She is not ready! Can't you see that? She told me. She knows she can't—"

Startled by the disturbance, Rinya turned her head, but the proctors had already activated the pumps. A gush of potent chemical odor stung the air just as Janess tried to yank the syringe out of her sister's mouth.

With surprising speed for her bulk, Bellonda shouldered Janess aside, knocking her to the floor.

"Janess, stop this!" Murbella snapped with all the command she could muster. When her daughter continued to struggle, she used Voice. "*Stop!*" At this, the young woman's muscles involuntarily froze.

"You're wasting an insufficiently prepared Sister," Janess cried. "My sister!"

Murbella said in a withering voice, "You must not interfere with the Agony in any way. You have distracted Rinya at a vital moment."

One of the proctors announced, "We succeeded, despite the disturbance. Rinya has taken the Water of Life."

The poison began to act.

DEADLY EUPHORIA BURNED through her veins, challenging her cellular ability to deal with it. Rinya began to see her own future. Like a Guild Navigator, her mind was able to negotiate a safe path through the veils of time, avoiding obstacles and curtains that blocked her view. She saw herself on the table, along with her mother and twin sister, who were unable to hide their concern. It was like looking through a blurred lens.

I will permit it to pass over me and through me . . .

Then, incontrovertibly, as if curtains had been pulled from a window to reveal a flood of blinding light, Rinya beheld her own death— and could do nothing to prevent it. Nor could Janess, who shouted. And Murbella realized: She *knew.*

Locked away inside her body, Rinya experienced a powerful lance of pain from the core of her body to her brain.

And when it has gone past me I will turn the inner eye to see its path. Where the fear has gone there will be nothing. Only I will remain . . .

Rinya had recalled the entire Litany. Then she felt nothing at all.

RINYA CONVULSED ON the table, trying to rip free of the restraints. The teenager's face had become a contorted mask of shock, pain, and terror. Her eyes were glazed . . . almost gone.

Murbella could not cry out, could not speak. She stood utterly still as a fierce storm churned within her. Janess had known! Or had she caused it?

For a moment Rinya lapsed into quiescence, her eyelids fluttered, and then she let loose a horrendous scream that cut through the room with a knife of sound.

In slow motion, Murbella reached for her dead daughter and touched the still-warm skin of her cheek. In the background, she heard Janess's anguished cry fill the room, alongside her own.

It is only through constant and diligent practice that we are able to achieve the potential—the perfection—of our lives. Those of us who have had more than one life have had more opportunity to practice.

—DUNCAN IDAHO,
A Thousand Lives

Duncan faced his opponent in the neutral-walled chamber, holding a short-sword in one hand, a kindjal dagger in the other. Miles Teg, steely eyed, did not blink. The room's padding and insulation swallowed most sounds.

It would be a mistake to view this youth as a mere boy. Teg's reflexes and speed could match, or even defeat, any fighter pitted against him . . . and Duncan could sense something *more* about him, a mysterious skill set that the young Bashar kept well hidden.

But then, Duncan thought, *we all do the same thing.*

"Activate your shield, Miles. Always be prepared. For anything."

The two men reached to their belts and touched the power buttons. A small, humming half-shield appeared, a rectangular blur in the air that adjusted to its wearer's movements, swinging to protect vulnerable areas.

These walls and the hard floor held many memories for Duncan, like indelible stains on the impermeable plates. He and Murbella had used this as their practice room, improving their methods, fighting, colliding . . . and often ending in a sexual tumble. Because he was a

Mentat, those individual memories would never fade, keeping him strongly connected to Murbella, as if by a fish hook caught in his chest.

Now, as part of the training dance, Duncan eased forward and touched his shield to Teg's. The crackle of polarized fields and sharp smell of ozone answered them. The two stepped back, raised their blades in a salute, and began.

"We will review the ancient Ginaz disciplines," Duncan said.

The young man slashed with his dagger. Teg reminded him very much of Duke Leto—intentionally so, thanks to generations of Bene Gesserit breeding.

Expecting a feint, Duncan parried upward, but the teenage Bashar reversed his feint and turned it into a real attack, punching the blade against the half shield. He had moved too quickly, though. Teg still wasn't accustomed to this odd method of fighting, and the Holtzman field deflected the dagger.

Duncan skipped back, cracked Teg's shield with his short-sword just to show that he could, and took a step in retreat. "It is an archaic duel-ing method, Miles, but one with many nuances. Though it was devel-oped long before the time of Muad'Dib, some might say it came from a more civilized time."

"No one studies the methods of Swordmasters anymore."

"Exactly! Therefore, you will have skills in your repertoire that no one else possesses." They clashed again, the metal-clattering of sword against sword, dagger fending off dagger. "And, if Scytale's nullentropy tube truly contains what he says it does, we may soon have others who are familiar with those ancient times."

The recent and unexpected revelation by the captive Tleilaxu Mas-ter had resurrected a flood of memories from Duncan's past lives. A small implanted nullentropy capsule—perfectly preserved sample cells taken from great figures of history and legend! Sheeana and the Bene Gesserit Suk doctors had been analyzing the cells, sorting and labeling them, determining what sort of genetic treasures the Tleilaxu had given them in exchange for his freedom, in exchange for a ghola of his own.

Supposedly Thufir Hawat was in there, and Gurney Halleck, along with a number of Duncan's other long-lost comrades. Duke Leto the

Just, Lady Jessica, Paul Atreides, and the "Abomination" Alia, who had once been Duncan's lover and consort. Haunted by them now, he felt achingly alone, yet filled with hope. Was there really such a thing as the future, or was it just the past, returning over and over?

His life—*lives*—had always seemed to carry a definite direction. He was the legendary Duncan Idaho, a paragon of loyalty. But more than ever before, he had been feeling lost. Had the escape from Chapterhouse been the right thing to do? Who were the old man and woman, and what did they want? Were *they* truly the great Outside Enemy, or another threat entirely?

Not even Duncan knew where the *Ithaca* was going. Would he and his shipmates eventually find a destination, or would they simply wander until the end of their days? The very idea of fleeing and hiding grated on him.

Duncan actually knew more about being hunted than anyone aboard; he'd earned a visceral understanding of it long ago. As a child in his very first lifetime under the Harkonnens, he had been used as prey in Beast Rabban's hunts. Rabban and his henchmen had turned the boy loose in a large forest preserve, where young Duncan had finally outwitted his rivals, finding a smuggler pilot who provided him with safe passage. *Janess* . . . that had been her name. He recalled telling Murbella about the escape years ago, as they lay on sweat-dampened sheets.

Sensing his distraction, Teg cut, pushed, and slid his kindjal partway through the shield before Duncan retreated, smiling with satisfaction. "Good! You are learning to control yourself."

Teg's expression did not change. Lack of control was not one of the Bashar's weak points. "You seemed distracted, so I took advantage of it."

As he looked at the young man before him, sweat dripping down his brow, Duncan saw a strangely doubled image. As an old man, the original Bashar had raised and trained the Duncan ghola child; later, after Teg's death on Rakis, the mature Duncan Idaho ghola had raised the reborn boy. Was this to be an endless cycle? Duncan Idaho and Miles Teg as eternal companions, alternating as mentor and student, each filling the same role at separate times in their lives?

"I remember when I instructed young Paul Atreides in Swordmaster techniques. We had a training mek in Castle Caladan, and Paul learned to defeat it at any setting we chose. Even so, he did better against a live opponent."

"I prefer an enemy that bleeds when I defeat it."

Duncan laughed. "Paul once said something just like that, too."

He and Teg continued to fight for the better part of an hour, but Duncan found himself preoccupied with, and reminded of, long-past training duels. If what the Tleilaxu Master said was true and they could bring back gholas of the key comrades in Duncan's past, then these daydreams need no longer be tedious memories for him. They could become real again.

Illusion, Miles. Illusion is their way. The fashioning of false impressions to achieve real goals, that is how the Tleilaxu work.

—JANET ROXBROUGH-TEG,
mother of Miles Teg

Now broken by the Face Dancers and bound by fear to do exactly as they commanded, an anxious Uxtal was dispatched to Tleilax for "an important assignment." Khrone had been expressionless as he explained to the small, frightened man, "The Honored Matres have found something in the ruins of Bandalong that interests us. We require your expertise."

Sacred Bandalong! For a moment, the thrill eclipsed his intimidation. Uxtal had heard legends of this once-great place, the heartland of his people, but he had never been there. Few of the Lost Tleilaxu had been welcomed by the suspicious original Masters. He had always hoped to make a hajj at some point in his life, a pilgrimage. But not like this . . .

"W-what can I do?" The Lost Tleilaxu researcher shuddered to think what the turncoat Face Dancers would demand of him. Right before his eyes, they had killed Elder Burah. By now they might well have replaced every member of the Council of Elders! Every moment was a nightmare for Uxtal; he knew that each person around him could be another hidden shape-shifter. He jumped at any startling sound, any sudden movement. He could trust no one.

But at least I am alive. He clung to that. *I am still alive!*

"You can work with axlotl tanks, correct? You have the knowledge necessary to grow a ghola, if we wish it?"

Uxtal knew they would kill him if he gave the wrong answer. "It requires a female body, specially adapted so that her womb becomes a factory." He swallowed hard, wondering how he could make himself appear more intelligent, more confident. A ghola? Lower-caste Tleilaxu knew nothing about the Language of God required to grow flesh, but as a member of a higher caste, Uxtal should be able to accomplish it. They would discard him otherwise. Perhaps if the Face Dancers got him just a little assistance, someone with additional knowledge . . .

Uxtal still cringed at the recollection of blood oozing from Elder Burah's crushed eyes, and the sickening *snap* as the Face Dancers broke the older man's neck. "I will do as you command."

"Good. You are the only sufficiently trained Tleilaxu still alive."

The only . . . ? Uxtal gulped. What had the Honored Matres found in Bandalong? And what did the Face Dancers want with it? He had not dared to ask Khrone anything else, though. He didn't want to know. Having too much knowledge could get him killed.

The Honored Matres frightened Uxtal almost as much as the turncoat Face Dancers did. The Lost Tleilaxu had been allies of the whores against the original Masters, and now Uxtal could see that Khrone and his fellow shape-shifters had made bargains of their own. He had no idea whom these new Face Dancers served. Could they possibly be . . . independent? Inconceivable!

ARRIVING AT THE core world of Tleilax, Uxtal was shocked at the extent of the damage. Using their terrible, unstoppable weapon, the female attackers had burned every original Tleilaxu planet in a series of horrific holocausts. Though Bandalong itself had not been completely incinerated after all, it had been beaten nearly to death, its buildings scarred, its Masters rounded up and executed. Lower-caste workers were ground under the boot heel of the new rulers. Only the strongest structures in the capital city, including the Palace of Banda-long, had survived, and Honored Matres now occupied them.

Stepping out into the terminal of the reconstructed main shuttle station, Uxtal wavered at the unwelcome sight of the tall, dominant women. They strode about everywhere in their leotards and gaudy capes, but did no work beyond supervising and guarding the various operations. The real labor was done by surviving members of the unclean lower castes. At least Uxtal was better off than that. Khrone had chosen him for important work.

The shuttle station was hastily put together with obvious construc-tion defects such as gaps in walls, uneven places in the floor, and door-ways that did not appear to be plumb. The Honored Matres worried only about superficial impressions, paying little attention to details. They did not expect, or require, anything to last for long.

Two women approached him, tall and severe in their blue-and-red tights. The more dangerous-looking of the pair eyed him deprecat-ingly. He was not cheered by the fact that they seemed to know who he was. "Matre Superior Hellica awaits you." Uxtal followed at a brisk pace, eager to show his cooperation. The two women seemed to be watching—hoping?—for him to make a wrong move.

Honored Matres enslaved males through unbreakable sexual tech-niques. Uxtal feared they would try to do the same to him—a process with these powindah women that he found horrifyingly unclean and disgusting. Before sending Uxtal to Tleilax, Khrone had mutilated his Lost Tleilaxu slave "as a precaution" against the women, though Uxtal wondered if the preventive measures had not been as awful as the Honored Matres themselves. . . .

The two women shoved him into the rear passenger compartment of a groundcar and drove off. Uxtal tried to occupy himself by looking out the windows, pretending to be a sightseer or a hajji, a tourist mak-ing a pilgrimage to the most sacred of Tleilaxu cities. The newly erected buildings had a bright vulgarity, quite unlike the grandeur of Bandalong as described in the legends. Construction activities were ongoing in every direction. Slave crews operated ground equipment, and suspensor cranes put up more buildings, working at a frenzied pace. Uxtal found it all rather disheartening.

Some shells of buildings had been reconditioned to suit the purposes of the occupying army. The groundcar sped past what once must have been a holy temple, but which now looked like a military building. Armed women filled the front plaza. An ornate statue stood blackened and forlorn, perhaps left that way as a sign of the Honored Matres' conquest.

Uxtal felt bleaker by the moment. How was he ever going to get out of this? What had he done to deserve his fate? While observing his surroundings, integers filled his mind as he tried to decipher codes and find a sacred mathematical explanation for what had occurred here. God always had a master plan, which could be determined if one knew the equations. He tried to count the number of holy sites that had been defiled, how many blocks they passed, how many turns they took on a winding road that led to the former Palace. It rapidly became a calculation far too complex for him to solve.

He was alert, absorbing as much information as possible, to ensure his own survival. He would do whatever was necessary to keep himself alive. It only made sense, especially if he was one of the last of his kind. God would want him to survive.

Above the west wing of the Palace, a suspensor crane floated high, lowering a bright red section of roof into place. Uxtal shuddered at the garish new look of the structure—pink columns, scarlet roofs, and lemon yellow walls. The Palace looked more like a carnival structure than a holy residence for the Masheikhs, the greatest masters.

His two escorts took Uxtal past snaking energy cables and crews of lower-caste Tleilaxu operating power tools, mounting wall hangings, installing rococo glowpanels. Uxtal entered an immense room with a high domed ceiling, which made him feel even smaller than he was. He saw charred panels and the remnants of quoted scripture from the Great Belief. The monstrous women had covered many of the verses with their sacrilegious decorations. Even hidden by lies, though, the word of God remained supremely powerful. Someday, after all this was over and he could come back, maybe he would do something about it. Make things right again.

With a noisy clatter, an ostentatious throne emerged from an opening in the floor. An older blonde woman sat back, looking like a once-beautiful queen who had been poorly preserved. The throne rose higher, until the regal woman glowered down at him. Matre Superior Hellica.

Her eyes flickered with an undertone of orange. "At this meeting, I decide whether you live or die, little man." Her words boomed so loudly that her voice must have been augmented.

Uxtal remained petrified as he prayed silently, trying to look as insignificant and conciliatory as possible. He wished he could disappear through an opening in the floor and escape into an underground tunnel. Or, if only he could defeat these women instead, and fight—

"Do you have vocal cords, little man? Or have they been removed? You have my permission to speak, as long as you say something intelligent."

Uxtal summoned his courage, being as brave as Elder Burah would have wanted him to be. "I—I do not know exactly why I am here, only that it is an important genetic assignment." His mind raced for a way out of his predicament. "My experience in that field is unsurpassed. If you need someone to do the work of a Tleilaxu Master, there can be no better choice."

"We have no other choice at all." Hellica sounded disgusted. "Your ego will diminish after I bond you to me sexually."

Trying not to cringe, Uxtal said, "I-I must stay focused on my work, Matre Superior, rather than be distracted by obsessive erotic thoughts."

She obviously enjoyed watching him suffer, but the Matre Superior was just toying with him. Her smile gaped red and raw, as if someone had cut a gash across her face with a razor blade. "The Face Dancers want something from you, and so do the Honored Matres. Because all Tleilaxu Masters are now dead, your specialized knowledge grants you a certain importance by default. Perhaps I won't tamper with you. Yet."

She leaned forward and glared. His two escorts stepped back, as if afraid to be in Hellica's targeting zone. "It is said you are familiar with axlotl tanks. The Masters knew how to use those tanks to create melange. Incredible wealth! Can you do that for us?"

Uxtal felt his feet turn to ice. He couldn't stop shaking. "No, Matre Superior. The technique was not developed until after the Scattering, when my people were gone from the Old Empire. The Masters did not share that information with their Lost brothers." His heart pounded. She was obviously displeased, *murderously* displeased, so he continued quickly, "I *do* know how to grow gholas, however."

"But is that knowledge useful enough to save your life?" She heaved a disappointed sigh. "The Face Dancers seem to think so."

"And what do the Face Dancers want, Matre Superior?"

Her eyes flashed orange, and he knew he had made a mistake by blurting his question. "I have not yet finished *telling* you what the Honored Matres want, little man. Though we are not so weak as to be addicted to spice, like the Bene Gesserit witches, we do understand its value. You would please me most if you rediscovered how to create melange. I will provide as many women as you need for brainless wombs." Her words carried a cruel undertone.

"There is, however, an alternative substance we use, an orange adrenaline-based chemical that is derived primarily from *pain*. We will show you how to manufacture it. That will be your first service for us. A repaired laboratory building will be made available to you. We can add modules, if necessary."

When Hellica rose from her throne, her presence was even more intimidating. "Now, as for what the Face Dancers want from you: When we conquered this planet and liquidated the despicable Masters, we discovered something unusual during our autopsy and analysis of one burned corpse. A damaged nullentropy capsule was cleverly hidden inside the Master's body. It contained cellular samples, mostly destroyed, but with a small amount of viable DNA. Khrone is very interested to learn what was so important about those cells, and why the Masters protected and hid them so well."

Uxtal's mind spun forward. "He wants me to grow a ghola from those cells?" He could barely cover his relief. This was something he could indeed do!

"I will allow you to do so, provided you also create our orange spice substitute. If you succeed in producing actual melange from the axlotl tanks, then we will be even more pleased." Hellica's eyes narrowed. "From this day forth your solitary goal in life is to see how well you can please me."

DESPERATELY RELIEVED TO be away from the volatile Matre Superior—and still alive—Uxtal followed the two female escorts to his purported research center. Bandalong was so full of chaos and destruction, he wasn't sure what sort of facility to expect. Along the way, he and his two looming companions passed a large military convoy of purple-uniformed women, groundtrucks, and demolition equipment.

When they arrived at the commandeered lab, a locked door stood against them. While the stern-looking females tried to deal with the problem, growing more befuddled and angry by the moment, Uxtal slipped away on trembling legs. He made a show of inspecting the grounds, primarily to keep his distance from the dangerous women as they pounded on the door and demanded entrance. He had no hope of escaping, even if he found a weapon, attacked them, and raced back to the Bandalong spaceport. Uxtal cringed, thinking up excuses if the women should challenge what he was doing.

Grasses and weeds already grew in the charred ground surrounding the facility. He peered over a split bar fence to the adjacent property where an elderly, low-caste farmer tended to immense sligs, each larger than a man. The ugly creatures rooted around in mud, eating steaming piles of garbage and debris stripped from the burned buildings. Despite the creatures' filthy habits, slig meat was considered a delicacy. At the moment, however, the stench of excrement robbed Uxtal of all appetite.

After having been bullied for so long, he was pleased to see someone weaker than himself for a change, and shouted officiously to the low-caste slig farmer, "You! Identify yourself." Uxtal doubted if the filth-smeared worker could provide any useful information, but Elder Burah had taught him that all information was useful, especially in unfamiliar surroundings.

"I am Gaxhar. I've never heard an accent like yours." The farmer limped over to the fence and looked at Uxtal's formal high-caste uniform, which was, thankfully, much cleaner than the slig farmer's. "I thought all the Masters were dead."

"I'm not a Master, not technically." Struggling to maintain his haughty position of authority, Uxtal added sternly, "But I am still your superior. Keep your sligs away from this side of the property. I cannot afford to have my important laboratory contaminated. Your sligs carry flies and disease."

"I wash them down every day, but I will keep them away from the fences." In their pen, the wide, sluglike animals rolled over each other, slithering and squealing.

At a loss for anything else to say, Uxtal gave a weak-sounding and unnecessary warning. "You had better watch yourself around the Honored Matres. I am safe because of my special knowledge, but they might turn on a mere farmer in an instant and tear you to pieces."

Gaxhar made a snort that was halfway between a laugh and a cough. "The old Masters were no kinder to me than the Honored Matres are. I've just gone from one cruel overlord to another."

A groundtruck rumbled up to the sligs. With a dump mechanism, it released a load of wet, reeking garbage. The hungry creatures swarmed to the putrid feast, while the farmer crossed his arms over his scrawny chest. "Honored Matres send the body parts of high-caste men for my sligs to eat. They think the flesh of my superiors makes the slig meat taste sweeter." The barest hint of a disrespectful sneer was quickly hidden by the man's generally blank expression. "Perhaps I will see you again."

What did he mean? That Uxtal would be dumped here, too, when the whores were finished with him? Or was it just innocuous conversation? Uxtal frowned, unable to take his eyes from the sligs crawling over the body parts, chewing them efficiently with their multiple mouths.

Finally, his two Honored Matre escorts came to fetch him. "You may enter your laboratory now. We have destroyed the door."

There is no escape—we pay for the violence of our ancestors.
—from "Collected Sayings of Muad'Dib" by the
PRINCESS IRULAN

R inya's been gone for a month now. I miss her terribly." Walking beside Janess toward the acolytes' bungalows, Murbella could see her struggling to mask the anguish on her face.

Despite the feelings in her own heart, the Mother Commander maintained a distant expression. "Do not make me lose another daughter, or another potential Reverend Mother. When the time comes, you must be certain you are prepared for the Agony. Do not let your pride rush you."

Janess nodded stoically. She would not speak ill of her lost twin, but she and Murbella both knew that Rinya had not been as confident as she had claimed. Instead, she had covered her doubts with a veneer of false bravado. And that had killed her.

A Bene Gesserit had to hide her emotions, to drive away any vestiges of distracting love. Once, Murbella herself had been trapped by love, tangled and weakened by her bond with Duncan Idaho. Losing him had not freed her, and the thought of him still out there in the void, unimaginably far away, gave her a constant ache.

Despite their stated position, the Sisterhood had long known that love could not be eliminated completely. Like ancient priests and nuns from some long-obsolete religion, Bene Gesserits were supposed to give up love entirely for a greater cause. But in the long run, it never worked to discard everything in order to protect against one perceived weakness. One could not save humans by forcing them to surrender their humanity.

By remaining in close contact with the twins and observing their training, even revealing the identities of their parents, Murbella had broken the Sisterhood's tradition. Most daughters taken into Bene Gesserit schools were told to reach their potential "without the distractions of family ties." The Mother Commander did keep herself separate and aloof from the two younger daughters, Tanidia and Gianne, however. But she had lost Rinya and refused to cut herself off from Janess.

Now, following a training session in combined Bene Gesserit and Honored Matre fighting skills, the two of them made their way across the Keep's west garden, heading toward where Janess and her fellow acolytes lived. The girl still wore her rumpled and sweat-stained white combat suit.

The Mother Commander kept her voice neutral, though she, too, felt the pang in her heart. "We must go on with our lives. We still have many enemies to face. Rinya would want us to."

Janess straightened as she walked. "Yes, she would. She believed you about the Enemy, and so do I."

Some Sisters doubted the Mother Commander's urgency. Honored Matres had come running back into the Old Empire, sure that the sky was falling. But before Murbella stripped away all the foundations of the Bene Gesserit, a few of the women had demanded proof that such a terrible opponent truly existed out there. No Honored Matre had ever gone deep enough into Other Memory to remember much of her past; even Murbella could not recall their origin out in the Scattering, and could not say how they had first encountered their Enemy or what had provoked them to genocidal fury.

Murbella couldn't believe such blindness. Had the Honored Matres just imagined hundreds of planets eradicated by plague? Had they simply wished into existence the great Weapons used to obliterate Rakis and so many other planets?

"We need no further evidence to know the Enemy is out there," Murbella said curtly to her daughter, as they followed a dry, thorny hedge. "And they are now coming after us. All of us. I doubt the Enemy will make any distinctions among the factions of our New Sisterhood. Chapterhouse itself is certainly within their targeting crosshairs."

"If they find us," Janess said.

"Oh, they will find us. And they will destroy us, if we are not prepared." She looked at the young woman, seeing so much potential in her daughter's face. "Which is why we need as many Reverend Mothers as possible."

Janess had thrown herself into her studies with a determination that would have surprised even her obsessive, driven twin. Fighting with her hands and feet, spinning, rolling, dodging, the girl could strike an adversary from all sides, encircling her with speed and power.

Earlier that day Janess had faced off against a tall, wiry girl named Caree Debrak. Caree had come in as a young student from the newly conquered Honored Matres swarming toward Chapterhouse. Harboring resentment against the Mother Commander's daughter, Caree had used the competitive event as an excuse to vent her anger. She intended to *hurt*. Janess had practiced the lesson's moves and expected to beat the girl in fair combat, but the youthful Honored Matre had unleashed a raw form of violence, breaking the rules and nearly breaking Janess's bones. The female bashar in charge of personal combat training, Wikki Aztin, had dragged the pair apart.

The incident troubled Murbella greatly. "You lost to Caree because the Honored Matres have no inhibitions. You must learn to match them in that, if you mean to succeed here."

In the past several months, Murbella had detected an ugly undertone, especially among the younger trainees. Though all were supposedly part of a united Sisterhood, they still insisted on segregating themselves, wearing colors and badges, separating into cliques clearly defined by their heritage as either Bene Gesserit or Honored Matre.

Some of the more severe malcontents, disgusted with conciliation and refusing to learn or compromise, continued to disappear to their own settlements far to the north, even after the execution of Annine.

As they approached the acolytes' barracks, Murbella heard a clamor of angry voices through the brittle brown hedges. Rounding a turn in the garden path, they came to the commons, an expanse of withered grass and gravel walkways fronting the bungalows. Normally the acolytes gathered there for games, picnics, and sporting events, though an unexpected dust storm had left a layer of grit on the benches.

Today, most of the class was arrayed on the parched lawn as if it were a battlefield—more than fifty girls in white robes, all acolytes. The girls, divided into distinct groups of Bene Gesserits and Honored Matres, threw themselves upon each other like howling animals.

Murbella recognized Caree Debrak amidst the combatants. The girl knocked a rival down with a hard kick to the face and then pounced upon her like a hungry predator. While the fallen acolyte thrashed and fought back, Caree grabbed her hair, stepped hard on her chest, and yanked upward with enough force to uproot a tree. The sickening snap of the girl's neck carried even above the frenzy of the melee.

Grinning, Caree left the corpse on the dry ground and whirled to go after another opponent. Acolytes with orange Honored Matre armbands attacked their Bene Gesserit rivals with wild abandon, punching, kicking, gouging, even using teeth to rip skin. Already, more than a dozen young women lay sprawled like bloody rags on the dry grass. Shrieks of anger, pain, and defiance welled up from undisciplined throats. This was no game, nor was it practice play.

Appalled at the behavior, Murbella shouted, "Stop this! All of you!"

But the acolytes, their adrenaline surging, continued to tear and scream at each other. One girl, a former Honored Matre, staggered forward, her hands hooked into claws that lashed out at any noise; her eye sockets were unseeing, bloody pits.

Murbella saw two young Bene Gesserits knock down a thrashing Honored Matre and tear the orange band from her arm. With hard punches strong enough to shatter their victim's sternum, the Bene Gesserit acolytes killed her.

Caree flew feet first at the aggressive pair. She slammed into them simultaneously and sent them rolling away. A kick crushed the larynx of one, but the other ducked a follow-through blow. While her companion collapsed, gurgling and choking, the other rolled and sprang to her feet, clutching a broken chunk of rock that had been part of the landscaping.

Guards, proctors, and Reverend Mothers came running from the Keep. Bashar Aztin led her own troops, and Murbella noticed that they all carried heavy stunner weapons. The Mother Commander shouted into the mayhem, using Voice to make her words strike the listeners like projectiles. But the din was so great that none of the acolytes seemed to hear her.

Side by side, Janess and Murbella waded into the acolytes who were still fighting and rained blows on them, paying no attention to whether their targets wore orange bands or not. Murbella noticed her daughter increasing her intensity, pouring her entire body into fighting moves.

Murbella tucked her own head and slammed into a gleefully victorious Caree Debrak, driving her hard to the ground. The Mother Commander could easily have landed a fatal blow, but restrained herself enough to merely knock the wind out of the girl.

Gasping and retching, Caree rolled over and glared at Murbella and Janess. She climbed to her feet, wavering. "Didn't you get enough from me earlier, Janess? You want more of the same?" She swung a fist.

With obvious effort, Janess controlled herself, easily dodging but not retaliating. "'There is more skill in avoiding confrontations than in engaging in them.' That's a Bene Gesserit axiom."

Caree spat. "What do I care for witches' axioms? Do you have any thoughts of your own? Or only your mother's, and quotes from an old book?"

Caree barely had the words out before she lashed out with a powerful kick. Anticipating it, Janess darted to the left and came around on her opponent's side, striking her temples with a sharp fist. The young Honored Matre went down, and Janess gave her a stunning kick in the forehead that slammed her backward.

Finally, the skirmish petered out as more women arrived to pull the fighters apart. The whole commons was littered with the remnants of the bloody brawl. A volley of stun fire dropped several of the still-fighting acolytes together into a heap on the ground, unconscious but alive.

Heaving great breaths, Murbella surveyed the bloody field in disgust and fury. She shouted at the young Honored Matres, "Your orange bands caused this! Why flaunt your differences instead of joining us?"

Glancing to her side, Murbella saw Janess had taken up a stance to protect the Mother Commander. The girl might not be ready for the Spice Agony yet, but she was ready for this.

The surviving acolytes began slinking toward their respective bungalows. Voicing her mother's thoughts, Janess shouted at them, over the dead bodies strewn on the brown grass, "Look at all the wasted resources! If we keep this up, the Enemy won't need to kill any of us."

Once a plan is conceived, it takes on a life of its own. Merely considering and constructing a scheme puts a certain stamp of inevitability upon it.

—BASHAR MILES TEG,
summary debriefing after the victory on Cerbol

When she was confrontational, Garimi could be as stubborn as the most hardened old Bene Gesserit. Sheeana let the sober-faced Sister stand in the assembly chamber and vent against the proposed historical ghola project, hoping that she would lose steam before she reached her conclusion. Unfortunately, many of the Sisters in the seats behind Garimi muttered and nodded, agreeing with the points she raised.

And so we give birth to even more factions, Sheeana thought with an inner sigh.

In the no-ship's largest meeting chamber, more than a hundred of the refugee Sisters continued their seemingly endless debate over the wisdom of creating gholas from Scytale's mysterious cells. There seemed no room for compromise. Because they had departed from Chapterhouse to retain Bene Gesserit purity, Sheeana insisted on preserving open discourse, but the argument had already gone on for more than a month. With so much dissent, she did not want to force a vote. Not yet. *At one time, we were all bound together by a common cause. . . .*

From the front row, Garimi said, "You suggest this ill-conceived scheme as if we have no other option. Even the most unschooled acolyte knows there are as many options as we choose to make."

Duncan Idaho's words glided cleanly into the brief silence, though no one had called upon him. "I did not say we had no choice. I merely suggested that this may be our *best* choice." He and Teg sat beside Sheeana. Who knew better the dangers, difficulties, and advantages of gholas than these two? Who understood these historical figures better than Duncan himself?

Continuing, Duncan said, "The Tleilaxu Master offers us the means to strengthen ourselves with key figures from an arsenal of past experts and leaders. We know little about the Enemy we might face, and it would be foolish to turn our backs on any possible advantage."

"Advantage? These historical figures are a veritable pantheon of shame for the Bene Gesserit," Garimi said. "Lady Jessica, Paul Muad'Dib—and, worst of all, Leto II, the Tyrant."

As Garimi's voice grew shrill, one of her companions, Stuka, added firmly, "Have you forgotten your Bene Gesserit training, Duncan Idaho? Your reasoning is not logical. All of the gholas we're talking about are relics of the past, straight out of legend. What relevance can they possibly have to our crisis now?"

"What they lack in current relevance, they gain in perspective," Teg pointed out. "The sheer living history in those cells is enough to make religious scholars and academics dizzy. Surely, among all of those heroes and geniuses we will find useful knowledge for any situation we might encounter. The fact that the Tleilaxu worked so hard to obtain and preserve such cells for all these centuries argues for how special they must be."

Reverend Mother Calissa expressed a valid concern; she had not given any hint as to the way she intended to vote. "I am worried that the Tleilaxu modified the genetics in some way—just as they tampered with Duncan. Scytale is counting on our awe. What if there is another plan at work here? Why does he really want the gholas brought back?"

Duncan drew his gaze across the seated women. "The Tleilaxu Master is in a vulnerable position, so he must ensure that any gholas we test are perfect. Otherwise he loses what he most wants from us. I don't trust him, but I do trust his desperation. Scytale will do anything to get what he needs. He is dying and is frantic for a ghola of himself, so we should use that to our advantage. In our perilous situation, we dare not let our fears guide our policy."

"*What* policy?" Garimi snorted, looking around at all the Sisters. "We wander through space, going nowhere, running from an invisible threat that only Duncan Idaho can see. For most of us, the real threat was the whores from the Scattering. They took over our Sisterhood, and we exiled ourselves to save the Bene Gesserit. We need to find a place where we can establish a new Chapterhouse, a new order where we can grow strong. That is why we have begun having children, cautiously expanding our numbers."

"And thereby straining the *Ithaca*'s limited resources," Sheeana said.

Garimi and many of her supporters made rude noises. "This no-ship has enough supplies to keep ten times our number alive for a century. To preserve our Sisterhood, we need to increase our number and expand our gene pool, in preparation for colonizing a planet."

Sheeana smiled craftily. "Yet another reason to introduce the gholas."

Garimi rolled her eyes in disgust. From behind her, Stuka called out, "The gholas will be inhuman abominations."

Sheeana had known someone would say this. "I find it curious how superstitious some of you conservative women are. Like illiterate peasants! I have heard very little rational argument from you."

Garimi looked back at her equally stern followers and seemed to draw strength from them. "Rational argument? I resist this proposal because it is patently dangerous. These are people we know from history. We *know* them, and what they are capable of doing. Do we dare unleash another Kwisatz Haderach upon the universe? We made that mistake once already. We should know better now."

When Duncan spoke, he had only his convictions, lacking the Bene Gesserit ability of Voice or their subtle manipulations. "Paul Atreides was a good man, but the Sisterhood and other forces sent him spinning in dangerous directions. His much-maligned son was good and brave himself, until he allowed the worm of the desert to dominate him. I knew Thufir Hawat, Gurney Halleck, Stilgar, Duke Leto, and even Leto II. This time, we can protect them from the flaws in their pasts and let them achieve their potential. *To help us!*"

As the women shouted, Garimi raised her voice loudest of all. "Through Other Memory, we know what the Atreides did as well as you do, Duncan Idaho. Oh, the cruelties committed in the name of Muad'Dib, the billions who died in his jihad! The Corrino Empire that had lasted for thousands of years fell! But even the disasters of Emperor Muad'Dib were not enough. Then came his son the Tyrant and thousands of years of crushing terror! Have we learned nothing?"

Raising her voice, Sheeana used a hint of command, enough to silence the other Bene Gesserits. "Of course, we have learned. Until today, I thought we had learned wise caution. Now it seems that history has only taught us unreasoning fear. Would you discard our greatest advantage just because someone might be unintentionally injured? We have enemies who will do us intentional violence. There is always a risk, but the ingenuity in our cellular banks at least offers us a chance."

She tried to calculate how many passengers Garimi had brought over to her side. Identifying and categorizing them in her mind, Sheeana found few surprises; all were traditionalists, ultraconservatives among the conservatives. At the moment, their numbers remained a minority, but that could change. This debate must end before more damage occurred.

Even once the project began in earnest, each ghola child would require a full gestation period, and then it must be raised and trained, with an eye toward the *possibility* of awakening its internal memories. It would take years. In the next decade or more, how many times would their no-ship fly headlong into crisis? What if they collided with the mysterious Enemy tomorrow? What if they were trapped in the shimmering net that Duncan said always followed them, always sought them out?

Long-term planning was what the Sisterhood did best.

Finally, Sheeana drew her generous mouth back in a firm line and stood her ground. This was a fight she did not intend to lose, but the debate had run its course, whether or not Garimi would admit it. "Enough of these circular arguments. I call for a vote. *Now.*"

And she carried the motion. Just barely.

Even our ship's no-field cannot protect us from the prescience of Guild Navigators as they search the cosmos. Only the wild genes of an Atreides can completely veil the ship.

—THE MENTAT BELLONDA,
addressing a convocation of acolytes

His mind numb after the shouting match among the Bene Gesserits, Duncan Idaho went through a round of solo exercises on the practice floor. To sort out his thoughts, he felt a compulsion to go to this familiar place where he had spent so many enjoyable hours. With Murbella.

In attempting to exert supreme control over his muscles and nerves, he became more conscious of his failures. There were always reminders. Employing his Mentat abilities, he recognized when he missed certain advanced prana-bindu movements by the merest hair's breadth; few observers would have noticed the errors, but he saw them. With the whole matter of the new gholas weighing heavily on him, he felt out of balance.

Again, he completed the ritualistic steps. Holding a short-sword, he tried to achieve the relaxed preparedness of prana-bindu, that inner calmness that would enable him to defend himself and strike with lightning speed. But his muscles stubbornly refused to comply with the impulses of his mind.

Fighting is a matter of life and death . . . not of mood. Gurney Halleck had taught him that.

Taking two deep breaths, Duncan closed his eyes and slipped into a mnemonic trance in which he arrayed the data involved with this dilemma. In his mind's eye, he saw a long scratch on an adjacent wall that had previously escaped his attention. Odd that no one had repaired it in so many years . . . odder still that he had not noticed it in all that time.

Almost a decade and a half ago Murbella had slipped and fallen there during a knife-fighting practice with him—and very nearly died. When she'd gone down in slow motion, twisting her knife hand and falling in such a way that the blade would have penetrated her heart, Duncan had envisioned the full range of possible outcomes in his Mentat mind. He saw the many ways that she could die . . . and the few in which she could be saved. As she fell, he thrust a powerful kick at her, knocking the weapon away and scraping the wall.

A scratch on the wall, unnoticed and forgotten until now . . .

Only moments after that near tragedy, he and Murbella had made love there on the floor. It had been one of their most memorable coital collisions, with his Bene Gesserit–enhanced masculine abilities pitted against her Honored Matre sexual bonding techniques. Superhuman stud against amber-haired temptress.

Did she still think of him after nearly four years?

In his private cabin and in the common areas of the no-ship, Duncan continued to find reminders of his lost love. Before the escape he had been intent on making secret plans with Sheeana, hiding necessary items aboard the vessel, surreptitiously loading the volunteer pilgrims, equipment, supplies, and seven sandworms—keeping Duncan so busy that he had been able to forget Murbella for a while.

But immediately after the no-ship successfully tore away from the old couple and their clinging web, Duncan had too much time and too many opportunities to stumble upon previously unnoticed emotional land mines. He found a few of Murbella's keepsakes, training garments, toiletry items. Though he was a Mentat and could not forget details, simply finding these leftovers of her presence had hit him hard, like memory time bombs, worse than the explosive mines that had once been rigged around the no-ship at Chapterhouse.

For his own sanity, Duncan had finally gathered every scrap, from rumpled exercise clothes caked with her dried sweat, to discarded towels she had used, to her favorite stylus. He had thrown them all into one of the no-ship's unused small storage bins. The intact nullentropy field would keep the items exactly as they were forever, and the lock would seal them away. There, they had remained for years.

Duncan never needed to see them again, never needed to think about Murbella. He had lost her, and could never forget.

Murbella might be gone forever, but Scytale's nullentropy tube could bring back Duncan's old friends. Paul, Gurney, Thufir, and even Duke Leto.

Now, as he toweled himself off, he felt a surge of hope.

FOUR YEARS AFTER

ESCAPE FROM CHAPTERHOUSE

It is not cowardly or paranoid to jump at shadows if a real threat exists.

> —MOTHER COMMANDER MURBELLA,
> private journals

The large unidentified battleship appeared in dead space far outside of the Chapterhouse system. It hung there, scanning cautiously before moving closer. Using long-range sensors, an incoming Guildship detected the vessel beyond any planetary orbit, a strange ship lurking where it shouldn't have been.

Always concerned about the Enemy, never knowing when or how the first attacks might occur, the Mother Commander dispatched two Sisters in a swift scout ship to investigate. The women approached tentatively, making their intention apparent in a nonthreatening way.

The strange battleship opened fire and destroyed the scout as soon as it came within range. The pilot's last transmission said, "It's a warship of some kind. Looks like it's been through seven hells, severely damaged—" And then the message cut off in a flash of static. . . .

In a grim mood, Murbella assembled her military commanders to formulate a swift and massive response. No one knew the identity or armaments of the intruder, whether it was the long-expected Outside Enemy or some other power. But it was a definite threat.

Many of the former Honored Matres, including Doria, had been spoiling for a fight in the four years since the Battle of Junction. Sim-mering with violence, the Honored Matres felt that their military abil-ities were growing stagnant. Now, Murbella would give them a chance to make up for it.

In a matter of hours, twenty attack ships—which had been part of the Chapterhouse space navy since the days of Bashar Miles Teg—accelerated out of the system. Murbella led them, despite the warnings and complaints of some of her more timid Bene Gesserit advisors, who wanted her to stay out of danger. She was the Mother Commander, and she would take charge of the mission. It was her way.

As the New Sisterhood's ships swooped closer, Murbella studied the images resolving on her screens, noting the dark scoring along the intruder's hull, the bright emissions of power leakage from damaged engines, the large holes blasted where contained atmosphere had vented into space.

"It's a wreck," transmitted Bashar Wikki Aztin from her own attack ship.

"But a deadly one," noted an adjutant. "It can still shoot."

Like a wounded predator, Murbella thought. It was a large craft, much bigger than her attack ships. Studying scanner screens, she recognized part of the design as well as a battle sigil on the heat-damaged hull. "It's an Honored Matre ship, but not from any of the assimilated groups."

"Does it belong to one of the rebel enclaves?"

"No . . . this is from beyond the edge of the Scattering," she trans-mitted. "From far beyond."

Over the decades, a great many Honored Matres had swept into the Old Empire like locusts, but their numbers were far greater out among the distant worlds. Honored Matres existed in independent cells, iso-lated from other groups not only for their own protection, but from a natural xenophobia.

Apparently the strange vessel had blundered into this section of space. Judging by its appearance, the battleship had been too severely damaged to make it all the way to its intended destination. Chapter-house, specifically? Or just any habitable planet?

"Remain outside of firing range," she warned her commanders, then adjusted her commsystem. "Honored Matres! I am Murbella, the legitimate Great Honored Matre, having assassinated my predecessor. We are not your enemy, but we do not recognize your ship or its markings. You destroyed our scouts unnecessarily. Open fire again at your own peril."

Only silence and static answered her.

"We're going to board you. This is my command as Great Honored Matre." She edged her ships forward, still receiving no response.

Finally a haggard, stern-looking woman appeared on the communications screen, her expression as sharp as broken glass. "Very well, Honored Matre. We will not open fire—yet."

"*Great* Honored Matre," Murbella said.

"That remains to be seen."

Moving cautiously, with their weapons systems powered up and ready to respond, the twenty New Sisterhood ships closed in around the large battle-scarred hulk. On a private channel, Doria signaled, "We could easily just crawl through a hole in the hull."

"I'd rather not be seen as attackers," Murbella replied, then transmitted on an open channel to the unnamed captain of the Honored Matre battleship, "Do your docking bays still function? How severe is your damage?"

"One docking bay is serviceable." The captain provided instructions.

Murbella told Bashar Aztin and half of her ships to remain outside as guardians while she guided the other ten in to face the survivors of what must have surely been a horrific battle.

When she and her comrades emerged in the docking bay, Murbella faced thirteen battered-looking women, all of them in colored leotards. Many still sported bruises, barely healed injuries, and medical patches.

The woman with the broken-glass expression had her left hand wrapped in healing strips. Ever suspicious, Murbella suspected she might be hiding a weapon in the bandaging, but it was unlikely; Honored Matres considered their own bodies to be weapons. This one glowered at Murbella and her team, some of whom were dressed as Bene Gesserits, others in the trappings of Honored Matres.

"You look different . . . strange," the captain said. Orange flecks appeared in her eyes.

"And you look defeated," Murbella snapped. Honored Matres responded to force rather than conciliation. "Who did this to you?"

The woman answered with scorn. "The Enemy, of course. The Enemy who has been hounding us for centuries, spreading plagues, destroying our worlds." She showed skepticism in her face. "If you do not know this, then you are no Honored Matre."

"We are aware of the Enemy, but we have been in the Old Empire for a long time. Much has changed."

"And apparently much has been forgotten! You look as if you've grown soft and weak, but we know the Enemy has been in this sector. We have explored to the best of our abilities in this damaged ship. We found several planets that were clearly charred by Obliterators."

Murbella did not correct her, did not tell the captain that those planets—no doubt Tleilaxu or Bene Gesserit worlds—had been destroyed by Honored Matres themselves, and not by the Outside Enemy.

Warily, Murbella stepped forward, wondering if these thirteen Honored Matres were all that had survived on the entire battleship. "Tell us what you know of our mutual Enemy. Any information will help us in our defenses."

"Defenses? You cannot defend against an invincible foe."

"Nevertheless, we shall try."

"No one can stand against them! We must flee, seize whatever we can for our survival, and move faster than the Enemy can pursue us. You must know this." Her bruised eyes narrowed; the broken glass of her expression seemed to sharpen even more. "Unless you are not truly an Honored Matre. I do not recognize these others or their strange clothing, and you have a foreign manner about you . . ." She looked as if she wanted to spit. "We all know that our Enemy has many faces. Is your face among them?"

The Honored Matre strangers tensed and coiled, then flung themselves upon Murbella and her followers. These outside Honored Matres did not know the superior fighting abilities of the unified New Sister-hood, and they were also weary and scarred. Even so, desperation heated their violence.

After the bloodbath, four of Murbella's comrades lay dead on the deck before the rest of her crew subdued and killed all of the Honored Matres, except for the captain.

When it was clear that her women would be slain, the Honored Matre leader bolted through the docking bay door toward a lift. The Bene Gesserits with Murbella were astounded. "She is a coward!"

Murbella was already running toward the lift. "Not a coward. She's going to the bridge. She'll scuttle this ship before she lets it fall into our hands!"

The nearest lift tube was damaged and wouldn't operate. Murbella and several Sisters ran until they found a second elevator that sped them up toward the command deck. The captain could easily destroy all navigation records and perhaps blow up the engines (if they remained intact enough to respond to a self-destruct order). She had no idea how many of the battleship's systems were still functional.

By the time Murbella, Doria, and three others burst onto the com-mand deck, the Honored Matre captain was already hammering at the panels with such force that her fingertips were bloody. Sparks and smoke curled up, erupting from short-circuited control stations. Murbella reached the woman in a flash, grabbed her shoulders and hurled her away from the station. The captain lunged back toward them, but a single reflexive blow from the Mother Commander broke her neck. No time for slow interrogations.

Doria reached the panel first and impetuously used her bare hands to rip out the control boards, disconnecting the console. Afterward, she frowned down at the smoking panels, unable to stop the damage that was already underway. Extinguishers smothered the electrical fires.

Bene Gesserit experts combed over the systems while Murbella waited, worried that the whole battleship was still going to explode around them. One of the Sisters looked up from a navigation station. "Self-destruct sequence successfully interrupted. Most of the records were destroyed by the captain, but I was able to retrieve at least one set of coordinates from outside the Old Empire—the last place this ship went before fleeing here."

Murbella made up her mind. "We must learn what we can about what has occurred so far out there." The mystery had been gnawing at her for years. "I'll send scouts to retrace the course. After this, let no one dare suggest that I'm merely imagining the Enemy is coming to get us. If the Enemy is finally on the move, we need to know."

Naively, the Honored Matres think they have the loyalty of their enslaved Lost Tleilaxu. In reality, many of these Tleilaxu from the Scattering have their own plans. As Face Dancers, it is our task to ruin all of their schemes.

—KHRONE,
message to the Face Dancers

E ven by Lost Tleilaxu standards, the laboratory built in the ashes of Bandalong was primitive. Uxtal had only the most basic equipment scavenged from ruined facilities once used by old Masters, and this was the first time he had actually managed such a complex project by himself. He did not dare let the Honored Matres or Face Dancers suspect that the task might be beyond him.

Useless lab assistants were assigned to help him, generally weak-willed and low-caste males who had been sexually subjugated by the dreadful women. None of the assistants possessed any special knowledge or hints that might help. Already, because of some imagined slight, the mercurial Honored Matres had killed one of the pathetic men, and his replacement did not seem any more talented.

Uxtal struggled not to show his anxiety, trying to appear knowledgeable, though he was confused about many things. Khrone had ordered the little researcher to obey the Face Dancers, and the Face Dancers had told him to do whatever the Honored Matres commanded. Uxtal wished he understood more of what was going on. Were the new Face Dancers really allied with the violent whores? Or was it another trick within a trick, cleverly veiled? He shook his aching head in dismay. The ancient scriptures warned of the impossibility of serving two masters, and now he understood that only too well.

At night Uxtal rarely had more than a few hours to rest, and when he did, his anxiety was too great to allow any real sleep. He had to fool the whores and the Face Dancers. He would grow the new ghola that Khrone insisted upon—he could do that!—and he would try to make the adrenaline-based spice alternative the Honored Matres needed, using their own formula. The manufacture of genuine melange, however, was far beyond even his imagined capabilities.

In a magnanimous gesture, Hellica had given him plenty of female bodies to use as axlotl tanks, and he had already converted the one he needed (after botching the job three times previously). So far, so good. Along with all the equipment inside the primitive laboratory, the tank should be enough for him to achieve success. Now he simply had to create the ghola and deliver it, and Khrone would reward him (he hoped).

Unfortunately, that meant his ordeal here would last a minimum of nine months. He didn't know if he could stand it.

Suspecting Face Dancers everywhere, he started growing a child from the mysterious cells salvaged from a dead Tleilaxu Master's damaged nullentropy capsule. Meanwhile, on a daily basis, the Matre Superior made her impatience known for her supply of melange substitute. She was jealous of every second he diverted his attention from *her* needs. Panicked and exhausted, Uxtal was forced to satisfy both obligations, even though he had no experience at doing either.

As soon as the unidentified ghola baby was implanted in the first functional axlotl tank, Uxtal turned his efforts toward making the spice alternative. Since the whores already knew how to create the substance, Uxtal required no breakthroughs or flashes of genius in that area. He simply needed to manufacture the chemical in great quantities. The Honored Matres couldn't be bothered to do it for themselves.

Gazing through a one-way security window into the gray sky, Uxtal felt as if the landscape of his soul was like the charred, lifeless hills he saw in the distance. He didn't want to be here. Someday, he would think of a way out of this.

Born to an insular religious circle, Uxtal was deeply uncomfortable around dominant women. Among the Tleilaxu race, females were raised and then converted into brainless wombs as soon as they reached reproductive maturity. That was their only purpose. Honored Matres were the polar opposite of what Uxtal considered right and proper. No one knew the origin of the whores, but their propensity for violence seemed to have been bred into them.

He wondered if some foolish renegade Tleilaxu Master had actually *bred* the Honored Matres to hunt down the Bene Gesserits, much as Futars were supposedly bred to hunt down Honored Matres. What if the newly grown female monsters had gotten out of control, and the result was the destruction of all sacred worlds, the enslavement of a handful of Lost Tleilaxu, everything gone wrong?

Now, trying to look like a commanding administrator, Uxtal paced through the laboratory and watched two white-smocked lab assistants tend the special ghola tank.

A new modular building had just been brought in on a lift suspensor mechanism. The new laboratory wing was three times the size of the original facility, and required tearing down the neighboring slig farmer's fences and appropriating a portion of his land. Uxtal had expected him to object and thus incur the wrath of the Honored Matres, but he had seen the fellow—was his name Gaxhar?—meekly move his sligs to another section of land. The women also demanded that the farmer provide them with a constant supply of fresh slig meat, which he did. Uxtal took a quiet pleasure in seeing someone so downtrodden, in knowing that he was not the only one helpless in Bandalong.

In the older laboratory, captured women were chemically loboto-mized and converted into breeding vats. From separate operations in the new wing, Uxtal heard the muted screams of women being tor-tured, because *pain* (technically, the adrenaline, endorphins, and other chemicals the body produced in response to pain) was a primary ingre-dient in the special spice the Honored Matres craved.

Matre Superior Hellica had already gone to the new chambers to oversee the niceties. "Our facility will be ready as soon as I have properly christened it." She wore a tight-fitting gold-and-silver leotard that revealed the generous curves of her body, along with a matching cape and a jeweled headdress that looked like a crown mounted on her blonde hair.

He didn't particularly want to know what that meant. Each time he saw the Matre Superior, Uxtal struggled not to reveal his loathing, though she must recognize it on his grayish face. For his own survival, he tried to show just the right amount of fear in her presence, but not too much. He did not grovel—at least he didn't think so.

After a particularly loud volley of screams came from the new wing, Hellica swept through a doorway and into the laboratory section where the impregnated axlotl tank lay on its chromed table. She enjoyed looking at the single mound of sweating, odorous flesh. The Matre Superior nudged Uxtal roughly enough to knock him off balance, as if he were her comrade in arms. "Such an interesting way to treat the human body, don't you think? Only suitable for women who are worthy of nothing else."

Uxtal had not asked where the donor women came from. It was none of his business, and he didn't want to know. He suspected the whores had captured several of their hated Bene Gesserit rivals out on other planets. Now, that would have been interesting to see! As bloated axlotl tanks, at least these women had gone to their proper place, to be receptacles for offspring. The ideal of a Tleilaxu female . . .

Hellica scowled upon seeing both laboratory assistants tending the one pregnant tank. "Is that project more important than mine? We are in need of our drug—do not delay!"

Both assistants froze. Bowing before her, Uxtal said immediately, "Of course not, Matre Superior. We await your pleasure."

"My pleasure? What would you know of my pleasure?" She loomed over the little man, regarding him with her predatory gaze. "I wonder if you have the stomach for this work. All the original Masters are dead as punishment for their past crimes. Do not make me add you to that number."

Crimes? Uxtal didn't know what the original Tleilaxu had done to the Honored Matres to earn a hatred strong enough to warrant complete extinction. "I only know genetics, Matre Superior. Not politics." He quickly bowed and scuttled out of her reach. "I am perfectly happy to serve you."

Her pale eyebrows arched. "Your lot in life is to serve."

*When the past returns to us with all its glory and pain, we don't
know whether to embrace it or to flee.*

—DUNCAN IDAHO,
More Than a Mentat

The two axlotl tanks in the no-ship's medical center had once
been Bene Gesserit females. Volunteers. Now all that remained
of the women were gross mounds of flesh, their arms and legs flabby,
their minds completely vacated. They were living wombs, biological
factories for the creation of spice.

Teg could not look at them without feeling bleak. The air in the med
center smelled of disinfectants, medicinal chemicals, and bitter cinnamon.

The Acolytes' Manual said, "A defined need leads to a solution." In
the first year of their odyssey, the Tleilaxu Master had revealed how to
manufacture melange with axlotl tanks. Knowing what was at stake,
two of the refugee women had offered themselves. The Bene Gesserit
always did what was necessary, even to this extent.

Years ago on Chapterhouse, Mother Superior Odrade had permitted
the creation of axlotl tanks for the Sisterhood's own ghola experiments.
Volunteers were found, females who could serve the order in no better
way. Fourteen years ago, his own reborn body had emerged from one of
them.

The Bene Gesserit know how to demand sacrifices of us. Somehow they make us want to do it. Teg had defeated many enemies, using his tactical genius to achieve victory after victory for the Sisterhood; his death on Rakis had been the ultimate sacrifice.

Teg continued to look at the axlotl tanks—at these *women*. These Sisters had also given their lives, but in a different way. And now, thanks to Scytale and his hidden nullentropy capsule, Sheeana needed more tanks.

When studying the contents of the nullentropy capsule, the Suk doctors had also discovered Face Dancer cells, which immediately cast suspicion upon the Tleilaxu Master. The frantic Scytale insisted that the process was controllable, that they could identify and select only those individuals they wished to resurrect as gholas. With his life beginning to ebb, the little Master had lost all of his bargaining power. In a moment of vulnerability, he explained how to separate Face Dancer cells from the others.

Then, once again, he begged to be allowed to grow a ghola of himself before it was too late.

Now, Sheeana paced the floor beside him in the medical center. Shoulders stiff and neck arched, she looked over at Scytale. The Tleilaxu Master was not yet comfortable with his new freedom. He seemed nervous inside the med-center, as if drowning in guilt because he had revealed so much. He had surrendered everything, and now he no longer had any control.

"Three more tanks would be best," Scytale said, as if discussing the weather. "Otherwise, creating the group of desired gholas will take too long, one at a time, each with nine months of gestation."

"I am confident we will find willing volunteers." Sheeana's voice was cold.

"When you finally begin this program, my own ghola must be first." Scytale looked from one pale-skinned axlotl tank to the other like a doctor inspecting test tubes in a lab. "My need is greatest."

"No," Sheeana said. "We must first verify that what you claim is true, that these cells are indeed samples of who you say they are."

Scowling, the diminutive man looked at Teg as if to find support from a person who claimed to worship honor and loyalty. "You know the genetics have been verified. Your own libraries and chromosome sequencers have had months to compare and catalog the cellular material I gave you."

"Simply sifting through all those cells and choosing the first candidates is quite a task." Sheeana sounded pragmatic. All of the identified cells had been separated into secure storage drawers in the genetic library, code-locked and placed under guard so that no one could tamper with them. "Your people were extremely ambitious in the cells they stole, dating all the way back to the Butlerian Jihad."

"We *acquired* them. My people may not have had a breeding program such as yours, but we did know to watch the Atreides line. We understood that great events were about to unfold, that your long-standing search for a superhuman Kwisatz Haderach was likely to reach fruition around the time of Muad'Dib."

"So how did you get all the cells?" Teg asked.

"For millennia, Tleilaxu workers have been handlers of the dead. Though many consider that an unclean and despised profession, we did have unprecedented access. Unless a body is completely destroyed, it is simple enough to acquire a skin scraping or two."

At fourteen, Teg was still gangly and on his way to becoming a tall man. His voice cracked at embarrassing moments, though the thoughts and memories in his head belonged to an old man. He spoke just loudly enough for Sheeana to hear, "I would like to meet Paul Muad'Dib and his mother, the Lady Jessica."

"That is just the beginning of what I offer," Scytale said, aiming his glare at Sheeana. "And you did agree to my terms, Reverend Mother."

"You will have your ghola. But I am not inclined to hurry."

The elfin man bit his lower lip with tiny, sharp teeth. "There is a ticking clock. I must have time to create a Scytale ghola and raise it so that I can trigger his memories."

Sheeana gave a dismissive wave. "You said yourself that you had at least a decade left, possibly fifteen years. You'll have the best medical care. Our Bene Gesserit doctors will keep watch over your condition. The Rabbi is a retired Suk doctor, if you don't want females tending you. In the meantime, we will test the new cells you offer us."

"That is why you'll need three more axlotl tanks! The conversion process will take some months, then the implantation of the embryo, then gestation. We will need to perform many tests. The sooner we produce enough gholas to allay your suspicions, the sooner you will see the truth of what I have told you."

"And the sooner you can have your own ghola," Teg added. He stared intently at the two axlotl tanks until he could picture the women they had been before the hideous conversion process, real females with hearts and minds. They'd had lives and dreams, and people who cared about them. Yet, as soon as the Sisterhood had declared its need, they'd offered themselves without hesitation.

Teg knew that Sheeana had only to ask for more. New volunteers would consider it an honor to give birth to heroes from the legendary days of Dune.

We are the wellspring of human survival.
— MOTHER COMMANDER MURBELLA

Murbella's scouts returned ashen-faced from a flyby of the intact coordinates found in the scuttled Honored Matre ship. Racing out to a distant star system far beyond the known limits of the Scattering, they discovered evidence of great carnage.

When Murbella received the recordings from the scouts, she watched them in her private chamber along with Bellonda, Doria, and the old Archives Mother Accadia.

"Utterly wiped out," said the scout. Young and intense, she was a former Honored Matre named Kiria. "Even with all their military might and violence . . ." She couldn't seem to believe what she was saying or what she had seen. Kiria installed a shigawire spool into a viewer and projected holograms in the middle of the room. "See for yourselves."

The unidentified planet, now a charred tomb, was obviously a former Honored Matre population center, with the remnants of dozens of large cities laid out in their characteristic fashion. The inhabitants were all dead, buildings blackened, entire metropolitan sections turned to glassy craters, structures melted, spaceports cracked, and the atmosphere turned into a dark stew of soot and poisonous vapors.

"This is worse. Look." Deeply disturbed, Kiria switched to images that showed a battlefield in space. Strewn through the orbital zone floated the wreckage of thousands of large, heavily armored ships. Bristling with weapons, these were the Honored Matres' great vessels—all of them destroyed, littering space in a wide ring. "We scanned the wreckage, Mother Commander. All of the craft were of a similar design to the Honored Matre battleship we encountered here. We found no other types of ships. Unbelievable!"

"What is the significance of that?" Bellonda said.

Kiria snapped at her, "It means that the Honored Matres were annihilated—thousands of their best battleships—*and they didn't manage to take out a single one of the Enemy!* Not a one!" She brought a fist down on the table.

"Unless the Enemy removed their own damaged warships, to keep their workings secret," Accadia said, though the explanation did not seem likely.

"You discovered no clues about the nature of the Enemy? Or of the Honored Matres themselves?" Murbella had tried again to search through Other Memory, striving to delve into her Honored Matre past, but had encountered only mysteries and dead ends. She could trace back along the Bene Gesserit lines, following life upon life all the way back to Old Earth. But in the Honored Matre line, she found almost nothing at all.

"I gathered enough evidence to be frightened," Kiria said. "This is clearly a force we cannot defeat. If that many Honored Matres were wiped out, what hope does the New Sisterhood have?"

"There is always hope," old Accadia said unconvincingly, as if quoting a platitude.

"And now there is incentive as well as a dire warning," Murbella said. She looked at all of her advisors. "I will call a gathering immediately."

ALMOST A THOUSAND Sisters had been invited from all over the planet, and the receiving hall had to be substantially modified for the event. The Mother Commander's throne and all symbols of her office had been removed; soon the meaning of that gesture would become apparent to all. On the walls and vaulted ceiling, she had ordered all frescoes and other ornamentation to be covered, leaving the huge chamber with a starkly utilitarian character. A signal that they needed to focus on bare necessities.

Without explaining why, Odrade-within reminded Murbella of a Bene Gesserit axiom: "'All life is a series of seemingly insignificant tasks and decisions, culminating in the definition of an individual and her purpose in life.'" And she followed that with another: "'Each Sister is part of the larger human organism, a life within a life.'"

Remembering the stew of discontent that simmered among the factions even here on Chapterhouse, Murbella saw what Odrade was getting at. "When our own Sisters kill each other, more than just individuals die."

At a recent supper, an altercation had left a Bene Gesserit dead and an Honored Matre in a deep coma. Murbella had decided to convert the comatose one into an axlotl tank to set an example, though even that was inadequate punishment for such continued, petty defiance.

As she paced the speaking hall, the Mother Commander forced herself to recall the progress she had made over the past four years since their forced fusion. She herself had required years to make the fundamental change, to accept the core teachings of the Sisterhood and see the flaws in Honored Matre methods of violence and short-term goals.

When she was held captive among the Bene Gesserit, even she had naively assumed her strength and abilities would prove to be greater than that of the witches. Such arrogance! At first she had schemed to destroy the Sisterhood from within, but the more Bene Gesserit knowledge and philosophy she received, the more she began to understand—and frown upon—her former organization. Murbella was merely the first convert, the first hybrid of Honored Matre and Bene Gesserit . . .

On the morning of the gathering, the mixed representatives assumed their marked seats, dark green cushions arranged on the floor in ever-expanding concentric circles, like the petals of a blossoming flower. The Mother Commander placed her own cushion down among the Sisters, rather than looming over them from a high throne.

Murbella wore a simple black singlesuit that gave her perfect freedom of movement, but without the flashy ornamentation, cape, or bright colors the Honored Matres preferred; she also eschewed the concealing robes the Bene Gesserits usually draped over themselves.

As the representatives situated themselves in a clash of mismatched clothes and colors, Murbella decided abruptly that she would impose a dress code. She should have done so a year ago, following the bloody school-yard brawl that had left several acolytes dead. Even after four years, these women still clung to their old identities. No more armbands, no more gaudy colors or capes, no more flowing ravenlike robes. From now on, a simple black singlesuit would do for everyone.

Both sides would have to accept changes. Not compromise, but synthesis. Compromises only drove both ends of the curve to an unacceptable and weaker average; instead, both sides must take the best from the other and discard the rest.

Sensing their palpable uneasiness, Murbella rose to her knees and stared the women down. She had already heard of more former Honored Matres slipping away to join the outcasts in the northern regions. Other rumors—no longer so absurd—suggested that some had even joined the largest group of rebels led by Matre Superior Hellica on Tleilax. In light of what they had all just learned about the Enemy, such distractions could not be tolerated any longer.

She knew that many of the gathered Sisters would automatically argue against the changes Murbella planned to impose. They already resented her for the turmoil she had caused in the past. For a chilling moment, she compared herself to Julius Caesar standing before the Senate to propose monumental reforms that would have benefited the Roman Empire. And the Senators had voted with their daggers.

Before speaking, Murbella performed a Bene Gesserit breathing exercise to calm herself. She became conscious of a change in the air currents around her, something intangible. Narrowing her eyes, she took note of details, of the placement of seated and standing women.

After activating the receiving hall's sound system with a wave of her hand, Murbella spoke into a microphone that dropped on a suspensor and hovered in front of her face. "I am unlike any leader the Sisterhood or the Honored Matres have ever had. It is not my purpose to please everyone, but instead to forge an army that has a chance— however slight—of survival. *Our* survival. We cannot afford the time for gradual changes."

"Can we afford changes at all?" grumbled one Honored Matre. "I cannot see how they have benefited us."

"That is because you cannot *see*. Will you open your eyes, or congratulate yourself on your blindness?" The other woman's eyes flashed, though the orange flecks had long ago gone away from the lack of orange spice substitute.

Just behind her, a Bene Gesserit Sister arrived late. She approached along a narrow aisle, scanning the area around her as if searching for her seat. But every woman knew her assigned place. The latecomer should not be going in that direction.

Watching with peripheral vision as she spoke, Murbella gave no sign that she had noticed anything amiss. The dark-haired and high-cheekboned woman looked unfamiliar. *Not someone I know.*

She kept her gaze forward, internally counting the seconds as she mentally mapped the newcomer's approach. Then, without looking back, using the full reflexes wired into her from both Honored Matre and Bene Gesserit training, Murbella sprang to her feet. With breathtaking speed, she spun in the air to face the woman. Before her feet could touch the floor again, the Mother Commander bent backward, just as the attacker moved in a blur, pulling something from the pocket of her robe and slashing out in a single fluid motion. Milky white and crystalline-sharp—an ancient crysknife!

Murbella's muscular responses bypassed conscious thought. She dipped with one flattened hand, avoiding the tip of the plunging crysknife and drove upward to strike the wrist. A thin bone popped with a sound like dry wood breaking. The would-be assassin's fingers opened, and the crysknife began to fall, but so slowly it seemed to hang suspended, like a feather. When the woman raised her other arm to fend off a second blow, Murbella hit her with a smashing punch to the throat, crushing her larynx before she could cry out.

As Murbella's adversary collapsed, the crysknife clattered to the floor, its blade shattering. A dim part of Murbella's mind was pleased to see both Sisters and Honored Matres leap from their cushions, instinctively jumping up to aid the Mother Commander in case the coup attempt was more widespread. In their motions, she recognized truth, just as she had seen the lies in the motions of the would-be assassin.

Both fat Bellonda and wiry Doria pounced on the fallen woman, holding her down. *Now* those two worked together! Still on her feet, Murbella scanned the large room and catalogued the faces, assuring herself that there were no interlopers present and no threats.

Though the lone attacker thrashed, trying to breathe, or maybe forcing herself to die, Bellonda pressed the woman's throat, opening her air passage to keep her alive. Doria roared for a Suk doctor.

The broken crysknife lay on the floor by the writhing woman. Murbella assessed it with a glance and understood. Traditional weapon . . . ancient ways. The symbolism of the gesture was clear.

Murbella used Voice, hoping the injured woman was too weak to use standard defenses against the command. "Who are you? Speak!"

With cracked and broken words rattling through her damaged throat, the woman forced out her answer. She seemed glad to do so and wildly defiant. "I am your future. Others like me will emerge from shadows, drop from ceilings, come at you out of thin air. One of us will get you!"

"Why do you wish to kill me?" The other Bene Gesserits in the audience had fallen into an utter hush, straining to hear the attacker's words.

"Because of what you did to the Sisterhood." The woman managed to turn her head toward Doria as a symbol of the Honored Matres. If she'd had the strength, she might have spat. "As Mother Commander you raise the alarm about an Outside Enemy, while you welcome real enemies into our midst. Fool!"

Scowling grimly, Bellonda provided the attacker's name after ransacking her Mentat mind. "She is Sister Osafa Chram. One of the orchard workers, a new arrival from across the planet."

A Bene Gesserit has tried to kill me. No longer was it just the power-hungry Honored Matres who sought to seize her position of power.

"Sheeana was right to flee . . . and leave the rest of us to rot here!" Looking up at the Sisters, then giving a final glare at Murbella, Osafa Chram summoned the necessary courage and willed herself to die.

As the assassin began her final spasms, Murbella shouted, "Bellonda! Share with her! We must discover what she knows! How widespread is this conspiracy?"

The Reverend Mother reacted with unexpected speed and grace, slapping her hands to the woman's temples and pressing their foreheads together. "She resists me even with her dying breath! Not letting her thoughts flow." Bellonda winced, then withdrew. "She's gone."

Doria leaned closer and grimaced. "Smell that. Shere, and lots of it. She's made sure we can't even use a mechanical probe to pry loose her thoughts."

The gathered Sisters murmured uneasily. Murbella wondered if she needed to subject everyone to Truthsayer interrogation. A thousand of them! And if this Bene Gesserit Sister had tried to kill the Mother Commander, could Murbella trust even her Truthsayers?

Marshaling her concentration, she gave a dismissive wave toward the dead woman on the floor. "Remove that. Everyone else, resume your seats. A gathering is serious business, and we have fallen behind schedule."

"We're with you, Mother Commander!" a young woman shouted from the audience. Murbella couldn't tell who said it.

Doria quietly returned to her seat, watching Murbella with grudging respect. Some of the former Honored Matres in the audience were clearly surprised—some smug, others indignant—that a knife blade could have come from the coldly pacifistic Bene Gesserits.

Murbella gave no more than an annoyed glance as women hustled away with the bundled body of the dead woman. "I have fended off assassination attempts before. We have important work to do here, and we must quash these petty rebellions among us, erasing all vestiges of our past conflicts."

"For that, we would need collective amnesia," Bellonda snorted.

A thin wave of laughter spread through the room, and dissipated quickly.

"I will force it upon you," Murbella said with a glare, "no matter how many heads I have to knock together."

An insistent communication seized Khrone through the tachyon net as the Guildship departed Tleilax, where he had secretly inspected the progress of the new ghola in its axlotl tank.

His lackey Uxtal had indeed implanted an embryo made from the cells hidden in the burned body of the Tleilaxu Master. So, the Lost Tleilaxu was not completely incompetent. The mysterious child was growing even now. And if the ghola's identity was as Khrone suspected, the possibilities were interesting, indeed.

A year ago, Khrone had deposited Uxtal in Bandalong with strict orders, and the terrified researcher had obeyed in every way. A Face Dancer replica might have been adequate to the task, given a clear enough mental imprinting of Uxtal's knowledge, but the squirming assistant had been performing with an edge of desperation that no Face Dancer could match. Ah, the predictable instinct of humans to survive. It could easily be used against them.

As the Guildship drifted around to the nightside of Tleilax, the ship's viewers showed black scars where cities had been erased. Only a few weakly shining lights marked struggling towns that clung to life. Somewhere down there, the greatest works of the Tleilaxu had their origins, even the primitive versions of Face Dancers, so many millennia ago. But those shape-shifting mules were little more than hand-daubed cave paintings compared to the masterpieces that Khrone and his fellows had become.

Face Dancers had taken over the crew positions on this ship, killing and replacing a handful of Guildsmen, leaving only the oblivious Navigator in his tank. Khrone was not certain whether a Face Dancer could imprint and replace a grandly mutated Navigator. That was an experiment to be considered at some later date. In the meantime, no one would know that he had come to Tleilax just to observe.

No one, except for his distant supposed controllers who watched the Face Dancers at all times.

Now, as Khrone walked down the corridor of the cruising ship, his step faltered. The burnished metal walls blurred and became less distinct. His whole view tilted at an angle, then sideways. Abruptly, the reality of the Guildship vanished, leaving him standing in an empty, cold void, with no surface visible beneath his feet. Sparkling, colorful lines of the tachyon net writhed around him, connections extending everywhere, woven through the universe. Khrone froze, his eyes widening as he looked around. He stopped himself from speaking.

In front of him he discerned a crystal-sharp image of the forms that the two entities chose for him to see: a calm and friendly looking old couple. Actually, they were anything but gentle and harmless. The two had bright eyes, white hair, and wrinkled skin that radiated a warm glow of health. Both wore comfortable clothes: the old man a red plaid shirt, the matronly woman gray gardening overalls. But though she had assumed the shape of a woman's body, she had not the slightest air of femininity. In the vision that trapped Khrone, the two stood among fruit trees bursting with blossoms, so laden with white petals and buzzing bees that Khrone could smell the perfume and hear the sounds.

He didn't understand why this bizarre pair insisted on such a façade, certainly not for his benefit. He did not at all care about their appearance, nor was he impressed.

Despite his grandfatherly face, the old man's words were harsh. "We grow impatient with you. The no-ship got away from us when it vanished from Chapterhouse. We caught another glimpse of it a year ago, but the craft slipped away from us again. We continue our own search, but you promised that your Face Dancers would find it."

"We will find it." Khrone could no longer feel the Guildship around him. The air smelled like sweet blossoms. "The fugitives cannot evade us forever. You will have them, I assure you."

"We do not have that long to wait. The time is nearly upon us after all these millennia."

"Now, now, Daniel," the old woman chided. "You have always been so goal-oriented. What have you learned in pursuing the no-ship? Hasn't the journey itself provided many rewards?"

The old man scowled at her. "That is beside the point. I have always worried about the unreliability of your distracting pets. Sometimes they feel the need to become martyrs. Don't they, my *Martyr*?" He said the name with dripping sarcasm.

The old woman chuckled as if he had merely been teasing her. "You know I prefer Marty to Martyr. It's a more human name . . . more personal."

She turned toward the blossom-laden fruit trees behind her, reached up with a tough brown hand and plucked a perfectly round portygul. The rest of the blossoms disappeared, and now the trees were full of fruit, all of it ripe for the picking.

Lost in this strange illusory place, Khrone stood boiling inside. He resented that his alleged masters could come upon him so unexpectedly, wherever he might be. The Face Dancer myriad was a widely extended network. The shape-shifters were everywhere, and they would catch the no-ship quarry. Khrone himself wanted control of the lost vessel and its valuable passengers as much as the old man and woman did. He had his own agenda, which these two never guessed. The ghola being grown on Tleilax could be an important component of his secret plan.

The old man adjusted a straw hat on his head and leaned closer to Khrone, though his image came from impossibly far away. "Our detailed projections have provided us with the answer we need. There is no possibility for error. Kralizec will soon be upon us, and our victory requires the Kwisatz Haderach, the superhuman bred by the Bene Gesserit. According to the predictions, the no-ship is the key. He is— or will be—aboard."

"Isn't it amazing that mere humans reached the same conclusion thousands of years ago with their prophecies and their writings?" The old woman sat on a bench and began to peel the portygul. Sweet juice dripped from her fingers.

Unimpressed, the old man waved a callused hand. "They laid down so many millions of prophecies, they couldn't possibly have been wrong all the time. We know that once we acquire the no-ship, we acquire the Kwisatz Haderach. That has been proven."

"*Predicted*, Daniel. Not proven." The woman offered him a section of the fruit, but the old man declined.

"When there is no doubt, then a thing is proven. I have no doubt."

Khrone did not need to pretend confidence. "My Face Dancers will find the no-ship."

"We have faith in your abilities, dear Khrone," the old woman said. "But it has been nearly five years, and we need more than mere assurances." She smiled sweetly as if she meant to reach out and pat him on the cheek. "Don't forget your obligations."

Suddenly the multicolored lines of force around Khrone grew incandescent. Through all the nerves of his body, penetrating every bone and muscle fiber, he felt a searing agony, an indescribable pain that went beyond his cells and beyond his mind. With his intrinsic Face Dancer control, he tried to shut down all of his receptors, but he could not escape. The agony continued, yet the old woman's voice remained exceptionally clear in the back of his thoughts: "We can keep this up for ten million years if we choose."

Abruptly the pain was gone, and the old man reached over to take half of the peeled fruit the woman offered him. Tearing off a section, he said, "Do not give us an excuse to do it."

Then the illusory world wavered. The bucolic orchard disappeared, and the bright network of lines faded, leaving only the metal-walled corridors of the Guildship again. Khrone had collapsed to the deck, and no one else was around. Shaking, he climbed to his feet. The throbbing agony still burst out in cellular echoes from dark afterimages behind his eyes. He drew several breaths to regain his strength, using his outrage as a crutch.

During the wash of pain, his features had shifted through numerous assumed guises and reverted to their blank Face Dancer appearance again. Gathering himself, Khrone vengefully formed his face into an exact replica of the old man's. But that was not enough for him. Feeling petty rage, he drew back his lips to expose teeth that he transformed into brown and decayed stumps. Khrone's imitation of the old man's wrinkled face became decayed. Flesh hung in sagging folds, then turned yellow before separating from the muscles. Vindictively leprous blotches covered the skin, and the face became a mass of boils, the eyes milky and blind.

If only he could project the condition, it was what the old bastard deserved!

Khrone reasserted himself again, restoring his normal appearance, though the anger remained unquenched within him. Then his smile gradually returned.

Those who considered themselves the rulers of the Face Dancers had been fooled again, just like the original Tleilaxu Masters and their offshoots, the Lost Ones. Still shaking, Khrone chuckled now as he walked along the Guildship's corridor, regathering his strength. He looked like an average crewman again. No one could possibly understand the fine art of deception better than he did.

I am its greatest practitioner, he thought.

*Damn your analyses and your infernal projections! Damn your
legal arguments, your manipulations, your subtle and not-so-
subtle pressures. Talk, talk, talk! It all comes down to the same
thing: When a difficult decision must be reached, the real choice is
obvious.*

—DUNCAN IDAHO,
ninth new ghola, shortly before his death

In the bright chamber that served the Jews as their temple, in a ceremony as traditional as the no-ship's stores could provide, the old
Rabbi led the Seder. Rebecca watched with her new understanding of
the root meanings behind the ancient ritual. She had *lived* it herself in
her memories, ages ago. Though he would never admit it, even the
Rabbi did not grasp some of the nuances, despite a lifetime of study.
Rebecca would not correct him, however. Not in front of the others,
not even in private. He was not a man who wished for a refinement of
his understanding, not as a Suk doctor, nor as a Rabbi.

Here, isolated from many of the strict requirements of the ancient
Passover service, the Rabbi followed the rule of the Seder as best he
could. His people acknowledged the difficulties, accepted the truth in
their hearts, and convinced themselves that everything was correct
and proper, lacking in no detail.

"God will understand, so long as *we* do not forget," the Rabbi said
in a low voice, as if uttering a secret. "We have had to make do before."

For the private observance in the Rabbi's extended quarters, which
also served as their temple, they had matzahs, maror—or bitter herbs—

and something resembling the right kind of wine . . . but no lamb. A processed meat substitute from the ship's stores was the closest he could come. His followers did not complain.

Rebecca had celebrated the Passover all her life, participating without questioning. Now, however, thanks to those millions from Lampadas in her head, she could delve through countless paths of memory across a wide web of generations. Buried within her were recollections of the first true Passover, lives as slaves in an incredibly ancient civilization called Egypt. She knew the truth, understood which parts were the strictest historical fact and which had slowly strayed into ritual and myth, despite the best efforts of rabbis to keep faith with previous generations.

"Perhaps we should smear blood over the lintel on our quarters," she said quietly. "The angel of death is different from before, but it is death nevertheless. We are still being pursued."

"If we can believe what Duncan Idaho says." The Rabbi did not know how to respond to her often-provocative comments. He protected himself by retreating into the formal order of the Seder. Jacob and Levi helped him with the blessing on wine, the washing of hands. They all prayed again and read from the Haggadah.

These days the Rabbi frequently grew angry with Rebecca, snapping at her, challenging her every statement because he saw the work of evil within it. If he had been a different sort of man, Rebecca could have talked with him for hours, describing her memories of Egypt and Pharaoh, the awful plague, the epochal flight into the desert. She could have recounted real conversations to him in the original tongue, shared her impressions of the living man Moses. One of her myriad ancestors had actually heard the great man speak.

If only the Rabbi were a different sort of person . . .

His flock was small; not many of them had gotten away from the Honored Matres on Gammu. For millennia upon millennia, their people had been persecuted, driven from one hiding place to another. Now, as they let themselves be swept up in the festive Passover ritual, their voices were few, though strong. The Rabbi would not allow himself to admit defeat. He doggedly did what he believed he must do, and he saw Rebecca as a foil against whom to test his mettle.

She did not ask for his censure or suggest a debate. With all the memories and lives within her, Rebecca could easily counter any erroneous statement he might make, but she had no wish to make him look like a fool, did not want him to grow even more resentful and defensive.

Rebecca had not yet told him of her recent decision to take on a greater responsibility, an even greater pain. The Bene Gesserits had called, and she had responded. She already knew what the Rabbi would say about it, but she had no intention of changing her mind. She could be as stubborn as the Rabbi, if she so chose. The horizon of her thoughts extended to the edge of history, while his thoughts were bounded by his own life.

By the time grace was spoken after their meals, then the happy Hallel and the songs, she discovered that her cheeks were wet with tears. Jacob saw this with a hushed awe. The service was moving, and with her perspective it seemed more meaningful than ever. Her weeping, though, came from the knowledge that she would not see another Seder. . . .

Much later, after the benediction and the last reading, when the small party had finished eating and departed, Rebecca remained behind in the Rabbi's quarters. She helped the old man put away the paraphernalia of the service; the awkward distance between them told her that he knew something was troubling her. The Rabbi held his silence, and Rebecca didn't offer to speak. She could sense him looking at her with his flashing eyes.

"Another Passover service aboard this no-ship. Four so far!" he finally said, falsely conversational. "Is this any better than being hidden like rodents under the ground while Honored Matre searchers try to uncover us?" When the old man was uncomfortable, Rebecca knew he resorted to complaints.

"How quickly you have forgotten our months of terror cramped in that hidden chamber with our air systems failing, the waste-recycling tanks overfull, the food supplies dwindling," she reminded him. "Jacob couldn't fix it. We would all have died soon, or been forced to slip away."

"Maybe we could have eluded the terrible women." His words were automatic, and Rebecca could tell he didn't believe them himself.

"I think not. Overhead in the ash pit, the Honored Matre hunters were using their scanning devices, probing the soil, digging for *us*. They were close. They suspected. You know it was only a matter of time before they discovered our hiding place. Our enemies always find our hiding places."

"Not all of them."

"We were lucky the Bene Gesserit chose to attack Gammu when they did. It was our chance, and we took it."

"The Bene Gesserit! Daughter, you always defend them."

"They saved us."

"Because they were obligated to. And that obligation has now made us lose you. You are forever tainted, girl. All those memories you took within your mind corrupted you. If only you could forget them." He hung his head in a melodramatic gesture of misery, rubbing his temples. "I shall forever feel guilt because of what I made you do."

"I did it willingly, Rabbi. Do not go looking for guilt that you did not earn. Yes, all those memories wrought great changes in me. Even I did not guess the magnitude of that weight from the past."

"They rescued us, but now we are lost again, wandering and wandering on this ship. What is to become of us? We have begun to have children, but what good does it do? Two babies so far. When will we find a new home?"

"This is like our people's sojourn in the desert, Rabbi." Rebecca actually remembered parts of it. "Perhaps God will lead us to the land of milk and honey."

"And perhaps we will vanish forever."

Rebecca had little patience for his constant moaning, his wringing of hands. It had been easier to tolerate the old man before, to give him the benefit of the doubt and let her faith counsel her. She had respected the Rabbi, believed everything he said, never thought to question. She longed for that innocence and confidence again, but it was gone. The Lampadas Horde had made sure of that. Rebecca's thoughts were now clearer, her decision irrevocable.

"My Sisters have asked for volunteers. They have . . . a need."

"A *need?*" The Rabbi raised his bushy eyebrows, pushed his spectacles back up.

"The volunteers will submit to a certain process. They will become axlotl tanks, receptacles to bear the children they have determined are necessary for our survival."

The Rabbi looked angry and revolted. "It is clearly the work of evil."

"Is it evil if it saves all of us?"

"Yes! No matter what excuses the witches give."

"I do not agree, Rabbi. I believe it is the work of God. If we are given tools for our survival, then God must want us to survive. But the evil inclination tricks us by sowing seeds of fear and suspicion."

As she had expected, he bridled. His nostrils flared, and he grew indignant. "Do you suggest that *I* am following an evil inclination?"

Her counterblow was strong enough to knock him off his feet. "I'm saying that I have decided to volunteer. I will become one of their womb tanks. My body will provide a necessary receptacle so the gholas can be born." A softer voice now, kinder words. "I trust you will look upon those children I bear and give them whatever aid and counsel they might require. Teach them if you can."

The Rabbi was aghast. "You—you cannot do this, daughter. I forbid it."

"It is Passover, Rabbi. Remember the blood of the lamb on the door-post."

"That was allowed only during the days of the Solomonic temple in Jerusalem. It is forbidden to do it anywhere else, at any time."

"Nevertheless, though I am far, far from untainted, this may be enough." She remained calm, but the Rabbi was shaking.

"It is folly and pride! The witches have lured you into their trap. You must pray with me—"

"My mind is made up, Rabbi. I've seen the wisdom of this. The Bene Gesserits *will* have their tanks. They *will* find their volunteers. Consider all the other women aboard, younger and stronger by far. They have their futures ahead of them, while I have had countless lives inside my head. That is more than enough for any person, and I am content. By offering myself, I save someone else."

"You will be cursed!" His hoarse voice cracked before it could rise to a scream. She wondered if he would tear his sleeve and cast her out, disavowing any further connection with her. Right now, the Rabbi was too horrified by what she had told him.

"As you so often remind me, Rabbi, I have millions already within me. In all my pasts a great many of them were devout Jews. Others followed their own conscience. But make no mistake, this is a price I can willingly pay. An honorable price. Don't think about losing me—think instead of the girl I am saving."

Grasping at straws, he said, "You are too old. You are past child-bearing years."

"My body only needs to provide the incubator, not the ovaries. I have already been tested. The Sisters assure me that I can adequately serve." She rested her hand on his arm, knowing that he cared for her. "You were a Suk doctor once. I trust the Bene Gesserit physicians, but I would feel better if I knew that you would also watch over me."

"I . . . I—"

She went to the door of the temple chamber and gave him a last smile. "Thank you, Rabbi." She slipped away before he could marshal his scrambled thoughts and continue arguing with her.

To the loving eye, even an Abomination can be a beautiful child.

—MISSIONARIA PROTECTIVA,
adapted from the Azhar Book

For months under the stern and watchful eyes of the Honored Matres, Uxtal worked at monitoring the axlotl tank while also attending the pain laboratories. He felt wrung out in his struggle to satisfy those who controlled him.

Khrone had come to visit him twice in the past half year (twice that he knew about, though a Face Dancer could move unnoticed whenever he liked). In his squalid quarters, the Lost Tleilaxu researcher kept his own calendar, marking off each day as a small victory, as if survival itself were a matter of keeping score.

In the meantime, he had also begun to produce enough of the orange melange alternative to make the whores believe he had value to them after all. Unfortunately, his successes were more a result of repeated attempts than any genuine skill on his part. In spite of his uncertainties and hastily covered blunders, Uxtal had stumbled upon a serviceable manufacturing method; though inefficient, it was good enough to keep the whores from killing him, for the time being.

And meanwhile the ghola baby continued to grow.

When the male fetus reached a point where he could take samples sufficient to run analyses, he compared the DNA to genetic records that Khrone had provided. He still didn't know what the Face Dancers had in mind with this child; in fact, he wasn't even convinced the shape-shifters had a plan at all, beyond their own curiosity.

Initially, Uxtal was able to isolate the general bloodline, then narrow it down to specifics, a planet of origin, an extended family . . . and then a definite family. Finally he backtracked the lineage to a specific historical person. The result startled him, and he nearly deleted the answer before anyone could see. But he was sure someone must be observing him, and if he was caught trying to hide information, the Honored Matres would treat him very harshly.

Instead, he faced his own dizzying questions. Why had the old Tleilaxu Masters preserved those particular cells? What possible purpose could they have imagined? And what other remarkable cells had been inside the destroyed nullentropy capsule? Too bad the Honored Matres had destroyed all the bodies, burning them or feeding them to sligs.

Khrone would return soon enough. Then maybe the Face Dancers would take their ghola baby away, and Uxtal could be free. Or maybe they would just kill him and be done with it. . . .

After its carefully monitored gestation period, the decanting of the infant was imminent. Quite imminent. Uxtal spent most of his days now in the axlotl room, both fearful and fascinated. He bent over the bloated female tank, testing the unborn baby's heartbeat, his movements. The child frequently let loose vicious kicks, as if he hated the fleshy cell that contained him. Not surprising, but alarming nevertheless.

When the day arrived, Uxtal summoned his assistants. "If the baby is not born healthy, I will send you to the torture wing—" He suddenly gasped, remembering other duties, and left the befuddled assistants standing by the pregnant tank as he rushed into the new adjacent laboratory wing.

There, among the screams, moans, and a tiny trickle of precursor chemicals for spice alternative, Hellica was waiting impatiently for him. For some time she had amused herself by watching the spice "harvesting" process, but now, seeing Uxtal, she snaked toward him.

He averted his eyes, stammered. "I am s-sorry, Matre Superior. The ghola is about to be born, and I was distracted. I should have ignored all other responsibilities as soon as you arrived." He muttered a silent, frantic prayer that she wouldn't murder him then and there. The Face Dancers would be quite upset if she killed him before he could decant the child, wouldn't they?

When Hellica's eyes flashed dangerously, he wanted to run. "I do not believe you are sufficiently convinced of your place in this new order, little man. It is time you are bonded—before that ghola is born. I need to rely on you. You will never again lose track of your priorities."

Uxtal became more aware of the swell of her breasts and the way she moved in the tight leotard. She seemed to project a hypnotic sexuality. Their gazes locked, but he experienced no arousal.

"Once I make you dependent on my pleasures," she continued, massaging his face gently with her fingers, "I will have your full dedication to my project. With the ghola baby out of the way, you will have no other excuses."

Uxtal felt his pulse accelerate. What would she do once she found out what Khrone had done to him?

A shout came from the main laboratory, followed by the brief indignant squall of a baby. Uxtal's heart leapt into his throat. "The child has been born! How could they do it without me?" Uxtal tried to pull away from Hellica. Terrified that his assistants had proved they could do their work independently, he didn't dare let anyone believe he might be unnecessary. "Please, Matre Superior, let me make certain my foolish assistants did nothing wrong."

Fortunately, Hellica seemed as interested as he was. The Tleilaxu man scuttled out of the new wing and rushed to the now deflated axlotl tank. With a shy but confused smile, one of the assistants held up the dripping, apparently healthy infant by one foot. The Matre Superior strode over, her cape fluttering behind her.

Uxtal snatched the baby from the assistant, though he found the whole birthing process disgusting. He was sure that Khrone would kill him (and slowly) if he allowed anything to happen to this child.

He showed the infant to Hellica. "There, Matre Superior. As you see, this distracting job will be over as soon as the Face Dancers take the child away. My work for them is done. I can now devote much more of my time and energy to creating the orange spice you want so much. Unless . . . unless you would just like to let me go free?" He raised his eyebrows pleadingly.

She gave a dismissive sniff and stalked back into the new wing, where sounds of screaming echoed through the corridors.

Uxtal stared down at the newborn boy, amazed at his own luck. By some miraculous numerical alignment, he had achieved success. Now Khrone could not complain, or punish him. A quiver of dread shuddered down his spine. What if the Face Dancers insisted that he restore the ghola's memories as well? So many more years!

Seeing the newborn now, so simple, innocent, and "normal" puzzled Uxtal. Having reviewed the historical records, he couldn't imagine what this ghola's destiny would be, what Khrone would do with him. It must be part of a cosmic plan that he could understand, but only if he ascertained all the numbers that pointed to the truth.

He held the ghola baby out before him, looked at the tiny face, and shook his head. "Welcome back, Baron Vladimir Harkonnen."

SIX YEARS AFTER

ESCAPE FROM CHAPTERHOUSE

We all have a beast within us, hungry and violent. Some of us can feed and control the predator within, but it is unpredictable when unleashed.

—REVEREND MOTHER SHEEANA,
Ithaca logs

Mulling over her duties and dilemmas, Sheeana walked alone down quiet and isolated passageways. Now that the ghola resurrection program had been decided upon, the long wait had begun. After a year and a half of preparations, three more axlotl tanks were ready, bringing the total to five. The first of the precious embryos now gestated inside one of the new augmented wombs. Soon, the near-mythical figures from history would return.

The Tleilaxu Master Scytale eagerly attended to the axlotl tanks, utterly committed to ensuring that the first ones turned out perfectly, so that Sheeana would allow him to create a ghola of himself. Since the little man had so much to gain from the success of the process, she trusted him—to a certain extent, and only for the time being.

No one knew what the Enemy wanted or why they were so interested in this particular no-ship. "One must understand an enemy to fight that enemy," the first incarnation of Bashar Miles Teg had once written. And she thought, *We know nothing about this old man and woman that only Duncan can see. Whom do they represent? What do they want?*

Preoccupied, she continued to walk the lower decks. During their years on the *Ithaca*, Duncan Idaho had kept an anxious watch outside, searching for any sign of the Enemy's endlessly questing net. The ship seemed to have remained safe since the narrow escape more than two years ago. Maybe she and the other passengers were safe, after all. Maybe.

As month after month of daily routine passed without any overt threat, Sheeana had to remind herself to fight against complacency, against the natural tendency to grow soft. Through the lessons in Other Memory, especially in her Atreides bloodline, she knew the perils of lowering her guard.

Bene Gesserit senses should always be alert for subtle dangers. Sheeana stopped in midstep in an isolated corridor. She froze as a scent touched her nostrils, a wild animal odor that did not belong in the processed and air-conditioned corridors. It was mixed with a coppery smell.

Blood.

A primal inner sense told her she was being watched, and perhaps even stalked. The invisible gaze burned like a lasgun against her skin. Goose bumps prickled the back of her neck. Realizing that this was a precarious moment, she moved slowly, holding out her hands and spreading her fingers—partly in a placating gesture, partly in preparation for hand-to-hand combat.

The no-ship's winding corridors were wide enough to accommodate the movement of heavy machinery such as Guild Navigator tanks. Built out in the Scattering, much of the vessel's design was driven by needs and pressures that were no longer relevant. Support struts curved overhead like the ribs of a huge prehistoric beast. Adjoining passages plunged off at angles. Storage chambers and unoccupied quarters were dark, and most of the doors to the main passenger areas were sealed but not locked. With only their own refugees aboard, the escaping Bene Gesserits rarely felt the need for locks.

But something was here. Something dangerous.

Inside her head, the voices from Sheeana's past clamored for her to be careful. Then they backed off into necessary mental silence so that she could concentrate. She sniffed the air, took two steps farther down the hall, and stopped as the warning instinct grew more potent. *Danger here!*

One of the storeroom doors was dark and almost closed, but not quite sealed. The tiny crack was just wide enough that an observer hiding within could keep watch on anyone who passed by.

There! That was where the scent of blood came from, and a rank, musky, animal smell. Intent on her discovery, she could not hide her reaction.

The door burst open, and a muscular dynamo stood there naked, pale flesh dusted with reddish-brown hair, a mouth widened to accommodate thick, tearing fangs. The muscles beneath the tight skin were as tight as coiled shigawire. One of the Futars! His curved claws and dark lips were stained with a bright splash of fresh blood.

With all the force of Voice she could put behind a single word, Sheeana snapped, "*Stop!*"

The Futar froze as if a leash around his neck had suddenly been yanked taut. In the bright corridor light, Sheeana stood motionless, non-threatening. The creature glared at her, his lips drawn back to expose long teeth. She used Voice again, though she was aware that these creatures might have been bred to resist known Bene Gesserit skills. Sheeana cursed herself for not spending more time studying the beasts to understand their motivations and vulnerabilities. "*Do not harm me.*"

The Futar remained poised for attack, a bomb ready to explode. "You Handler?" He took a deep sniff. "Not Handler!"

In the dim storeroom that the Futar had chosen for his den, Sheeana caught a glimpse of white flesh and torn dark robes. She saw pale fingers curled toward the ceiling, loose, in a repose of death. Who had it been?

Until now, the four captive Futars had been surly and restless, but not murderous. Even when they had been held prisoner by the Honored Matres—their natural prey—they had not killed the whores, because apparently they would not act without instructions from their true masters. *Handlers.* But after their rough treatment by the Honored Matres, and then years of being held in the brig of the no-ship, could the Futars be breaking down? Even the harshest inbred training could grow fuzzy around the edges, allowing "accidents."

Sheeana focused on her adversary, forcing herself not to see the creature as something unstable or broken. *Don't underestimate him!* At the moment she could not concern herself with how the creature had escaped from its high-security brig cell. Had all four broken free to roam the halls, or was this the only one?

In a careful gesture, she lifted her chin and turned her head to one side, baring her throat. A natural predator would understand the universal signal of submission. The Futar's need for dominance, to be the leader of a pack, required him to accept the gesture.

"You are a Futar," Sheeana said. "I am not one of your old Handlers."

He crept forward to draw a deep sniff. "Not Honored Matre either." He growled, a low, bubbling sound that demonstrated his hatred for the whores who had enslaved him and his comrades. But Bene Gesserit Sisters were something else entirely. Even so, he had killed one.

"We are your caretakers now. We give you food."

"Food." The Futar licked blood from his dark lips.

"You asked us for sanctuary on Gammu. We rescued you from the Honored Matres."

"Bad women."

"But we are not bad." Sheeana remained motionless, nonthreatening, facing the coiled danger of the Futar. As a child she had confronted a giant sandworm and shouted at it, heedless of her peril. She could do this. She made her voice as soothing as possible. "I am Sheeana." She spoke in a lilting, hushed voice. "Do you have a name?"

The creature growled—at least she thought it was a growl. Then she realized that the confined rumble in his larynx was actually his name. "*Hrrm.*"

"Hrrm. Do you recall when you came to this no-ship? When you escaped from the Honored Matres? You asked us to take you away."

"Bad women!" the Futar said again.

"Yes, and we saved you." Sheeana edged closer. Though she wasn't entirely sure of its efficacy, she controlled her body chemistry to increase her scent, trying to match some of the markers exuded by the Futar's musk glands. She made sure he smelled that she was *female*, not a threat. Something to protect, not attack. She was also careful not to give off any odor of fear, to keep this predator from thinking of her as its prey.

"You shouldn't have escaped from your room."

"Want Handlers. Want *home*." With a longing in his feral eyes, Hrrm glanced back at the dark storage room where the torn body of the hapless Sister lay. Sheeana wondered how long Hrrm had been feeding on the corpse.

"I need to take you back to the other Futars. You must stay together. We protect you. We are your friends. You must not hurt us."

Hrrm grumbled. Then, taking a big chance, Sheeana reached out and touched his hairy shoulder. The Futar stiffened, but she stroked carefully, seeking pleasure centers along his vivid nerves. Though startled by her attentions, Hrrm did not draw away. Her hands drifted upward, moving with a gentle intensity. Sheeana touched Hrrm's neck, then behind his ears. The Futar's suspicious growl became a sound more like a purr.

"We are your friends," she insisted, applying just a hint of Voice to reinforce it. "You should not hurt us." She looked meaningfully into the den chamber, at the dead Sister on the floor.

Hrrm stiffened. "My kill."

"You should not have killed. That is not an Honored Matre. She was one of my Sisters. She was one of your friends."

"Futars should not kill friends."

Sheeana stroked him again, and his coarse body hair bristled. She began to lead him down the corridor. "We feed you. There is no need for you to kill."

"Kill Honored Matres."

"There are no Honored Matres on this ship. We hate them, too."

"Need to hunt. Need Handlers."

"You can't have either right now."

"Someday?" Hrrm sounded hopeful.

"Someday." Sheeana could make no more of a promise than that.

She took him away from the dead Bene Gesserit, hoping the two of them would encounter no one else on the way back to the brig, no other potential victims. Her hold on this creature was far too tenuous. If Hrrm was startled, he might attack.

She took side passages and service lifts that few others would use, until they arrived at the deep brig level. The Futar seemed disconsolate, reluctant to go back into his cell, and she pitied him his endless confinement. Just like the seven sandworms in the hold.

Reaching the door, she saw that a minor security circuit had failed after so many years. At first she had dreaded a systemic problem and expected to find all the Futars loose. Instead, this proved to be a minor glitch resulting from poor maintenance procedures. An accident on an old vessel.

The year before there had been another breakdown involving a water recycling reservoir, when a corroded pipe flooded a corridor. They had also experienced recurring problems with the algae vats that were used for food and oxygen production. Maintenance was growing lax. *Complacent.*

Sheeana controlled her anger, not wanting Hrrm to smell it on her. Though the Bene Gesserits lived in constant intangible peril, the danger no longer seemed immediate. She had to impose much stricter discipline from now on. A breakdown like this could have led to disaster!

Hrrm looked saddened and beaten as he shuffled into the confinement chamber. "You must stay in there," Sheeana said, trying to sound encouraging. "At least for a while longer."

"Want home," Hrrm said.

"I will try to find your home. But right now I have to keep you safe."

Hrrm plodded to the far wall of the brig chamber and squatted on his haunches. The other three Futars approached the barriers of their separate cells to peer out with hungry, curious eyes.

Fixing the door shield mechanism was a simple thing. Now all would be safe, Futars and Bene Gesserits. Sheeana feared for them, though. Wandering aimlessly in the no-ship, her people had been too long without a goal.

That would have to change. Perhaps the birth of the new gholas would give them what they needed.

To the Sisterhood, Other Memory is one of the greatest blessings and greatest mysteries. We understand only shadows of the process by which lives are transferred from one Reverend Mother to another. That vast reservoir of voices from the past is a brilliant but mysterious light.

—REVEREND MOTHER DARWI ODRADE

Over the course of two years, the New Sisterhood had started to become a single unified organism, and all the while the planet of Chapterhouse continued to die. Mother Commander Murbella walked briskly through the brown orchards. One day this would all be desert. On purpose.

As part of the plan to create an alternative to Rakis, sandtrout worked furiously to encapsulate water. The arid belt expanded, and now only the hardiest apple trees with the deepest roots clung to life.

Nevertheless, the orchard was one of Murbella's favorite places, a joy she had learned from Odrade—her captor, teacher, and (eventually) respected mentor. It was mid-afternoon, and sunlight filtered through the sparse leaves and brittle branches. Even so, it was a cool day, with a stiff breeze from the north. She paused and bowed her head out of respect for the woman who lay buried beneath a small Macintosh apple tree, which struggled to grow even as the environment wasted into harsh aridity. No braz plaque identified the Mother Superior's resting place. Though Honored Matres preferred ostentation and dramatic memorials, Odrade would have been appalled by any such gesture.

Murbella wished her predecessor could have lived long enough to see the results of her great plan of synthesis: Honored Matres and Bene Gesserits living together on Chapterhouse. The groups had learned from their differences, drawing strength from each other.

But renegade Honored Matres on outside planets continued to be a thorn in her side, refusing to join the New Sisterhood, causing turmoil while the Mother Commander needed to face the much larger threat of the Outside Enemy. Those women rejected her as their leader, saying that she had tainted and diluted their ways. They wanted to wipe out Murbella and her followers, to the last Sister. And some of those rebels might still have their terrible Obliterators—though certainly not many, or they would have used them by now.

When her newly formed group of fighters completed their training, Murbella intended to seize the renegades and bring them into the fold, before it was too late. The New Sisterhood would eventually have to go up against large contingents of Honored Matre holdouts on Buzzell, Gammu, Tleilax, and other worlds.

We must break them and assimilate them, she thought. *But first, we must be certain of our unity.*

Bending down, Murbella scooped up a handful of dirt near the base of the small tree. Holding the dry soil in the palm of her hand, she lifted it to her nose and inhaled the pungent, earthy aroma. At times, she wondered if she could detect, ever so faintly, the infinitesimal scent of her mentor and friend.

"Someday I may join you here," she said aloud, looking at the struggling tree, "but not yet. First, I have important work to finish."

Your legacy, murmured Odrade-within.

"*Our* legacy. You inspired me to heal the factions and bring together women who were mortal enemies. I didn't expect it to be so hard, or to take so long." In her head Odrade remained silent.

Murbella walked farther from the fortresslike Keep, putting it behind her, and all of her responsibilities with it. She identified the passing rows of dying trees: apples giving way to peaches, cherries, and oranges. She decided to order an active program of planting date palms, which would survive longer in the changing climate. But did they even have years?

Climbing a nearby hill, she noted how much harder and drier the soil was. In grasslands beyond the orchards, the Sisterhood's cattle still grazed, but the pasture was sparse now, forcing the animals to range farther. She saw the flicker of a lizard running across the warm ground. Sensing danger, the tiny reptile scurried up a large stone to look back at her. Suddenly a desert hawk swooped down, snatched the creature, and carried it into the sky.

Murbella responded with a hard smile. For some time now, the desert had been approaching, killing all growing things in its path. Windblown dust painted the normally blue skies with a constant brownish haze. As the sandworms grew out in the arid belt, so did their desert, to accommodate them. An ever-expanding ecosystem.

In the encroaching desert ahead of her, and the faltering orchards behind her, Murbella saw two great Bene Gesserit dreams crashing into one another like opposing tides, a beginning absorbing an ending. Long before Sheeana brought a single aging sandworm here, the Sisterhood planted this orchard. The new plan, however, had far greater galactic importance than any symbolism represented by the orchard graveyards. Through their bold action, the Bene Gesserits had saved the sandworms and melange, before the ravages of the Honored Matres.

Wasn't that worth the loss of a few fruit trees? Melange was both a blessing and a curse. She turned and strode back to the Keep.

The conscious mind is only the tip of the iceberg. A vast mass of
subconscious thoughts and latent abilities lies beneath the surface.
                                        —The Mentat Handbook

Back when Duncan Idaho was held prisoner at the Chapterhouse spaceport, enough deadly mines had been placed on the no-ship to destroy it three times over. Odrade and Bellonda had planted the explosives throughout the grounded no-ship, ready to be triggered should Duncan try to escape. They had assumed that the deadly mines would be a sufficient deterrent. The loyal Sisters had never dreamed that Sheeana herself and her conservative allies might deactivate those mines and steal the ship for their own purposes.

The passengers aboard the *Ithaca* were theoretically trustworthy, but Duncan, staunchly supported by the Bashar, insisted that these mines were simply too dangerous to leave unprotected. Only he, Teg, Sheeana, and four others had direct access to the armory.

During his routine check, Duncan unsealed the vault and viewed the wide selection of weapons. He drew reassurance from observing his options, tallying the ways that the *Ithaca* could fight back, should it ever become necessary. He sensed that the old man and woman had not stopped searching, though he had not encountered the shimmering net for three years now. He could not let his guard down.

He inspected rows of modified lasguns, pulse rifles, splinter guns, and projectile launchers. These weapons represented an edgy potential for violence that made him think of Honored Matres. The whores would not want distant and impersonal stunners; they preferred weapons that caused extreme damage up close, where they could see the carnage, and smile. He had already gained far too much insight into their tastes when he'd discovered the sealed torture chamber. He wondered what else the terrible women might have hidden aboard the great vessel.

For the entire time Duncan had been a prisoner aboard the grounded no-ship, these weapons had been stored here, securely locked but still within reach. Had he wanted to, he surely could have broken into the armory and stolen them. He was surprised that Odrade had underestimated him . . . or trusted him. In the end, she had given him what history called the "Atreides choice," explaining the consequences and allowing him to decide whether or not to stay with the no-ship. She trusted his loyalties. Anyone who knew him, either personally or from history, understood that Duncan Idaho and Loyalty were synonymous.

Now he considered the compact, sealed mines that had been meant to bring the no-ship down in a flaming collapse. A fail-safe.

"Those aren't the only ticking bombs aboard this ship." The voice startled him, and he spun about, instinctively assuming a fighting stance. Dour, curly-haired Garimi stood at the hatch. In spite of all his experience with them, Duncan was still astonished by how silently the damned witches could move.

Duncan struggled to regain his composure. "Is there another armory, a secret stash of weapons?" It was possible, he supposed, given the thousands of chambers aboard the giant ship that had never been opened or searched.

"I was speaking metaphorically. I meant those gholas from the past."

"That has already been discussed and decided." In the medical center, the first ghola from Scytale's sample cells would soon be decanted.

"Simply making a decision does not make the decision correct," Garimi said.

"You harp on it too much."

Garimi rolled her eyes. "Even you haven't seen any sign of your hunters since the day we consigned our five tortured Sisters to space. It's time for us to find a suitable world and establish a new core for the Bene Gesserit Sisterhood."

Duncan frowned. "The Oracle of Time also said the hunters were searching for us."

"Another encounter that only you experienced."

"Are you suggesting I imagined it? Or that I'm lying? Bring me any Truthsayer you like. I will prove it to you."

She grumbled. "Even so, it has been years since the Oracle purportedly warned you. We have eluded capture all this time."

Leaning against one of the shelves of weapons, Duncan gave her a cool stare. "And how do you know the Enemy isn't patient, that they won't just wait for us to make a mistake? They want this ship, or they want someone aboard it—probably me. Once these new gholas regain their knowledge and experience, they may be our greatest advantage."

"Or an unrecognized danger."

He realized he would never convince her. "I knew Paul Atreides. As the Atreides Swordmaster, I helped to raise and train that boy. I will do so again."

"He became the terrible Muad'Dib. He began a jihad that slaughtered trillions, and he turned into an emperor as corrupt as any in history before him."

"He was a good child and a good man," Duncan insisted. "And while he shaped the map of history, Paul was himself shaped by the events around him. Even so, in the end he refused to follow the path that he knew led to so much pain and ruin."

"His son Leto did not have such reservations."

"Leto II was forced into a Hobson's choice of his own. We cannot judge that decision until we know everything that was behind it. Perhaps not enough time has passed for anyone to say whether or not his choice was ultimately correct."

A storm of anger crossed Garimi's face. "It's been five thousand years since the Tyrant began his work, fifteen hundred years since his death."

"One of his most prominent lessons was that humanity should learn to think on a truly long time scale."

Uncomfortable with allowing the Bene Gesserit woman so close to so many tempting weapons, he eased her back out into the corridor and sealed the vault door. "I was on Ix fighting the Tleilaxu for House Vernius when Paul Atreides was born in the Imperial Palace on Kaitain. I found myself embroiled in the first battles of the War of Assassins that consumed House Ecaz and Duke Leto for so many years. Lady Jessica had been summoned to Kaitain for the last months of her pregnancy because Lady Anirul suspected the potential of Paul and wanted to be present at the birth. Despite treachery and assassinations, the baby survived and was brought back to Caladan."

Garimi stepped away from the armory, still obviously disturbed. "According to the legends, Paul Muad'Dib was born on Caladan, not on Kaitain."

"Legends are just that, sometimes fraught with errors, sometimes distorted intentionally. As an infant, Paul Atreides was christened on Caladan, and he considered that planet his home, until his arrival on Dune. You Bene Gesserits wrote that history."

"And now you plan to rewrite it with what you assure us is the truth, with your precious Paul and other ghola children from the past?"

"Not rewrite it. We intend to *re-create* it."

Clearly dissatisfied, but seeing that any further argument would simply carry them in circles, Garimi waited to see which direction Duncan would walk. Then she turned the opposite way and stalked off.

The unknown can be a terrible thing, and is often made more mon-
strous by human imagination. The real Enemy, however, may be far
worse than any we can possibly imagine. Do not let your guard
down.

—MOTHER SUPERIOR DARWI ODRADE

The fat Reverend Mother and the feral Honored Matre stood stiffly together, as far apart as they thought they could without being too obvious. Even an observer without specialized Bene Gesserit training would have noticed their dislike for each other.

"You two will have to work together." Murbella's voice allowed for no argument. "I have decided that we must devote more of our efforts to the desert belt. Never forget that melange is the key. We will call in outside researchers to set up observation bases out in the deepest worm territories. Maybe we can find a few old experts who actually visited Rakis before it was destroyed."

"Our melange stockpiles are still significant," Bellonda pointed out.

"And the sandtrout seem to be destroying all fertile land," Doria added. "The flow of spice is secure."

"Nothing is ever secure! Complacency can be a worse threat than the rebel Honored Matres themselves—or the Outside Enemy," Murbella said. "To oppose either adversary, we must have the absolute cooperation of the Spacing Guild. We need their immense ships, fully armed to transport us to and from anywhere we choose. We can use the

Guild and CHOAM as carrot and stick to force planets, governments, and independent military systems to follow our lead. For that, our most effective tool is melange. With no other source, they will have to come to us for spice."

"Or they can fly other ships from the Scattering," Bellonda said.

Doria snorted. "The Guild would never stoop to that."

With a sideways glance at her rival and partner, Bellonda added, "Because we only let the Guild obtain small amounts of spice from us, they also pay exorbitant prices for black-market melange from other stockpiles. Once we force them to exhaust their spice supplies, we will bring the Guild to its knees, and they will do whatever we ask of them."

Bellonda nodded. "The Guild is probably desperate already. When Administrator Gorus and the Navigator Edrik came here three years ago, they were nearly frantic. We have kept them on a tight leash since then."

"They could well be on the verge of irrational action," Doria warned.

"The spice must flow, but only on our terms." Murbella turned to the women. "I have a new assignment for you two. When we offer our generous forgiveness in exchange for Guild cooperation in the coming war, we'll need to be extravagant in our payment. Doria and Bellonda, I place you in charge of managing the arid zone, the spice extraction process, and the new sandworms."

Bellonda looked shocked. "Mother Commander, could I not serve you better here, as your advisor—and guardian?"

"No, you could not. As a Mentat you have shown great skill in handling details, and Doria has the edge to push where it is needed. Make sure our sandworms produce spice in the quantities we—and the Guild—will need. From now on, the deserts of Chapterhouse are your responsibility."

AFTER THE UNLIKELY pair left for the desert, Murbella went to see the old Archives Mother Accadia, still seeking essential answers.

In a large and airy wing of Chapterhouse Keep, the ancient librarian had arranged numerous tables and booths where thousands of Reverend Mothers toiled. Under normal circumstances, the Keep's archives would have been a quiet place for study and meditation, but Accadia had taken on a special mission that gave the New Sisterhood a wealth of unexpected hope.

The Bene Gesserit library world of Lampadas had been among the many planetary casualties from Honored Matre depredations. Knowing their imminent fate, the doomed women had Shared among each other, distilling the experience and knowledge of an entire population into only a few representatives. Eventually, all of those memories, and the entire library of Lampadas, had been placed in the mind of the wild Reverend Mother Rebecca, who had managed to Share again with many others, thus saving the memories of all those people.

Accadia's grand new scheme was to re-create the lost Lampadas library. She gathered Reverend Mothers who had obtained the knowledge and experiences of the Lampadas horde. The ones who were Mentats were able to remember word for word everything those previous lives had read and learned.

The archives wing was a drone of conversation and background noise, women sitting before shigawire spool recorders and dictating from memory, reading aloud page after page of rare books that their experiences recalled. Other women sat with their eyes closed, sketching on crystal sheets the diagrams and designs that were locked away in memory. Murbella watched volume after volume being re-created before her eyes. Each woman had a specific assignment, to reduce the likelihood of duplicating efforts.

Accadia seemed content as she greeted her visitor. "Welcome, Mother Commander. With great effort, we are managing to undo more and more losses."

"I can only hope that the Enemy does not obliterate Chapterhouse and render your efforts in vain."

"Preserving knowledge is never a pointless exercise, Mother Commander."

Murbella shook her head. "But we don't seem to have certain vital knowledge. Key elements are missing, the simplest, most straightforward information. Who or what is our Enemy? Why would they cause such appalling destruction? For that matter, who are the Honored Matres? Where did they come from, and how did they provoke such wrath?"

"You yourself were an Honored Matre. Do your Other Memories give you no clues?"

Murbella gritted her teeth. She had tried and tried, with no success. "I can study the course of the Bene Gesserit lines I have acquired, but not the Honored Matres. Their past is a black wall before my eyes. Each time I delve into it, I reach an impassable barrier. Either the Honored Matres do not know their own origins, or it is such a terrible secret that they have managed to block it completely."

"I've heard that is true for all of our Honored Matres who have passed through the Spice Agony."

"Every one." Murbella had received the same answer again and again. The origins of the Honored Matres, and of the Enemy, were no more than dim myths in their past. Honored Matres had never been reflective, pondering consequences or tracing events back to first principals. Now, it seemed they would all suffer for it.

"You will have to find the information some other way, Mother Commander. If we discover any clues while reproducing the Lampadas library, I will inform you."

Murbella thanked her, yet sensed that the information she needed did not lie here.

SHORTLY BEFORE JANESS decided to undergo the Spice Agony—three years after her twin sister had failed—the Mother Commander went to her room in the acolytes' barracks.

"I deceived myself about Rinya's chances in the ordeal." The words did not come easily to Murbella. "I never dreamed that a daughter of mine and Duncan's could possibly fail. My old Honored Matre hubris showed itself."

"This daughter won't fail, Mother Commander," Janess said, sitting straight. "I have trained hard, and I am as ready as anyone can be. I am frightened, yes, but only enough to maintain my edge."

"Honored Matres believe there is no place for fear," Murbella mused. "They do not consider that one can be strengthened by admitting weakness, instead of trying to hide it or bulldoze your way over it."

" 'If you do not face your weaknesses, how do you know where to be strong?' I read that quote in the archival writings of Duncan Idaho."

Over the years, Janess had studied the many lives of Duncan Idaho. Though she would never meet her father, she had learned much from the combat techniques of the great Swordmaster of House Atreides, classic fighting abilities that had been recorded and passed on to others.

Setting aside the distraction of Duncan, Murbella looked down at her oldest surviving daughter. "You don't need my help. I can see it in your eyes. Tomorrow you face the Spice Agony." She rose and prepared to go. "I have been looking for someone whose loyalties and skills I can trust completely. After tomorrow, I believe you will be that person."

No land or sea or planet is forever. Wherever we stand, we are only stewards.

—MOTHER SUPERIOR DARWI ODRADE

Carrying two passengers, the ornithopter flew over the newborn desert and rock formations, heading away from Chapterhouse Keep. Looking back from her wide seat in the rear compartment, Bellonda watched the rings of dying crops and orchards disappear behind the dunes. From the small cabin ahead of her, Doria controlled the aircraft. The brash former Honored Matre rarely let Bellonda pilot a 'thopter, though she was certainly competent. The two spoke little during their hours of flying.

Farther south, the barren regions continued to expand as the planet itself dried up. Over the course of nearly seventeen years, the water-hoarding sandtrout had drained the large sea, leaving a dust bowl and an ever-widening arid band. Before long, all of Chapterhouse would become another Dune.

If any of us survives to see it, Bellonda thought. *The Enemy will find us, and all our worlds, sooner or later.* She was not superstitious, nor an alarmist, but the conclusion was a Mentat certainty.

Both women wore plain black singlesuits designed for permeability and cooling. Since the assassination attempt at the gathering,

Murbella had made the uniform dress code mandatory across the New Sisterhood, no longer allowing the women to flaunt their different origins. "During times of peace and prosperity, freedom and diversity are considered absolute rights," Murbella said. "With a monumental crisis facing us, however, such concepts become disruptive and self-indulgent."

Every Sister on Chapterhouse now wore a black singlesuit, without any obvious identifiers of whether she originated from the Honored Matres or Bene Gesserits. Unlike the heavy, concealing Bene Gesserit robes, the fine mesh of the formfitting fabric hid none of Bellonda's lumpy bulk.

I look like the Baron Harkonnen, she thought. She felt an odd sort of pleasure whenever the ferally lean Doria looked at her with disgust.

The former Honored Matre was in a foul mood because she didn't want to go on this inspection trip—especially not with Bellonda. In perverse response, the Reverend Mother made an effort to be overly cheery.

No matter how much Bellonda tried to deny it, the two of them had similar personalities: both obstinate and fiercely loyal to their respective factions, yet grudgingly acknowledging the greater purpose of the New Sisterhood. Bellonda, always quick to notice flaws, had never hesitated to criticize Mother Superior Odrade either. Doria was similar in her own way, unafraid of pointing out faults in the Honored Matres. Both women tried to hold on to the outdated ways of their respective organizations. As the new Spice Operations Directors, she and Doria shared stewardship of the fledgling desert.

Bellonda wiped perspiration from her brow. They were almost to the desert, and with each passing moment, the heat outside increased. She raised her voice above the drone of the 'thopter's wings. "You and I should make the best of this trip—for the good of the Sisterhood."

"*You* make the best of it." Doria shouted her sarcasm. "For the good of the Sisterhood."

Bellonda grabbed a safety strap as the ornithopter passed through turbulence. "You are mistaken if you think I agree entirely with what the Mother Commander is doing. I never thought her mongrel alliance would survive the first year, much less six."

Scowling, Doria steadied the controls. "That does not make us in any way alike."

Below, patches of sand and dust swirled, temporarily obscuring the ground. The dunes were encroaching on a line of already dead trees. Comparing the coordinates on a bulkhead screen with her notebook, Bellonda estimated that the desert had advanced by almost fifty kilometers in only a few months. More sand meant more territory for the growing worms, and consequently more spice. Murbella would be pleased.

When the air currents smoothed, Bellonda spotted an interesting exposed rock formation that had previously been obscured by thick forest. On a sheer side of the rock, she saw a magnificent splash of primitive paintings in red and yellow ochre that had somehow endured the passage of time. She had heard of these ancient sites, supposedly indications of the mysterious, vanished Muadru people from millennia past, but she had never seen evidence of them before. It surprised her that the lost race had reached this obscure planet. What had drawn them all the way out here?

Not surprisingly, Doria showed no interest whatsoever in the archaeological oddity.

Presently the aircraft landed on a flat section of rock, near one of the first worm observatories Odrade had established. The small, blocky structure towered above them as they disembarked. When the 'thopter's canopy opened and the two stepped out onto the drifting dunes near Desert Watch Station, Bellonda felt perspiration at her temples and in the small of her back, despite the cooling properties of the black singlesuit.

She took a long sniff. The parched landscape smelled dead with all the vegetation and soil gone. This desert band was dry enough for sandworms to grow, though it had not yet achieved the flinty, sterile cleanness of the real desert on lost Rakis.

Taking a lift tube to the top of the station tower, Bellonda and Doria entered the reinforced observatory. In the distance they could see a small spice-harvesting operation where a mixed crew of men and women worked a vein of rust-colored sand.

Doria used a high-powered viewing scope to gaze out over the dunes. "Wormsign!"

Through her own scope, Bellonda watched a mound in motion just beneath the sand. Judging from the size of the moving ripple, the worm was small, only five meters or so. Farther out in the dune sea, she spotted another small sand-dweller churning in toward the spice operations. These new-generation worms did not yet have the power and ferocity to mark out their territories.

"Larger worms will create more melange," Bellonda said. "In a few years, our specimens may pose a genuine danger to the spice crews. We may have to institute the more expensive hovering harvesters."

Updating charts on her handheld data screen, Doria said, "Soon we will be able to export large enough quantities of spice to make ourselves rich. We can buy all the new equipment we like."

"The purpose of the spice is to increase the power of our New Sisterhood, not to line your pockets. What good is wealth, if none of us survives the Enemy? Given enough spice, we can build a powerful army."

Doria shot her a hard glare. "You parrot the Mother Commander so well." Gazing through the angled windows toward the faint shadows of forests smothered beneath the sand, Doria shielded her eyes against the glare. "Such devastation. When Honored Matres did a similar thing to your planets with their Obliterators, you called it senseless destruction. Yet on your own planet, you Sisters take pride in it."

"Transformation is often a messy business, and not everyone sees the end result as a good thing. It is a matter of perspective. And intelligence."

Evil can be detected by its smell.

—PAUL MUAD'DIB,
the original

Khrone received regular reports on the child Baron's progress from his many Face Dancers in Bandalong. At first he had asked for the creation of the ghola out of mere curiosity, but by the time the baby was two years old, he had developed plans to make use of it. Face Dancer plans.

Baron Vladimir Harkonnen. What an interesting choice. Even he didn't know why the old Masters had preserved the cells of the ancient, deviously brilliant villain. But Khrone had come up with his own ideas for the ghola.

First, though, the child must be raised and analyzed for special talents. It would be another decade or so before the latent memories of the Baron's original life could be triggered. That would be another assignment for Uxtal, if the little man could possibly keep himself from getting killed for that long.

So many of the components in his overall scheme had interlocked over decades, even centuries. Khrone could see how those pieces fit together, like the thoughts of the Face Dancer myriad. He could discern the smaller patterns and larger ones, and during each step he played his appropriate part. No one else on the great stage of the universe—not the audience, not the directors, not his fellow cast members—knew the extent to which the Face Dancers controlled the whole operation.

Content that all was under control in Bandalong, Khrone slipped away to Ix for his next important opportunity there. . . .

AFTER THE PRIZED Vladimir Harkonnen ghola was born, hapless Uxtal's first difficult task was complete. Still, his oppression did not end.

The simpering Lost Tleilaxu researcher had not disappointed the Face Dancers. Even more surprising, Uxtal had managed to keep himself alive among the Honored Matres for nearly three years now. He had marked off every single day on the makeshift calendar in his quarters.

He lived in terror, and he always felt cold. He could barely sleep at night, shuddering, alert for any stalking noise, dreading the appearance of any Honored Matre who might come to make good on the threat to sexually bond him. He looked under his bed for any Face Dancers that might be hiding there.

He was the only one of his kind still alive. All the Lost Tleilaxu elders had been replaced by Face Dancers, all the old Masters murdered outright by the Honored Matres. And he, Uxtal, was still breathing (which was more than he could say about any of those others). Even so, he was utterly miserable.

Uxtal wished the Face Dancers would just take the diminutive Vladimir away. Why didn't they relieve him of at least one impossible burden? How long was Uxtal supposed to be responsible for the brat? What more did they want? More and more and more! One of these days he was sure to make a fatal error. He couldn't believe he had succeeded for so long.

Uxtal wanted to shout at the Honored Matres, at any person he encountered, hoping it might be a Face Dancer in disguise. How could he do his work? But he simply kept his eyes averted and tried to put on a convincing show that he was working extremely hard. Being miserable was far preferable to being dead.

Still alive. But how to remain that way?

Did even the Matre Superior know how many shape-shifters lived among her people? He doubted it. Khrone probably had insidious plans of his own. Maybe if Uxtal uncovered them and exposed the Face Dancer schemes to the Honored Matres, then Hellica would be indebted to him, would reward him—

He knew, however, that would never happen.

Sometimes Matre Superior Hellica brought visitors into the torture laboratory, preening Honored Matres who apparently ruled other worlds that still resisted the New Sisterhood's attempts to assimilate them. Hellica sold them the orange drug that Uxtal now produced in great quantities. Over the years, he had perfected the technique of harvesting their adrenaline and catecholamine neurotransmitters, dopamine, and endorphins, a cocktail used as the precursor for the orange spice substitute.

In a superior tone, Hellica explained, "We are Honored Matres, not slaves to melange! Our version of spice comes as a direct consequence of pain." She and the observers looked down at the writhing subject. "It is more suited to our needs."

The pretender queen bragged (as she often did) about her lab programs, exaggerating the truth by increments, much as Uxtal overemphasized his own questionable skills. As she told her lies, he always nodded in agreement with her.

Since his work producing the melange substitute had expanded, he now supervised a dozen lower-caste laboratory assistants, along with a leathery, long-in-the-tooth Honored Matre named Ingva, whom he was sure served more as a spy and snitch than a helper. He rarely asked the crone to do anything, because she constantly feigned ignorance or offered some other excuse. She resented taking instructions from any male, and he was afraid to make demands.

Ingva came and went at unpredictable times, undoubtedly to keep Uxtal off balance. More than once, overdosed on some intoxicant, she had pounded on his door in the middle of the night. Since the Matre Superior had never claimed him for herself, Ingva threatened to bond him to her sexually, but hesitated to openly defy Hellica. Looming over him in the dimness, the old Honored Matre ranted threats that chilled him to the bone.

Once, when she had consumed too much artificial spice stolen from the fresh laboratory supplies, Ingva had actually been near death, her delirious eyes completely orange, her vital signs weak. Uxtal had very badly wanted to let her die in front of him, but he was afraid to do so. Losing Ingva would not have solved his problems; it would have cast suspicion on him, with unknown and terrifying repercussions. And the next Honored Matre spy might be even worse.

Thinking quickly, he had given her an antidote that revived her. Ingva had never thanked him for the rescue, never acknowledged any debt whatsoever. Then again, she had not killed him, either. Or bonded with him. That was something, at least.

Still alive. I am still alive.

AS HE GREW, the child ghola of Vladimir Harkonnen lived in a guarded nursery chamber on the laboratory grounds. The toddler had virtually everything he asked for, including pets to "play with," many of which did not survive. Obviously, the Baron had bred true.

His mean streak greatly amused Hellica, even when he turned his nascent rage against her. Uxtal didn't understand why the Matre Superior paid attention to the ghola boy, or why she cared about the incomprehensible Face Dancer plans.

The little researcher was uneasy about leaving Hellica alone with the child, sure that she would harm him in some way, thus leaving *Uxtal* to suffer severe punishment. But he had no way of preventing her from doing anything she pleased. If he made so much as a peep of complaint, she could wither him with a glare. Fortunately, she actually seemed to like the little monster. She treated her interactions with the boy as a game. Over at the neighboring slig farm, they happily fed human body parts to the large, slow-moving creatures that chewed the flesh into paste, which their multiple stomachs digested.

After seeing the cruel streak already manifesting itself in the toddler Vladimir, Uxtal was glad the remaining cells in the dead Master's hidden nullentropy capsule had been destroyed. What other beasts had the heretic old Tleilaxu hoarded from ancient times?

The origins of the Spacing Guild are shrouded in cosmic mists, not unlike the convoluted pathways a Navigator must travel.
                    —Archives of the Old Empire

N ot even the most experienced Guild Navigator could begin to comprehend this altered, nonsensical universe where reality held its mysteries close to its chest. But the Oracle of Time had summoned Edrik and his many fellows here.

Agitated, the Navigator swam in his tank of spice gas atop the immense Heighliner, peering anxiously through the windows of his chamber into the landscapes of space and his inner mind. Around him, as far as he could see and imagine, he beheld thousands of enormous Guildships. Such a grouping had not been assembled for millennia.

Following their summons to an unremarkable set of coordinates between star systems, Edrik and his fellow Navigators had waited for the otherworldly voice to provide further instructions. Then, unexpectedly, the fabric of the universe had folded around them and cast all of them into this vast and deeper void, with no apparent way back out.

Perhaps the Oracle knew of their desperate need for spice, because Chapterhouse kept a stranglehold on supplies to "punish" the Guild for cooperating with the Honored Matres. The vile Mother Commander, flaunting her power yet ignorant of how much damage she could truly cause, had threatened to destroy the spice sands if she didn't get her way! Madness! Perhaps the Oracle herself would show them another source of melange.

The Guild's stockpiles dwindled daily as Navigators consumed what they needed in order to guide ships through folded space. Edrik did not know how much spice remained in their numerous hidden storage bunkers, but Administrator Gorus and his ilk were definitely nervous. Gorus had already requested a meeting on Ix, and Edrik would accompany him there in a matter of days. The human administrators hoped that the Ixians could create or at least improve a technological means to circumvent the shortage of melange. More nonsense.

Like a breath of fresh, rich spice gas, Edrik sensed something rising from the depths of his mind, filling his consciousness. A tiny point of sound expanded from within, growing louder and louder. When it finally emerged as words in his mutated brain, he heard them simultaneously thousands of times over, overlapping with the prescient minds of other Navigators.

The Oracle. Her mind was unimaginably advanced, beyond any level even a Navigator's prescience could attain. The Oracle was the ancient foundation of the Guild, a comforting anchor for all Navigators.

"This altered universe is where I last saw the no-ship piloted by Duncan Idaho. I helped his ship break free, returning him to normal space. But I have lost them again. Because the hunters continue to search for them with their tachyon net, we must find the ship first. Kralizec is indeed upon us, and the ultimate Kwisatz Haderach is aboard that no-ship. Both sides in the great war want him for their victory."

The echoes of her thoughts filled Edrik's soul with a cold terror that threatened to unwind him. He had heard legends of Kralizec, the battle at the end of the universe, and had dismissed them as no more than human superstitions. But if the Oracle was concerned about it . . .

Who was Duncan Idaho? What no-ship was she speaking of? And, most amazing of all, how could even *the Oracle* be blinded to it? Always in the past, her voice had been a reassuring and guiding force. Now Edrik sensed uncertainty in her mind.

"I have searched, but I cannot find it. It is a tangle through all the prescient lines I can envision. My Navigators, I must make you aware. I may be forced to call upon you for assistance, if this threat is what I think it is."

Edrik's mind reeled. He felt the dismay of the Navigators around him. Some of them, unable to process this new information that shook their fragile holds on reality, spun into madness within their tanks of spice gas.

"The threat, Oracle," Edrik said, "is that we have no melange—"

"The threat is Kralizec." Her voice boomed through every Navigator's mind. "I will summon you, when I require my Navigators."

With a lurch, she hurled all of the thousands of great Heighliners back out of the strange universe, scattering them into normal space. Edrik reeled, trying to orient himself and his ship.

The Navigators were all confused and agitated.

Despite the Oracle's call, Edrik clung to a far more selfish concern: *How can we help the Oracle, if we are all starved for spice?*

*The young reed dies so easily. Beginnings are times of such great
peril.*

—LADY JESSICA ATREIDES,
the original

I t was a royal birth, but without any of the customary pomp and cir-
cumstance. Had this occurred at another time, on faraway Rakis,
fanatics would have run through the streets shouting, "Paul Atreides is
reborn! Muad'Dib! Muad'Dib!"

Duncan Idaho could remember such fervor.

When the original Jessica gave birth to the original Paul, it was a
time of political intrigues, assassinations, and conspiracies that
resulted in the death of Lady Anirul, wife of Emperor Shaddam IV, and
the near murder of the baby.

According to legend, all the sandworms on Arrakis had risen above
the dunes to herald the arrival of Muad'Dib. The Bene Gesserit had
never been beyond manipulating the masses with trumpets and omens
and delirious celebrations about prophecies come true.

Now, however, the decanting of the first of the gholas from history
seemed utterly mundane, more like a laboratory exercise than a religious experience. Yet this was not just any baby and not merely a
ghola, but Paul Atreides! Young Master Paul, who was later the
Emperor Muad'Dib, and then the blind Preacher. What would the

child become this time? What would the Bene Gesserit *force* him to become?

While waiting for the completion of the decanting process, Duncan turned to Sheeana. He saw satisfaction in her eyes, and uneasiness as well, though this was exactly what she had argued for. He was fully aware of what the Bene Gesserit feared: Paul had the potential in his bloodline. Almost certainly he could become the Kwisatz Haderach again, perhaps with even greater powers than before. Did Sheeana and her Bene Gesserit followers hope to control him better this time, or would it be a disaster of even greater proportions?

On the other hand, what if Paul was the one who could save them from the Outside Enemy?

The Sisterhood had played their breeding games to create a Kwisatz Haderach in the first place, and in return Paul had stung them terribly. Since Muad'Dib, and the long and terrible reign of Leto II (himself another Kwisatz Haderach), the Bene Gesserit had been terrified of creating such a one again.

Many fearful Reverend Mothers saw hints of the Kwisatz Haderach in any remarkable skill, even in precocious Duncan Idaho. Eleven previous Duncan gholas had been killed as children, and some of the proctors had made no secret of the fact that they wanted to kill *him* as well. To Duncan, the very idea that he might fit the mold of a messiah, like Paul, was absurd.

When the Bene Gesserit Suk doctors held up the infant, Duncan caught his breath. After cleaning sticky fluids from the fresh skin, the somber doctors subjected the baby to numerous tests and analyses, then wrapped him in sterile thermal cloths. "He is intact, undamaged," one of them reported. "A successful experiment."

Duncan frowned. An experiment? Was that how they saw this? He could not tear his gaze away. A veil of memories about young Paul nearly blinded him: how he and Gurney had taught the boy his first sword-and-shield lessons, how during the Duke's War of Assassins Duncan had taken the boy off to hide among the Caladan primitives, how the family had moved from their ancestral home to Arrakis and into a trap set by the Harkonnens. . . .

But he felt more than that. Looking at the healthy infant, he tried to see the face of the great Emperor Muad'Dib. Duncan knew the special pain and doubts this ghola child would experience. The ghola Paul would know about his past life but would remember none of it, at least not for years.

Taking the infant Paul into her arms, Sheeana spoke quietly. "To the Fremen he was the messiah who came to lead them to victory. To the Bene Gesserit, he was a superhuman who emerged under the wrong circumstances and escaped our control."

"He is a baby," the old Rabbi said. "An unnatural one."

The Rabbi, himself trained as a Suk doctor, attended the birth, though only reluctantly. He had a pronounced aversion to the tanks, but he looked somewhat defeated. With his brow furrowed and his eyes troubled, he had mumbled to Duncan, "I feel duty bound to be here. I made a promise to watch over Rebecca."

The woman was all but unrecognizable on the med-center table, hooked up to tubes and pumps. Was she dreaming of her other lives? Lost in a sea of ancient memories? The old man seemed to see something of his personal failure in her sagging face. Before the Bene Gesserit doctors had extracted the child from the augmented womb, he prayed for Rebecca's soul.

Duncan focused on the baby. "Long ago, I gave my life to save Paul. Would the universe have been better off if he had died that day under Sardaukar knives?"

"Many Sisters would make that argument. Humanity has been recovering for millennia from how he and his son changed the universe," Sheeana said. "But now we have a chance to raise him properly and see what he can do against the Enemy."

"Even if he changes the universe again?"

"Change is preferable to extinction."

Master Paul's second chance, Duncan thought.

He reached down with a strong hand, a Swordmaster's hand, to touch the baby's tiny cheek. If a miracle was created by technology, was it still a miracle? The infant smelled of medicinals, disinfectants, and melange that had been added to the surrogate mother's vat for months, a precise mixture that old Scytale had told them was necessary.

The baby's eyes seemed to focus on Duncan for a moment, though such a young infant could not possibly see clearly. But who could say what a Kwisatz Haderach might or might not see? Paul had foreseen the future of humankind after journeying in his mind to a place others could not go.

Like Magi, three Bene Gesserit Suk doctors crowded closer, chattering with awe over the baby they had worked so hard to create.

In disgust, the Rabbi turned and swept past Duncan, heading for the med-center's door, muttering "Abomination!" before he slipped out into the corridor.

Behind him, the Bene Gesserit doctors adjusted their life-support machinery and announced that the now deflated axlotl tank was ready to be impregnated with another ghola baby from the Tleilaxu Master's stored cells.

For millennia, the Ixians had managed to deliver miracles, providing what no one else could, and they rarely failed to live up to
expectations. The Spacing Guild had no choice but to go to Ix when
they needed an unorthodox solution for the melange shortage.

The technocrats and fabricators on Ix continued their industrious
research, pushing technological boundaries with their inventions. During the chaos of the Scattering, Ixians had achieved significant
progress in developing machines that had previously been considered
taboo because of ancient restrictions imposed in the wake of the Butlerian Jihad. By purchasing devices that were suspiciously close to
"thinking machines," the customers themselves became complicit in
breaking the age-old laws. In this atmosphere, it was in the best interest of everyone to maintain complete discretion.

When the desperate Guild delegation arrived on Ix, members of
the Face Dancer myriad were everywhere, in secret. Posing as an Ixian
engineer, Khrone attended the meeting—another step in a dance so
well-choreographed that the participants could not see their own

movements. The New Sisterhood and the Guild would dig their own graves, and Khrone considered that a good thing.

The Guild representatives were ushered into one of the giant underground manufactories where copper shielding and scan-scramblers concealed them from view. No one would ever know this group had come here except for the Ixians. And the Face Dancers. After decades of infiltration, Khrone and his improved shape-shifters easily fit in. They looked exactly like scientists, engineers, and fast-talking bureaucrats.

Now, filling his role as a skilled deputy fabricator, Khrone wore short brown hair and a heavy brow. The lines around his mouth indicated that here was a hardworking functionary, someone whose opinion could be trusted and whose conclusions would stand up to any amount of double-checking. Three others in the largely silent assembly were also Face Dancers, but the spokesman for the Ixians was (for the time being at least) a true human. So far, Chief Fabricator Shayama Sen had given them no reason to replace him. Sen seemed to want the same things Khrone did.

Ixians and Face Dancers shared a barely concealed disdain for foolish fears and fanaticism. Was it truly an invasion and a conquest, Khrone wondered, if the Ixians would have accepted the new order anyway?

Inside the immense hall, the air was filled with the hissing of production lines, vaporous plumes of cold baths, and the acrid fluids of imprinting chemicals. Others might have found the clamor of sights, sounds, and smells distracting, but the Ixians considered it soothing white noise.

Edrik the Navigator's armored tank drifted on suspensors, flanked by four gray-clad escorts. Khrone knew that the Navigator would be the greatest problem here, for his faction had the most to lose. But the mutated creature did not take charge of the negotiations. That task was left to the sharp-eyed Guild spokesman, Rentel Gorus, who stepped forward on willowy legs. His long white braid hung ropelike from his otherwise bald scalp. The visitors covered themselves with a veneer of importance and entitlement, which revealed a great deal about the extent of their anxiety. True confidence was quiet and invisible.

"The Spacing Guild has needs," said Administrator Gorus, sweeping the room with his milky but not-blind eyes. "If Ix can fulfill them, we are willing to pay any reasonable price. Find us a way out of the manacles the New Sisterhood has placed on us."

Shayama Sen folded his hands together and smiled. "And what is it you need?" The nails on his two forefingers were metallic and patterned with the kaleidoscopic lines of circuitry.

Edrik swam close to the speaker in his thick-walled tank. "The Guild needs spice so that we may guide our ships. Can Ix's machinery create melange? I see no point in coming here."

Gorus gave the Navigator a glare of pure annoyance. "I am not so skeptical. The Spacing Guild wonders if Ixian technology could be used regularly and reliably for navigation—at least during this difficult transition period. Since the time of the God Emperor, Ix has produced certain calculating machines that can take the place of Navigators."

"Only in part. The machines have always been inferior," Edrik said. "Poor copies of a real Navigator."

"Nevertheless, they proved useful in times of great need," Shayama Sen pointed out. "During the various waves of Scatterings, many ships used the primitive devices to travel without the benefit of spice or Navigators."

"And a vast number of those ships were lost," Edrik interrupted. "We will never know how many blundered through suns or dense nebulae. We will never know how many were simply . . . lost, arriving in unknown star systems and unidentified worlds, never able to find their way back."

"Recently, when melange was plentiful—thanks to Tleilaxu tank-manufactured spice—the Guild had no qualms about relying solely on our Navigators," Administrator Gorus said, sounding quite reasonable. "Now, however, times have changed. If we can prove to the New Sisterhood that we don't rely entirely on them, then their monopoly has no teeth. Then, perhaps, they will not be so haughty and intractable, and they will be more willing to sell us spice."

"That remains to be proved," grumbled the Navigator.

"Navigation devices have remained in use among certain parties," Shayama Sen added. "When the Honored Matres began to return from the outside fringes, they did not have Navigators. Only when they needed to know the full landscape of the Old Empire did they rely upon the services of the Guild."

"And you cooperated with them," Khrone said, using his words like a needle. "Is that not why the Sisterhood is displeased with you?"

"The witches also used their own ships, bypassing the Guild," Gorus said, in a huff. "Until recently, they did not trust even us with the coordinates of Chapterhouse, fearing we would have sold the location to the Honored Matres."

"And would you have?" Sen seemed amused. "Yes, I think so."

"This has nothing to do with the discussion of navigation machines." The Guild Administrator abruptly cut off further discussion.

The Chief Fabricator smiled and tapped his fingernails together, unleashing a flurry of sparks along the circuit paths like tiny phosphorescent rats scurrying through a maze. "Though such artificial devices were not accurate, or practical, or necessary, we still installed them in a few ships, even in recent times. Though neither Guildships nor independent vessels relied upon them, their primary purpose was to demonstrate to the Tleilaxu and the Priests of the Divided God that we could indeed function without their spice. However, the plans have been shelved for many centuries."

Gorus continued, "Perhaps given sufficient monetary incentive, you could revisit that old technology and develop it to a higher level?"

Khrone required all the control of his fluid facial muscles to keep the smile off his face. This was exactly what he had hoped for.

Chief Fabricator Sen also looked extremely pleased. He examined Edrik's armored tank, intrigued by its engineering. "Perhaps Navigators should have used their prescience to see this melange shortage coming."

"That is not how our prescience works."

Gorus pointed out, "The New Sisterhood is now the sole provider of melange—and their Mother Commander Murbella will not yield, despite our entreaties."

Edrik added, "We have met with her. She is not rational."

"It seems to me that Murbella is perfectly aware of her power and her bargaining position," the Chief Fabricator said, speaking mildly.

"We would like to take that bargaining chip from the witches, but we can only do so with your help," said the Guild Administrator. "Give us another option."

Khrone knew that adding his support would do little; however, by expressing straw-man doubts, he would forge a closer alliance between these others. "To develop a navigation machine of such sophistication—and to use it as more than a mere symbol—would require technology dangerously close to thinking machines. There are the restrictions of the Butlerian Jihad to consider."

Sen, Gorus, and even the Navigator responded with scorn. "The people will forget the ancient commands of the Jihad soon enough if Guildships are unable to fly, if all space travel is crippled," the Administrator said.

Khrone turned to the Chief Fabricator, who was ostensibly his boss. "I would be honored if Ix accepted this challenge, sir. My best teams can begin work on adapting numerical compilers and mathematical projection devices."

Shayama Sen chuckled at the Guildsman. "The price will be high. A percentage, perhaps. The Spacing Guild and CHOAM are among our best customers . . . and our ties could grow stronger still."

"CHOAM is sure to contribute to the cost, if they see that it is necessary to keep interstellar trade functioning," Gorus admitted.

How these Guildsmen tried to hide their desperation! Khrone decided it was best to give them a different target. "While the Bene Gesserits and the Honored Matres were at each other's throats, the Guild and CHOAM continued commercial activities unmolested. Now, the New Sisterhood claims that a far worse enemy is coming at them, at *us*, from outside."

Gorus made a rude snort, as if he had much to say on the subject, but swallowed his opinions like thick lumps of phlegm.

The Chief Fabricator gazed down his nose. "Is there evidence that this enemy exists at all? And is the enemy of the Sisterhood and the Honored Matres necessarily the enemy of Ix, the Guild, or CHOAM?"

"Trade is trade," Edrik said in a bubbling voice. "Everyone requires it. The Guild requires Navigators, and we require spice."

"Or navigation machines," Gorus added.

Khrone nodded placidly. "And thus we return to the necessary price for Ixian services."

"If you can produce what we ask, then our profits—and indeed the shift in the balance of power—will be of incalculable value. I believe we can make it a viable prospect for both of us." As the Administrator spoke, the Navigator continued to look uncomfortable.

Khrone allowed the faintest of satisfied smiles on his false face. From the far-distant overlords who always watched him through the tachyon net, he already had access to any navigational calculators the Guild could need. Such technology was quite basic compared to what the "Enemy" could command. For Khrone it would be a simple matter of pretending to develop such technology on Ix and then selling it at great cost to the Guild.

Around them, the fabrication plant continued to produce the sounds and smells of vigorous industry. "I still do not like the implications of technology superceding true Navigators." Edrik seemed trapped in his tank.

"Your loyalty is to the *Spacing Guild*, Edrik," Gorus brusquely reminded him. "And we will do what we must to survive as an organization. We have little choice in the matter."

The treatment of an injury may hurt more than the wound itself. Do not allow a sore to fester because you are unwilling to tolerate the momentary pain.

—BENE GESSERIT SUK DOCTOR FLORIANA NICUS

Murbella walked with Janess—now *Reverend Mother* Janess—through the stony remnants of the dying gardens around the Keep. They stood by the rocky bed of a dry stream, all the moisture stolen by the dramatically changing climate of Chapterhouse. The polished stones were a poignant reminder of the fast-flowing water that had once rushed along this channel.

"You are my lieutenant now, no longer my daughter." She knew her words must sound harsh to the young woman, but Janess did not flinch. Both of them understood that from now on an appropriate emotional separation had to be maintained, that Murbella must be Mother Commander, not mother. "Both the Bene Gesserits and the Honored Matres have tried to prohibit love, but they can only prohibit the expression of it, not the thought or emotion. Mother Superior Odrade was called a heretic among her Sisters because she believed in the power of love."

"I understand, Mother . . . Commander. Each of us must give up something for the sake of the new order."

"I shall teach you to swim by hurling you into the raging waters, a metaphor that I fear will not be relevant here much longer. I am counting on you to advance more quickly than either of our factions. It has taken six years of struggle, dragging both sides toward the center, for the women to learn to live with each other. Fundamental change may take generations, but we have made great strides."

"Duncan Idaho called it 'compromise by swordpoint,'" Janess quoted.

Murbella raised her eyebrows. "Did he?"

"I can show you the historical record, if you like."

"An apt description. The New Sisterhood is not yet the smoothly running machine I had hoped for, but I have convinced the Sisters to stop killing each other. Most of them, at least."

She thought quickly of Janess's old nemesis, Caree Debrak, who had disappeared from the student bungalows only days before she'd been scheduled to undergo the Agony; Caree had renounced the conversion as brainwashing and slipped away into the night. Few of the Sisters would miss her.

"Under normal circumstances," Murbella continued, "I could overlook the fact that some Honored Matres don't accept my rule. Freedom of discourse and the airing of opposing philosophies. But not now."

Janess drew herself straight, showing that she was ready for her assignment. "Renegade Honored Matres still control much of Gammu and a dozen other worlds. They have seized the soostone operations on Buzzell and gathered their most powerful forces on Tleilax."

Over the past year, the Mother Commander had assembled a force of Sisters and vigorously trained them in the combined fighting techniques of Honored Matres and Bene Gesserits. The bond between the two factions was best forged in the crucible of personal combat. "Now it is time to give my trainees a target."

"Stop training and start fighting," Janess said.

"Another quote from Duncan?"

"Not that I'm aware of . . . but I think he'd agree with the sentiment."

Murbella smiled wryly. "Yes, he probably would. If the renegades will not join us, they must be eliminated. I will not have them slip knives into our backs when we are concentrating on real battles."

"They have had years to entrench themselves, and they will not fall without a terrific battle."

Murbella nodded. "Of more immediate concern is the enclave of dissidents right here on Chapterhouse. It hurts me like a splinter in my hand. In the best case, it causes troublesome pain; in the worst, it festers and spreads an infection. Either way, the splinter must be removed."

Janess narrowed her eyes. "Yes, they are much too close to home. Even if the Chapterhouse dissidents do nothing overt against us, they demonstrate a weakness to outside observers. The situation brings to mind another wise observation from Duncan Idaho's first life. In a report he submitted when he lived among the Fremen on Dune, he said, 'A leak in a qanat is a slow but fatal weakness. Finding the leak, and plugging it, is a difficult task, but it must be done for the survival of all.'"

The Mother Commander was both proud and amused. "In citing so many of Duncan's writings, do not forget to think for yourself. Then someday others will begin quoting you." Her daughter wrestled with that idea, then nodded. Murbella continued. "You will help me plug the leak in the qanat, Janess."

THE BASHAR OF the New Sisterhood's main forces, Wikki Aztin, devoted her time and her best resources to training Janess for her first tough assignment. Wikki had a ready sense of humor and a story for every occasion. A stooped and narrow-faced woman of uncommon energy, she suffered from a congenital heart defect that prevented her from attempting the Agony; thus, Wikki had never become a Reverend Mother. Instead, she was assigned to the Sisterhood's military operations, where she had risen through the ranks.

Outside the Mother Commander's shelter in the isolated training fields, spotlights illuminated the attack 'thopters Janess was preparing for their vigorous assault the following day.

Housecleaning, Murbella called it. These rebels had betrayed her. Unlike outsiders who had never heard the Sisterhood's teachings, or misguided women who did not know the threat of the oncoming Enemy. Murbella hated the Honored Matre holdouts on Buzzell, Gammu, and Tleilax, but those women didn't know any better. These dissidents, however—she considered their betrayal far worse. It was a personal affront.

When Janess was out of earshot, tending to her duties, Murbella came up to stand with the bashar. Wikki said, "Did you know that some of the Sisters are betting against your pup, Mother Commander?"

"I suspected as much. They feel I gave her too much responsibility too soon after becoming a Reverend Mother, but it's only making her work harder."

"I've seen her digging in with a new resolve, trying to prove them wrong. She's got your spirit, and she reveres Duncan Idaho. With all eyes on her, she looks forward to an opportunity to shine, to set an example for others." Wikki looked out into the night. "You sure you don't want me to come along on the assault tomorrow? This engagement is close to home, small but important. A real exercise would be . . . gratifying."

"I need you to stay here and watch things. While I'm away from the Keep, someone could attempt a coup."

"I thought you had gotten them to settle their differences."

"It is an unstable equilibrium." Murbella sighed. "Sometimes, I wish the real Enemy would just attack us—and force those women to all fight on the same side."

THE FOLLOWING MORNING, Murbella and her squadron took off. Janess rode with her in the lead 'thopter as they flew over the surface of the planet. Despite her training, and the confidence her mother placed in her, Janess was still a green lieutenant, not yet ready to assume command.

After turning a reluctant blind eye to them for several years, the Mother Commander could no longer tolerate deserters and malcontents. Even in the remote regions, the settlement was too great a weak spot, a magnet for potential saboteurs as well as a possible foothold for a larger force of renegade Honored Matres from elsewhere.

Murbella had no doubts about what she had to do, and no sympathy. Because the New Sisterhood was desperate for competent fighters, she would invite the deserters back into the fold, but she did not have high hopes that any of them would accept. As cowards and complainers, these women had already shown their true colors. She wondered what Duncan would have done in a situation like this.

As the squadron approached the reported location of the encampment, Janess reported that she had picked up heat and transmission signatures. Without prompting, she ordered all of the aircraft to activate their shields, in case the rebels fired at them with weapons stolen from the Chapterhouse armories.

When Janess and her tactical officers scanned the area in their initial high-altitude sweep, however, they found no competing aircraft or military equipment in the vicinity, just a few hundred lightly armed women trying to hide in the thick conifer forests below. Although patches of snow made for wide variances in the thermal map of the area, the human bodies stood out like bonfires.

Converting the image to optical, Murbella panned across the deserters, many of whom she recognized; some had been gone for years, even before she had executed one of their vocal proponents, Annine.

She addressed the rebels below over the 'thopter's booming loudspeaker. "This is Mother Commander Murbella, and I come offering an olive branch. We have transport 'thopters at the rear of our formation, ready to bring all of you back to the Keep. If you disarm and cooperate, I will grant you amnesty and the opportunity for retraining."

She saw Caree Debrak on the ground. The bitter young woman pointed a farzee rifle at them. Tiny pinpoints of fire spat out, and the fast molten projectiles struck harmlessly against the 'thopter's shields.

"Damn lucky it's not a lasgun," Murbella said.

Janess looked astonished. "Lasguns are forbidden on Chapterhouse."

"Much is forbidden, but not everyone follows the rules." Working her jaw angrily, Murbella spoke over the loudspeaker again, in a sharper tone. "You have deserted your Sisters in a time of crisis. Put this divisiveness behind you and return with us. Or are you cowards, afraid to face our true Enemy?"

Caree fired the farzee rifle again, splattering more molten projectiles against the 'thopter's shields.

"At least we didn't fire the first shot." Janess looked at her mother. "In my opinion, Mother Commander, negotiating with them is a waste of time. With well-placed sedative darts, we could disarm them, force them back to the Keep, then try to win them over." Below, many of the other rebels grabbed their weapons and shot ineffectively at the Sisterhood's assault force.

Murbella shook her head. "We will never make them see reason— and we can never trust them again."

"Should we try a limited military engagement then, just enough to strike fear into them? It would give our new squadron practice in the field. Land the soldiers and use them to attack and humiliate the holdouts. If our hand-to-hand combat skills can't defeat this lot, we won't have a chance against the real whores who have had years to build up their planetary defenses."

Seeing the malcontents firing at them with rifles, Murbella felt increasing anger. Her voice broke like glass in her own ears. "No. Doing so would only risk more of our loyal Sisters. I won't lose a single fighter here." She shuddered to think of how much damage these women could cause if they pretended to surrender and then spread their poison from within. "No, Janess. They have made their choice. We can never trust them again. Never again."

Her daughter's eyes flashed with understanding. "They're no more than insects. Shall we exterminate them?"

Below, more dissidents were running through the trees and emerging from the dense pines carrying heavier weapons.

"Drop shields and open fire," Murbella shouted into the commsystem that connected all of the attack vessels. "Use incendiaries to light the woods." An officer in one of the other 'thopters protested that the response was too severe, but Murbella cut her off. "There will be no debate."

Her handpicked squadron opened fire, and the blazing bloodbath left no survivors. She took no joy in it, but the Mother Commander had showed that she would strike like a scorpion if provoked. She hoped that such knowledge would prevent further discontent and opposition.

"Let this be an example that will long be remembered," she said. "An enemy among us can cause damage as surely as the Enemy outside."

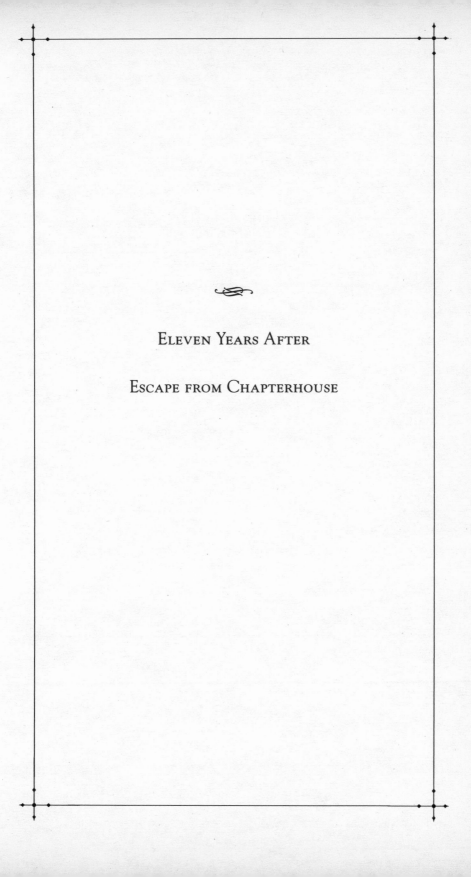

ELEVEN YEARS AFTER

ESCAPE FROM CHAPTERHOUSE

Caladan: third planet of Delta Pavonis; birthworld of Paul Muad'Dib. The planet was later renamed Dan.

—Terminology of the Imperium (Revised)

When the ghola of Baron Vladimir Harkonnen was seven years old, the Face Dancers commanded Uxtal to take him to the ocean world of Dan.

"Dan . . . Caladan. Why are we going there?" Uxtal asked. "Does this have something to do with the fact that it was once the home-world of House Atreides, enemy of House Harkonnen?" In his joy to be going away from Matre Superior Hellica, the Lost Tleilaxu researcher found the courage to view the Face Dancer as his rescuer.

"We have found something there. Something that could allow us to use the resurrected Baron." The Face Dancer escort raised a hand, stopping the question Uxtal was about to ask. "That is all you need to know."

While he had prayed fervently for the day when he could relinquish the difficult ghola child, Uxtal now worried that Khrone might consider his usefulness to be at an end. Maybe the Face Dancers would come up behind him, place fingers over his eyes, and *squeeze*, as they'd done to Elder Burah. . . .

He hurried toward the shuttle that would take him and the brat away from Tleilax. He mumbled to himself, like a personal mantra: *I am still alive. Still alive!*

At least he would be away from Ingva and Hellica, the stench of sligs, and the screams of torture victims being wrung dry of their pain-induced chemicals.

IN THE INTERVENING years, Hellica had continued to enjoy young Vladimir Harkonnen. They were birds of a feather. Uxtal found it chilling to hear the seven-year-old boy and the Matre Superior laugh together as they discussed people who didn't deserve to live anymore, choosing victims for the torture laboratories.

The treacherous little boy reported constantly to the pretender queen, informing her of purported mistakes or indiscretions committed by laboratory assistants. Uxtal had lost many of his best helpers that way, and the scheming child fully comprehended the power he held. Uxtal could barely master his own terror in the ghola's presence. Though only a child, Vladimir was nearly the same size as the diminutive Tleilaxu.

Unexpectedly, though, Uxtal had managed to endear himself to the ghola in a way that had the benefit of driving a wedge between the boy and Hellica. As a Tleilaxu, he had many personal habits that outsiders considered revolting, such as his proclivity to emit coarse bodily noises. Seeing the Baron's delight in such grossness, Uxtal began to embellish his own habits around the child, which gave the two of them a peculiar bond.

Miffed at Vladimir's fickle attentions and showing no more maturity than the child ghola, Hellica had stopped associating with the boy. She reacted with haughty indifference when the Guildship came to take Uxtal and the ghola away to Dan. But the anxious researcher knew she would be there waiting when he returned. . . .

AFTER A FOLDSPACE journey, the Tleilaxu and his charge rode a shuttle down to the watery planet. En route they played a private game, competing with one another to see who could be the most disgusting, to see if they could get a reaction out of the bland and stony Face Dancers accompanying them. Vladimir, with an amazing repertoire of scatological talents, made more revolting sounds and noxious odors than anyone Uxtal had ever encountered. After each display, the cherubic boy grinned fiercely.

Uxtal conceded defeat, knowing it was safer to lose to a Harkonnen than to win, even without Matre Superior Hellica leering over their shoulders.

One of the Face Dancers stood at the shuttle's viewport, pointing outside. "The ruins of Castle Caladan, the ancestral home of House Atreides." The edifice lay in broken fragments of stone at the edge of a seaside cliff, with a landing field not far away on the outskirts of a nearby fishing village.

The Face Dancer obviously intended to bring Vladimir to a place that might evoke a visceral reaction, but Uxtal detected no glimmer of recognition in the boy's spider-black eyes, no spark of recollection. The Baron ghola was far too young to access his memories yet, but by placing him in the environment of his archenemies, with so many potential memory triggers, maybe they would awaken something after all, or at least lay a good foundation for success.

Perhaps that was what Khrone wanted of them. Uxtal hoped so, wishing he could stay here on Dan permanently. Though somewhat austere and damp, the ocean world seemed a great improvement over Bandalong.

As soon as they stepped off the shuttle onto the paved field, Vladimir stared toward the ruined castle. His shaggy hair blew in a sea breeze. "My enemies lived here? This is where Duke Leto Atreides was from?"

Though Uxtal didn't know the answer for certain, he knew what the ghola boy wanted to hear. "Yes, he must have been where you are standing, breathing the same air that fills your lungs now."

"Why can't I remember? I want to remember. I want to know more than you told me, more than I can see in filmbooks." He stamped a foot on the ground.

"And one day you will. One day it will all come back to you."

"I want it now!" The child looked up with a peevish expression, puckering his lips. This, Uxtal knew, signified dangerous potential.

He took the boy's hand and led him quickly toward a waiting groundcar before the childish temper could explode. "Come, let's see what the Face Dancers have found."

Knowing the decisions and the mistakes made by others can be frightening. More often, though, I find it comforting.

—REVEREND MOTHER SHEEANA,
Ithaca logs

The van Gogh painting hung on a metal wall of Sheeana's cabin. She had stolen the masterpiece from the Mother Superior's quarters before escaping from Chapterhouse. Of all the crimes she had committed during her flight, taking the van Gogh was her only selfish and unjustified act. For years, she had drawn comfort from this great work of art and everything it represented.

With the glowpanels adjusted to perfect illumination, Sheeana stood unblinking before the masterpiece. Though she had studied the painting meticulously many times, she still gained new insight from the daubs of bright paint, the thick brushstrokes, the chaotic flurry of creative energy. A deeply disturbed man, van Gogh had turned these splotches and smudges of color into a work of genius. Could pure, cold sanity have done as much?

Thatched Cottages at Cordeville had survived the atomic destruction of Earth ages ago, the Butlerian Jihad and ensuing dark ages, then Muad'Dib's Jihad, thirty-five hundred years of the Tyrant's rule, the Famine Times, and the Scattering. Without doubt, this fragile piece of art was blessed.

But its creator had been driven to the brink of madness by his passions. Van Gogh had channeled his vision into color and form, a representational splash of reality so intense that it could only be conveyed on canvas.

One day she would show the painting to the ghola children. Paul Atreides, the oldest, was now five years old and showed every sign of being just a normal little boy. His "mother" Jessica was a year younger, the same age as the ghola of the warrior-Mentat Thufir Hawat. Paul's love, Chani, was only three, while the historic traitor to House Atreides, Wellington Yueh, was two, born at the same time that Sheeana had finally allowed Scytale to create a ghola of himself. The great planetologist and Fremen leader Liet-Kynes was a year-old baby, and the Naib Stilgar had just been born.

It would be years before the Bene Gesserit had any chance of triggering those ghola memories, before the historical re-creations could become the weapons and tools Sheeana needed. If she showed them the van Gogh painting right now, would they react based on some instinct from their past lives, or would they view the images with fresh eyes?

A genius from Ix had restored and enhanced the original; an invisibly thin but tough coating of plaz sealed and protected the masterwork from further aging. The Ixian restorer had not only returned the painting to its original glory, he had added interactive simulations so that an appreciative observer could go through the process of every brushstroke, seeing the complex and primitive marvel as it had been created from layer upon layer of paint. Sheeana had experienced the instructional simulation enough times that she felt she could have repainted the cottages herself with her eyes closed. But even if she'd made a perfect copy, it wouldn't have been the same as the original.

Sheeana backed up to her bed and sat down, never taking her eyes from the painting. The voices in Other Memory seemed to appreciate it, though she kept the constant clamor under control.

Odrade-within spoke to her now in a scolding tone. *I am sure other Sisters consider the theft of Vincent's painting to be more serious than stealing the no-ship or sandworms from the desert belt. Those things could be replaced, but not a masterpiece.*

"Maybe I am not the person you thought I was. But then, I—more than anyone else—can't live up to the myth built around me. Does the Cult of Sheeana still have followers out there in the Old Empire? Does your manufactured religion still revere me as an angel and a savior?"

The Bene Gesserit knew the powers of unflagging belief among vast populations. The Sisters harnessed religions as weapons—created them, guided them, and turned them loose as one might aim an arrow from a bow.

Religions were odd things. They were born with the emergence of a strong and charismatic leader, yet somehow they grew more powerful after that keystone figure died, especially if martyred. No army ever fought harder without its bashar, no government grew stronger without its king or president, yet a religion without Sheeana spread faster as soon as the converts believed she was dead. Sheeana's unique background had given the Missionaria Protectiva plenty to work with, enough raw material to attract fanatics in droves.

Here in her quiet, peaceful quarters, she was glad to be far from all that.

At the thought of being a supposed martyr around whom a powerful religion had grown, she felt another life awaken and rise up within her, a distant, ancient voice: *Both Muad'Dib and Liet-Kynes spoke against the dangers of following a charismatic hero.*

When the lives within permitted it, she liked to delve deeply into lines of Other Memory, looking farther and farther back in time, into the backwash and whitewater rapids of the river of history. "I agree. That is why those who would throw away their lives in such a cause must be watched and guided."

Guided? Or manipulated?

"The difference is only a matter of words, not substance."

There are times when manipulating the masses is the only way to form an adequate defense. A fighting force of fanatics can surpass any number of enemy weapons.

"Paul Muad'Dib proved that. His bloody jihad rocked the galaxy."

The other voice chuckled within her. *He was by no means the first to use such tactics. He learned much from the past. He learned much from me.*

Sheeana cast her inner vision deep into her mind. "Who are you?"

I am one who knows this subject better than most. Better than almost anyone. The voice paused. *I am Serena Butler. I started the mother of all jihads.*

WITH SERENA BUTLER'S warning fresh in her mind, Sheeana strode through a lower-level corridor. Considering all the factions aboard the *Ithaca*, each with their own agendas and distortions, Sheeana knew of an innocent, yet impenetrable, source of information: the four captive Futars.

The creatures had caused no further trouble in the five years since one had escaped from the brig and killed a Sister, a minor proctor. Sheeana had visited them on occasion and talked to all of them, but so far she had been frustrated in her attempts to gain useful information. Nevertheless, Serena Butler had given her a new idea—to use religious awe as a tool.

Confident that she could protect herself if necessary, she released the one that called himself Hrrm from the large holding chamber where the Futars now lived. Years ago, after she had found Hrrm loose in the lower corridors, she had done everything possible to give him and his companions a larger space. They were predators, feral things, and they needed to run and roam. So, Sheeana had added security systems to an armor-walled storage bay, then instructed several proctors and a few of the Rabbi's hardworking Jews to construct a simulated environment. The new enclosure did not fool the Futars, but it comforted them. Though not quite freedom, it was far preferable to the stark, separated brig cells.

During the construction of the special arboretum, Sheeana had done her best to find out what their original home with the Handlers had been like, but the Futars offered few details. Their vocabulary was quite limited. When they said "trees," she could not get them to describe the size or species. Instead, she resorted to showing them images until they finally grew excited, pointing to a tall, silver-barked aspen.

Now, after ensuring that the nearby corridors and lift tubes were empty of distractions or threats, Sheeana took the tense beast-man to the observation chamber above the sand-filled hold.

Hrrm paced warily along beside her. The Honored Matres had abused him so terribly that he was reluctant to extend trust, but in the years since Sheeana had begun visiting the Futars, Hrrm had come to accept her.

In order to draw information out of them, Sheeana decided she needed to make a stronger impression. Although it went against her usual principles, she decided to portray herself as the Missionaria Protectiva did—as a religious figure who wielded mystical powers. The Futars would see her in a different light. Perhaps if she could impress Hrrm, he would answer the same questions, but in a more useful manner. The Futars were too simple and direct to keep secrets, but they plainly did not comprehend the implications of the things they understood.

Inside the observation chamber, the Futar stepped closer to the plaz window and looked down toward the sand inside the cargo hold. His pupils dilated and his nostrils flared when he saw movement there, the stirring dunes. One of the large sandworms rose up, its cavernous mouth yawning open as sand streamed from its rings. The blind head of a second worm rose, as if the creatures could sense Sheeana's presence high above them.

Hrrm backed away, his lips curling in a half snarl. His breathing sounded like a growl. "Monsters."

"Yes. My monsters." The Futar seemed confused and intimidated. Hrrm could not take his eyes from the worms. "My monsters," she repeated. "You stay here, and watch."

Sheeana slipped away from the chamber and code-locked the door behind her before taking a lift directly down to the cargo hold level. She opened the hatch and stepped out onto the temperature-controlled sands under artificial-yellow sunlight. The sandworms came toward her, shaking the hold with their weight and friction. Unafraid, Sheeana marched out and climbed up the dunes to face them.

With a burst of sand, the largest worm rose up, followed by a second one beside it, and a third behind her. Sheeana stared up toward the small, dark observation window through which she hoped Hrrm would be watching her with awe.

She ran toward the nearest worm, and the giant backed away, scuttling through the sand. She ran at another, and it also retreated; then she stood in the middle and began to twirl. She waved her hands at the worms and began swaying back and forth in a lissome dance. The worms followed, weaving and swaying.

Around her she could smell fresh spice, the bitter yet stimulating aroma that had no other natural origin. The worms circled her like sycophants. Finally Sheeana collapsed onto the sand and let them continue their circling, until all seven of the creatures reared up around her, and she dismissed them.

Turning tail, the creatures rippled through the contained dunes, leaving her. Sheeana struggled to her feet, brushed herself off, and went to the hatch. By now, Hrrm should be sufficiently impressed.

When she reentered the observation chamber, the Futar turned to her, then backed away and raised his face, baring his own throat in a gesture of submission. Sheeana felt the warmth of the moment thrill through her. "My monsters," she said.

"You stronger than bad women," Hrrm said.

"Yes, stronger than Honored Matres."

The beast-man seemed to force the words from his throat. "Better than . . . Handlers."

Sheeana pounced. "Who are the Handlers?"

"Handlers."

"Where are they? Who are they?"

"Handlers . . . control Futars."

"What are Futars?" She needed to know more, needed to pin him down. There were too many questions about what the whores had brought from the Scattering and how they were all connected to the Outside Enemy.

"We are Futars," Hrrm said, sounding indignant. "Not fish people."

Ah, an intriguing new nugget of information. "Fish people?"

"Phibians." Hrrm growled with disgust. His mouth had trouble forming the word.

Sheeana frowned, imagining a modification that combined amphibious genes with humans, the same way feline DNA had been used to create Futars. Hybrids. "Did the Handlers create Phibians?"

"Handlers made Futars. We are Futars."

"Did they also create Phibians?"

Hrrm seemed to grow angry. "Handlers made *Futars*. Kill Honored Matres."

Sheeana fell silent, processing the information. The chromosomal tinkering that had created Futars might be similar to what was used to breed aquatic-dwelling "Phibians." While the Handlers had used those techniques to breed creatures who would target Honored Matres, someone else had made Phibians. To what purpose?

She wondered if Lost Tleilaxu from the Scattering had sold their skills to the highest bidder. If the Futars hated Phibians, then were the "fish people" somehow allied with the Honored Matres? Or was Sheeana simply reading too much into the crude utterances of the beast-man?

"Who are the Handlers?" she said again.

"You better," Hrrm answered. It was all the response she could get. Though he looked at her in a different way, Sheeana had achieved no insights or vital information. Just clues, without the necessary context.

She took him back to his holding cell and turned him loose among the other Futars. She didn't know how well they communicated with one another, but she was certain Hrrm would share what he had learned. He would tell his fellows about the woman who controlled the worms.

The best method of attack is to make a quick kill. Always be ready to strike your opponent's jugular. If you want to provide a performance, be a dancer.

—MOTHER COMMANDER MURBELLA,
rally before troop deployment

When the Enemy came, the New Sisterhood would not fight every battle alone. Murbella refused to allow that. Though there was no central leadership in the disjointed civilizations of the Old Empire, she vowed that she would compel those civilizations to participate. They could not be allowed to sit on the sidelines when so much was at stake for humanity.

Under the instruction of her daughter Janess, as well as the veteran bashar Wikki Aztin, the Sisterhood's deadliest fighters were being trained, but Murbella needed access to powerful weapons, and a great many of them. Therefore, she went to Richese, the primary competitor of Ix.

After Murbella's small shuttle landed in the main Richesian commercial complex, the Factory Commissioner arrived to meet her. He was a short man with a round face, close-cropped hair, and a sincere-looking smile that he could mount on his face at will. Two women and three men accompanied him, all wearing identical smart-looking business attire. They carried projection pads and easily revised papers, contracts, price lists.

"The New Sisterhood wishes to do business with you, Commissioner. Please show me everything you have in the way of weaponry—offensive and defensive."

Beaming, the round-faced man reached forward to clasp her hand, which she reluctantly allowed him to shake. "Richese is glad to be of service, Mother Commander. We can manufacture anything from a dagger to a fleet of battleships. Are you interested in explosives, hand weapons, projectile launchers? We have defensive space mines that can be hidden by no-fields. Please tell me, what is your particular need?"

Murbella met him with a hard gaze. "Everything. We're going to need the whole list."

For thousands of years Richese and Ix had been technological and industrial rivals, each with their own areas of expertise. Ix had made its name doing groundbreaking research, producing creative designs and pioneering new technologies. Though many of their projects failed spectacularly, the successful ones generated sufficient profits to more than pay for the mistakes.

Richese, on the other hand, was better at imitation than innovation. They were more conservative in the risks they took, yet increasingly ambitious in their output and efficiency. By taking advantage of economies of scale, cutting profit margins, and pushing automated factory lines to the very limits of what the strictures of the Butlerian Jihad allowed, Richese was able to produce sought-after items in enormous quantities at low cost. Murbella selected them over Ix because the New Sisterhood needed huge numbers of weapons—as soon as possible.

The business complex where the Factory Commissioner always met his potential customers included lush landscaping with parks and fountains; the buildings were clean, stylized, and welcoming. Any unsightly industrial zones remained far from view. Walking down spacious hallways lined with showcases of items that Richese could produce on a moment's notice, Murbella felt as if she were wandering through an unending exhibit hall of marketing displays.

Giving her plenty of time to examine the merchandise, the Commissioner chattered as they walked from one display case to another. "Since the death of the Tyrant and the Famine Times, Richese has been called on to provide defensive armaments for any number of brushfire wars. You will be satisfied with what we can produce."

"If we survive the coming conflict, then I will be satisfied."

She studied body armor and ship armor, pseudoatomics, lasguns, projectile launchers, microexplosives, pulse cannons, blasters, poison dusts, shard-daggers, flechette guns, disruptors, mind scramblers, offensive X-probes, hunter-seeker assassination tools, deceptives, energizers, burners, dart launchers, stun grenades, even genuine atomics "for display purposes only." A holo-model of Richese's southern continents showed vast shipyards producing space yachts and military no-ships.

Murbella said, "I want all of those space yachts converted into warships. In fact, we need to commandeer all of your factory systems. You must completely devote your production lines to producing the weapons we need."

The attorneys and salespeople gasped, then consulted with each other. The Factory Commissioner seemed alarmed. "That is quite an astonishing request, Mother Commander. We do have other customers, you know—"

"None more important than we are." She fixed him with a cold glare. "We will pay for the privilege, of course—in melange."

The Commissioner's eyes lit up. "It has long been said that wartime is hard on people, but good for business. Doesn't the Guild have a standing order for all the spice your new desert belt produces?"

"I have severely restricted Guild purchases, though their demand remains high," Murbella said. The Richesian was already aware of this, of course. He was simply playing a game.

The hovering attorneys and sales representatives were mentally going through some preliminary calculations. After they were paid in melange, the Richesians could turn around and sell the spice to the desperate Guild for ten times the already steep value the New Sisterhood had placed on it. They would reap profits backward and forward.

Murbella crossed her arms over her chest. "We will need a military force such as humanity has never before seen, because we face an Enemy unlike any other."

"I've heard rumors. Who is this foe and when will they strike? What do they want?"

She blinked as a flicker of anxiety passed through her. "I wish I knew."

First, though, her fighting squads would face the rebel Honored Matres in their dispersed enclaves, and for that she needed armored 'thopters, assault ships, heavy groundcars, personal projectile launchers, pulse rifles, and even razor-sharp mono-blade knives. Many of the battles against the dissidents would involve close-in fighting.

"We can provide certain items immediately from our stockpiles, a few ships, some space mines. One warlord customer recently suffered from . . . um, an assassination. Therefore his completed order remains unclaimed, and we can offer you all of it."

"I'll take it with me now," she said.

THE MOTHER COMMANDER continued to train her troops, honing them into a razor-sharp weapon. Wearing a black singlesuit uniform, Murbella stood beside Janess on a suspensor platform that floated low over the largest training field. Below, in midday sunlight, her hand-picked troops went through increasingly difficult personal combat routines, never resting, never tolerating the smallest mistake.

Upon hearing that Murbella's special squad had crushed the encampment of dissidents on Chapterhouse, her advisors had been shocked at the swift brutality, but the Mother Commander stood firm against the uproar. "I am not Bashar Miles Teg. He could have used his reputation to subtly manipulate the malcontents, and might have reached a compromise that skated past violence. But the Bashar is no longer with us, and I fear his clever tactics will not be effective against the Armageddon forces of the Enemy. Violence will become more and more necessary."

The women had found no effective counterargument.

After that first decisive battle, the Mother Commander's crack forces took a new name for themselves: Valkyries.

Murbella challenged her Valkyries to master a type of fighting that Janess had rediscovered in the archives: the techniques of the Swordmasters of Ginaz. By resurrecting that training discipline and arming her Sisters with skills that no one alive remembered, the Mother Commander intended to produce fighters better equipped than any before them to neutralize the entrenched Honored Matres.

At the moment, the squads were executing a complex maneuver in which they fought against mock enemy troops on the ground, attacking them in spinning star formations. Viewed from the high suspensor platform, the show was quite impressive as the five points of each star rotated and surged against the opposing force and sent them fleeing in disarray. It was something Murbella called the "choreography of personal combat." She could not wait to test it in battle.

Like her mother, Janess plunged into her work with fervor. She had even adopted the surname of her father, calling herself Lieutenant Idaho. It sounded right to her, and to Murbella. Mother and daughter were becoming quite a formidable force. Some Sisters jokingly claimed that they didn't need an army—those two were dangerous enough on their own.

Wearing a satisfied look, the Mother Commander reviewed the troop formations. Janess, too, was clearly proud of the trained fighters. "I will pit our Valkyries against any army the Honored Matres can raise against us."

"Yes, Janess, you will—and soon. First, we will conquer Buzzell."

Muad'Dib could indeed see the Future, but you must understand the limits of this power. Think of sight. You have eyes, yet cannot see without light. If you are on the floor of a valley, you cannot see beyond your valley. Just so, Muad'Dib could not always choose to look across the mysterious terrain. He tells us that a single obscure decision of prophecy, perhaps the choice of one word over another, could change the entire aspect of the future. He tells us "The vision of time is broad, but when you pass through it, time becomes a narrow door." And always, he fought the temptation to choose a clear, safe course, warning "That path leads ever down into stagnation."

—from "Arrakis Awakening" by the
PRINCESS IRULAN

The planet Dan was full of Face Dancers. Just by looking at the natives in the settlement near the ruined Atreides castle, Uxtal could sense them everywhere. His skin crawled, but he didn't dare show fear. Maybe he could slip away, run to hide in the wilderness of the headlands, or pretend to be a simple fisherman or cliff-farmer.

But if he tried any of that, the Face Dancers would hunt him down and capture him, punish him. He didn't dare risk their wrath. So he meekly followed along.

Maybe Khrone would be so pleased to see the Baron child that he would simply free Uxtal, reward him for his service, and send him away. The Lost Tleilaxu researcher could cling to unrealistic hopes. . . .

He and young Vladimir were taken to temporary quarters in a hostelry on the outskirts of the village. The boy ghola complained that he wanted to throw rocks in the water and at the boats, or poke into the market stalls where sellers gutted the fish, but Uxtal made excuses, delaying the restless child while they waited in their chilly, rustic room. Vladimir began to ransack every cabinet and hiding place he could find. Uxtal clung to the knowledge that at least the Honored Matres were far away.

A nondescript man appeared at the door of their room. He looked like any other villager, but a rash of goose bumps stippled Uxtal's skin. "I have come to take the Baron ghola. We must test him."

He heard an odd sound, as of bones cracking and shifting. The man's face metamorphosed until the blank cadaverous face of Khrone stared back at him with ink-pit eyes.

"Y-yes," Uxtal said. "The boy is progressing quite nicely. Seven years old now. However, it would be very helpful to me if I knew what you want him for. Very helpful."

Vladimir watched the Face Dancer with curious awe. He had never seen one of the shape-shifters revert to its blank state. "Great trick. Can you teach me to change my face like that?"

"No." Khrone turned back to the Tleilaxu. "When I originally asked you to grow this ghola, I did not know who he was. When I learned his identity, I still did not know if the Baron Harkonnen would do us any good, but I thought that he might. Now I have discovered a wonderful possibility." He took the boy's hand, and led him away. "Wait here, Uxtal."

So the diminutive researcher remained alone in his primitive room, wondering how much longer he would be permitted to live. In another situation he might have enjoyed the moment of peace, the quiet relaxation, but he was too afraid. What if the Face Dancers found some flaw in the ghola? Why did they need him here on Dan? Would Khrone throw him back into the clutches of Matre Superior Hellica? The Face Dancers had left him among the Honored Matres for years. Uxtal didn't know how much more he could stand. He couldn't believe Hellica had let him live, or that the withered old Ingva hadn't yet tried to bond him sexually. He closed his eyes and swallowed the moan in his throat. So many things could go wrong if he went back there. . . .

To calm himself, he began a traditional cleansing ritual. Standing next to an open window and facing the ocean, he dipped a white cloth into a bowl of water and washed his naked chest. It had been so long since he'd been able to adequately perform the personal bodily ablutions required by his religion. People were always spying on him, intimidating him. After he finished, Uxtal meditated outside on a small wooden balcony that overlooked the fishing village. He prayed by mentally rearranging numbers and signs, searching for the truth in the holy patterns.

The door of the room burst open and the ghola child ran in, flushed and laughing. He carried a dripping knife and dodged among the rough furniture as if playing some sort of game. His clothes were covered in wet mud and blood.

Khrone followed the boy into the room at a more sedate pace, carrying a small parcel in his arms. He had reverted to his innocuous guise of a bland-featured man. Chuckling, young Vladimir called for Khrone to hurry.

Uxtal quickly intercepted the boy. "What are you doing with that knife?" He extended a hand to take the weapon away.

"I was playing with a baby slig. They have a little pen of them in the village, but none of them are big, like back home." He grinned. "I jumped in with them and stabbed a few." He wiped the blade on his own trousers and handed it to the Tleilaxu, who set it out of reach atop a tall wardrobe.

Khrone looked contemplatively at the bloodstains. "I am not averse to violence, but it must be directed violence. Constructive violence. This ghola has little self-control. He is in need of behavioral modifications."

Uxtal tried to deflect the conversation from the implied criticism. "Why did he grab a knife and jump into a slig pen?"

"He was influenced by our conversation. I was discussing our discovery with my comrades, and the boy drew inspiration from the object. He seems to have a fondness for knives."

"Matre Superior Hellica taught him that." Uxtal swallowed hard. "I have read his cellular history. The original Baron Harkonnen was—"

"I know everything about the original. He has excellent potential for what I have in mind now. Our plans have changed because of what we've discovered here on Dan."

Uxtal stared at the mysterious parcel in the Face Dancer's hands. "And what have you found?"

Though his gash-mouth did not smile, Khrone seemed very

pleased. He began to unwrap the object. "Another solution to our crisis."

"Which crisis?"

"One you cannot understand."

Feeling chastised, Uxtal bit back further questions, and stared as Khrone revealed another knife, this one ornate and sealed inside a clear plaz container. The weapon had a jeweled handle with intricate designs carved into it; the blade itself bore etched letters and symbols from an ancient language, but the words were obscured by a thick smear of crimson. Blood, barely oxidized. He leaned closer. It still looked moist inside its preservative cover.

"This is an ancient weapon—thousands of years old—sealed inside a nullentropy field until today, hidden and protected over the centuries by a succession of religious fanatics."

"Is that blood?" Uxtal asked.

"I prefer to call it genetic material." Gingerly, the Face Dancer set the artifact on the table. "We discovered it in a long-sealed religious shrine here on Dan, watched over by remnants of the Fish Speakers, who have now joined the Cult of Sheeana. The dagger is stained with the blood of Paul Atreides."

"Muad'Dib! The father of the Prophet Himself, Leto II, the God Emperor."

"Yes, the messiah who led Fremen warriors in a great jihad. A Kwisatz Haderach. We need him."

"Because of the nullentropy field, the blood of Muad'Dib is still wet . . . fresh," Uxtal said, quivering in excitement. "Perfectly preserved."

"Ah, so you see where this is leading. There is hope for you yet. You may be useful after all."

"Yes, I am useful! Let me show you. But . . . but I need to know more about what you want."

At a hand gesture from their leader, two more Face Dancers entered the room, leading a wrung-out woman who wore a deep blue dress; her brown hair hung in stringy clumps. As she drew near, Uxtal noted the famous Atreides crest of long ago, a red braided hawk, on the left breast of her dress. When she saw the preserved dagger, the woman struggled against her captors. She didn't seem to care about the Face Dancers or anyone—only the knife.

Khrone prodded her. "Speak, Priestess. Tell this man the story of your holy knife so that he may understand."

She looked at Uxtal briefly, then turned her worshipful gaze back toward the dagger. "I am Ardath, formerly a Fish Speaker priestess, now servant of Sheeana. Long ago, the evil Count Hasimir Fenring attempted to assassinate the blessed Muad'Dib with this dagger. The weapon belonged to Emperor Shaddam IV, was given to Duke Leto Atreides as a gift, and then returned to Shaddam during his trial before the Landsraad. Later, Emperor Shaddam offered the dagger to Feyd-Rautha for his duel with Muad'Dib." Priestess Ardath seemed to be reciting often-rehearsed scripture.

"Later, during Muad'Dib's jihad, an exiled Hasimir Fenring— himself a failed Kwisatz Haderach—acquired the dagger. In a vile plot, he stabbed Muad'Dib deeply in the back. Some say that he died that day from the wound, but that Heaven sent him back among the living, for his work was not yet done. In a miracle he returned to us."

"And Muad'Dib's fanatics preserved the bloody knife as a religious artifact," Khrone finished impatiently. "It was taken to a shrine here on Caladan, home of House Atreides, where it remained hidden for all these years. You can already guess what we want you to do, Tleilaxu. Deactivate the nullentropy field, take cell samples—"

Ardath tore herself free of her guards and dropped to her knees in prayer, leaning toward the ancient relic. "Please, you cannot tamper with such a holy article."

At a gesture from Khrone, one of the Face Dancers grabbed her head and twisted it sharply, snapping her neck. He dropped her to the floor like a discarded doll. As they dragged the dead priestess away, Uxtal gave the female no more than a passing thought, since she was irrelevant. Instead, he was intrigued by the possibilities of the lovely, preserved dagger. Her prattling had been distracting anyway.

He came closer and picked up the sealed dagger with shaking hands, tilting it so that light glistened off the wet blade. The cells of Muad'Dib! The possibilities astounded him.

Khrone said, "Now you have another ghola project to work on,

along with raising Baron Harkonnen. Back to Tleilax with you both—
for as many years as it takes." More Face Dancers came into the room.
"When the time is right, we will have a much more useful purpose for
the Baron."

The first new armored vessels arrived from Richese exactly as
Murbella had ordered, sixty-seven warships designed for space
combat and troop transport, heavily loaded with weaponry. The
Mother Commander had also paid the appropriate bribes in spice for a
Guildship to transport them directly and unexpectedly to Buzzell. It
was the first of what she hoped would be many conquests over the
renegade Honored Matres.

The weapons shops of Richese, thrilled with the enormous order
for armaments, worked overtime to create military equipment of every
possible design and efficacy. When the outside threat did arrive in the
Old Empire, they would not find the human race unprepared or undefended.

First, however, the restructured Sisterhood had to quash the
destructive resistance here at home. *We must clean the slate before the
real Enemy arrives.*

In deep consultation with Bellonda, Doria, and Janess, Murbella
had chosen this first campaign carefully. Now that her Valkyries had
eradicated the malcontents on Chapterhouse, the well-trained women

were ready for another target. Buzzell was perfect, both for its strategic and its economic importance. The Honored Matres were haughty and overconfident, making their defenses vulnerable. Murbella intended to show them no mercy.

She did not know the precise disposition or distribution of Honored Matre defenses around Buzzell, but she could guess. Sitting inside their ships lurking within the hold of the great Guildship, all of her Valkyries were ready to be deployed.

As soon as the Guildship emerged from foldspace, its lower doors yawned open. The women neither asked for nor received further instructions, since they knew what to do: Find priority targets and destroy them. Sixty-seven vessels, all equipped with cutting-edge weapons technology, poured out and opened fire with projectiles and targeted explosives that began shredding the fifteen large Honored Matre frigates stationed in orbit. The Honored Matres had no time to react—and barely enough time to bellow their outrage over the commsystems. In ten minutes, the bombardment turned every single vessel into lifeless, floating scrap metal. Buzzell was now undefended.

"Mother Commander! A dozen unaligned ships are flying away from the atmosphere. A different design . . . they don't appear to be combat craft."

"Smugglers," Murbella said. "Soostones are valuable, so there will always be smugglers."

"Shall we destroy them, Mother Commander? Or seize their cargoes?"

"Neither." She watched the tiny ships flitting away from the ocean world. If the smugglers had proved to be a significant drain on the soostone wealth, the Honored Matres would never have let them survive. "We have a more important target down there. We'll oust the Honored Matres and negotiate with the smugglers afterward."

She led the warships to their formal conquest of the few specks of habitable land on the vast, fertile ocean.

Buzzell had long been used as a Bene Gesserit punishment planet where the Sisterhood discarded those who had disappointed them, women who had failed the ancient order in some manner. The ocean world wasn't much to look at, but the rich, deep sea was home to shelled creatures, called cholisters, that produced elegant gems.

Soostones. Noble women flaunted them; collectors and artisans paid inflated prices for them.

Like Rakis, she thought. *Ironic, that the worst places produce the items of greatest value.*

The Honored Matres' inexorable search for wealth had drawn their attentions to Buzzell years ago. After the whores overran the islands on the vast oceans, they had killed most of the disgraced Bene Gesserit Sisters and forced the survivors to harvest soostones for them.

Now, assisted by orbital surveillance, Murbella easily determined which were the main inhabited landmasses barely poking above the waves. The New Sisterhood would recapture the nerve centers of soostone activity from the Honored Matres. Soon, Buzzell would have different leaders.

The Richesian battle craft landed around the primary soostone-processing encampment. Such a great number of vessels overwhelmed the tiny landing area and most were forced to rely on inflatable pontoons, raft piers, and simple suspensor fields on the water. Ships encircled the rocky island like a noose.

As it turned out, apart from the frigates in orbit, barely more than a hundred of the whores held the facilities of Buzzell in their iron grip. When the Valkyries arrived, the Honored Matres who lived on this island in the finest (though still spartan) buildings, rushed out, fully armed. Though they fought viciously, the women were greatly outnumbered and outmatched. Murbella's fighters easily assassinated half of them before the rest capitulated. The losses were expected.

The Mother Commander strode out into the biting, salty air to begin surveying the sparse world she had just conquered.

When the fighters rounded up the surviving Honored Matres, Murbella discovered nine women who clearly did not belong among them, downtrodden yet proud in tattered black robes. Bene Gesserit. *Only nine!* Buzzell had been a punishment planet for well over a hundred Sisters . . . and only nine had survived the whores.

Murbella stalked back and forth, looking at the gathered women.

Her Valkyries stood in formation behind her, their black singlesuit uniforms embellished with sharp black spikes, used as ornamentation and as weapons. The Honored Matres looked defiant, murderous—exactly as Murbella expected. The captive Sisters averted their eyes, having spent so many years in the yoke of oppressive mistresses.

"I am your new commander. Who among you claimed to lead these women?" She swept a whipsaw gaze across them. "Who will be my underling here?"

"We are not underlings," one sinewy Honored Matre sneered, spoiling for a fight. "We don't know you, nor do we recognize your authority. You act like an Honored Matre, but you have the smell of witches about you. I don't think you are either."

So Murbella killed her.

The Honored Matre leader had persecuted Sisters here for years. Her kicks and blows were swift, but insufficient in the face of Murbella's combined training. With a broken neck, snapped ribs, and blood oozing from burst eardrums, the arrogant woman dropped dead to the black stones of the reef settlement.

Murbella never broke a sweat. She turned to the others. "Now, who speaks for you? Who will be my first underling?"

One of the other Honored Matres stepped forward. "I am Matre Skira. Ask your questions of me."

"I will know about the soostones and your operations here. We need to know how to extract profits from Buzzell."

"The soostones are ours," Skira said. "This planet is—"

Murbella dealt her a blow across the chin so swiftly that it sent the woman reeling backward before she could raise a hand to defend herself. Looming over her like a bird of prey, Murbella said, "I ask again: Explain the soostone operations to me."

One of the downtrodden Bene Gesserits broke from her line. A middle-aged woman with ash-blonde hair, she had a worn face that must once have been strikingly beautiful. "I can explain it to you."

Skira scuttled like a crab onto her elbows trying to get to her feet. "Don't listen to that cow. She's a prisoner, fit for beating and nothing else."

"I am called Corysta," the blonde said, ignoring Skira.

Murbella nodded. "I am Mother Commander of the New Sisterhood. Mother Superior Odrade herself chose me as her successor before she was killed in the Battle of Junction. I have unified Bene Gesserits and Honored Matres to stand against our common, deadly Enemy." She nudged Skira with her foot. "Only a few renegade Honored Matre enclaves such as this remain. We will either assimilate them or grind them to dust."

"Honored Matres are not so easily defeated," Skira insisted.

Murbella looked down her nose at the woman on the ground. "You were." She focused on Corysta. "You are a Reverend Mother?"

"I am, but I was exiled here for the crime of love."

"Love!" The wiry Skira spit the word out, as if expecting agreement from her conqueror. She began to talk about Corysta in a derisive, hard-edged voice, calling her a baby stealer and a criminal to both the Bene Gesserits and the Honored Matres.

Murbella gave the Sister a quick, appraising glance. "Is that true? Are you a notorious stealer of babies?"

Corysta kept her eyes averted. "I could not steal what was already mine. No, I was the *victim* of theft. I nurtured both children out of love, when no one else would."

Murbella made up her mind on the spot, knowing she had to learn quickly. "In the interests of speed and efficiency, I will Share with you." That way, she could gather all the information from Corysta in an instant.

The other woman hesitated only for a moment, then bowed her head and leaned forward so that Murbella could touch her, brow to brow, mind to mind. In a flood, the Mother Commander drew in everything she needed to know about Buzzell and far more than she had wanted to learn about Corysta.

All of the other woman's experiences, her daily life, her knowledge, her painful memories and intense loyalties to the Sisterhood, became part of Murbella, as if she had lived them herself.

In the interior vista, she saw through Corysta's eyes as she worked alongside other slaves at a sorting and cleaning table on a dock near the edge of the rugged reef. A breeze carried the biting odors of the sea to her nostrils. The morning sky was typically dreary and overcast.

White gulls hopped along the fauxwood dock, looking for crustacean fragments and tiny morsels of meat that might fall off during the processing operations.

A scaly, intimidating Phibian overseer walked up and down the sorting line, his body reeking of rotted fish. He watched the work and periodically checked to make certain that none of the Bene Gesserit slaves had stolen anything. Corysta wondered where she could possibly go if she did try to steal a soostone fragment.

She had been in exile on Buzzell for almost two decades, first cast out by the Sisterhood as a young woman, then trapped as a slave to the whores from the Scattering. Corysta had been sentenced to Buzzell for what the Bene Gesserits called a "crime of humanity." She had been ordered to breed with a spoiled, petulant nobleman who pranced about in a different outfit every time she saw him. Following the orders of her Breeding Mistresses, Corysta had seduced the fop—whom she could not imagine loving—and had manipulated her internal chemistry to ensure that the resulting child would be a daughter.

From the moment of conception, the daughter had been destined for the Bene Gesserit order. Corysta had known that intellectually, but not in her heart. As the child grew in her womb, Corysta began to have misgivings, especially when the baby started to move and kick. Alone with herself, she got to know her daughter before she was born and began to imagine raising the girl as her own, being a traditional mother to her, a practice that was forbidden in the Sisterhood. In spite of the strictness of the various breeding programs, there had to be room for exceptions, for some degree of love. Each day, Corysta talked soothingly to the baby in her womb, uttering special blessings. Gradually, she began to think about escaping from her oppressive obligations.

One night as she sang mournfully to her unborn child, Corysta made the fateful decision to keep her baby. She would not turn the little girl over to the Breeding Mistresses, as ordered. Corysta fled into seclusion, giving birth alone in an unlit shelter, like an animal. A stern Breeding Mistress named Monaya discovered where she was and stormed in, accompanied by a black-robed squadron of enforcers. After knowing only a few hours of her mother's love, the newborn daughter was taken away, and Corysta never saw her again.

She hardly remembered the subsequent journey to Buzzell, where she was abandoned with the other discarded Sisters to remain for the rest of her life in the "penance program." During all the years Corysta spent here on patches of black land no larger than a prison yard, surrounded by oceans, she never stopped thinking about her lost daughter.

Then the Honored Matres had swept in like savage carrion birds, slaughtering thousands of Bene Gesserit exiles on Buzzell. Only a handful of Sisters were spared to be put to work as slaves.

Whenever the rank iodine smell announced the presence of the Phibian overseers, Corysta worked faster to sort the precious stones by color and size. Behind her, the damp amphibious man moved on, breathing heavily from gills that worked to suck oxygen from air instead of seawater. Fearing punishment, Corysta never looked at the Phibian.

In her first year of captivity she fumed, wishing she could find some way to get her child back. As time passed, she lost all hope of that and began to accept her circumstances. For years she lived from moment to moment, only rarely picking at the mistakes of her past like someone worrying at a loose tooth. The deep waters of Buzzell became the limits of her universe.

She and her fellow survivors did not actually dive for the deep water stones; Phibians did that. Genetically modified hybrids created out in the Scattering, the human-amphibian creatures had bullet-shaped heads, lean and streamlined bodies, and slick green skin that shone with oily iridescence. Corysta was fascinated by them, and feared them.

Then, years ago, Corysta had rescued an abandoned Phibian baby from the sea, concealing and tending it in her simple hut for months. She nurtured her "Sea Child" back to health, but then, in a cruel echo of her earlier experience, Honored Matres had snatched the hybrid baby from her.

Having heard of her previous experience, the whores taunted Corysta, calling her "the woman who lost two babies." They openly ridiculed her, while her fellow exiled Sisters quietly admired her. . . .

SHAKEN, MURBELLA WITHDREW from contact with the disgraced Sister, to find that only a moment had passed. In front of her, Corysta blinked back at her in amazement at the flood of news and information. Sharing went both ways, and now the punished Bene Gesserit woman knew everything the Mother Commander knew. It was a gamble Murbella had been willing to make.

Considering how swiftly her Valkyries had succeeded in securing all vulnerable points, Murbella was certain that the New Sisterhood could easily run the operations here. She would leave a defensive force in orbit, convert or kill the remaining Honored Matres, and get back to work. She glanced around for Phibian guards, but they had all vanished into the deep water with the arrival of the Valkyries. They would return. Sharing with Corysta had told her all she needed to know.

"Reverend Mother Corysta, I appoint you overseer of the Sisterhood's soostone operations. I know that you are aware of many flaws, as well as the ways the work process could be improved."

The woman nodded, her eyes shining with pride that Murbella had entrusted her with these new responsibilities. Red-faced with rage, Matre Skira was barely able to control herself.

"If any other Honored Matres prove to be a problem, you have my permission to execute them."

TWO DAYS LATER, satisfied with the changes under way and ready to return to Chapterhouse, Murbella walked back through the weathered settlement at dusk. She passed between locked soostone holding sheds and a hodgepodge of living quarters and administrative buildings. Glowglobes surged on inside the buildings, as night swiftly fell under a coppery orange blanket of sunset.

Four Honored Matres emerged from the deep shadows of an equipment shed and the doorway of a dark building. Though they crept forward, clearly intending to be stealthy, Murbella spotted them immediately. Their violent intent rose from them like noxious fumes.

Tingling and ready for a fight, she regarded them with disdain. The four women stalked forward, confident in their numbers, though Honored Matres rarely managed to fight efficiently as a team. Combat with several of them would simply be a brawl.

The Honored Matres rushed her. In a blur of motion, Murbella kicked and spun repeatedly, cutting through all four of them. A choreographed synthesis of Bene Gesserit combat methods and Honored Matre fighting tricks, overlaid with a pattern of Duncan's Swordmaster techniques—any one of her Valkyries could have done the same.

In less than a minute, the attackers lay dead. Another group of angry Honored Matres boiled out of the equipment sheds. Murbella prepared for a grander fight and laughed aloud. She could feel her body singing with the call of combat. "Will you make me kill all of you? Or should I leave one alive as a witness, to discourage further nonsense? Who else will try?"

Two more did, and two more died. Confused, the rest of the Honored Matres hung back. To be sure that her message had sunk in, Murbella taunted them. "Who else will face me?" She pointed to the fallen bodies. "These six have learned the lesson."

No one accepted the challenge.

Thirteen Years After

Escape from Chapterhouse

On a moment's notice a friend can become a competitor, or a dangerous enemy. It is essential to analyze the probabilities at all times, to avoid being taken by surprise.

—DUNCAN IDAHO,
Mentat observation

The Rabbi hurried down the corridor with a scroll under his arm, muttering, "How many more will you create?" He had built his arguments, compiling proofs from Talmudic writings, but the Bene Gesserits were not impressed. They could quote as many obscure prophecies back at him and baffle him with mysticism that went far beyond his own.

As Duncan Idaho strode past the spry, bespectacled man, the Rabbi was too preoccupied even to notice him. The sight of him in the corridor outside the med-center and the ghola crèche had become commonplace over the years. Several times a week the Rabbi looked in on the axlotl tanks, praying over the woman he had known as Rebecca and peering in at the group of strange, tank-incubated children. Though entirely harmless, the poor fellow seemed out of touch, clinging to a reality that manifested only in his mind and in his guilt. Even so, Duncan and the others tried to show him the respect he deserved.

After the Rabbi left, Duncan also watched the ghola children as they interacted with one another like normal children, all extremely bright, but unaware of their previous personalities. The Tleilaxu Master Scytale kept his ghola apart from the other children, but the eight historical gholas, ranging in age from one to seven years, were raised together. They were all flawless cellular matches.

Duncan was the only one who remembered them the way they had been. Paul Atreides, Lady Jessica, Thufir Hawat, Chani, Stilgar, Liet-Kynes, Dr. Yueh, and the baby Leto II. They were just children now, innocent and sweet, an unorthodox group with mismatched ages. Right now in one of the bright chambers, Paul and his oddly younger mother were playing together, happily arranging toy soldiers and military equipment around a mock castle.

The oldest ghola, Paul was calm, full of intelligence and curiosity. He looked exactly like the images in the Bene Gesserit archives of the child who had spent his early years at Castle Caladan. Duncan remembered him well.

The decision to create the next ghola—Jessica—had sparked much debate on the no-ship. In her first life, Lady Jessica had thrown the Sisterhood's careful breeding plans into complete turmoil. She had made rash decisions based on her conscience and her heart, forcing the Sisterhood to revise centuries-old schemes. Some among Sheeana's followers felt that Jessica's advice and input could prove invaluable; others disagreed—vehemently.

Next, Teg and Duncan had lobbied strongly for the return of Thufir Hawat, knowing that the warrior-Mentat could assist them in a critical battle situation. They also wanted Duke Leto Atreides, another great leader, though initially there had been difficulties with the cellular material.

Muad'Dib's beloved Chani had also been one of the early priorities, if only as a mechanism to control the potential Kwisatz Haderach, should he show signs of becoming what they most feared. But they knew very little about the original girl. As the daughter of a Fremen, Chani's early life had made no mark in the Bene Gesserit records, and therefore much of her past remained a mystery. Their sketchy information came from her later association with Paul and the fact that she was the daughter of Liet-Kynes, the visionary planetologist who had rallied the people of Dune to turn their desert world into a garden.

Yes, Liet-Kynes was also there, and two years younger than his own daughter. . . . *We must dispense with our preconceptions of family*, Duncan thought. Details of age and convoluted parentage were no odder than the existence of these children at all.

The Bene Gesserit committee had chosen to bring back Kynes for his abilities in long-term thinking and large-scale planning. For similar reasons, they restored the great Fremen leader Stilgar a year later.

There was also a ghola of Wellington Yueh, the great traitor who had caused the downfall of House Atreides and the death of Duke Leto. History reviled Yueh, so Duncan didn't understand the Sisterhood's rationale behind resurrecting him. Why Yueh, and not yet, for example, Gurney Halleck? Perhaps the Bene Gesserits simply considered him an interesting experiment, a test case.

So many historical figures here, Duncan thought. *Including myself.*

He glanced up at a panel of surveillance imagers high on the walls. The crèche chamber, the med-center, the library rooms, and the play chamber were closely monitored by such equipment. As Duncan watched silently, he saw the gholas take notice of him one by one. They looked at him with adult eyes in children's bodies, and then they went back to playing, wrestling, making up games, experimenting with toys.

Though the activities seemed perfectly ordinary, a group of proctors diligently recorded every interaction and toy selection, every childish brawl. They noted preferences in colors, blossoming friendships, and analyzed each result for possible significance.

The Bashar Miles Teg, another reincarnated legend, entered the chamber. Standing half a head taller than Duncan, he wore dark trousers and a white shirt with a gold starburst insignia on the collar, the symbol of his past rank as the Bashar.

"I never get over how strange it is to see them like this, Miles. It makes me think we played God, voting on which ones to resurrect and which to keep under cellular lockup."

"Some decisions were obvious. Though the cells were there, we chose not to bring back another Baron Harkonnen, Count Fenring, or Piter de Vries." He frowned in disapproval as the black-haired baby Leto II cried after losing a sandworm toy to a three-year-old Liet-Kynes.

Duncan said, "I loved little Leto and his sister Ghanima when they were orphaned twins. And as the God Emperor, Leto killed me time and again. Sometimes when that ghola baby looks at me, I think he already has his Tyrant memories." He shook his head.

Teg said, "Some of the most conservative Sisters already say we have created a monster." Leto II, though smaller than Kynes, fought fiercely for the toy. "His death resulted in the Scattering, the Famine Times . . . and now because of that great, reckless dispersal of people, we have provoked an Enemy to come after us. Is that really an acceptable end to his Golden Path?"

Duncan raised his eyebrows and mused at Teg, Mentat to Mentat, "Who is to say the Golden Path is at an end? Even after all this time, this may still be *part* of Leto's plan. I would not underestimate his prescience."

As gholas themselves, he and Teg had assumed many of the responsibilities for the program. The real difficulties wouldn't arise for years yet, when the children reached a level of maturity sufficient to prepare them for reawakening their memories. Instead of hiding information from the gholas, Duncan insisted that they be granted full access to data about their previous lives, in the hope of turning them into effective weapons more quickly.

These children were all double-edged swords. They could hold keys to saving the no-ship from future crises, or they could raise dangers of their own. The new gholas were more than flesh and bone, more than individual personalities. They represented a stunning array of potential talents.

As if making a command decision, Teg marched into the room, separated the two quarreling children, and found additional toys to keep them content. As Duncan watched, he recalled how many times he had tried to assassinate the God Emperor himself, and how many times Leto II had brought him back as a ghola. Gazing at the one-year-old child, Duncan thought, *If anyone could find a way to live forever, it would be him.*

Every judgment teeters on the brink of error. To claim absolute knowledge is to become monstrous. Knowledge is an unending adventure at the edge of uncertainty.

—LETO ATREIDES II,
the God Emperor

From ocean to desert, blue world to brown sand. Leaving newly conquered Buzzell, Murbella returned to Chapterhouse to oversee the growing wasteland.

From the Keep on Chapterhouse, she took an ornithopter, piloting it herself. Perfectly self-sufficient, she flew the 'thopter out over the fast-growing dunes where the worms' domain was spreading. She gazed down at the brittle and leafless branches of what had been a thick forest. The trees reached upward like drowning men trying to fend off a slow tidal wave of obliterating sand. Soon, the new desert—beautiful in its own way—would engulf the whole planet, just like Rakis.

I chose to make the ecosystem die as swiftly as possible, said the voice of Odrade-within. *It was the humane thing to do.*

"It is easier to create a wasteland than a garden."

There was nothing easy about this. Not easy on Chapterhouse, and not easy on my conscience.

"Or on mine." Murbella stared down at the sterile emptiness. The bones of an environment lay down there, desiccating in the hot afternoon sun. All part of the detailed Bene Gesserit plan. "But it is what we have to do for spice. For power. For control. To make the Spacing Guild, CHOAM, Richese, and all planetary governments do as we command."

That is what survival is all about, child.

Only a few months ago, this area had been forest. Careful not to waste their dwindling resources, the Sisters had begun logging in the area after the trees died, but the desert had spread too quickly for them to finish. Now, with Bene Gesserit efficiency, work teams cut transient roads through the sand and drove large haulers into the dead forest. They dug out the trunks, cut the dry boughs, and removed the wood for construction material and fuel. The dead trees were no longer part of a viable ecosystem, so the Sisterhood would make use of the lumber. Murbella abhorred waste.

She veered off into the broader region of dunes that stretched in seemingly endless succession like immense ocean waves frozen in time. Sand dunes, though, were always on the move, churning countless silica particles in an excruciatingly slow tsunami. Sand and fertile land had always engaged in a great cosmic dance, each trying to lead. As Honored Matres and Bene Gesserits were doing now.

The Mother Commander's thoughts turned to Bellonda and Doria, both forced to cooperate for the good of the Sisterhood. For years the two had jointly overseen spice operations, though she knew they still hated working together. Now, unannounced, Murbella flew far out over the sand in her unmarked 'thopter.

Below, she spotted Chapterhouse workers as well as offworlder support staff setting up a temporary spice-harvesting camp on a patch of orange sand. The vein of fresh spice was large for Chapterhouse, minuscule by the former standards of Rakis, and a mere speck compared to what the Tleilaxu had once produced in their axlotl tanks. But the patches were growing, and so were the worms that produced them.

Choosing a landing site, the Mother Commander banked the aircraft and slowed the flapping motion of the wings. She saw her two Spice Ops Directors standing together on the sand, taking silicon or bacteriological samples for laboratory analysis. Several isolated research stations had already been established far out in the desert belt, allowing scientific teams to analyze possible spice blows. Harvesting equipment waited to be deployed—small scrapers and gatherers, not the monstrous hovering carryalls and factories that had once been used on Rakis.

After landing the ornithopter, Murbella just sat in the cabin, not yet ready to emerge. Bellonda trudged over, brushing gritty dust from her work clothes. With an expression of annoyance on her sunburned face, Doria followed, squinting into the sunlight that reflected off the cockpit.

Finally emerging, Murbella drew a warm, dry breath that smelled more of bitter dust than of melange. "Out here in the desert, I feel a sense of serenity, of eternal calmness."

"I wish I did." Doria dropped her heavy pack and kit onto the dirt. "When will you assign someone else to work the spice operations?"

"I am quite content with my responsibilities," Bellonda said, primarily to irritate Doria.

Murbella sighed at their petulant competitiveness and bantering. "We need spice and soostones, and we need cooperation. Show me you are worthy, Doria, and perhaps I will send you to Buzzell, where you can complain about the cold and damp, rather than the arid heat. For now, my command is that you work here. With Bellonda. And, Bell, your assignment is to remember what you are and to make Doria into a superior Sister."

The wind blew stinging sand into their faces, but Murbella forced herself not to blink. Bellonda and Doria stood side by side, wrestling with their displeasure. The former Honored Matre was the first to give a curt nod. "You are the Mother Commander."

BACK IN THE Keep that evening, Murbella went to her workroom to study Bellonda's meticulous projections of how much spice they could expect to harvest in coming years from the fledgling desert, and how swiftly productivity would rise. The New Sisterhood had expended spice widely enough from their stockpiles that outsiders believed they had an inexhaustible supply. In time, though, their secret hoards could dwindle to nothing more than a cinnamony aftertaste. She compared the amount to the soostone profits starting to roll in from Buzzell, and then to the payments the Richesian weapons shops demanded.

Outside, through the Keep's windows, she saw distant, silent flashes of lightning, as if the gods had muted the sounds of the changing weather. Then, as if in response to her thoughts, dry wind began to pummel the Keep, accompanied by claps of thunder. She went to the window, looked out at the twisting tongues of dust and a few dead leaves swirling along a footpath between buildings.

The storm intensified, and a startling patter of large raindrops struck the dusty plaz, leaving streaks in the blown grit. The weather of Chapterhouse had been in upheaval for years, but she didn't recall Weather Control planning a rainstorm over the Keep. Murbella couldn't remember the last time rain had come down like this. An unexpected storm.

Many dangerous storms were out there—not just the oncoming Enemy. The most powerful strongholds of the Honored Matres remained on various worlds like festering sores. And still no one knew where the Honored Matres had come from, or what they had done to provoke the relentless Enemy.

Humanity had evolved in the wrong direction for too long, wandering down a blind path—the Golden Path—and the damage might be irreversible. With the Outside Enemy coming, Murbella feared they might well be on the threshold of the greatest storm of all: Kralizec, Arafel, Armageddon, Ragnarok—by any name, the darkness at the end of the universe.

The rain outside lasted for only a few moments, but the howling wind continued long into the night.

Do our enemies occur naturally, or do we create them through our own actions?

—MOTHER SUPERIOR ALMA MAVIS TARAZA,
Bene Gesserit Archives, open records for acolytes

The very existence of the Leto II ghola was an offense to Garimi. Little Tyrant! A baby with the destruction of the human race in his genes! How many more reminders of Bene Gesserit shame and human failure must they face? How could her fellow Sisters refuse to learn from mistakes? Blind hubris and foolishness!

From the very beginning Garimi and her staunchly conservative allies had argued against the creation of these historical gholas, for obvious reasons. Those figures had already lived their lifetimes. Many had caused great damage and turned the universe upside down. Leto II—the God Emperor of Dune who became known as the Tyrant—was the worst, by far.

Garimi shuddered to think of the unspeakably huge risks Sheeana was taking with all of them. Not even Paul Atreides, the long sought-after and yet uncontrolled Kwisatz Haderach, had caused as much damage as Leto II. Paul had at least maintained an element of caution, keeping part of his humanity and refusing to do the terrible things that his own son had later embraced. Muad'Dib at least had the good grace to feel *guilty*.

But not Leto II.

The Tyrant had sacrificed his humanity from the beginning. Without remorse, he had accepted the awful consequences of merging with a sandworm and he forged ahead, plowing through history like a whirlwind, casting innocent lives around him like discarded chaff. Even he had known how hated he would be when he said, "I am necessary, so that never again in all of history will you need someone like me."

And now Sheeana had brought the little monster back, despite the risk that he might do even more damage! But Duncan, Teg, Sheeana, and others felt Leto II might be the most powerful of all the gholas. Most powerful? Most dangerous, instead! At the moment, Leto was just a one-year-old baby in the crèche, helpless and weak.

He would never be this vulnerable again.

Garimi and her loyal Sisters decided to make their move without delay. Morally, they had no choice but to destroy him.

She and her broad-shouldered companion Stuka slipped along the dim corridors of the *Ithaca*. In deference to ancient human biological cycles, Duncan the "captain" had imposed a regular diurnal shifting of bright lights and dimness to simulate days and nights. Though it was not necessary to adhere to such a clock, most people aboard found it socially convenient to do so.

Together, the two women stalked around corners and dropped through tubes and lift platforms from one deck to the next. Now, as most of the passengers prepared for sleep, she and Stuka entered the silent crèche near the expansive medical chambers. Two-year-old Stilgar and three-year-old Liet-Kynes were in the nursery, while the other five young gholas were with proctors. Leto II was the only baby currently in the crèche, though the axlotl tanks were sure to create more, eventually.

Using her knowledge of the ship's controls, Garimi worked from the hall station to bypass the observation imagers. She wanted no record of the supposed crime that she and Stuka were about to commit, though Garimi knew she could not keep her secret for long. Many of the Reverend Mothers aboard were Truthsayers. They could ferret out the murderers with proven methods of interrogation, even if they had to question all the refugees aboard.

Garimi had made her choice. Stuka, too, swore she would sacrifice her life to do what was right. And if the two of them didn't succeed, Garimi knew of at least a dozen other Sisters who would gladly do the same, given the chance.

She looked at her friend and partner. "Are you ready for this?"

Stuka's wide face, though young and smooth, seemed to carry an infinite age and sadness. "I have made my peace." She took a deep breath. "I must not fear. Fear is the mind-killer." The two Sisters intoned the rest of the Litany together; Garimi found that it had never ceased to be useful.

With the surveillance imagers successfully deactivated, the pair entered the crèche, using all of the Bene Gesserit stealth and silence they could manage. Baby Leto lay in one of the small monitored cradles, by all appearances an innocent little child, looking so human. *Innocent!* Garimi sneered. How deceptive appearances could be.

She certainly did not need Stuka's assistance. It should be simple enough to smother the little monster. Nevertheless, the two angry Bene Gesserits shored up each other's confidence.

Stuka looked down at Leto and whispered to her companion. "In his original life, the Tyrant's mother died in childbirth, and a Face Dancer tried to murder the twins when they were only hours old. Their father went off blind into the desert, leaving the babies to be raised by others. Neither Leto nor his twin sister were ever held warmly in their parents' arms."

Garimi shot her a sour glance. "Don't start going soft on me," she husked. "This is more than just a baby. In that crib lies a beast, not a mere child."

"But we do not know where or when the Tleilaxu acquired the cells to make this ghola. How could scrapings have been stolen from the immense God Emperor? If that was truly where the cells came from, why wasn't he born as a half man, half sandworm? More likely, they kept secret samplings of the boy Leto's cells from before he underwent his transformation. That means this child is technically still an innocent, his cells taken from an innocent body. Even when he gets his memories back, he will not be the hated God Emperor."

Garimi glowered at her. "Do we dare take that risk? Even as children, Leto II and his twin sister Ghanima had special and awesome powers of prescience. No matter what else, this is still an Atreides. He still has all the genetic markers that led to two dangerous Kwisatz Haderachs. That cannot be denied!" Her voice began to grow too loud. Glancing down at the stirring child, Garimi saw his bright eyes looking at her with a startling sentience, his mouth slightly open. Leto seemed to know why she was there. He recognized her . . . and yet he did not flinch.

"If he is prescient," Stuka said uncertainly, "then maybe he knows what we're going to do to him."

"I was thinking exactly the same thing."

As if in response, one of the monitoring alarms bleeped, and Garimi raced to the controls in order to bypass them. She could not allow a signal to alert the Suk doctors. "Quickly! We have no more time. Do it now—or I will!"

The other woman picked up a thick pillow and raised it above the baby's face. Garimi frantically worked at the alarm panel as Stuka pushed the pillow down to smother him.

Then Stuka screamed, and Garimi whirled to see a brief flash of tan segments, a writhing shape that rose up from the monitoring cradle. Stuka recoiled in panic. The pillow in her hands was shredded, its fabric spraying out in tatters.

Garimi couldn't believe what she was seeing. Her vision seemed to be doubled, as if two separate things were occurring in the same place at the same time. A wide-ringed mouth of tiny crystalline teeth lashed out from the crib, striking the broad-shouldered woman in the side. There was a splash of blood. Gulping panicked breaths, Stuka clutched at a gash that ripped through her robes and laid open the skin down to the ribs.

Garimi stumbled forward, but by the time she got to the small bed she saw only the quietly resting child Leto. The boy lay back, gazing up at her calmly with his bright eyes.

Ceasing her cries of pain, Stuka used her Bene Gesserit abilities to stop the flow of blood from the jagged tear in her side. She fought for balance as she reeled away from the crib, her eyes wide. Garimi looked from her back to the child in its cradle. Had she truly seen Leto transform into a sandworm?

There were no surveillance images. Garimi could never prove what she thought she had seen. But how else to explain Stuka's wound?

"What are you, little Tyrant?" Garimi saw no blood on the small fingers or mouth. Leto blinked back at her.

The crèche door burst open, and Duncan Idaho swept in, followed by two proctors and Sheeana. Duncan stood there, his face dark with anger, saw the blood, the shredded pillow, the baby in its crib. "What in the seven hells are you doing here?"

Garimi backed away from the crib, keeping her distance, afraid that little Leto might turn into the vision worm again and attack. Looking at Duncan's fiery eyes, she almost concocted a lie that Stuka had come to kill the baby and that she, Garimi, had arrived in time to defend the child. But that lie would crumble quickly upon further examination.

Instead, she drew herself up straight. A Suk doctor arrived in response to the alarms Duncan had triggered. After checking the baby, she went to where Stuka had collapsed in fatigue. Sheeana peeled away the tattered robe to expose the deep gash that had bled extensively before Stuka—in a surge of energy—managed to staunch the flow. Duncan and the proctors stared at it in awe.

Garimi tore her gaze away, now more fearful of Leto II than ever. She gestured angrily at the cradle. "I suspected this child was a monster before. Now I have no doubt whatsoever."

Despite the words of egalitarians, all humans are not the same. Each of us contains a unique mix of hidden potential. In times of crisis, we must discover these abilities before it is too late.

— BASHAR MILES TEG

During the uproar that followed the attempt on young Leto's life, Miles Teg watched the predictable power plays among the Bene Gesserit.

The initial escape from Chapterhouse had made them set aside their differences for a time, but over the years factions had formed, and festered like unhealed wounds. The schism grew as time passed and the ghola children provided a powerful wedge. In recent years, Teg had observed smoldering embers of uneasiness and resistance among Garimi's faction, centered around the new gholas. The crisis over Leto II had been like touching an igniter to kindling soaked with accelerant.

Teg's mother had raised him on Lernaeus, guiding him in Bene Gesserit ways. Janet Roxbrough-Teg was loyal to the Sisterhood, though not mindlessly so. She taught her son useful skills, showed him how to protect himself from Bene Gesserit tricks, and made him aware of how the ambitious women schemed. A true Bene Gesserit would take any necessary action to achieve a desired goal.

But the attempted murder of a child? Teg was concerned that even Sheeana had miscalculated the risks.

Garimi and Stuka stood defiantly in the boxes of the accused, not bothering to hide their guilt. The heavy doors of the large audience chamber were sealed, as if someone feared the two women might try to flee the no-ship. The thick air in the confined room had the sour, pungent odor of melange exuded from perspiration. The other women were quite agitated, and even most of the conservative faction had turned against Garimi, for now.

"You have acted against the Sisterhood!" Sheeana gripped the edge of the podium. Her voice projected loud and clear as she raised her chin, her blue-within-blue eyes flashing. She had tied back her thick, copper-streaked hair, revealing the dusky skin of her face. Sheeana was not much older than Garimi, but as acting leader of the shipboard Bene Gesserits, she projected the authority of much greater age. "You have broken a trust. Do we not have enough enemies already?"

"It seems you do not see all of them, Sheeana," Garimi said. "You create new ones in our own axlotl tanks."

"We have welcomed disagreement and discussion, and we have made our decision—as *Bene Gesserits!* Are you a tyrant yourself, Garimi, whose wishes simply tread over the will of the majority?"

Even the staunch conservatives grumbled at that. Garimi's knuckles turned white as she stood there.

From the front row next to Duncan, Teg observed with his Mentat abilities. The plazmetal bench beneath him was unyielding, but he hardly felt it. Young Leto II had been brought into the gathering chamber. An eerily quiet child, his bright eyes watched all activities around him.

Sheeana continued, "These historical gholas may be our chance for survival, and you tried to kill the one who could be the greatest help of all!"

Garimi scowled. "My dissent is a matter of record, Sheeana."

"Disagreement is one thing," Teg said aloud, his voice carrying the weight of command. "Attempted assassination is quite another."

Garimi glared at the Bashar for interrupting. Stuka spoke. "Is it assassination when one kills a monster instead of a human?"

"Have a care," Duncan said. "The Bashar and I are also gholas."

"I do not call him a monster because he is a *ghola,*" Garimi said, gesturing toward the toddler. "We saw him! He carries the Worm within him. That innocent baby transformed into a creature that attacked Stuka. You have all seen her wounds!"

"Yes, and we have heard your imaginative explanation." Sheeana's voice dripped with skepticism.

Garimi and Stuka looked deeply offended and turned to the Sisters in the raised benches, lifting their hands for support. "We are still Bene Gesserit! We are well-trained in observation and in the manipulation of beliefs and superstitions. We are not frightened children. That . . . abomination transformed into a worm to defend himself from Stuka! Ask us to repeat our stories before a Truthsayer."

"I have no doubt that you believe what you say you saw," Sheeana said.

Speaking with utter calm, Duncan interjected, "The ghola baby has been tested—as have all the new gholas. His cellular structure is perfectly normal, exactly as we expected. We checked and double-checked the original cells from Scytale's nullentropy capsule. This is Leto II, and nothing more."

"Nothing more?" Garimi let out a sarcastic laugh. "As if being the Tyrant is not enough? The Tleilaxu could have tampered with his genetics. We found Face Dancer cells among the other material. You know not to trust them!"

The Tleilaxu Master was not there to defend himself against the accusations.

Looking at Duncan, Sheeana admitted, "Such tampering has been done before. A ghola can have unexpected abilities, or an unexpected time bomb inside."

Teg watched their attention turn to him. He was an adult now, but they still remembered his origin from the first Bene Gesserit axlotl tanks. There could be no question about his genetics. Teg had been produced under the direct control of the Bene Gesserit; no Tleilaxu had ever had an opportunity to meddle.

None of the refugees here, not even Duncan Idaho, knew that Teg could move at impossible speeds, and that he sometimes had the ability to see no-fields that were invisible even to the most sophisticated scanners. Despite the Bashar's proven loyalty, though, the Sisterhood had too many suspicions. They saw nightmare hints of another Kwisatz Haderach everywhere.

The Bene Gesserit are not the only ones who can keep secrets.

He spoke up, "Yes, we all have hidden potential within us. Only fools refuse to use their potential."

Sheeana looked hard at the stern, dark-haired Garimi, who had once been her close friend and protégée. Garimi crossed her arms, trying to control her obvious indignation.

"Under other circumstances, I might have imposed banishment and exile. However, we cannot afford to diminish our numbers. Where would we send you? To execution? I think not. We have already split from Chapterhouse, and we've had few enough children in the intervening thirteen years. Do I dare eliminate you, Garimi, and your supporters? Crumbling factions are what one would expect from a weak and power-mad cult. We are *Bene Gesserit*. We are better than that!"

"Then what do you suggest, Sheeana?" Garimi stepped out of the box of the accused and strode toward the podium where Sheeana stood. "I cannot simply ignore my convictions, and you cannot ignore our supposed crime."

"The gholas—all of them—will be tested again. If you are proved correct that this child is a threat, then there was no crime committed. In fact, you will have saved us all. However, if you are wrong, then you will formally rescind your objections." She crossed her own arms, mirroring Garimi.

"The Sisterhood has made its decision, and you defied it. I am fully prepared to grow another ghola of Leto II—or another ten gholas—to ensure that at least one survives. Eleven gholas of Duncan were killed before we charged the Bashar with protecting him. Is that what you want us to do, Garimi?" The look of horror in the other woman's eyes was the only answer Sheeana needed.

"In the meantime, I assign *you* to watch over Leto II, as his guardian. In fact, you are now responsible for all of the gholas, as the official Proctor Superior."

Garimi and her followers were stunned. Sheeana smiled at their disbelief. Everyone in the chamber knew that responsibility for the one-year-old boy's life now lay solely with Garimi. Teg could not con-

trol his faint smile. Sheeana had devised a perfect Bene Gesserit punishment. Garimi did not dare let anything happen to him.

Recognizing that she was trapped, Garimi nodded curtly. "I will
watch, and I will discover what dangers lurk within him. When I do, I
expect you to take the necessary action."

"*Necessary* action, only."

Leto II sat innocently in his padded chair, a small, helpless-looking
baby—with thirty-five hundred years of tyrannical memories locked
away inside of him.

AFTER STARING AGAIN at "Cottages at Cordeville," Sheeana lay
in her quarters, drifting in and out of sleep, her thoughts troubled and
overactive. Neither Serena Butler nor Odrade had come back to whisper to her in some time, but she felt a deeper disturbance churning in
Other Memory, an uneasiness. As fatigue fuzzed her thoughts, she
sensed an odd sort of trap enfolding her, a vision that drew her under,
more than a dream. She tried to awaken to the alarming change, but
could not.

Browns and grays swirled around her, and she saw a brightness
beyond that drew her closer, pulling her body through the colors
toward the light. Sounds intruded like a screaming wind, and a dry
dustiness invaded her lungs, making her cough.

Abruptly, the turmoil and noise subsided, and she found herself
standing on sand, with great rolling dunes extending from the foreground to the farthest horizons. Was it the Rakis of her childhood? Or
perhaps an even older planet? Oddly, though she stood barefoot in her
sleeping clothes, she could not feel the surface beneath her, nor did
she feel the heat from the bright sun overhead. Her throat, however,
was parched.

Surrounded by empty dunes, it seemed pointless to walk or run in
any direction, and so she waited. Sheeana bent over and picked up a
handful of sand. Lifting her hand high, she spilled the sand, letting it
fall—but it formed an odd hourglass in the air, particles filtering
slowly through an imaginary constricted opening. She watched the

invisible bottom chamber begin to fill. Did it mean that time was running out? For whom?

Convinced that this was more than a dream, she wondered if she could be experiencing a journey into Other Memory that was not just voices, but actual experiences. Tactile visions encompassed all of her senses, like reality. Had she taken a path to some other place . . . just as the no-ship had once slipped through into an alternate universe?

As she stood in the middle of the wasteland, the sand continued to trickle through the ethereal hourglass. Would a sandworm come, if this landscape was meant to replicate the planet Dune?

She saw a distant figure on one of the dune tops, a woman moving over the sand with a well-practiced and intentionally uneven gait, as if she had spent all her life doing it. The stranger glided down the dune face toward Sheeana, then disappeared in a valley between the undulating dunes. Moments later she reappeared on top of a closer mound of sand. The woman went down one dune and up another, coming closer to her, growing larger. In the foreground, sand continued to whisper through the bottleneck of the invisible hourglass in the air.

Finally, the woman crested the last dune and hurried down the visible face directly toward Sheeana. Oddly, she left no footprints and spilled no loose sand.

Now Sheeana could see that she wore an old-style stillsuit, with a black hood. Even so, a few strands of gray hair drifted around a face so dry and leathery it looked like driftwood. Her rheumy eyes were the deepest blue-within-blue Sheeana had ever seen. She must have consumed a great deal of spice for many years; she seemed incredibly ancient.

"I speak with the voice of the multitude," the crone said in an eerie, echoing voice. Her teeth were yellow and crooked. "You know what I mean?"

"The multitude of Other Memory? You speak for dead Sisters?"

"I speak for eternity, for all who have lived and all who are yet unborn. I am Sayyadina Ramallo. Long ago, Chani and I administered the Water of Life to Lady Jessica, the mother of Muad'Dib." She pointed a gnarled finger toward a distant formation of rocks. "It was over there. And now you have brought them all back."

Ramallo. Sheeana knew of the old woman, a key figure in the epic of recorded history. In sending Jessica through the Agony in a Fremen sietch, not realizing she was pregnant, Ramallo had unknowingly changed the fetus inside. The daughter, Alia, had been called an Abomination.

The Sayyadina seemed remote, a mere mouthpiece for the turmoil in Other Memory. "Hear my words, Sheeana, and heed them closely. Be careful what you create. You bring back too much, too quickly. A simple thing can have great repercussions."

"You want me to stop the ghola project altogether?" On the no-ship, Alia's cells were also among those preserved in the Tleilaxu Master's nullentropy capsule. Ramallo in Other Memory must have seen the infamous Abomination as her greatest, most tragic error, though the old Sayyadina had not lived to know Alia.

"You want me to avoid Alia? One of the other gholas?" Alia was to be the next ghola child created, the first of a new batch that included Serena Butler, Xavier Harkonnen, Duke Leto Atreides, and many others.

"Caution, child. Heed my words. Take time. Proceed cautiously over dangerous terrain."

Sheeana moved closer to the figure. "But what does that mean? Should we wait a year? Five years?"

Just then the sand in the imaginary hourglass ran out, and old Ramallo faded to a ghostly image that lingered like a dust devil before disappearing entirely. With her, the landscape of ancient Dune dissolved as well, and Sheeana found herself in her bedchamber again, staring into the shadows with a sense of uneasiness, and no clear answers.

Like minds do not always blend. They can be an explosive mixture.
— MOTHER COMMANDER MURBELLA

For more than thirteen years now, from the time she had arrived with her Honored Matre conquerors intending to rule Chapterhouse, Doria had played the game of getting along with the witches. By now, she was quite good at it. Doria had tried to tolerate their ways and learn from them in order to turn such information against the Bene Gesserit. Gradually, she had accepted some compromises in her thought patterns, but she could not alter her fundamental core.

Out of grudging respect for the Mother Commander, she struggled to do her best with the spice operations, as she was ordered to. Intellectually, she understood the broad plan: to increase spice wealth which, along with the flow of soostones from Buzzell, would fund the unimaginable expense of building a giant military force that could stand against all renegade Honored Matres and then the Enemy.

Still, Honored Matres often acted on impulse, not logic. And she had been raised, trained, even *programmed* to be an Honored Matre. Her cooperation wasn't always easy, especially around that corpulent, supercilious witch, Bellonda. Murbella had made a grave mistake in her belief that forcing Doria and Bellonda to work together would make them grow and adapt—like an ancient atomic physicist slamming nuclei together, hoping to force a fusion reaction.

Instead, in the years that she and Bellonda had worked in the expanding arid zone, their mutual hatred had grown. Doria found it intolerable. Together in a scout 'thopter, the two women completed yet another desert survey. The close company only made Doria detest her bovine partner more—with her wheezing and sweating and tendency to annoy. The crowded cabin had become a pressure chamber.

When Doria finally piloted the 'thopter back to the main Keep, she flew with reckless speed, anxious to be away from the other woman. Beside her, clearly aware of her partner's discomfort, Bellonda sat with a smug smile. Her sheer bulk seemed to throw the 'thopter off balance! In her tight black singlesuit, she looked like a lumpy zeppelin.

All afternoon, they had exchanged tense words, vicious smiles, and sharp glances. Chief among Bellonda's personality defects, her training as a Mentat caused her to act as if she knew everything about every conceivable subject. But she didn't know everything about the Honored Matres. Far from it.

Doria's life had never been under her control. Since birth, she had been at the beck and call of one harsh mistress after another. In the Honored Matre way, she had been raised communally on Prix, out in the vast territory settled in the Scattering. Honored Matres didn't care about the science of genetics; they let breeding take its course, depending upon which male a particular matre seduced and bonded.

Honored Matre daughters were segregated according to their fighting abilities and sexual prowess. From an early age, girls faced repeated tests, life-or-death conflicts that "streamlined" the pool of candidates. Doria desperately wanted to *streamline* the bloated old Reverend Mother beside her.

She smiled as a new image came to her. *She looks like an ambulatory axlotl tank.*

Ahead, the Keep was profiled against the orange splash of the setting sun. The ever-present dust created spectacular colors across the sky. But Doria could see no beauty in the sunset, and obsessed instead on the sweating pile of flesh beside her.

I can't stand the smell of her. She's probably thinking of ways to kill me, before I can stick her like the pig she is.

As the 'thopter came in for a landing, Doria let a melange pill dissolve in her mouth, though it brought her only hints of the drug's usual calming effects. She'd lost count of the pills she'd taken over the past several hours.

Seeing her hunched over the controls, Bellonda said in her baritone voice, "Your small thoughts have always been transparent to me. I know you want to remove me, and you're just waiting for the opportunity."

"Mentats like to calculate probabilities. What is the probability that we will land and walk calmly away from each other?"

Bellonda considered the question seriously. "Very low, due to your paranoia."

"Ah, psychoanalysis! The benefits of your companionship are endless."

The ornithopter's flapping wings slowed, and the craft settled with a rough jolt on the flat pavement. Doria waited for the other woman to criticize her rough landing; instead, Bellonda dismissively turned her back and fumbled with the latch on the passenger compartment door. The moment of vulnerability lit a fuse in Doria, setting off a visceral, predatory response.

Though cramped in the craft's cockpit, she lashed out in a snapping blow with her legs. Bellonda sensed her coming and struck back, using her greater weight to knock Doria against the pilot's hatch just as it was opening. The Honored Matre fell through and tumbled embarrassingly onto the landing pad. Humiliated and furious, Doria looked up.

"Never underestimate a Reverend Mother, no matter what she looks like," Bellonda called cheerfully from the ornithopter's cockpit door. She eased out of the 'thopter like a whale being born.

At the rear of the landing pad, the Mother Commander waited to meet them and receive their report. Seeing the brewing altercation, however, Murbella swept toward them like an approaching thunderstorm.

Doria didn't care. Unable to control her rage, she sprang to her feet, knowing that all semblance of civility between them had ended forever. As the big woman dropped to the landing pad, Doria circled, ignoring Murbella's shout. This would be a fight to the death. The Honored Matre way.

Doria's black singlesuit was torn and her knee scraped bloody from the awkward tumble to the rough pavement. She limped, exaggerating her injury. Also deaf to the Mother Commander, Bellonda moved with surprising speed and grace. Seeing her seemingly lamed opponent, she closed for the kill.

But as Bellonda sprang forward in a combination fist-and-elbow attack, Doria dropped flat on the ground to let her adversary storm past—a feint—then flipped to her feet and sprang, using her whole body like a thrown kindjal. Now momentum worked against the heavyset Sister. Before she could turn, Doria slammed into her back, using hard fists to pound her kidneys.

With a roar, Bellonda turned, trying to face her attacker, but Doria remained like a shadow on her tail, hammering hard-knuckled punches into her. Hearing ribs crack, Doria slammed harder, hoping the sharp bone shards would puncture Bellonda's liver and lungs through all those folds of flesh. She matched each move Bellonda made, always remaining out of reach.

Finally, when dark blood bubbled from the big woman's mouth, Doria allowed the face-off. Bellonda charged forward like an enraged bull. Though she was already suffering from massive internal bleeding, Bellonda feigned an attack, then sidestepped Doria, striking her with a hard kick in the side. The smaller woman skidded away, thrown to the ground.

Murbella and several other Sisters approached them from all sides.

Glowering, Bellonda circled to Doria's left, looking for the next opportunity to strike. The Honored Matre leaned into her opponent's strength, a tactic designed to confuse the Reverend Mother.

Doria had only a fraction of a second. Seeing the muscles of her adversary slacken just a little, she sprang like a coiled serpent and plunged her fingers into Bellonda's neck, digging her nails through padded folds of skin until she reached the jugular. With a yank, she tore the blood vessel, and crimson fluid jetted upward, spurting with the force of a pounding heart.

Doria stepped back, frozen in delighted horror as the spray struck her face and dark bodysuit. The lumbering woman's face wore a look of surprise, as she lifted a hand to the gushing neck wound. She could not stop the flow, or adjust her internal chemistry against such a grievous wound.

In disgust, Doria shoved her away, and Bellonda collapsed to the ground. Smearing her opponent's blood from her eyes, Doria stood over her in triumph, watching the life drain away. A traditional duel, the way she had been raised. Her skin flushed with the thrill. This opponent would not recover.

Holding her bleeding neck with feebly twitching fingers, Bellonda stared up in disbelief. The fingers slipped away.

Mother Commander Murbella gave Doria a spinning kick, bloodying her mouth. "You've killed her!" Another kick drove her to the ground.

The former Honored Matre scrambled to her hands and knees. "It was a fair challenge."

"She was useful! You do not get to decide which of our resources we discard. Bellonda was your fellow Sister—and I needed her!" She fought to articulate words through her anger. Doria was sure the Mother Commander wanted to kill her. "*I needed her, dammit!*"

Grabbing Doria by the material of her black singlesuit, Murbella dragged her closer to Bellonda and the red pool spreading around her body on the ground. "Do it! It is the only way you can make up for what you have done. It is the only way I will let you live."

"What?" The dead woman's eyes were already starting to grow glassy.

"*Share.* Do it now, or I'll kill you myself and Share with both of you!"

Bending over the warm corpse, Doria grudgingly placed her forehead against her opponent's. She fought back her disgust and revulsion. In a matter of seconds, Bellonda's life began pouring into her own, filling her with all the secret vitriol that this vile woman had felt for her, along with her thoughts and experiences and all of the Other

Memories lodged deep in her awareness. Soon Doria possessed all of the disgusting data that made up her rival.

She could not move until the process was complete. Finally, she tumbled backward onto the hard pavement. Silent and growing cold, Bellonda wore a maddening, oddly victorious smile on her thick, dead lips.

"You will carry her with you always," Murbella said. "Honored Matres have a long tradition of promotion through assassination. Your own actions gave you this job, so accept it . . . a fitting Bene Gesserit punishment."

Rising to her knees, Doria looked in anguish at the Mother Commander. Feeling dirty and violated, she wanted to vomit and disgorge the intrusion, but that was impossible.

"Henceforth, you are the sole Spice Operations Director. All sandworm functions are your responsibility, so you'll have to work twice as hard. Do not disappoint me again, as you did today."

A woman's deep voice surfaced inside Doria's head, annoying and taunting. *I know you don't want my old job,* said Bellonda-within, *and you're not qualified to accomplish it. You will need to consult with me constantly for advice, and I may not always talk to you nicely.* Baritone laughter filled Doria's skull.

"Shut up!" Doria glared vindictively at the corpse that lay at the foot of the still-cooling 'thopter.

Murbella remained cold to her. "You should have tried harder before. It would have been much easier for you." She scowled in disgust at the scene. "Now clean up this mess and prepare her for burial. Listen to Bellonda—she will tell you her wishes." The Mother Commander marched away and left Doria alone with her inescapable new inner partner.

*One must always keep the tools of statecraft sharp and ready.
Power and fear—sharp and ready.*

—BARON VLADIMIR HARKONNEN,
the original, 10,191 B.G.

B ack again in the laboratories of Bandalong, enduring the nerve-
wracking daily grind, Uxtal stood before the grossly pregnant
axlotl tank. The nine-year-old child beside him stared with an intense,
unsettling fascination. "That's how I was born?"

"Not quite. That is how you were *grown*."

"Disgusting."

"You think that's disgusting? You should see how natural humans
procreate." Uxtal could barely keep the revulsion from his voice.

The air smelled of chemicals, disinfectants, and cinnamon. The
skin of the tank pulsed gently. Uxtal found it both hypnotic and repellent. To be working with the axlotl tanks again, growing another ghola
for the Face Dancers, at least he felt like a real Tleilaxu speaking the
Language of God—somebody important! It was more fulfilling than
just creating fresh drugs for the constantly demanding whores. After
two years of preparation and effort—and more than one time-
consuming mistake—he would be ready for the next vital ghola to be
decanted within a month.

Then, maybe they would leave him alone. But he doubted it.

Khrone seemed to be running out of patience, as if he guessed that the delays might have been caused by Uxtal's bumbling and ineptitude.

Matre Superior Hellica was obviously not pleased that the Lost Tleilaxu researcher would take his attentions from the production of the orange spice substitute, but she had granted him another axlotl tank with only halfhearted complaints. Uxtal wondered what kind of hold the Face Dancers had over her.

Checking the pregnant tank for the tenth time in the past hour, Uxtal studied the readings. There was nothing more to do but wait. The fetus was growing perfectly, and he had to confess his own curiosity about this one. A ghola of Paul Atreides . . . Muad'Dib . . . the first man to ever become a Kwisatz Haderach. Now he had brought back the Baron Harkonnen, then Muad'Dib. What could the Face Dancers possibly want with those two?

After returning from Dan with the preserved bloody knife, the process of growing the requested ghola had taken longer than Uxtal had expected. As soon as he switched off the nullentropy field, finding viable cells on the blade had not been difficult, but the first attempt at implanting a ghola in an old axlotl tank had failed. He had intended to grow a new Paul Atreides in the same womb that had given birth to Vladimir Harkonnen—it had a certain delicious historical irony—but the used-up axlotl tank had not been properly tended over the years and it rejected the first fetus. Then the womb actually died. A waste of female flesh.

Ingva had watched accusingly, growing bolder in her resentment toward the little man. She seemed to think she herself was as important as the Matre Superior because of her work in the torture laboratories. Strangely deluded by her sexual prowess, Ingva also believed herself attractive. Apparently her own mirror had malfunctioned! To Uxtal, she looked like a lizard dressed up as a woman.

After the first axlotl tank had perished, Uxtal was terrified, though he did his best to cover any errors by leaving evidence that his assistants had caused the problem. They were expendable, after all, and he wasn't. But the repercussions never came.

Matre Superior Hellica flippantly gave him a damaged woman for a replacement tank. The skull and brain were injured, but her body remained alive. She was an Honored Matre . . . nearly killed in an assassination attempt gone awry, perhaps? Nevertheless, her reproductive systems—the only important parts of the female anatomy, as far as he was concerned—functioned perfectly well. So Uxtal had started again, first converting the body into an axlotl tank, running meticulous and redundant tests, and then selecting more genetic material from the preserved blood on the dagger. This time there would be no mistake.

The nine-year-old's dark eyes gleamed. "Will he be my playmate? Like my new kitten? Will he do everything I command?"

"We shall see. The Face Dancers have great plans for him."

Vladimir looked angry. "They have plans for me, too! I'm important."

"That may be. Khrone tells me nothing."

"I don't want another ghola here. I want a new kitten. When do I get a new kitten?" Vladimir pouted. "The other one is broken."

Uxtal gave an exasperated sigh. "You killed another one?"

"They break too easily. Get me a new one."

"Not now. I have work to do. I told you, this new ghola is very important." He studied the tubes and pumps, making sure the readings were all acceptable. Suddenly fearing that Ingva might be watching, he added aloud, "But not more important than my work for the Honored Matres."

Even with the production lines moving smoothly, Hellica required increased amounts of the adrenaline spice, insisting that her women had to be stronger and more alert, now that the New Sisterhood had begun rooting them out so fiercely. The witches of Chapterhouse had already seized Buzzell and several smaller Honored Matre strongholds.

In the meantime, needing a source of income after losing their soostone operations, Hellica insisted that he rediscover the old Tleilaxu technique of producing real melange. He had quailed at the challenge, which was impossibly difficult—far more so than making mere gholas—and so far he had failed in every attempt. The task was simply beyond his capabilities. Every month when Uxtal had to deliver the same pathetic report, the same lack of results, he was sure someone would execute him on the spot.

Ten years—how have I survived this nightmare for ten years?

The boy Vladimir poked the distended flesh of the tank with his finger, and Uxtal slapped his hand away. With this child in particular, it was necessary to establish clear boundaries. If there was any way of hurting the unborn Atreides child inside, the brat would find it.

Vladimir recoiled and glowered, first at his stung hand, then at Uxtal. Obviously, his little mind was churning as he turned away peevishly. "I'm going outside to have fun. Maybe I'll kill something."

LEAVING THE AXLOTL tank and counting down the time remaining until the baby could be decanted, Uxtal went to the "pain encouragement rooms." There, closely monitored by Honored Matres, his assistants siphoned chemicals from writhing torture victims. Over the years, Uxtal had learned that certain types of pain led to differences in the purity and potency of the resulting substance. Hellica rewarded him for that sort of research and analysis.

Unsettled by Vladimir's near tantrum, he threw himself into the work, snapping orders to his assistants, monitoring the dull-eyed fear on the faces of the strapped victims being milked for pre-spice chemicals. At least *they* were cooperating. He wasn't going to give lizardlike Ingva anything to report to the Matre Superior.

Hours later, exhausted and anxious for a few moments of privacy in his quarters where he could complete his ritual ablutions and prayers, then mark off another day that he had survived, Uxtal left the pain laboratories. By now, the boy Vladimir had either gotten himself into trouble or found the Matre Superior to exchange cruelties with her. Uxtal didn't care.

Though weary, he headed toward the smaller laboratory section to check on the pregnant axlotl tank one final time, but the young Baron blocked the way, standing with his hands on his hips. "I want another kitten. Right now."

"I already said no." Uxtal tried to go around, but the nine-year-old moved to block his way again.

"Or something else. A lamb! Get me a little lamb. Sligs are boring."

"Stop this," Uxtal snapped. Drawn by the commotion of voices, Ingva slinked out of the torture wing and watched them hungrily. He looked away from her, swallowing hard.

When the boy saw the old Honored Matre spy, his attention spun in another direction, like a projectile ricocheting off thick armor. "Ingva told Matre Superior Hellica that my sexuality is very powerful for my age—and quite perverse." He seemed to know the comment would be provocative. "What did she mean by that? Do you think she wants to bond with me?"

Uxtal looked over his shoulder. "Why don't you ask her yourself? In fact, why don't you go do that right now?" As he tried to step around the boy yet again, he became aware of an unusual sound in the laboratory. Splashing noises came from somewhere by the axlotl tank.

Startled, Uxtal roughly shoved Vladimir aside and hurried toward the tank. "Wait!" the boy said, hurrying to catch up.

But Uxtal had already reached the mounded female form. "What have you done?" He ran to the flex-tube nutrient connections. Ripped loose, they were gushing red and yellow fluids all over the floor. The sympathetic nervous system in the womb-body caused the jellylike flesh to shudder. A thin squealing and sucking sound came from the slack remnants of its mouth, an almost-conscious sound of desperation. A surgical knife from the pain-encouragement rooms lay on the floor. An alarm klaxon went off.

In panic, Uxtal struggled to reconnect the lines. He whirled to grab the smug child by the shirt and shook him. "Did you do this?"

"Of course. Don't be stupid." Vladimir kicked at Uxtal's groin, but succeeded only in hitting his thigh, though it was enough to make the Tleilaxu release him. The boy ran off, shouting, "I'm going to tell Hellica!"

Torn between his fears of the Matre Superior and the Face Dancers, Uxtal looked in dismay at the tank's mangled life-support systems. He couldn't let the womb—and the critically important child within—die. That poor baby . . . and poor Uxtal!

Drawn by the alarm, two lab assistants rushed in—competent ones, thankfully, instead of Ingva. Maybe if they worked swiftly enough . . .

Under Uxtal's direction, he and his assistants frantically installed new flexible tubing, refilled the reservoirs, pumped in stimulants and stabilizing drugs, and reconnected the monitors. He wiped sweat from his grayish brow.

Ultimately, Uxtal saved the tank. And the unborn ghola.

VLADIMIR THOUGHT HE'D been clever. In contrast, his punishment was swift, severe, and, for him, most unexpected.

He went directly to Hellica to tattle on Uxtal for his abuses, but the Matre Superior's face was already flushed hot with anger. Ingva had been swifter, racing to the Palace to make her damning report.

Before the boy could tell his lying version of the story, Hellica grabbed him by the front of his shirt with fingers as sharp and strong as a tiger's claws. "For your sake, you little bastard, the new ghola had better not be harmed. You wanted to kill him, didn't you?"

"N-no. I wanted to play with him. Right now." Terrified, Vladimir backed up a step. He tried to look as if he might cry. "I wasn't trying to hurt him. I was trying to make him come out. I'm tired of waiting for my new playmate. I was going to cut him free. That's why I took the knife."

"Uxtal interrupted him before he could succeed." Ingva slinked out from behind a hanging where she had been eavesdropping.

Her eyes flashing orange, the Matre Superior gave him a stern lecture. "Don't be such a fool, boy! Why would you destroy when you can *control*? Is that not a better revenge against House Atreides?"

Vladimir blinked; this had not occurred to him.

Hellica discarded him, as if he were a bothersome insect. "Do you know what exile means? It means you're going back to Dan—or wherever Khrone wants to stash you away. As soon as I can obtain a Guildship, you will be in his hands."

"You can't! I'm too important!" Even at a young age, his twisted little mind was beginning to understand plots and schemes, but he didn't yet grasp the deep intrigues of the politics that prevailed all around him.

Hellica silenced him with a threatening frown. "Unfortunately for you, the ghola baby is far more important than you are."

FOURTEEN YEARS AFTER

ESCAPE FROM CHAPTERHOUSE

The human body can achieve many things, but perhaps its greatest role is to act as a storage mechanism for the genetic information of the species.

—TLEILAXU MASTER WAFF,
at a kehl meeting on the Duncan Idaho ghola project

His ghola son was himself . . . or would be, once the memories within were brought to the surface. But that could not happen for several years yet. Scytale hoped his aging body would last long enough.

Everything the Tleilaxu Master had experienced and learned in countless sequential lifetimes was stored in his own genetic memory and reflected in the same DNA that had been used to create the five-year-old Scytale duplicate who stood before him. This was actually a clone, not a true ghola, because the cells had been taken from a living donor. The child's predecessor was not dead. Yet.

But old Scytale could feel the increasing physical degeneration. A Tleilaxu Master should not fear death, because it had not been a real possibility for millennia—not since his race had discovered the means to immortality through ghola-reincarnation. Though his ghola child was flourishing, he was still much too young.

Year by year, the inevitable march of death paraded through his body's systems, making his organs function less efficiently than they once had. *Planned obsolescence.* For millennia, the Masheikh elite of his race had met in secret councils, but never had they imagined a holocaust such as they now faced—such as Scytale now faced, as the last living Master.

Realistically, he did not know what he could accomplish alone. With unrestricted access to axlotl tanks, Scytale might have restored other Masters like himself, the true geniuses of his race. Cells of the last Tleilaxu Council had been stored within his nullentropy capsule, but the Bene Gesserit refused to consider creating gholas of those men. In fact, after the uproar surrounding the baby Leto II, as well as an ominous vision Sheeana claimed to have received in Other Memory, the witches had halted the entire ghola program. "Temporarily," they said.

At least the powindah women had finally granted him his son, his copy. Scytale might achieve continuity after all.

The boy was with him now in the portion of the ship that had once been Scytale's prison. Since revealing the last of his secrets, Scytale's restrictions had been eased, and he could move about wherever he wished. He could observe the other eight ghola children undergoing whatever training the Bene Gesserit considered necessary. Reluctantly placed in charge of the young gholas, Proctor Superior Garimi had offered to instruct his son as well, but Scytale refused, not wishing to have him contaminated.

The Tleilaxu Master gave his son private instruction to prepare him for his great responsibility. Before the elder incarnation died, a great deal of important information needed to be passed on, much of it secret.

He wished he had the witches' ability to Share their memories. *Human downloading*, he called it. If only he could awaken his son that way, but the Sisterhood kept that particular secret to themselves. No Tleilaxu had ever been able to determine the method, and such information was not for sale. The witches claimed it was a power they held as women, that no male could ever achieve it. Ridiculous! The Tleilaxu knew, and had proved, that females were as unimportant as the pigment on a wall. They were just biological vessels to produce offspring, and a conscious brain was not necessary for that process.

Alone, he faced the challenge of teaching the boy the most sacred rituals and cleansings. Though he spoke in whistles and whispers, using a coded tongue that no one except Masters should be able to speak, he still feared the witches could understand him. Years ago, Odrade had tried to entrap him by speaking that ancient language to prove she deserved his trust. To Scytale it only proved that he should never underestimate their wiles. He suspected that the witches had installed listening devices in his quarters, and no powindah must be allowed to hear the deep mysteries.

Desperation had painted him into smaller and smaller corners. His body was dying, and this child was his only option. If he did not take the risk that some of his words might be overheard, then those holy secrets might die with him. Wondrous knowledge, vanished forever. Which was worse, discovery or extinction?

Scytale leaned forward. "You carry a great burden. Few in our glorious history have ever borne such a responsibility. You are the hope of the Tleilaxu race, and my personal hope."

The familiar boy seemed both intimidated and eager. "How am I to do it, Father?"

"I will show you," Scytale said in Galach, before again reverting to the old language. The boy had shown an exceptional aptitude for it. "I will explain many things, but it is only a preparation, a foundation for your understanding. Once I restore your memories, you will know it all intuitively."

"But how will you restore my memories? Will it hurt?"

"There is no greater agony, and no greater satisfaction. It cannot be described."

The boy responded quickly, "The essence of s'tori is to comprehend our unknowability."

"Yes. You must accept both your inability to understand and your importance in keeping the keys to such knowledge." Old Scytale sat back on his cushion. The boy was already nearly as tall as he was. "Listen while I tell you of lost Bandalong, our beautiful, sacred city on holy Tleilax, where our Great Belief was founded."

He described the glorious towers and minarets, and the secret chambers where fertile females were kept to produce the desired offspring, while others were converted into axlotl tanks for Tleilaxu laboratory needs. He talked about how the Council of Masters had quietly preserved the Great Belief through so many millennia. He explained that the sly Tleilaxu had fooled the evil outsiders by pretending to be weak and greedy so that all Tleilaxu would be seriously underestimated, a ploy to sow the seeds of eventual victory.

His ghola son drank it all in, a rapt audience for a talented storyteller.

Old Scytale had to trigger his duplicate's inner memories as soon as he could. It was a race against time. The Master's skin already showed blemishes, while his hands and legs had developed a noticeable tremor. If only he had more time!

The boy shifted restlessly. "I'm hungry. Will we eat soon?"

"We cannot afford to take a break! You must absorb everything possible."

The boy drew a deep breath, put his small, pointed chin in his hands, and gave the Master his full attention. Scytale spoke again, faster this time.

I know who I was. The historical record is quite clear on the facts.
A more pertinent question to answer, though, is who I am.

—PAUL ATREIDES,
no-ship training sessions

From outside the instructional chamber, peering through a spyplaz window, Duncan found himself staring at the past. The eight students of varying ages and historical significance were all earnest, continuing their daily instruction with changing degrees of restlessness, intimidation, and fascination.

Paul Atreides was a year older than his "mother," his son Leto II was a precocious toddler, and his father Duke Leto had not yet been born. *One thing is certain: never in history has there been a family such as this.* Duncan wondered how they would deal with the peculiar situation when their memories were restored.

Most days, Proctor Superior Garimi took each of the young gholas through a well-structured regimen of prana-bindu training, physical exercise, and mental acuity challenges. The Bene Gesserit had molded their acolytes for millennia, and Garimi knew exactly what she was doing. She had no love for her duties in charge of the ghola children, but she accepted her role, knowing she would face an even worse punishment should harm come to any of them. With such intensive physical training and mental instruction methods, these children had been rushed along in their development, making them far more mature and intelligent than equivalent boys and girls of the same age.

Today, Garimi had placed the small group in a large faux solarium and given them materials and an assignment. Though Duncan observed them surreptitiously, the group seemed to be alone. The chamber was bathed in warm yellow light, supposedly a spectrum similar to the sun of Arrakis; the smooth ceiling projected an artificial blue sky, and a coating of soft sand from the hold had been strewn on the floor. This room was meant to suggest a memory of Dune, without the harsh realities.

The perfect place for their assignment.

Using blocks of neutral sensiplaz, shapers, and historical blueprint grids, the ghola children were expected to complete a compelling and ambitious project. Working together, the gholas would assemble an accurate model of the Grand Palace of Arrakeen, which had been built by the Emperor Muad'Dib during his violent reign.

The *Ithaca*'s archives contained a variety of images, accounts, tourist brochures, and often contradictory construction drawings. From his second life, Duncan remembered that the real Grand Palace had many secret passages and hidden rooms, necessitating falsified diagrams.

Paul bent to pick up a shaper glove, and looked at it skeptically. Testing his abilities, he began to spread the free-form material in a whisper-thin but firm layer: the foundations of his palace. The other children distributed raw-material blocks of sensiplaz; the no-ship's stores could always provide more.

In previous training sessions, the gholas had studied biographical summaries of their historical predecessors. They read and reread their own histories, familiarizing themselves with the available details, while searching their minds and hearts to understand the undocumented motivations and influences that had shaped them.

Starting out with a clean slate, would any of these cellular offspring turn out the same as they had in the past? They were certainly being raised differently.

The children reminded him of actors learning roles in a play with an immense cast. The children were forming friendships and alliances.

Stilgar and Liet-Kynes already demonstrated signs of friendship. Paul sat by Chani, while Jessica kept to herself, without her Duke; Paul's son Leto II, missing his twin sister, also showed distinct signs of being a loner.

Little Leto II should have had his twin sister. The boy wasn't destined to become a monster, but without Ghani this time, he could be even more vulnerable. One day, after watching the quiet boy, Duncan had marched up to Sheeana and demanded answers. Yes, Ghanima's cells were in Scytale's reservoir, but for whatever reason, the Bene Gesserits had not brought her from the new axlotl tanks. "Not at this time," they'd said. Of course they could always do so later, but Leto II would remain separated in years from a person who should have been his twin, his other half. He felt sorry for the boy's needless pain.

Drawn together by their shared past, as well as their own instincts, Paul and six-year-old Chani sat side by side. He hunkered down on the floor, studying the layout. A holo blueprint shimmered in the air, giving far more detail than he needed. He focused on the structural walls, the main parts of the complex that was the largest man-made structure ever built.

Duncan knew that Garimi's assignment for the children had many layers of purpose, some artistic, some practical. By making a scaled-down replica of Muad'Dib's Grand Palace, these gholas could touch history. "Tactile sensations and visual stimuli evoke a different understanding than mere words and archival records," she had explained. Most of the eight gholas had been inside the actual structure in their previous lives; maybe this would feed their inner memories.

Though too small to help, Leto II could walk about clumsily and observe with fascination. Only a year earlier, Garimi and Stuka had tried to kill him in the crèche. Placid and interested, Leto II spoke little, but showed a frightening level of intelligence and seemed to absorb everything around him.

The toddler sat down on the sandy floor and rocked back and forth in front of the Palace's projected main entrance, holding his knees. The two-year-old seemed to understand certain things as well as the other children did, perhaps even better.

Thufir Hawat, Stilgar, and Liet-Kynes worked together to raise the outer fortress walls. They laughed and played, seeing the task as a game instead of a lesson. Since reading of his original heroic life, Thufir had developed a bold personality. "I wish we'd just find the Enemy and get on with it. I'm sure the Bashar and Duncan could fight them."

"And now they have us to help," Stilgar said brashly and nudged his friend Liet, inadvertently knocking some of the blocks down.

Watching, Duncan muttered, "We don't exactly have you—not the *you* we want."

Jessica created more blocks from the sensiplaz, and Yueh dutifully helped her. Chani paced the boundaries, marking the general outline projected on the plan. Then she and Paul set up a scale representation of the huge Annex that had housed all the Atreides attendants and their families—thirty-five million of them, at one time! The records had not been exaggerated, but the scope was difficult for any person to grasp.

"I can't imagine us living in a home like that," Chani said, pacing around the newly marked boundaries.

"According to the Archives, we were happy there for many years."

She smiled mischievously, understanding much more than a girl should have. "This time, can we just eliminate Irulan's quarters?"

Secretly hearing this, even Duncan chuckled.

The cells of Irulan, daughter of Shaddam IV, were among those in Scytale's treasure trove, but the med-center axlotl tanks would not produce her anytime soon. No other gholas were scheduled, though Duncan had mixed feelings to know that Alia would have been next. Garimi and her conservatives certainly hadn't complained about putting a cautious halt to the ghola project.

Inside the model Palace, the children blocked out an independent structure, the Temple of St. Alia of the Knife. The temple had supported a burgeoning religion around the living Alia, and its priesthood and bureaucrats had brought down Muad'Dib's legacy. Duncan saw the great louvered window through which Alia—possessed and driven mad—had thrown herself to her death.

Studying the blueprints again, the gholas—each wearing shaper gloves—worked the sensiplaz into a quick approximation of the Palace's framework. They extruded representations of the immense entrance pillars and the capitol arch, leaving the numerous statues and staircases for later, as finishing touches. Accurately including all of the ornamentation, the gifts and adornments presented by pilgrims from hundreds of worlds conquered in Muad'Dib's jihad, would have been an impossible task. But that was another part of the training: Rub their faces in an impossible task to see how far they would carry it forward.

Tired of feeling like a voyeur, Duncan turned from the spyplaz and walked into the training room. Glancing at him, the gholas noted his presence, and then went back to work. But Paul Atreides walked right up to him.

"Excuse me, Duncan. I have a question."

"Only one?"

"Can you tell me how our memories will be restored? What techniques will the Bene Gesserit use, and how old will we be when it happens? I'm already eight. Miles Teg was only ten when they reawakened him."

Duncan stiffened. "They were forced to do that. A time of extremis."

Sheeana had done it herself, using a twisted variation of sexual imprinting techniques. Miles had been in the body of a ten-year-old boy, with the buried mind of an old, old man. The Bene Gesserits were willing to risk scarring his psyche because they had needed his military genius to defeat the Honored Matres. The young Bashar had been given no say in the matter.

"Aren't we in a time of extremis right now?"

Duncan studied the front of the model palace. "You need know only that the restoration of your memories will be a traumatic process. We know of no other way to accomplish it. Because you each have a separate personality"—he glanced around at the children—"the awakening will be different for each of you. Your best defense is to understand who you were, so that when the memories come flooding back, you're ready for them."

Young Wellington Yueh, five years old, piped up in a wavering childish voice. "But I don't *want* to be who I was."

Duncan felt the heaviness in his chest. "I'm sorry, but none of us has that luxury."

Chani always stayed close to Paul. Her voice was small but the words were large. "Do we have to live up to the Sisterhood's expectations?"

Duncan shrugged and forced a smile. "Why not exceed them?"

Together, they continued to build the walls of the Grand Palace.

Our aimless wandering is a metaphor for all of human history. The participants in great events do not see their place in the overall design. Our failure to see the larger pattern, however, does not dis- prove that one exists.

—REVEREND MOTHER SHEEANA,
Ithaca logs

S heeana walked the sands again. Her bare toes sank into the soft, grainy powder. The enclosed air held brittle flint odors and the fertile, cinnamony smell of fresh melange.

She had still not forgotten the strange Other Memory vision in which she had spoken to Sayyadina Ramallo and received her cryptic warning about the gholas. *Be careful what you create.* Sheeana had taken the admonition seriously; as a Reverend Mother, she could do nothing else.

But exercising caution was not the same as stopping entirely. What had Ramallo meant? Despite searching through her mind, she was unable to find the ancient Fremen Sayyadina again. The clamor was too loud. She did, however, again encounter the even-more-ancient voice of Serena Butler. The legendary Jihad leader offered much wise advice.

Inside the no-ship's kilometer-long great hold, Sheeana trudged across the stirred sand, not bothering to use the careful stutter-step of Fremen on Dune. The captive worms instinctively knew she had entered their domain, and Sheeana could sense them coming.

While waiting for the worms to charge toward her in a froth through the dunes, Sheeana lay down on the sand. She wore no still-suit as she had done as a little girl. Her legs and arms were bare. *Free.* She felt the sandy grains pressing against the skin of her arms and legs. Dust clung to the prickles of perspiration from her pores. With the soft dust all around her, she imagined what it would be like to be one of the sandworms in the wild, plunging beneath the surface like a big fish in a great arid sea.

Sheeana got to her feet as the first three worms arrived. She picked up the empty spice-gathering basket from where she had set it and stood to face the sinuous creatures. They extended their round heads, their mouths glittering with crystal teeth and tiny flickers of flame fueled by an inner friction furnace.

The original worms of Arrakis had been aggressively territorial. After the God Emperor went "back into the sand," each of the new worms he spawned contained a pearl of his awareness, and they could work together when they wished to do so.

She cocked her head and lifted her sealed basket to show them. "I have come to gather spice, Shaitan." Long ago, the priests on Rakis had been horrified to hear her speak thus to their Divided God.

Unafraid, Sheeana walked between their ringed bodies, as if they were only towering trees. She and the sandworms had always had an understanding. Few others aboard the no-ship dared to enter the hold now that the creatures had grown so large. Sheeana was the only one who could gather natural spice from the sands, some of which she added to the much greater supply of fresh melange created in the ship's axlotl tanks.

Sniffing, she followed the scent to where a fresh cinnamony bloom might be found. Children from her village had done the same thing long ago. The fragments of windblown melange they scavenged from the dunes helped to buy supplies and tools. Now that whole way of life was gone, as was Rakis itself. . . .

Inside her head, the fascinating and ancient voice of Serena Butler once again bubbled up from deep within her Other Memories. Sheeana carried on her conversation aloud. "Tell me one thing: How can Serena Butler be among my ancestors?"

If you dig deep enough, I am there. Ancestor after ancestor, generation after generation . . .

Sheeana was not so easily convinced. "But Serena Butler's only child was murdered by thinking machines. That was the trigger of the Jihad. You had no heirs, no other descendants. How can you be in my Other Memories, regardless of how far back I go?"

She looked up at the strange forms of the sandworms, as if the martyred woman's face might be there.

Because, Serena said, *I am.* The ancient voice said no more, and Sheeana knew she would get no better answer.

Brushing past the nearest worm, Sheeana stroked one of the hard, encrusted ring segments. She sensed that these worms dreamed of freedom, too, longing to find a great open landscape through which they could burrow, where they could claim their own territory, fight battles of dominance, and propagate.

Day by day, Sheeana observed them from the viewing gallery above. She saw the worms circling the hold, testing their boundaries, knowing that they must wait . . . *wait!* Just like the Futars pacing in their arboretum, or the refugee Bene Gesserits and Jews, or Duncan Idaho, Miles Teg, and the ghola children. They were all trapped here, caught in the odyssey. There must be someplace safe where they could go.

Finding a rusty blotch on the sand, she stooped to brush fresh melange into her impermeable basket. The worms produced only small amounts of melange, but because it was fresh and genuine, Sheeana kept much of it for her own uses. Though the axlotl-produced spice was chemically identical, she preferred the close connection to the sandworms, even if it was all in her imagination. Like Serena Butler? Or Sayyadina Ramallo?

The worms passed her and began to plow their great bodies through the sand. Sheeana bent to gather more spice.

INSIDE THE MEDICAL center—torture chamber, more like!—the Rabbi knelt beside the gross female form and prayed, as he did so often.

"May our Ancient God bless and forgive you, Rebecca." Though she was brain dead and her body no longer resembled the woman he had known, he insisted on using her given name. She had said she would be dreaming, living among those myriad lives within her. Was it true? Despite what he saw and smelled in this chamber of horrors, he would remember who she had been and honor her.

Ten years as a tank! "Mother of monsters. Why did you allow them to do this, daughter?" And now, with the ghola project on hiatus, her body no longer even served the purpose for which she had sacrificed it. What a terrible thing.

Her naked abdomen, adorned with tubes and monitors, was no longer swollen, but he had seen her several times as a mound carrying a pregnancy so unnatural that even God must turn his eyes from it. Rebecca and the other two Bene Gesserit women who had volunteered to become such horrors lay on sterile beds. Axlotl tanks! Even the name sounded unnatural, stripped of all humanity.

For years these "tanks" had produced gholas; now they simply secreted chemical precursors that were processed into melange. Their bodies had become nothing more than detestable factories. The women were maintained with a constant stream of fluids, nutrients, and catalysts.

"Is any goal worth such a price?" the Rabbi whispered, not sure if he was beseeching the Almighty in prayer or asking Rebecca directly. In either event, he received no answer.

With a shudder, he let his fingers touch Rebecca's belly. The Bene Gesserit doctors had often scolded him, telling him not to touch "the tank." But, though he despised what Rebecca had done to herself, he would never harm her. He was resigned to the fact that he could no longer save her, either.

The Rabbi had looked in on the ghola children. They seemed innocent enough, but he was not fooled. He knew why these genetically ancient babies had been born, and he wanted no part of such an insidious plan.

He heard someone arrive in the humming silence of the medical chamber and looked up to see a bearded man. Quiet, intelligent, and competent, Jacob had taken it upon himself to watch over the Rabbi, as Rebecca had once done.

"I knew I would find you here, Rabbi." His expression was stern and scolding—one the old man himself might have used when he disapproved of someone else's behavior. "We have been waiting for you. It is time."

The Rabbi glanced at a chronometer and realized how late it was. According to their calculations and the habits they followed, this was sunset on Friday, time to begin the twenty-four hours of Shabbat. He would say the prayers in their makeshift synagogue; he would read Psalm 29 from the original text (not the horribly bastardized version in the Orange Catholic Bible), and then his small group would sing.

Preoccupied with his prayers and wrestling with his conscience, the old man had lost track of time. "Yes, Jacob. I am coming. I'm sorry."

The other man took the Rabbi by the arm and helped him along, though he needed no assistance. Jacob leaned closer and reached out to brush unexpected tear streaks from the older man's cheeks. "You are crying, Rabbi."

The old man glanced back at what had once been a vibrant woman, Rebecca. He stopped for a long, uncertain moment, and then permitted his companion to lead him from the medical chamber.

Soostones: Highly valued jewels produced by the abraded carapace of a monoped sea creature, the cholister, found only on Buzzell. Soostones absorb rainbows of color, depending upon the touch of flesh or how light falls on them. Because of their high value and portability, the small and perfectly round stones—like melange— are used as hard currency, especially in times of economic turmoil and social upheaval.

—Terminology of the Imperium (Revised)

With the smell of salt air around her—so different from the Chapterhouse desert!—Mother Commander Murbella surveyed the continuing operations on Buzzell. In the past year, Reverend Mother Corysta had sent the New Sisterhood many shipments of soostones, which covered other expenses while the spice production was devoted to paying for the armaments Richese had begun to produce. Murbella had distributed her spies widely, gathering information about the remaining rebel Honored Matre strongholds, preparing her long-term plan. Soon, she would be ready to move against the main enclaves in earnest.

Recapturing Buzzell and seizing all soostone production had cut off the rest of the Honored Matres from a primary source of wealth. It had both provoked and weakened the strongest remaining bastions of rebellious women.

So far, the New Sisterhood had subsumed five rebel strongholds in addition to Buzzell. For every hundred thousand that her female soldiers killed, they captured only a thousand. For every thousand captured, maybe a hundred were successfully converted to the New

Sisterhood. Murbella had declared to her advisors, "Rehabilitation is never guaranteed, but death is certain. No one needs to remind us how Honored Matres think. Would they respect our pleas for unification? No! They need to be broken first."

The last strongholds of the violent women would be tough nuts to crack, but Murbella convinced herself that the Valkyries were up to the task. Not every conquest could be as clean and simple as the recapture of Buzzell.

Over the past several months, Corysta had made many changes to the operations on the ocean planet, and the Mother Commander approved. From the beginning, Corysta—"the woman who had lost two babies"—had been willing to help. Even before Sharing with Murbella, she seemed to remember a good deal about being a Bene Gesserit.

The Buzzell settlements consisted of only a few buildings and defensive towers on the patchy outcroppings of rock and hardscrabble islands, along with large boats, processing barges, and anchored rafts. Under Corysta's supervision, many of the resentful Bene Gesserit exiles had initially demanded to be transferred away from the rough soostone labor. Some had been petulant and wanted revenge on the vicious whores. Pointedly leaving the most strident exiles in their old assignments, Corysta—thinking much like Murbella—had promoted others to be special local advisors.

She had commandeered the reasonably comfortable quarters that Matre Skira and her whores had taken from the Bene Gesserit exiles and ordered the remaining handful of Honored Matres to erect their own thin tents on the rocky ground. Murbella understood that this was a means of control, rather than revenge. Skira and her group, as well as the Bene Gesserit exiles, had been isolated from outside politics for a long time. Clearly, uniting these particular women was another difficult task, and a significant challenge to Corysta's leadership abilities, but gradually the women were learning the benefits of working together. It was like a microcosm of what had happened at Chapterhouse.

Now, on the afternoon of the second day of her follow-up inspection, the Mother Commander toured the revamped soostone operations, accompanied by Corysta and the Honored Matre Skira. Nearby, a dozen workers—all Honored Matre survivors—continued washing and sorting stones according to their size and color, the work they had once forced the Bene Gesserit exiles to do. Phibian guards no longer stood over the workers; Murbella wondered if the aquatic people had noticed, or cared, that their female masters had changed.

Beneath the surface of the water, Phibian divers trapped and corralled the large slow-moving shellfish. Cholisters had a fleshy, probing body covered by a thick and lumpy carapace; persistent abrasions of that casing produced hard milky scars that could be chipped off like gems embedded in rock. The slow growth of the nodules, the scarcity of the sea creatures themselves, and the difficulty of harvesting deep underwater all contributed to the rarity and value of the gems.

When the Honored Matres brought in the hybrid Phibians, production increased dramatically. The amphibious people lived in the sea, swam deep without any special equipment, and ranged far from the island outcroppings as they hunted for the slowly wandering cholisters.

Standing on the dock with her new advisors, Murbella turned toward a large Phibian male who stood at the reef's edge; apparently he had once been a guard, for he still carried his barbed whip. Four other Phibian deep divers crouched together on the rocky beach, where they had just delivered a load of soostones.

The Honored Matres did not know exactly where the Phibians had come from, just "somewhere out in the Scattering, a long time ago." Skira said that the amphibious half-breeds were an insular species with only limited vocabularies, but Murbella's Bene Gesserit instincts told her otherwise. The memories she had Shared with Corysta added evidence to this; the Phibians were more than they appeared to be.

Ordering her two escorts to accompany her, Murbella descended a spray-slick rock stairway to the shingle beach.

"This is not safe." Skira ran to catch up with the Mother Commander. "Phibians can be violent. Last week, one of them drowned an Honored Matre. Took her out and pulled her underwater."

"She probably deserved it. Do you doubt that the three of us can defend ourselves?" Nearby, a squad of Murbella's Valkyries also watched over their commander, weapons at the ready.

Corysta pointed to the group. "The tallest one is our best producer. See the scar on his forehead? He dives the deepest and brings back the most soostones."

From a flash of Corysta's memory, Murbella recalled the abandoned Phibian baby she had rescued from a tide pool. He'd had a scar on his forehead, a claw mark. Could this be the same one, from so many years ago? The one she called "Sea Child?" She recalled other instances, other encounters. Yes, this aquatic male definitely knew who Corysta was.

The scarred Phibian was the first to notice the women approaching. All of the creatures turned warily, blinking their slitted eyes. Three smaller Phibians retreated into the foaming water, where they hovered out of reach. The scarred one, though, held his ground.

Murbella regarded him carefully, trying to read his alien body language for some clue as to what he was thinking. Though shorter than the creature, she assumed a confident fighting posture.

For a long moment, the Phibian regarded her with his membranous eyes. Then he spoke in a throaty voice that sounded like a dripping rag drawn through a pipe. "Boss boss."

"What do you mean?"

"You. Boss boss."

Corysta interpreted. "He knows you are the boss of all the bosses."

"Yes. I am your boss now."

He bowed his head deferentially.

"I think you're a good deal smarter than you let on. Are you a good Phibian?"

"Not good. *Best.*"

Boldly, Murbella took a step closer. Other than what she knew from Corysta, she had no idea about the Phibians' social inclinations or taboos. "You and I are both leaders in our own way. And as one leader to another, I promise that we will no longer treat you the way the Honored Matres did. You have already seen the changes. We won't use the lash on you, or let you use it on anyone else. Work for all. Benefit for all."

"No more lash." He lifted his chin, proud and stern. "No more soostones for smugglers."

Murbella tried to process what he was implying. Was it a promise, or a threat? Surely, after a year the Phibians must have noticed a significant difference in their lives.

"Smugglers are always a problem," Corysta explained to her. "We can't stop them from taking soostones out in the open water."

The nostrils flared in Skira's beaklike nose. "We have long suspected the Phibians also traded with smugglers, stealing our soostone harvests and providing for themselves."

"Not your soostones," the Phibian said with a long bubbling rumble.

Murbella felt she was on the verge of an interesting breakthrough. "You promise not to deal with smugglers if we treat you fairly? Is that what you mean?"

Skira sounded mortally offended. "Phibians are slaves! Subhuman creatures. They do what they are created to do—"

Murbella regarded her with a murderous glare. "Provoke me if you dare. I am perfectly willing to kill another arrogant whore to make my point."

Skira met her eyes like a mouse facing a rattlesnake. At last she bowed, and then took a small step back. "Yes, Great Honored Matre. I did not mean to offend."

The Phibian seemed amused. "No more smugglers."

Corysta explained, "The smugglers have always been smart enough to leave us most of the haul. They were an irritation to the Honored Matres, maybe, but not enough of a thorn to require massive retaliation."

Skira grumbled, "We would have crushed them sooner or later."

"What could the smugglers pay you?" Murbella asked the creature, ignoring Skira. "What do Phibians want?"

"Smugglers bring spice. We give soostones."

So that was it! Though the Guild was desperate for melange, and Murbella still refused to provide them with anything more than a trickle for their bare necessities, smuggling groups and black-market traders had begun to disseminate their own hoarded spice.

From her singlesuit pocket, she produced a small cinnamon-colored tablet and handed it to the Phibian. "We have more melange than smugglers could ever bring to you."

With a perplexed expression, the creature held it in his webbed hand, and then sniffed cautiously. The thick-lipped smile returned. "Spice. Good." With a very serious expression, he stared at the tablet of melange in his hand, but did not attempt to swallow it.

"You will get along just fine with the Sisterhood. We think the same way." Murbella pointed at the tablet of melange. "You keep."

"Trade?"

She shook her head. "No. A gift, for you."

"He doesn't understand the concept of a gift. It's not part of their culture," Skira said. "Slaves are not accustomed to having any possessions." Murbella wondered if all Honored Matres were so blind and simplistic and full of preconceptions.

The Phibian leader said, "Smugglers taught us."

Either not understanding, or refusing the gift, he handed the tablet back to her—reverently, rather than spitefully—and waded into the water next to his companions. Soon his head disappeared beneath the waves, and the other three deep divers followed.

Skira sniffed. "If your Sisterhood has so much melange, we can pay Phibians with it to stay away from smugglers, and give us all the soostones."

"As soon as I return to Chapterhouse, I'll issue new orders. We will provide melange to the Phibians if they need it." Murbella looked at Corysta, wondering how long it had been since the exiled Sister had received a dose herself. Surely during the Honored Matre domination, the exiled Sisters had been cut off. They would have gone through terrible withdrawal. But then, in her Shared memories with Corysta, she recalled instances where the scarred Phibian—Sea Child—had delivered some of the melange obtained from smugglers, secreting it among the rocks where Corysta could find it. "And we will give spice to any others here who may need it as well."

Superstitions and nonsense from the past should not prevent us from making progress. If we hold ourselves back, we admit that our fears are more powerful than our abilities.

—THE FABRICATORS OF IX

W hen the Ixian Chief Fabricator sent his message to the Guild announcing success with the new navigation machines, a small delegation raced to Ix. The speed with which they arrived told Khrone everything he needed to know. The Guild Administrators were much more desperate than they let on.

He and his Face Dancers had drawn out the "invention phase" for eight years now, the shortest time he could justify for the reintroduction of such a drastically sophisticated new technology. He could not afford to raise too many questions from the Guild, or even the Ixians. The extraordinary new device could guide any ship safely and efficiently. No Navigator—and hence, no spice—was necessary.

Khrone would have them eating out of his hand.

Wearing a gray formal suit made of a plazsilk that had an oily sheen, Khrone stood quietly beside Chief Fabricator Shayama Sen. Though the Baron Harkonnen ghola and the one-year-old Paul Atreides needed constant tending in their isolation on Caladan, Khrone had decided to come to Ix to observe this interaction for himself.

Administrator Gorus entered the room accompanied by six other men. In addition to Guild functionaries, Khrone noted a representative of the independent Guild Bank and a master merchant from CHOAM. It seemed that the Guild Administrators had pointedly not brought a Navigator to these discussions. Instead, the delegation had left him in his spice-filled chamber high above and isolated in his orbiting ship. Oh, how they must be thirsting after the new technology!

This time they met in a small intimate chamber, not the large manufacturing bay with the clamor of industrial noises that had so dominated their first meeting. Sen called for refreshments, drawing out the moment. He seemed to enjoy the anticipation. "Gentlemen, commerce across the galaxy is about to change forever. What you desire is in your hands, thanks to Ixian innovation."

Gorus tried to conceal his eagerness with a skeptical expression. "Your claims are impressive and extravagant, Chief Fabricator."

"They are also true."

Khrone played his meek role, serving sweet confections and a robust drink that was (ironically, considering the nature of the meeting) heavily laced with melange. As Administrator Gorus politely consumed the proffered treats, he scanned the technical reports and testing results provided by Khrone's team. "These new Ixian navigation machines seem to be a thousand times more accurate than the previous ones we incorporated into some of our Guildships. Much better than anything used in the Scattering."

The Chief Fabricator took a long sip of his hot melange beverage. "Never underestimate Ixians, Guildsman. We notice you did not include a Navigator in these discussions."

Gorus put on a haughty air. "He was not necessary."

Khrone suppressed a smile. That statement was true on several levels.

"Humanity has been searching for an accurate navigational system for . . . for millennia! Think of how many ships were lost during the Famine Times," the Guild banker said, his face suddenly florid. "We expected you would take decades to achieve such a dramatic overhaul from first principles."

Sen beamed proudly at Khrone. Even the Chief Fabricator assumed that the recent breakthroughs were based on real Ixian knowledge and ingenuity, not brought in from the Outside Enemy.

The CHOAM master merchant scowled at the Guild banker. "This is nothing new. Obviously, Ixians must have been working on forbidden technology in secret all along."

"And much to our benefit, I might add," Gorus interrupted, cutting off any possible argument.

"We Ixians do not rest on our laurels." Shayama Sen then quoted one of the tenets of Ix, "'Those who do not actively pursue progress and innovation soon find themselves at the tail end of history.'"

Khrone interceded before foolish questions could be raised. "We prefer to call these new devices 'mathematical compilers,' to avoid inadvertent confusion with thinking machines of any kind. These compilers simply automate the processes that a Navigator or even a Mentat can do. We do not wish to raise the ugly specter that led to the Butlerian Jihad."

He listened to his own euphemisms and rationalizations, knowing that these men would do exactly what they wanted to do anyway, regardless of laws and moral restrictions. They were just imaginative— and greedy—enough to provide any necessary justifications, should questions come up.

Shayama Sen added with a stern edge to his voice, "If you gentlemen had any doubts, you would not be here. By pretending uneasiness and citing ancient prohibitions against thinking machines, are you trying to bully us into lowering our price? That will never work." He set his cup down, but continued smiling.

"In fact, it makes commercial sense for us to offer this technology more widely. We believe the New Sisterhood would be particularly eager to obtain navigation devices of their own to build an autonomous fleet. They deal with the Spacing Guild now because they have little choice. How much would they pay for their independence, I wonder?"

At this, Administrator Gorus, the Guild banker, and the CHOAM representative all cried foul, an overlapping litany of protests. They had suggested this line of development in the first place; they had been promised exclusivity; they had already agreed to pay an exorbitant amount.

Khrone intercepted the comments before they could turn into an outright argument. He did not wish to let his carefully laid plans be sidetracked. "The Chief Fabricator is simply offering an example to make certain you understand the value of our technological development. While you gentlemen believe you have some claims to originating this work, you must also realize we could take bids from elsewhere. There will be no raising, or lowering, of the agreed-upon price."

Sen nodded briskly. "All right, let's not waste time with such ploys. Our price may be high, but you will pay it. No more outrageous melange expenditures, no more dependence on capricious Navigators. You are visionary businessmen, and even a child can see the immense profits that will accrue to the Guild once your ships are fitted with our"—he paused to recall the term Khrone had suggested—"mathematical compilers." Then he turned to the CHOAM man, who had eaten all of his confections and finished his hot spice beverage. "I trust I do not need to explain this to a master merchant."

"CHOAM has to keep up trade even during wartime. Richese is reaping huge profits by building a vast military force for the New Sisterhood."

The Ixian Chief Fabricator gave an annoyed grunt at the reminder.

Administrator Gorus seemed very excited. "Previously, when we installed primitive navigation machines on Guildships, we still carried a Navigator aboard each vessel." He looked apologetically at the Chief Fabricator. "We did not entirely trust your earlier machines, you see, but back then we didn't have to. There were questions of reliability, a few too many missing ships . . . Now, however, with the New Sisterhood's stranglehold on supplies and the proven accuracy of your . . . compilers, I see no reason not to rely on your navigation machines."

"So long as they work as well as you've promised," the Guild banker said.

When it was obvious that everyone believed in the new mathematical compilers, Khrone planted his seed of discord. "You know, of course, that this change will make Navigators obsolete. They are not likely to be pleased."

Administrator Gorus shifted uncomfortably and glanced from the banker to his fellow Guildsmen. "Yes, we know. That is most unfortunate."

Our motivations are as important as our goals. Use this to under-
stand your enemy. With such knowledge, you can either defeat him
or, even better, manipulate him into becoming your ally.

—BASHAR MILES TEG,
Memoirs of a Battle Commander

The crisis among the Navigators was so severe that Edrik sought
an audience with the Oracle of Time herself.

Navigators used prescience to guide foldspace ships, not to observe
human events. The Administrator faction had duped them, bypassed
them. The esoteric Navigators had never considered the activities and
desires of people outside the Guild to be relevant. What folly! The
Spacing Guild had been caught completely off-guard by the loss of
spice and the intractability of the only remaining suppliers. A quarter
century had passed since the destruction of Rakis; to make matters
worse, the Honored Matres had foolishly exterminated every Tleilaxu
Master who knew how to produce melange from axlotl tanks.

Now, with so many groups desperate for spice, the Navigators had
been forced to the brink of a treacherous cliff. Perhaps the Oracle
would offer a solution that Edrik could not see. In their earlier
encounter, she had hinted there might be a solution to their dilemma.
He was certain, however, that it did not involve navigation machines.

Faced with such a difficult situation, Edrik commanded that his
tank be delivered to the giant ages-old enclosure that held the Oracle

of Time whenever she chose to manifest in this physical universe. Intimidated in her presence, Edrik had spent a great deal of time planning his argument and marshaling his thoughts, knowing all the while it might be a pointless exercise. With prescience far superior and more expansive than any Navigator's, the Oracle must already have foreseen this encounter and imagined every word Edrik would speak.

Humbled, he looked out through his curved tank at the Oracle's translucent structure. Long ago, arcane symbols had been etched into the walls—coordinates, hypnotic designs, ancient runes, mysterious markings that only the Oracle comprehended. Her enclosure reminded him of a miniature cathedral, and Edrik felt like her supplicant.

"Oracle of Time, we face our greatest emergency since the time of the Tyrant. Your Navigators are starving for spice, and our own Administrators plot against us." He shuddered with the strength of his anger. The foolish lesser Guildsmen believed they could solve the problem by creating better Ixian navigation machines! Inferior copies. The Guild needed *spice*, not artificial mathematical compilers. "I beseech you, show us our path to survival."

He sensed an enormous thunderstorm of thoughts, the incredibly complex preoccupation of the churning mind hidden within the swirling mists. When the Oracle answered, Edrik felt that she was granting him only the tiniest fraction of her attention while her brain was focused elsewhere on much larger issues.

"There is always an insatiable hunger for spice. It is a small problem."

"A small problem?" Edrik said, incredulous. All of his arguments were washed away. "Our stockpiles are nearly exhausted, and the New Sisterhood doles out only a tiny fraction of what we need. Navigators could become extinct. What could be a more vital problem?"

"Kralizec. I will call all my Navigators again when I require them."

"But how can we assist you if we have no melange? How can we survive?"

"You will find another way to obtain spice—this I have foreseen. A forgotten way. But you must discover it yourself."

The sudden silence in his mind told Edrik that the Oracle was finished with this conversation and had gone back to pondering her greater questions. He clung to her startling pronouncement: *Another source of spice!*

Rakis was destroyed, the New Sisterhood refused to release their stockpiles, and the Tleilaxu Masters were all dead. Where else could the Navigators search? Since the Oracle herself had spoken it, he was confident there was a solution. As he drifted, Edrik let his thoughts spin out. Could there be another planet with sandworms? Another natural source of spice?

What about a new—or rediscovered—means of manufacturing melange? What had been forgotten? Only the Tleilaxu had known how to produce spice artificially. Was there a way to rediscover that knowledge? Did someone else still know the technique? That information had long ago been buried by the clumsy Honored Matres. How could it be dredged up again?

The Masters had carried their secrets to the grave, but even death did not always erase knowledge. Elders of the Lost Tleilaxu, shadow-brothers of the once-great Masters, did not know how to create melange, but they did know how to grow gholas. And gholas could have their memories triggered!

Suddenly, Edrik knew the answer, or thought he did. If he resurrected one of the old Masters, then he could wrest that knowledge free. And the damnable Sisterhood would be left without their advantage once again.

*The unexplored vastness into which humans fled in the Scattering
was a hostile wilderness, filled with unexpected traps and dangerous beasts. Those who survived were hardened and changed in
ways that we cannot fully comprehend.*

—REVEREND MOTHER TAMALANE,
Chapterhouse Archives,
Projections and Analyses of the Scattering

Sheeana sat cross-legged on the hard floor of the arboretum while
the four Futars prowled around her. She used Bene Gesserit skills
to slow her heartbeat and respiration rate. After the one called Hrrm
watched her dance with the sandworms, the shared awe among the
beast-men had kept her safe among them. Although she controlled the
scents that came from her body, she did not avert her gaze.

Most of the time the Futars walked on two feet, but occasionally
they reverted to a four-pawed pacing. Restless, always restless.

Sheeana had not moved for several minutes. The Futars twitched
each time she blinked, and then they went back to their restless prowling. Hrrm came close to her and sniffed. She lifted her chin and sniffed
back.

Despite the potential violence in these creatures, she knew it was
important for her to be with them inside this large chamber. After continued study, Sheeana was convinced the Futars could reveal much
more, if only she could sift the information out of them.

In the deep unknowns of the Scattering, they had been bred by

"Handlers" specifically to hunt down Honored Matres. But who were the Handlers? Did they know of the Enemy? Maybe she could winnow out a vital key to the origin of the whores and the nature of the old man and woman Duncan said were pursuing them.

"More food," Hrrm said, pacing around close to her. His wiry body hair was rank, and his breath smelled like partially digested meat.

"You've already eaten well today. If you eat too much, you will grow fat. Then you will be slow on the hunt."

"Hungry," one of the other Futars said.

"You are always hungry. Food will come later." It was a biological impulse for them to want to eat constantly, and their Honored Matre captors had kept them on the verge of starvation. The Bene Gesserit, however, maintained a regular, healthy feeding schedule.

"Tell me about the Handlers." She had asked the question hundreds of times, trying to get a few extra words out of Hrrm, another kernel of information.

"Where Handlers?" the Futar asked, his interest suddenly piqued.

"They are not here, and I can't find them unless you help me."

"Futars and Handlers. Partners." Hrrm stretched his muscles, snuf-fling. The other creatures bristled and flexed their cablelike muscles, as if proud of their physical appearance.

Apparently when the Futars had a focus, it was difficult to get them to consider other matters. In any event, Sheeana had convinced Hrrm (and to a lesser extent the other three) that the Bene Gesserits were different from Honored Matres. Hrrm had entirely forgotten that he had murdered a proctor years ago. Though the Sisters were not the much-anticipated Handlers, the Futars had finally accepted that these women were not to be killed and eaten, like Honored Matres. At least Sheeana hoped so. Slowly, she uncrossed her legs and rose to her feet.

"Hungry," Hrrm said again. "Want food now."

"You'll get food. We never forget to feed you, do we?"

"Never forget," Hrrm confirmed.

"Where Handlers?" another Futar asked.

"Not here. Far away."

"Want Handlers."

"Soon. As soon as you help us find them."

She left the arboretum enclosure as the Futars bounded through the artificial trees, searching relentlessly for something they would never find on the *Ithaca*. She took special care to lock the chamber securely behind her.

It is often easier for us to destroy each other than it is to resolve our differences. Such is the cosmic joke of human nature!

—MOTHER COMMANDER MURBELLA,
Chapterhouse meeting notes

In order to receive their small but desperately needed rations of melange, the Guild regularly sent Heighliners to Chapterhouse. The ships carried supplies, recruits for the New Sisterhood, and surveillance information collected from far-flung scouts. Murbella kept a careful watch on the rebel Honored Matre strongholds, preparing for her next major offensive with the Valkyries.

Six hours before the regular Guildship was scheduled to arrive, a smaller vessel careened into the system. Immediately upon emerging from foldspace, the ship began to broadcast an emergency warning.

The small craft from the Scattering had an unusual oval design, Holtzman engines, and its own no-field that flickered in and out of phase. Spewing out high levels of radiation in its exhaust, the ship had probably been damaged during its headlong flight to Chapterhouse. It maneuvered erratically as it approached.

Upon being notified, Murbella raced to the Keep's communications center, afraid this might be another embattled Honored Matre ship from far outside the Old Empire. On the screen, the crackling image was so filled with static that she could barely make out the vague outline of a pilot. Only after the ship burned all its remaining fuel to achieve a barely stable orbit did the transmission resolve enough that Murbella could discern the face of a Priestess of the Cult of Sheeana, who had been dispatched by the Missionaria Protectiva to promote the wild new religion.

"Mother Commander, we bring dire news! An urgent warning."

Murbella could see figures with her in the oval ship's crowded cockpit, but the Sister had not used any code words to denote that she was being forced or held captive. Knowing the others were listening, but not knowing who they were, Murbella carefully selected her words after identifying the young woman. "Yes . . . Iriel. Where have you come from?"

"Gammu."

With every moment, the transmitted images became clearer. Murbella could see five people inside the vessel's piloting chamber. Many of them wore the traditional clothing of Gammu. The anxious passengers appeared to be bruised and battered; dried blood caked their cheeks and clothes. At least two of those aboard appeared to be either dead or unconscious.

"No choice . . . no chance. We had to take the risk."

Murbella snapped at the nearest woman in the communications center. "Send up a retrieval ship. Get those people down here safely—now!"

"Not much time," the priestess transmitted; her whole body shook with utter weariness. "Need to warn you. We escaped from Gammu before the Heighliner departed, but the whores nearly killed us. They know what we discovered. When is the Guildship coming?"

"We still have several hours," Murbella said, trying to sound reassuring.

"It may be sooner, Mother Commander. They *know*."

"What do they know? What have you discovered?"

"Obliterators. The Honored Matres on Gammu still have four Obliterators. They received orders from their Matre Superior Hellica on Tleilax. They are coming here aboard the Guildship. They mean to destroy Chapterhouse."

THOUGH NOT SEVERELY injured, Priestess Iriel was exhausted and nearly starved. She had used all of her bodily reserves to help the small ship escape. Three of her six companions died before they could receive medical attention; the others were taken to the Keep's infirmary.

Before resting, Iriel insisted on finishing the report to her Mother Commander, even though she could barely remain upright. Murbella summoned potent melange drinks, and the stimulant temporarily revived the battered young woman.

Iriel told of her ordeal on Gammu. She had been assigned to that planet for several years now, given orders to prepare the populace for the coming conflict. By preaching the message of Sheeana and the need to stand against the Outside Enemy, Iriel had cultivated whole-hearted fanatical followers. The more concerned the people of Gammu grew about the danger from the outside, the more they wanted to hear Iriel's message of hope and urgency.

But the rebel Honored Matres also had one of their strongest enclaves there. As the cult spread, the entrenched whores had struck, hunting down Sheeana's followers. Perversely, the persecution made the cultists more resolute and determined. When Iriel had asked for their help in stealing this vital information and escaping from Gammu, she'd had no trouble finding volunteers. Fifteen of her brave followers had died before the warning ship could take off.

"You have done what was required of you, Iriel. You delivered your warning in time. Now go recover." Murbella held the Ridulian crystal sheets that the priestess had stolen from the Honored Matres.

Just then the Heighliner arrived—two hours ahead of schedule.

Iriel glanced knowingly at her Mother Commander. "Our work is only just beginning."

Murbella had hoped for more time, but had not counted on it. Only an hour earlier, suspensor-propelled launchers had placed hundreds of new-design Richesian space mines in orbit. Concealed by individual no-fields, they drifted in the orbital zones where Heighliners traditionally parked.

Her battle orders had already been issued, and as soon as the giant Guildship appeared, the members of the New Sisterhood went to work.

Her daughter Janess would lead one of the primary strike teams, but the Mother Commander intended to be in the fight right beside her. She would never let herself become a mere bureaucrat.

According to the priestess, the Honored Matres had bribed this Heighliner crew to transport them to Chapterhouse, which directly violated Spacing Guild prohibitions. Another example of how the Guild looked sideways whenever it was convenient for them. Was the Navigator even aware of the Obliterators on board the Honored Matre frigate? Even if the Guild wanted to punish the New Sisterhood for withholding melange, Murbella didn't think they were foolish enough to allow Chapterhouse to become a charred ball. This was their only source of spice, their last chance.

Murbella decided that one bribe deserved another, if only to show the Guild that Honored Matres could never hope to compete financially against the Sisterhood. With her soostones, her spice stockpiles, and the sandworms in the desert belt, Murbella could outbid anyone— and garnish it with a significant threat.

Before the great ship's cargo doors could open to disgorge any CHOAM vessels or hidden Honored Matre ships, Murbella transmitted an insistent call. She wore an implacable expression. "Attention, Guild Heighliner. Your sensors will show that I have just placed a swarm of Richesian mines around your vessel." She gave a signal, and the no-fields around the mines dropped away. Hundreds of the glittering, mobile explosives winked into view like diamond chips in space. "If you open your doors or release any ships, I will direct those mines to strike your hull and turn you into space dust."

The Navigator attempted to protest. Guild Administrators came on the commline, crying foul. But Murbella did not reply. She calmly transmitted copies of the Ridulian crystal sheets Iriel had brought and allowed two minutes of silence for them to absorb the information.

Then she said, "As you can see, we are perfectly justified in destroying your Heighliner, both to prevent the release of the Obliterators, and to impose a fitting punishment on the Guild. Our Richesian explosives could do the job without my having to risk the life of a single Sister."

"I assure you, Mother Commander, we have no knowledge of such heinous weapons aboard—"

"Even the most amateur Truthsayer could detect your lies, Guildsman." She cut off his protests, gave him a moment to regroup and become rational again, then continued in a more reasonable tone. "Another alternative—one which I prefer, because it would not destroy all those innocent passengers you carry—is for you to welcome us aboard and let us capture the Honored Matres and their Obliterators. In fact"—she ran a finger along her lips—"I will even be generous. Provided you cooperate without further delay, and don't insult our intelligence by protesting your innocence, we will grant you two full measures of spice—*after* our mission is successfully completed."

The Navigator hesitated for several moments, then accepted. "We will identify which small frigates in the hold came from Gammu. Presumably they carry Honored Matres and Obliterators. You will need to deal with those women yourselves."

Murbella flashed a predatory smile. "I wouldn't have it any other way."

WEARY AND SORE but exhilarated, the Mother Commander stood proudly beside her daughter in the blood-spattered hold of one of the unmarked Honored Matre ships. Eleven of the whores lay on the deck, their leotards torn, their bodies snapped. Murbella had not expected any of the Honored Matres to let themselves be captured alive. Six of her own Sisters had also died in the hand-to-hand combat.

One of the slain Bene Gesserits was, sadly, the brave priestess Iriel, who had begged to join in the fight despite her weariness. Driven by a fire of vengeance, she had killed two of the whores herself before a thrown knife caught her between the shoulder blades. As Iriel died, Murbella had Shared with her, in order to learn all that the woman knew about Gammu and the infestation of the whores there.

The threat was worse than Murbella had imagined. She would have to deal with it immediately.

Teams of male workers used suspensor pallets to remove the

ominous-looking spiked Obliterators, two from the hatches below each of the Honored Matre frigates. The angry rebels had no compunctions about destroying a whole planet and its inhabitants, just to decapitate the New Sisterhood. They would have to be punished.

"We need to study these weapons," Murbella said, excited by the prospect of duplicating them. "We must reproduce the technology. We will need thousands of them once the Enemy arrives."

Janess looked grimly at the dead body of the priestess on the floor and at the slaughtered whores strewn like dolls in the ship's corridors. Simmering anger colored her cheeks. "Perhaps we should use one of the Obliterators against Gammu and wipe out those women once and for all."

Murbella smiled with anticipation. "Oh, we will indeed move on Gammu next, but it will be a much more personal attack."

We never see the jaws of the hunter closing around us until the fangs draw blood.

—DUNCAN IDAHO,
A Thousand Lives

D uncan tapped the touchpads of the instrument console to alter course slightly as the *Ithaca* moved through empty space. Without charts or records, he had no way of knowing if any humans had gone this far in the Scattering. It made no difference. For fourteen years they had been flying blind, going nowhere. To reduce the risk of a navigational disaster, Duncan only rarely activated the Holtzman engines.

At least he had kept them safe. So far. Some of the passengers— especially Garimi and her faction, as well as the Rabbi's people—were growing increasingly restless. By now, dozens of children had been born, and were being raised by Bene Gesserit proctors in isolated sections of the *Ithaca*. They all wanted a home.

"We can't keep running forever!" Garimi had said during one of their recent all-hands meetings.

Yes we can. We may have to. The giant self-contained ship needed refueling only once or twice a century, since it was able to gather most of what it needed from the rarified sea of molecules scattered throughout space.

The no-ship had been cruising for years without making another leap through foldspace. Duncan had taken them farther than the imaginations of those who charted space. Not only had he eluded the Enemy, he had slipped away from the Oracle of Time, never knowing whom to trust.

In all that time, he had seen no sign of the glittering net, but it made him uneasy to remain in one area for long. *Why do the old man and woman want us so badly? Is it me they're after? Is it the ship? Or is it someone else aboard?*

As Duncan waited, letting his thoughts drift along with the vessel itself, he felt the overlappings of his own lifetimes, *so many lifetimes*. The mergings of flesh and consciousness, the flow of experience and imagination, the great teachings and the epic events he had experienced. He sifted through countless lifetimes, all the way back to his original boyhood on Giedi Prime under Harkonnen tyranny, and later on Caladan as the loyal weapons master of House Atreides. He had given his first life to save Paul Atreides and Lady Jessica. Then the Tleilaxu had restored him as a ghola called Hayt, and afterward many Duncan Idaho incarnations had served the capricious God Emperor. So much pain, so much exhilaration.

He, Duncan Idaho, had been present at many critical moments in human history, from the fall of the Old Empire and the rise of Muad'Dib, through the long rule and death of the God Emperor . . . and beyond. Through it all, history had been distilling events, processing and sifting them through the Duncans, renewing them.

Long ago, he had loved the beautiful, dark-haired Alia, even with all her strangeness. Centuries later, he had loved Siona deeply, though it was obvious the God Emperor had thrown them together intentionally. In all of his ghola lifetimes he had loved many beautiful, exotic women.

Why, then, was Murbella so difficult to get over? He could not break the debilitating bond she had with him.

Duncan had slept little in the past week because whenever he went to his cot and clasped his pillow, he could only think of Murbella, sensing the emptiness where her body *wasn't*. So many years—why wouldn't the ache and addictive longing fade?

Restless and wanting to put even more distance between himself and Murbella's siren call, he erased the current navigation coordinates, used his bold—or reckless—intuition, and made a random foldspace jump.

When they arrived at a new and uncharted portion of space, Duncan let his mind drift in a fugue state, deeper than a Mentat's trance. Though he did not admit it to himself, he was looking for any hint of Murbella's presence, though she could not possibly be here.

Obsession.

Duncan could not concentrate, and his woolgathering left them vulnerable to the gossamer yet deadly net that began to coalesce unnoticed around the no-ship.

TEG ARRIVED ON the navigation bridge, saw Duncan at the controls, and noted that the other man seemed consumed by his thoughts, as he often was, especially of late.

His glance went to the control modules, the viewscreen, the path the no-ship had taken along its projected course. Teg studied the patterns on the console, then the patterns in the emptiness. Even without the no-ship's sensors and viewscreens, he could grasp the sheer volume of empty space around them. A new void, a different starless region from where they had been.

Duncan had made a reckless jump through foldspace. But the nature of randomness was such that any new location was just as likely to be closer to the Enemy than farther away.

Something troubled him, something he could not ignore. His Atreides-based abilities allowed him to focus on those anomalies and discern what was not there. Duncan wasn't the only one who could see strange things.

"Where are we?"

Duncan answered with a distant riddle. "Who knows where we are?" He snapped out of his preoccupied trance, then gasped. "Miles! The net—it's closing in, tightening like a noose!"

Duncan had thrown the ship not into a safe wasteland, but directly into the vicinity of the Enemy. Like hungry spiders reacting to unexpected vibrations in their web, the old man and woman were closing in.

Already on edge from his premonition, Teg reacted with a burst of speed, without thinking. His body went into overdrive, his reflexes burning bright, his actions accelerating to indefinable speeds. Moving with a metabolism no human body was meant to withstand, he seized command of the navigation controls. His hands worked in a blur. His mind flashed from system to system, reactivating the Holtzman engines in the middle of their recharge. Immeasurably swift and alert, Teg became part of the ship—and guided them into a sudden and alarming foldspace jump.

He could feel the gossamer, *sentient* strands make one last futile grasp, but Teg tore the ship free, damaging the net as he lurched the huge vessel across a wrinkle in space, jumping to another place, and then another, wrenching the craft from the searchers' trap. Behind him he sensed pain, severe damage to the net and its casters, and then outrage at losing their prey again.

Teg streaked across the bridge, making adjustments, sending commands, moving so swiftly that no one—not even Duncan—would know he was covering for the other man's mistake. Finally, he slowed back to real time, exhausted, drained, and famished.

Astonished by what Teg had done in less than a second, Duncan shook his head to clear away the tar-pit memories of Murbella. "What did you just do, Miles?"

Slumped at a secondary console, the Bashar gave Duncan a mysterious smile. "Only what was necessary. We're out of danger."

A mere player should never assume he can influence the rules of a game.

—BASHAR MILES TEG,
strategy lectures

S nip!
     The blades of the hedge trimmer clacked together, severing random branches to alter the shape of the greenery. "You see how life persists in straying from its well-defined boundaries?" Annoyed, the old man moved methodically along the high shrub at the edge of the lawn, pruning the outlying stems and leaves, anything that detracted from geometrical perfection. "Unruly hedges are so unsettling."

With an insistent clicking of the blades, he attacked the tall shrubs. In the end, the planes were perfectly flat and smooth, according to his specifications.

Wearing an amused expression, the old woman sat back in her canvas lounge chair. She lifted a glass of fresh lemonade. "What I see is someone who persists in imposing order rather than accepting reality. Randomness has value, too."

Taking another sip, she thought about mentally activating a set of sprinklers to drench the old man, strictly as a demonstration of unpredictability. But that sort of prank, while amusing, would only provoke unpleasantness. Instead, she entertained herself by watching her companion's unnecessary work.

"Rather than drive yourself mad with adherence to a set of rules, why not change the rules? You have the power to do so."

He glared at her. "You suggest I am mad?"

"Merely a figure of speech. You have long since recovered from any sort of damage."

"You provoke me, Marty." A brief flicker of danger passed as the old man, with renewed vigor, returned his attention to the garden trimmers. He attacked the hedges again, shaping and molding, not satisfied until every leaf was in its desired place.

The old woman set her glass down and went to the flower beds where a profusion of tulips and irises added splashes of color. "I prefer to be surprised—to savor the unexpected. It makes life interesting." Frowning, she bent over to inspect a bristling weed that thrived among her plants. "There are limits, however." With a vicious yank, she uprooted the unwanted plant.

"You seem quite forgiving, considering that we still do not have the no-ship under our control. It angers me more each time they get away! Kralizec is upon us."

"That last time was very close." Smiling, the old woman moved through her flower garden. Behind her, the wilting blossoms suddenly brightened, infused with new color. The sky was a perfect blue.

"You aren't much concerned about the damage they just caused us. I expended a great deal of effort to create and cast the latest tachyon net. Lovely tendrils, far-reaching . . ." He twisted his lips into a scowl. "And now everything is torn, tangled, and frayed."

"Oh, you can re-create it with a thought." The woman waved a tanned hand. "You're just annoyed because something didn't happen the way you expected it to. Have you considered that the no-ship's recent escape provides evidence of the prophetic projection? It must mean that the one you expect—whom the humans call the Kwisatz Haderach—is truly aboard. How else could they have slipped away? Perhaps that is proof of the projection?"

"We always knew he was aboard. That is why we must have the no-ship."

The old woman laughed. "We *predict* he is aboard, Daniel. There is a difference. Centuries and centuries of mathematical projections convinced us that the necessary one would be there."

The old man jammed his sharp hedge trimmers point first into the grass, impaling the lawn as if it were an enemy.

The mathematical projection had been so sophisticated and complex that it was tantamount to a prophecy. The two knew full well that they required the Kwisatz Haderach to win the impending typhoon struggle. Previously, they would have considered such a prophesy no more than a superstitious legend spawned by frightened people cowering from the dark. But after the impossibly detailed analytical projections, along with millennia of eerily clever human prophecies, the old couple knew that their victory required possession of the wild card, the human loose cannon.

"Long ago, others learned the folly of trying to control a Kwisatz Haderach." The old woman stood up from her weeding. She put a hand to the small of her back as if she had a muscle ache, though it was only an affectation. "He nearly destroyed them, and they spent fifteen hundred years bemoaning what happened."

"They were weak." The old man took a half-full glass of lemonade from where he had set it on an ornate lawn table and drank it down in a single gulp.

She went to his side and looked through a razor-edged gap in the hedge toward the extravagant and complex towers and interlinked buildings in the faraway city that surrounded their perfect sanctuary. She touched his elbow. "If you promise not to pout, I can help you repair the net. You really must accept the fact that plans can be disrupted quite easily."

"Then we must make better plans."

Nonetheless he joined her in concentration, and they began to weave the gossamer strands through the fabric of the universe once more, reconstructing their tachyon net and sending it out at great speed, covering impossible distances in the blink of an eye.

"We will keep trying to catch that ship," the old woman said, "but we might be better off focusing our efforts on the alternative plan that Khrone has in mind. Thanks to what was found on Caladan, we do have another option, a second chance to assure our victory. We should pursue both alternatives. We know that Paul Atreides was a Kwisatz Haderach, and a ghola of the boy has already been born, thanks to Khrone's foresight—"

"Accidental foresight, I am sure."

"Nevertheless, he also has the Baron Harkonnen, who will be a perfect fulcrum with which to turn the new Paul to our purposes. Therefore, even if we do not capture the no-ship, we are guaranteed to have a Kwisatz Haderach in our possession. We win, either way. I will make certain Khrone does not fail us. I have sent special watchers."

The old man was powerful and rigid, but at times naïve. He did not suspect treachery enough. The old woman knew she needed to keep a better watch on their minions dispersed throughout the Old Empire. Sometimes the Face Dancers were too full of themselves.

She was happy to let each participant play his role, whether it be the old man, the Face Dancers, the passengers on the no-ship, or the vast herds of victims standing in the way in the Old Empire.

It amused her for now, but everything was changeable. That was the way of the universe.

Plans within plans within plans—like an infinite array of nested reflections cast by angled mirrors. It takes a superior mind to see all of the causes and effects.

—KHRONE,
message to the Face Dancer myriad

O n Caladan, the strange delegation from far, far outside arrived to see Khrone. They did not need to identify themselves when they demanded to learn of his progress with the Baron child and the Atreides ghola they called "Paolo." Khrone already had what the old man and woman needed, a little boy with all the necessary potential in his gene markers. A Kwisatz Haderach.

Instead of rewarding the Face Dancer, though, the distant puppet masters breathed down his neck, watching everything he did. They wanted complete control, and Khrone resented it. The Face Dancer myriad had suffered from too much domination by fools during the millennia of their existence.

Nevertheless, he bided his time. He could deal with these misfit spies.

According to the Guild manifest and the expertly doctored identi-fication glyphs they carried, the bizarrely augmented humans claimed to come from Ix. It was an acceptable cover story that would explain their odd appearance to any human who happened to see them. But Khrone knew that this technology sprang from an entirely different seed, and these ambassadors came from a much greater distance, where the breakwater fringes of the human Scattering had crashed against the bulwarks of the Enemy.

In the past, the meddling masters had pestered him via their interconnected net, but apparently since the net had recently sustained some damage, the two faraway watchers preferred a less vulnerable communication method. The old man and woman had sent these . . . monstrosities. He wondered if the supposed masters actually meant to intimidate him—*him!* The Face Dancer leader smiled at the very idea as he went to meet the delegation.

In the high-ceilinged foyer of the restored Castle Caladan, Khrone selected a guise that looked like an old archival painting of Duke Leto Atreides. He dressed in crisp gray clothes of an antique style, checked his appearance in a tall goldplaz-framed mirror, then clasped his hands behind his back as he descended the grand waterfall of stairs to the echoing hall. Stopping on the bottom step, he put on a bland smile, and waited coolly to receive the six men.

The scarred, pale-skinned representatives were clearly flustered by the physical effort of trudging up the steep walkway from the spaceport. Khrone had no incentive to make the journey easier for them, however. He had not asked for their presence, and did not intend to make them feel welcome. If the tachyon net was damaged, maybe the old man and woman would not transmit their waves of agony to goad him anymore. And then the Face Dancers could at last act with impunity.

Or maybe not. Uncertain, Khrone decided to maintain his docile charade just a while longer.

After the strange-looking ambassadors arranged themselves in a clump, Khrone looked down at them from the steps on which he stood. "Inform your superiors that you arrived safely." He unclasped his hands, brought them to the front, and cracked his knuckles. "And please inform them that the damage to your bodies was no fault of mine."

The men looked confused. "Damage?" The hairless men had pale skin with an oily appearance. Various devices were implanted in their skulls and chests: primitive electronic gauges, tubing, augmented memory chips, indicator lights. Raw red sores of unhealed wounds surrounded the implants. Everything had such a horrific, retrograde feel that Khrone had to wonder if this was a subtle and incomprehensible joke played by the old woman. *She* had a far quirkier sense of humor than her aged companion. "Damage? We were designed this way."

"Hmm. Interesting. My sympathies."

The mechanical additions were so primitive that they looked like a child's botched experiment. *Yes, Khrone thought, this has to be a joke. The old woman must be truly bored.*

"We have come to observe and record." The foremost man stepped away from the cluster. Dark fluid circulated through tubes in the thing's throat, extending to a pump behind his shoulders. His eyes were a deep metallic blue, showing no whites whatsoever. Another joke, suggesting that he was addicted to melange?

"They must be frustrated to have lost the no-ship. Again." Khrone gestured for the representatives to enter the castle's great hall. "I certainly hope our masters do not take it out on me. We Face Dancers are doing an exceptional job, as instructed."

"Face Dancers should have a greater sense of humility," said another of the augmented delegates.

Khrone raised his eyebrows. He wondered if his expression matched one the ancient Duke Leto might have made. "Am I remiss as a host? Come, would you care for refreshments? A feast?" He controlled his smile. "Or perhaps some much needed maintenance?"

"We prefer to spend our time collecting and analyzing data so that we can return with a full report."

"By all means, allow me to facilitate your departure as soon as possible." Khrone led the ambassadors to the castle's laboratory levels. "Fortunately, despite the escaped no-ship and the damaged net, everything else is going extremely well. Here in the Old Empire, my Face Dancers are undermining the foundations of all human civilization. We have infiltrated every major power group and have begun to turn them against each other."

"We require proof of this." A strange smell wafted from the first representative's body—caustic chemicals, halitosis, and a hint of rot.

"Then open your eyes!" Khrone paused in mid-step, calmed his voice, and continued in a more relaxed tone. "I invite you to travel among the worlds of the Old Empire. Your appearance may be alarming to most people, but enough anomalies have crawled back out of the Scattering that no one will question you too closely. I can provide a list of key planets and point out what you should look for. They will all be ready to fall like a house of cards as soon as the outside military forces arrive. Have our masters launched the battle fleet yet, or will they wait until they have the Kwisatz Haderach in hand?"

"That is not for us to say," three representatives said in unison, their augmented minds linked, their voices overlapping in an eerie echo.

"Then you make it difficult for me to conclude my activities. Why should our masters withhold vital information from me?"

"Perhaps they do not trust you," said another of the hodgepodge representatives. "Your progress has been unimpressive so far."

"Unimpressive?" Khrone snorted. "I have the Baron Harkonnen ghola, and I have the Paul Atreides ghola. It is guaranteed."

At the entrance to the thick-walled laboratory chambers, Khrone unsealed and hauled open a heavy door. Inside, a somewhat plump ten-year-old jerked to his feet, looking around warily with piggish eyes, as if he'd been caught doing something he shouldn't. Recovering quickly, the adolescent snickered at them, captivated by the horrifically mangled observers.

Khrone did not speak a word to the ghola, but turned back to the six representatives. "You see, the next phase of our plan is imminent. I expect to restore this Baron's memories soon."

"You can try to do it," the youth spat at him, "but you haven't yet convinced me that it's to *my* benefit. Why won't you let me play with little Paolo? I know you're keeping him here on Caladan."

"Exactly why do we need the Baron Harkonnen?" asked one of the hideous observers, ignoring the boy. "Our masters are interested only in the Kwisatz Haderach."

"The Baron will help us facilitate this. He will be like a wrecking bar to the Paolo ghola. After he becomes himself again, our Baron will be a valuable tool to unlock the powers of the superhuman. Historically, the problem with a Kwisatz Haderach is one of control. Once he helps me raise Paolo properly, I am confident the Baron can assure our hold on him."

The young man grinned at the newcomers. "You certainly are ugly. What happens if you pull out those tubes?"

"He does not seem cooperative," observed one of the spies.

"He will learn better. Reawakening a ghola's memories is a very painful process," Khrone said, still ignoring the young Harkonnen. "I greatly look forward to the task."

The Baron ghola let out an eager laugh that sounded like twisting metal. "I can't wait for you to *try*."

Khrone paused at the door, reminding himself to keep all security systems in place, especially with the mercurial Baron, who was quite prone to mischief. Khrone led the delegation of nightmarish humans into another room and carefully locked the chamber behind him. He did not want Vladimir Harkonnen to run loose.

"Our Atreides ghola is progressing nicely."

Before entering the castle's main chamber, Khrone turned a cool stare toward the hideous patchwork people. "Our victory is foreordained. Soon I will go to Ix to complete another step in the plan." Khrone meant victory for the *Face Dancers*, but the ambassadors would interpret it as they wished. "The rest is just a formality."

Reputation can be a beautiful weapon. It often spills less blood.

—BASHAR MILES TEG,
first incarnation

Foremost among the Mother Commander's weapons were her flesh-and-blood fighters. The rebel Honored Matres on Gammu wouldn't have a chance against the Valkyries. They had made a serious mistake in attempting to strike Chapterhouse with their Obliterators.

After their attack failed, the dissidents on Gammu had expected Murbella to overreact and retaliate instantly. But she had exercised the meticulous care and patience she'd acquired from her Bene Gesserit training. Now, striking back after a month's delay, she knew that every aspect of the plan was perfectly arranged.

Before setting off for Gammu, Murbella reviewed and revised her options based on the latest intelligence reports, as well as the information she had gleaned from Sharing with Priestess Iriel before she died. It was still unclear whether or not the renegade whores would make a suicidal stand on Gammu, triggering any last Obliterators they possessed, rather than let the world fall to the New Sisterhood. This would be Murbella's most critical battle to date, the toughest enclave of rebels.

Alone with the responsibilities of supreme command, she stood high atop the western rampart of Chapterhouse Keep. The attack itself, and victory, would occur swiftly. More than just excising the festering sore of rebel Honored Matres, the New Sisterhood needed the Gammu military-industrial complex for further defenses against the oncoming Enemy.

Murbella had already sent in operatives to soften the resistance: secret assassins, adept disseminators of propaganda, and members of the Missionaria Protectiva to rally the ever-growing religious groups against "the whores who killed the blessed Sheeana on Rakis." It was exactly what Duncan Idaho would have done.

The Honored Matres on Gammu were led by a charismatic and bitter woman named Niyela, who boldly claimed to trace her ancestry back to House Harkonnen—an obvious lie, since Honored Matres were unable to traverse the webs of Other Memory and could not remember their predecessors. Niyela had made her claim only after spending time digging through old records from the days when Gammu was a grimy industrial planet called Giedi Prime. Even after so long, the local population held a visceral hatred for the Harkonnens. Niyela apparently used that to her advantage.

The Honored Matres had set up extensive defenses on Gammu, including sophisticated scanners to detect and destroy incoming aircraft and missiles, specifically tailored to foil the New Sisterhood's traditional mode of attack. For the time being, small gaps remained in their coverage, especially in the least populated regions of the planet.

Janess assured the Mother Commander she could bring their forces in through one of the gaps and mount an overwhelming surprise attack. For the first time, her fighting women would rely primarily on their Swordmaster skills.

After gathering all their ships and summoning Guild transport, the Valkyries launched.

FROM THE NIGHT side of Gammu, scores of troop transports disembarked from an orbiting no-ship and headed down toward a region of broad, frigid plains. Flying only meters above the icy ground,

Murbella's ship raced overland toward the capital city of Ysai. Behind them, a formation of small troop shuttles cruised along like a school of hungry piranhas. Under her direction, the stealth shuttles paused just long enough to release their swarms of female commandos into the city, and then streaked off without firing a shot, triggering no alarms.

Just shy of dawn, Murbella and thousands of her black-uniformed Sisters filtered into Ysai to engage the defenders from the inside out, attacking where they were least expected. Although the entrenched whores had anticipated a large-scale lightning assault with attack 'thopters and heavy weaponry from above, the Sisterhood's commandos fought like scorpions from the shadows, striking, stinging, killing. The hand-to-hand combat made famous by the ancient Swordmasters of Ginaz required no technology more sophisticated than a sharp blade.

The Mother Commander chose her own target after reviewing the personal habits of Honored Matre Niyela. Accompanied by a small guard of fighters, Murbella ran directly to Niyela's ostentatious apartment near the central Guild Bank buildings in Ysai. The Valkyries in their combat singlesuits seemed to be cloaked in black oil. Half of the assassination operations were over before the whores managed to sound the first alarms.

Brightly clothed Honored Matres guarded the entrance to Niyela's dwelling, but Murbella and her companions struck in force, firing silent projectiles that hit their marks. Murbella bounded up an interior stairway, followed by Janess and her most trusted fighters. On the second level, a tall, athletic woman emerged from shadows in the hall. Dressed in a purple leotard and a cape adorned with chains and sharp crystal shards, she moved with the grace of a predatory feline.

Murbella recognized Niyela from Priestess Iriel's vivid memories. "Strange, you don't look at all like Baron Harkonnen," she said. "Perhaps some of his most prominent features did not breed true. Maybe that's a good thing."

As if springing an ambush, fully fifty Honored Matres emerged from doorways to take up protective positions around Niyela, arrogantly assuming the smaller assault squad would buckle and retreat upon seeing them. Like a deadly dance, the well-trained Valkyries paired off against them, flashing blades in their hands and sharp spines in their combat suits.

Murbella had eyes only for Niyela. The two leaders faced off, circling. The other women seemed to expect a "softened" Mother Commander to cringe at the prospect of combat.

The Honored Matre leader suddenly kicked out with a callused and deadly foot, but Murbella moved faster and eluded the blow. In a blur of motion, she counterattacked from one side with her fists and elbows, backing her adversary away. Then Murbella laughed, which unnerved her opponent.

In an unrestrained response, the Honored Matre threw herself at Murbella, fingers outstretched like knives, but Murbella thrust up with her left elbow, catching Niyela with the armored spine protruding from her combat suit. The slice shed blood down Niyela's arm. Murbella landed a solid kick in the other woman's solar plexus, driving her back into the wall.

Bumping into the stone barrier, Niyela slumped, as if beaten. She sprang to one side and darted back, but Murbella was ready for her, countering every move, driving Niyela backward until she had nowhere left to go. Even her Honored Matre followers could not resist the dizzyingly swift fighting techniques that the Mother Commander had drilled into her soldiers. All fifty of the guards were dead, leaving their leader alone and defeated.

"Kill me." Niyela spat the words.

"I'll do worse." Murbella smiled. "I will take you to Chapterhouse as my prisoner."

THE FOLLOWING DAY, the victorious Mother Commander marched through the streets of Ysai and mingled with curious crowds. The Cult of Sheeana had taken firm root here, and the Gammu natives saw their liberation as a miracle, interpreting the army of Sisters as soldiers fighting for their beloved martyr.

Noting various clear behavioral markers, Murbella suspected that some women in the crowd were actually Honored Matres who had changed their distinctive clothes. Were they cowards, or the seeds of a fifth column who would continue to resist on Gammu? Even with the signs of victory around her, Murbella knew that the fighting and consolidation would continue for some time, if not in Ysai itself then in the outlying cities. She would have to assign teams to root out any remaining nests of rebels.

She was not the only one to notice the lurking Honored Matres. Her agents surged forward, making arrests, thinning the crowd. Anyone captured would be given the opportunity to convert. Niyela herself would begin enforced training back on Chapterhouse. Those who didn't cooperate would be put to death.

Murbella's triumphant forces took more than eight thousand Honored Matres back to Chapterhouse, and more would follow after the mop-up operations were completed under the direction of Janess. The conversion process would be difficult, monitored closely by troops of Truthsayers and now-loyal Honored Matres—but no more difficult than the original forced unification. The Mother Commander could not afford to discard so many potential fighters, despite the risk.

Thus the New Sisterhood grew even stronger, with more and more numbers added to their forces.

SIXTEEN YEARS AFTER

ESCAPE FROM CHAPTERHOUSE

*Is Love born to us, as natural a part of our humanity as breathing
and sleeping? Or is Love something we must create within ourselves?*

       —MOTHER SUPERIOR DARWI ODRADE,
       private Bene Gesserit records (censored)

Two more years passed aboard the no-ship. Paul Atreides, his body
now ten years old, his mind stuffed full of all the external memories the library archives could provide and the histories of what he was
supposed to be, walked with the girl Chani.

She was rail-thin and petite, two years his junior. Though she had
grown up far from the arid wastelands of Arrakis, her body's metabolism, genetically adapted from her Fremen heritage, still did not squan-
der water. Chani wore her dark red hair pulled back in a braid. Her
brown skin was smooth and her mouth quick to flash a smile, especially
when she was with Paul.

Her eyes were a natural sepia, not the blue-within-blue eyes of
spice addiction, which Paul had seen in every historical image of an
older Chani, the beloved concubine of Muad'Dib and mother of his
twin children.

As they descended from one deck to another, making their way to
the aft engine section of the great no-ship, Paul let his hand slip into
hers. Though they were still just children, it seemed a comfortable
thing to do, and she did not pull away. All their lives they had played

together, explored together, and never questioned that they were supposed to be partners, just like in the old stories.

"Why do you find the engines so fascinating, Usul?" she said, calling him by the Fremen name that she had learned from her own diaries and journal recordings in the ship's archives.

In ancient, preserved poetry, the first Paul Muad'Dib had described Chani's voice as "the perfectly beautiful tones of fresh water chuckling over rocks." Listening to her now, the new Paul could see how he had once come to that conclusion.

"The Holtzman engines are so strange and powerful, able to take us anywhere we can imagine going." He reached out to tap her small, pointed chin with his fingertip, then said in a conspiratorial whisper, "Or maybe the real reason is because nobody watches us in the engine rooms."

Chani's brow furrowed. "On a ship this size, there are plenty of places for us to be alone."

Paul shrugged, smiling. "I didn't say it was a very good reason. I just wanted to go there."

They entered the giant engineering bay, where in normal times only certified Guildsmen could go. Under the present circumstances, Duncan Idaho, Miles Teg, and some Reverend Mothers knew enough about these foldspace engines to keep them functioning. Fortunately, no-ships were so exquisitely and sturdily built that little went seriously wrong, even after so many years without standard upkeep. The *Ithaca*'s major operating systems and self-repair mechanisms were sufficient to perform regular maintenance. The more important the component, the more redundancy was designed into it.

Nevertheless, both Teg and Duncan, using their Mentat abilities, had set about studying and memorizing all known specifications of the immense vessel to prepare themselves for any crisis that might occur. Paul supposed Thufir Hawat would also contribute his wisdom, once he grew up and became a Mentat again.

Now the boy and girl stood surrounded by throbbing machinery. Although the no-field projectors were located in different parts of the ship, with repeaters and reinforcing stations mounted throughout the hull, these giant engines were similar to the foldspace designs that had been used back in the time of Muad'Dib, and much earlier in the Butlerian Jihad. Tio Holtzman's then-dangerous foldspace engines had been the key to ultimate victory over the thinking machines.

Paul stared up at the massive machines, trying to sense their driving mathematical force, though he didn't understand it all. Chani, a few inches shorter than he, surprised him by standing on her tiptoes and kissing his cheek. He spun to face her, laughing.

She saw the surprise on his face. "Isn't that what I'm supposed to do? I've read all the files. We're destined for each other, aren't we?"

Growing serious, Paul held her small shoulders and gazed into her eyes. Then he reached out to stroke her left eyebrow, and drew his fingers down her cheek. He felt awkward doing this. "It's strange, Chani. But I can sense a tingle . . ."

"Or a tickle! I feel it, too. A memory just beneath the surface."

He kissed her on the brow, experimenting with the sensation. "Proctor Superior Garimi made us read our history in the archives, but those are just words. We don't know it here." He tapped his chest over the heart. "We can't know exactly how we fell in love before. We must have said a lot of private things to each other."

Her lips formed a frown, not quite a little girl's pout but rather an expression of concern. Her accelerated education and maturity made her seem much older than her years. "Nobody knows how to fall in love, Usul. Remember the story? Paul Atreides and his mother were in terrible danger when they joined the Fremen. Everyone you knew was dead. You were so desperate." She drew a quick breath. "Maybe that's the only reason we fell in love."

He stood close to her, embarrassed, not knowing what he was supposed to do. "How can I believe that, Chani? A love like ours was the stuff of legend. That doesn't happen by accident. I'm just saying that if we are to fall in love again when we get older, then we'll have to do it ourselves."

"Do you think we're getting a second chance?"

"All of us are."

She hung her head. "Of the things I've read, the saddest was the story of our first baby, our original son Leto."

Paul was surprised at the lump that automatically formed in his throat. He had read his old journals about their baby boy. He'd been so proud of their little son, but because of his damnable prescience, he had known that the first little Leto would be killed in a Harkonnen raid. That poor boy had never had a chance, hadn't even lived long enough to be christened Leto II, after Paul's father.

According to the records, his second son—the infamous one—had been willing to go down the dark and forbidding path where Paul himself had refused to go. Had Leto II made the right choice? The God Emperor of Dune had certainly changed the human race, and the course of history, for all time.

"I'm sorry, I made you sad, Usul."

He took a step away from her. Around them the engine room seemed to vibrate with anticipation. "Everyone hates our Leto II because of what he turned into. He did very bad things, according to history." The first Chani had died in childbirth, barely living long enough to see the twins.

"Maybe he'll get a second chance, too," she said. The ghola of the little boy was now four years old and already showing unusual acuity and talent.

Paul took her hand and impulsively kissed her on the cheek. Then they both left the engine room. "This time, our son could do things right."

The day hums sweetly when you have enough bees working for you.

—BARON VLADIMIR HARKONNEN,
the original

I n a state of high agitation, the twelve-year-old boy gazed out on a
pristine meadow of colorful flowers. A waterfall cascaded over a
rocky precipice and splashed into an icy blue pool. Too much of this
so-called "beauty" was painful and unsettling. The air carried no industrial chemicals; he hated even to breathe the stuff into his lungs.

To break the boredom and work off some of his energy, he had gone
for a long walk, kilometers from the compound where he had been sentenced to live on the planet Dan. *Caladan,* he reminded himself. The
curtailed name offended him. He had read his history and seen images
of himself as the old, fat Baron.

Exiled here for three years now, the young Vladimir Harkonnen
found he missed the laboratories of Tleilax, Matre Superior Hellica,
and even the smell of slig excrement. Trapped here, tutored and
trained and *prepared* by the humorless Face Dancers, the boy was impatient to make his mark. He was, after all, important to the plan (whatever it was).

Shortly after he'd been sent away to Caladan for the trivial crime of
sabotaging the axlotl tank holding the ghola of Paul Atreides, the new

baby had been born in Bandalong—healthy, despite Vladimir's best efforts. Khrone had whisked the infant Atreides away from Uxtal and brought him to Caladan for training and observation. Apparently, the Face Dancers had something vital for the Atreides to accomplish, and they needed a Harkonnen to help them achieve it.

The child, named Paolo to distinguish him from his historical counterpart, was three years old now. The Face Dancers took great care to keep him in a separate facility, "safe" from Vladimir, who couldn't wait until the two of them could . . . play together.

In times gone by, Caladan had been a world of simple fishermen, vintners, and farmers. With its immense ocean, Caladan had too much water and too little land to support large commercial industries. These days, most of the villages were gone, and the local population had dwindled to a small percentage of what it had once been. The Scattering had broken many threads that bound a multigalactic civilization together, and since Caladan produced little of commercial value, no one wanted to bring the planet back into the overall tapestry.

Vladimir had done a considerable amount of research in the reconstructed castle. According to the written history, House Atreides had ruled this place "with a firm yet benevolent hand," but the boy knew better than to believe that propaganda. History had a way of sanitizing the truth, and time distorted even the most dramatic events. The local files had obviously been padded with laudatory comments about Duke Leto.

Since the Atreides and Harkonnens were mortal enemies, he knew that his own house must have been the truly heroic of the two. When young Vladimir got his memories back, he would be able to recall such things firsthand. He wanted to reexperience the events with visceral truth. He wanted to know the treachery of the Atreides and the valor of the Harkonnens. He wanted to feel the adrenaline rush of real victory and taste the blood of fallen enemies on his fingers. He wanted the memories restored *now!* It galled him that he had to wait so long before having his past life triggered.

Alone in the meadow, he played with an inferno gun he had found at the castle compound. This lush natural environment of the seashore headlands disgusted him. He wanted machines to plow it under and

pave it over. Make way for real civilization! The only plants he wanted
to see were factory buildings sprouting up. He hated clean water
spilling all over the place, wanted to see manufactory chemicals
darken it and give it a sulfurous odor.

With a fiendish grin, Vladimir activated the gun and saw its muzzle
glow orange in his hands. He touched the yellow button for the first-
stage burner and watched a fine mist of concentrated incendiary particles spread over the meadow, the seeds of destruction. Moving to a
safer area of rock, he tapped the red second-stage button, and an immense blowtorch vomited from the weapon's barrel. The flammable
particles caught fire, transforming the entire meadow into a conflagra-
tion.

Beautiful!

Filled with malignant glee, he scurried to a higher vantage point
and watched the flames burn and crackle, sending smoke and sparks
hundreds of meters into the air. On the other side of the meadow, fire
licked up the rock face as if searching for prey. It burned with such
intensity that the heat cracked the stone itself, causing large chunks to
fall into the peaceful pool in a loud cascade.

"Much better!"

The ambitious young man had seen holopictures of Gammu and
compared them with images of its earlier incarnation as Giedi Prime
under the Harkonnens. Over the centuries his ancestral home had
been ruined, falling into a state of agricultural primitivity. The hard-
fought signs of civilization had faded into soft squalor.

Now, with the cleansing odors of fire and smoke filling his nostrils,
he wished he had bigger inferno guns and massive equipment: the
means to reshape this entire planet. Given time, tools, and a proper
workforce, he could turn backwater Caladan into a civilized place.

In the process he could torch vast expanses of the verdant landscape
to make way for new manufactories, landing fields, strip mines, and
metals-processing plants. The mountains in the distance were ugly, too,
with their white-capped summits. He would like to flatten the whole
range with powerful explosives, cover it with factories to produce goods
for export. And profit! Now *that* would really put Caladan on the galactic map.

He would not entirely destroy the ecosystem, of course—not the way the Honored Matres did with their planet-burners. In remote areas, unsuitable for industry, he would leave enough plants to maintain the oxygen levels. The seas would have to provide enough fish and kelp for food, because importing supplies from offworld was prohibitively expensive.

Caladan was such a waste now. How unadorned this world was . . . but how beautiful it could be with a little work. A great deal of work, actually. But it would be worth the effort, sculpting the homeworld of his mortal enemies—House Atreides—to his own vision. A Harkonnen vision.

These sensations and fantasies made him feel much, much better. Vladimir wondered if his memories might be ready to come back, a little at a time. He hoped so.

Hearing a clatter of stones behind him, he turned. "I've been watching you at play," Khrone said. "I am pleased to see you thinking along correct lines, just as the old Baron Harkonnen did. You will need some of these techniques when we place Paolo in your care."

"When do I get to play with him?"

"Your own survival depends on certain things. Understand this: helping us with the Paul Atreides ghola is the most important objective of your entire life. He is the key to our many plans, and your survival depends upon how well he does."

Vladimir formed a feral smile. "It is my destiny to be together with Paolo, and to succeed with him." He kissed the Face Dancer passionately on the mouth, and Khrone pushed him away.

Inside, Vladimir was not smiling at all. Even in this odd reenactment of his life, he still felt a need to strangle the Atreides ghola.

The meek see potential threats everywhere. The bold see potential profits.

—CHOAM administrative memo

M ore pain, more torture, more spice substitute. Still no success— not even anything that qualified as minor progress—in making melange with the axlotl tanks. In other words, business as usual.

Uxtal worked in his Bandalong laboratories, serving the needs of the Honored Matres. At least the two brats had been gone for years now, two less things to be terrified about. In his quarters, he had marked off more days and searched for ways to change his situation, to escape, to hide. But none of his solutions seemed remotely viable.

With the exception of God, he hated everyone who held authority over him. Beyond the things his superiors wanted from him, beyond the excuses and lies he told them concerning his work, Uxtal searched for signs and portents, numerical patterns, anything to reveal to him the significance of his own holy mission. He had survived for so long in this nightmare that there must be a purpose behind it!

Since taking away the newborn Paul Atreides ghola, the Face Dancers had not commanded him to do anything further for them, yet the little researcher felt no relief. He was not free. They were sure to come back and demand something even more impossible. The Honored Matres still pressured him to produce real melange with axlotl tanks, so he performed extravagant sham experiments to demonstrate how hard he was working—though completely without success.

Now that the Face Dancers no longer seemed to care about him, he was completely at the mercy of Matre Superior Hellica. He squeezed his eyes tightly shut and considered how difficult his life had been for so many years.

Since the New Sisterhood had conquered most of their other strongholds, the Honored Matres needed less and less of the adrenaline-based drug. That did not make life easier for him, though. What if the terrible women got it into their heads that they didn't require him at all anymore? He had achieved nothing new in quite some time and was sure they were convinced he would never make melange. (He had been convinced of that himself for several years now.)

Focused on business above all else, Guildships and CHOAM merchants flew in and out of the devastated zones on Tleilax. Necessarily neutral in the conflict, they traded without playing politics. Honored Matres required certain supplies and offworld items, especially with their extravagant tastes in clothing, jewels, rare foods.

Once, the whores had been fabulously wealthy, controlling the Guild Bank and carrying valuable currencies with them as they swept across star systems and planets, leaving scorched earth in their wake. Uxtal did not understand them, could not comprehend what could have created such monsters or what had chased them out of the Scattering. As usual, no one told him anything.

WHEN THE GUILD Navigators approached Hellica and her entrenched rebels on Tleilax with a proposal, Uxtal just knew his nightmare was about to get worse.

A messenger arrived in Bandalong from a high-orbiting Heighliner. Hellica herself came to escort Uxtal past the suspicious stares of Ingva and the browbeaten lab workers.

"Uxtal, you and I will travel to meet with Navigator Edrik. He awaits us aboard the Heighliner."

Though confused and intimidated, Uxtal could not argue. A Navigator? He gulped. He had never seen one of them before. He did not know why he was being singled out for such attention, but it couldn't be good news. How had the Navigator learned of his existence? Through prescience? He wondered if this might be an opportunity for him to escape, or get a reprieve . . . or be saddled with another impossible task.

Aboard the Guildship, though no one could overhear them inside the shielded chamber, Uxtal still did not feel safe. He stood silent, trembling, while Hellica strutted in front of the great armored tank. Behind the curved plaz walls, the mist-shrouded form of Edrik was so peculiar that Uxtal could not tell if the filtered voice carried an implied threat.

The Navigator spoke directly to him rather than to the Matre Superior, which was sure to set her off. "The old Tleilaxu Masters knew how to create melange with axlotl tanks. You will rediscover this process for us." The Navigator's distorted inhuman face floated behind the glass.

Uxtal groaned inside. He had already proved himself incapable of that.

"I have given him that command," Hellica said with a sniff. "For many years he has failed me."

"Then he must cease failing."

Uxtal wrung his hands. "It is not a trivial task. Worlds full of Tleilaxu Masters worked all throughout the Famine Times to perfect the complex process. I am only one man, and the old Masters did not share their secrets with the Lost Tleilaxu." He gulped again. Surely the Guild knew all this already?

"If your people are so ignorant, how did they create Face Dancers so superior to any previous ones?" the Navigator asked. Uxtal shuddered, knowing—now—that his people had not, after all, created Khrone or his superior breed of shape-shifters. Apparently, they had merely been found out in the Scattering.

"I am not interested in Face Dancers," Hellica snapped. She had always seemed at odds with Khrone. "I am interested in profits from melange."

Uxtal swallowed. "When the Masters all died, their knowledge died with the last one. I have been working diligently to reacquire the technique." He did not remind them that the Honored Matres themselves were responsible for losing those secrets; Hellica did not take even implied criticism well.

"Then use the indirect approach." Edrik delivered his words like a blow. "Bring one of them back."

The idea took Uxtal by surprise. He certainly had the ability to use an axlotl tank to resurrect one of the Masters, provided he had viable cells. "But . . . they are all dead. Even in Bandalong, the Masters were killed many years ago." He remembered the boy Baron and Hellica gleefully feeding body parts to the sligs. "Where am I to get cells for such a ghola?"

The Matre Superior stopped her tigerlike pacing and spun toward him as if to deliver a fatal thrust. "*That* is all you needed? A few cells? Thirteen years and you did not tell me you required only a few cells to solve this problem?" The orange in her eyes glowed like embers.

He quailed. The idea had never occurred to him. "I did not think it a possibility! The Masters are gone—"

She growled at him. "How stupid do you think we are, little man? We would not dispose of anything so valuable. If the Navigator's scheme will work—if we can create melange and sell it to the Guild— then I will give you the cells you need!"

Edrik's enormous head bobbed behind the plaz walls, and his bulging eyes glared at the quivering researcher. "You accept this project?"

"We accept it. This Lost Tleilaxu man works for us, and survives only at our pleasure."

Uxtal was still reeling from the revelation. "Then . . . then some of the old Masters are still alive?"

Her quirk of a smile was frightening. "Alive? After a fashion. Alive enough to provide the cells you need." She gave the Navigator a perfunctory bow and grabbed Uxtal by the arm. "I will take you to them. You must start right away."

AS THE MATRE Superior led him into a lower level of the commandeered Bandalong Palace, the stench grew worse with every step. He stumbled, but she dragged him along like a rag doll. Though Honored Matres decorated themselves with colorful fabrics and gaudy adornments, they were not particularly clean or fastidious. Hellica wasn't bothered by the stink wafting out of the dim chambers ahead; to her, it was the smell of suffering.

"They still live, but you won't get anything from their minds, little man." Hellica gestured for Uxtal to precede her. "That isn't what we kept them for."

With uncertain steps, he entered the shadowy room. He heard bubbling noises, the rhythmic hiss of respirators, gurgling pumps. It reminded him of the noisome lair of some foul beast. Ruddy light seeped from glowpanels near the floor and ceiling. He drew shallow breaths to keep himself from gagging as his eyes adjusted.

Inside he saw twenty-four small men, or what remained of them. He counted quickly before absorbing other details, searching for numerical significance. *Twenty-four—three groups of eight.*

The gray-skinned men had the distinctive features of old Masters, higher-caste leaders of the Tleilaxu. Over many centuries, genetic drift and inbreeding had given the Lost Tleilaxu a somewhat distinctive appearance; to outsiders, the gnomish men all looked alike, but Uxtal easily noted the differences.

All of them lay strapped to flat, hard tables, as if they'd been mounted on racks. Though the victims were naked, so many tubes and sensors were connected to them that he could see little of their gaunt forms.

"The Tleilaxu Masters had a nasty habit of constantly growing gholas of themselves as replacements. Like regurgitating food again and again." Hellica walked up to one of the tables, looked down at the slack-faced man there. "These were gholas of one of the last Tleilaxu Masters, spare bodies to be exchanged when he grew too old." She pointed. "This one was called Waff and had dealings with the Honored Matres. He was killed on Rakis, I believe, and never had the chance to reawaken his ghola."

Uxtal was reluctant to approach. Stunned, he looked at all the silent, identical men in the room. "Where did they come from?"

"We found them stored and preserved after we had eliminated all the other Masters." She smiled. "So, we chemically destroyed their brains and put them to a better use here."

The twenty-four sets of machinery hummed and hissed. Snakelike tentacles and tubes mounted to the groins of the mindless gholas began to pump; the strapped-down bodies twitched as the machinery made loud sucking sounds.

"Now the only thing they're good for is to provide sperm, should we ever decide to use it. Not that we particularly value your race's disappointing genetic material, but decent males seem to be in short supply here on Tleilax." Scowling, she turned away as Uxtal looked on in horror. She seemed to be hiding something; he sensed she hadn't told him all of her reasons.

"They are like your axlotl tanks, in a way. A good use for the males of your race. Isn't it what you Tleilaxu have done to females for so many millennia? These men deserved nothing better." She looked down her nose. "I'm sure you agree."

Uxtal struggled to cover his revulsion. *How they must despise us!* To do such a thing to *males*—even to a Tleilaxu Master, his enemy—was monstrous! The words of the Great Belief made clear that God had created females for the sole purpose of reproduction. A female could serve God in no greater way than to become an axlotl tank; her brain was merely extraneous tissue. But to think of males in similar terms was inconceivable. If he hadn't been so terrified of her, he might have told Hellica a thing or two!

This sacrilege would surely bring down the wrath of God. Uxtal had loathed these Honored Matres before. Now he could barely keep himself from fainting. The machines continued to milk the mindless males on the tables.

"Hurry up and take your cell scrapings," Hellica snapped. "I don't have all day, and neither do you. Guild Navigators aren't as pleasant to work with as I am."

Axlotl tanks have brought forth gholas and melange, as well as Face Dancers and Twisted Mentats. Out in the Scattering, Lost Tleilaxu genetic work was most likely responsible for creating Futars and Phibians. What other axlotl-grown creatures did they concoct in those fecund wombs? What else remains out there that is still unknown to us?

—Bene Gesserit Symposium, opening remarks by
MOTHER COMMANDER MURBELLA

In the two years since Gammu, one Honored Matre stronghold had fallen after another, a total of twelve smaller rebel enclaves eradicated in maneuvers that would have made even the best Swordmaster of Ginaz proud. Murbella's Valkyries had proven themselves time and again.

Soon, the last festering wound would be cauterized. Then humanity would be ready to face the far worse challenge.

Recently, Chapterhouse had made another substantial spice payment to the weapon shops of Richese. For years, the Richesian industries had been dedicated to building armaments for the New Sisterhood, retooling their manufacturing centers and ramping up to full-scale production. Although they regularly delivered warships and weaponry, their factories were still gearing up for the majority of items the Sisters had ordered. Within a few years, the Mother Commander would have an overwhelming armada of ships to stand together and defend against the Outside Enemy. She hoped it would be soon enough.

Inside her private chambers, working through reams of administrative matters, Murbella was relieved to be interrupted by a report from Gammu. Since the original crackdown there, Janess—promoted to regimental commandant—had been in charge of the consolidation, strengthening the Sisterhood's hold on the industries and population.

But her daughter was not among the three Valkyries who strode into her office. All three, she noted, had originally been Honored Matres. One was Kiria, the hard-edged scout who had investigated the distant Enemy-devastated planet, home of the damaged Honored Matre battleship that had come to Chapterhouse years ago. Given the opportunity, Kiria had been eager to help quash the insurgents on Gammu.

Murbella sat up straight. "Your report? Have you rooted out, killed, or converted the remaining rebel whores?"

The former Honored Matres flinched at the term, especially when used by someone who had previously been one of their own. Kiria stepped forward to speak. "The regimental commandant is not far behind us, Mother Commander, but she wanted us to report to you immediately. We have made an alarming discovery."

The other two women nodded, as if conceding Kiria's authority. Murbella noted one of them had a dark bruise on her neck.

Kiria turned toward the hall and barked orders to a pair of male workers standing outside. They entered carrying a heavy, lifeless form wrapped crudely in preserving sheets. Kiria tore the covering away from the head. The face was turned away, but the body had the shape and clothing of a man.

Intrigued, Murbella stood up. "What is this? Is he dead?"

"Quite dead, but it is not a man. Nor a woman."

The Mother Commander came around from behind her cluttered desk. "What do you mean? Is it not human?"

"It is whatever it chose to be, man or woman, boy or girl, hideous or pleasing in appearance." She turned the thing's head toward Murbella. The facial features were bland and humanoid, with staring black-button eyes, a pug nose, and pallid waxy skin.

Murbella narrowed her eyes. "I have never seen a Face Dancer so close. Nor one so dead. I presume this is their natural state?"

"Who can tell, Mother Commander? When we rooted out and

killed many of the rebel . . . whores, we found several shape-shifters among the dead. Alarmed, we brought in Truthsayers to interrogate the surviving Honored Matres, but found no more Face Dancers that way." Kiria pointed at the body. "This was one of the survivors. When she tried to escape, we killed her—and that is when her true identity came out."

"Undetectable by Truthsayers? Are you certain?"

"Absolutely."

Murbella wrestled with the complex implications. "Astounding."

Face Dancers were creatures made by the Tleilaxu, and the new ones who had returned with the Lost Tleilaxu were far superior to any the Bene Gesserit had previously encountered. Apparently, the new ones worked with, or for, the Honored Matres. And now she knew they could fool Truthsayers!

The questions fell faster than the answers. Why then had the Honored Matres destroyed the Tleilaxu worlds, attempting to exterminate all of the original Masters? Murbella had been an Honored Matre herself, and she still did not understand.

Intrigued, she touched the skin of the corpse, the coarse white hair on the head; each strand was rough against her fingertips. She inhaled deeply, sifting and sorting with her olfactory senses, but could find no distinctive smell. Bene Gesserit archives claimed that a Face Dancer could be detected by a very subtle odor. But she wasn't sure.

After a long silence, Kiria said, "We conclude that more of the rebel Honored Matres may indeed be Face Dancers, but we found no telltale indicators. No way to detect them whatsoever."

"Except for killing them," one of the other two Sisters said. "That was the only way to be sure."

Murbella frowned. "Effective, perhaps, but not entirely useful. We can't just execute everyone."

Kiria matched her frown. "That leads to a different kind of crisis, Mother Commander. Though we killed hundreds of Face Dancers among the rebels on Gammu, we were unable to capture a single one of them alive—not that we know of. They are perfect mimics. Absolutely perfect."

Deeply troubled, Murbella paced in her office. "You killed hundreds of Face Dancers? Does that mean you slaughtered thousands of rebels? What percentage of them are these . . . infiltrators?"

Kiria shrugged. "Posing as Honored Matres, they formed an attack squadron and tried to retake Gammu by force. They had a very complex and detailed plan, striking at vulnerabilities, and they rallied a great many of the rebel women to their cause. Fortunately, we found the viper's nest and struck. The Valkyries would have killed them either way, whether they were Face Dancers or whores."

One of the other women added, "Ironically, the Honored Matres who followed them were just as surprised as we were when their leaders turned into . . . this." She gestured toward the inhuman cadaver. "Even they did not know they had been infiltrated."

The third Sister said, "Regimental Commandant Idaho has placed the whole planet under quarantine, subject to your further orders."

Murbella kept herself from voicing the obvious security nightmare: *If that many Face Dancers have infiltrated the rebel whores on Gammu, do we have any among us here on Chapterhouse?* They had brought so many candidates for retraining. Her policy had been to absorb as many former Honored Matres as were willing to undergo the Sisterhood's instruction, their loyalty monitored by strict Truthsayers. After her capture on Gammu, their leader Niyela had killed herself rather than be converted. But what about the ones who claimed to cooperate?

Uneasily, Murbella studied the three women, trying to detect whether they were shape-shifters, too. But if that were true, why would they raise the suspicion in the first place?

Sensing the Mother Commander's suspicions, Kiria looked at her companions. "These are not Face Dancers. Nor am I."

"Isn't that exactly what a Face Dancer would say? I do not find your assurances terribly convincing."

"We would submit to Truthsayer interrogation," one of the other two said, "but you already know that is no longer reliable."

Kiria pointed out, "In pitched battle we noticed a strange thing. While some of the Face Dancers died quickly from their wounds, others did not. In fact, when two were on the verge of death, their features began to change prematurely."

"So, if we brought a subject to the *verge* of death, a Face Dancer would reveal itself?" Murbella sounded skeptical.

"Precisely."

With a sudden movement, Murbella flung herself at Kiria and hit her with a hard kick to the temple. The Mother Commander placed the blow precisely, shifting her foot a fraction of a centimeter from what would have been fatal.

Kiria fell to the floor like a stone. Her companions did not move.

On her back, Kiria gasped for breath, her eyes glazed. In a blur of motion, before they could run, Murbella felled the other two in the same manner, rendering them all helpless.

She loomed over the trio, ready to deliver the killing blows. But except for contortions of pain, their features did not change. In contrast, the ghoulish face of the dead shape-shifter was unmistakable in its preservation wrappings.

The Mother Commander tended to Kiria first, using Bene Gesserit healing holds to calm the victim's breathing. Then she massaged the woman's injured temple, her fingers finding the exact pressure points. The former Honored Matre responded quickly, and finally managed to sit up on her own.

Because the three women had not transformed meant either that they were not Face Dancers, or that the test did not work. Murbella's uneasiness grew as questions continued to rear up. She found herself in uncharted territory. Face Dancers could be anywhere.

Miles Teg arrived on the navigation bridge with a specific purpose in mind. He took a chair at the console beside Duncan, who only reluctantly turned his attention from the controls. Since his own distraction and preoccupation with Murbella had nearly allowed them to be trapped by the sparkling net, Duncan had been conscientious in his duties to the point of isolating himself. He refused to let down his guard again.

Teg said, "When I died the first time, Duncan, I was nearly three hundred standard years old. There were ways I could have slowed my aging—through massive consumption of melange, certain Suk treatments, or Bene Gesserit biological secrets. But I chose not to. Now I am feeling old again." He looked over at the dark-haired man. "In all your ghola lifetimes, Duncan, have you ever been truly old?"

"I'm more ancient than you can possibly imagine. I remember every one of my lives and countless deaths—so much violence against me." Duncan allowed himself a wistful smile. "But there were a few times when I had a long and happy life, with a wife and children, and I died peacefully in my sleep. Those were the exceptions, however, not the rule."

Teg looked at his own hands. "This body was no more than a child's when we left. Sixteen years! Children have been born, and people have died, but everything aboard the *Ithaca* seems stagnant. Is there more to our destiny than constant flight? Will it ever stop? Will we ever find a new planet?"

Duncan took another scan of space all around the drifting ship. "Where is it safe, Miles? The hunters will never give up, and each trip through foldspace is dangerous. Should I try to find the Oracle of Time and ask for her help? Can we trust the Guild? Should I take us into that other strange, empty universe again? We have more options than we admit, but nothing that makes a good plan."

"We should look for someplace unknown and unpredictable. We can travel routes that no mind can follow. You and I could do it."

Duncan stood from the pilot's chair and gestured to the controls. "Your prescience is as good as mine, Miles. Probably better, with your Atreides bloodline. You've never given me reason to doubt your competence. Go ahead and guide us there." His offer was sincere.

Teg's expression became uncertain, but he accepted the console. He could feel Duncan's confidence and acceptance, and it reminded him of his past military campaigns. As the old Bashar, he had led swarms of men to their deaths. They had accepted his tactics. More often than not, he had found a way to make violence unnecessary, and his men had come to think of his abilities as nearly supernatural. Even when he failed, his men died knowing that if even the great Bashar could not succeed, then the problem itself must be utterly unsolvable.

Studying the projections around him, Teg tried to get a feel for the space in which they roamed. In planning for this, before coming to the navigation bridge, he had consumed four days' ration of spice. Again, he had to do the impossible.

As the spice worked through him, he called up coordinates, letting the doubling vision of his innate prescience guide him. He would take the vessel where it needed to be. Without second-guessing himself or performing a backup navigational calculation, he lurched the *Ithaca* into the void. The Holtzman engines folded space, plucked them from one part of the galaxy and deposited them somewhere else. . . .

Teg delivered the no-ship to an unremarkable solar system with a yellow sun, two gas giant planets and three smaller rocky worlds closer to the star, but nothing within the habitable life zone. The readings were completely blank.

And yet his prescience had taken him to this place. *For a reason . . .* For the better part of an hour, he continued to study the empty orbits, probing with his intense senses, sure that his ability had not led them astray.

After the activation of the Holtzman engines, Sheeana had come to the navigation bridge, afraid that the net had located them again. Now she waited anxiously to see what he had found. She did not discount the Bashar's certainty.

"There's nothing here, Miles." Duncan leaned over his shoulder to study the same screens.

Though unable to disprove the statement, Teg did not agree with it. "No . . . wait a moment." His gaze blurred, and suddenly he spotted it—not with his real vision but with a dark and isolated corner of his mind. The potential had been stored deep in his complex genetics, awakened through the devastating T-probe torture that had also unlocked his ability to move at incredible speed. The instinctive capacity to *see* no-ships was another talent Teg had carefully guarded from the Bene Gesserits, afraid of what they might do to him.

The no-field he beheld now, however, was larger than the most mammoth ship he had ever seen. *Much larger.*

"Something's there." As he guided the no-ship closer, he sensed no danger, only a deep mystery. The orbital zone wasn't as empty as he had at first thought. The silent blot was merely an illusion, a blurry shroud large enough to cover a whole planet. A whole planet!

"I see nothing." Sheeana looked at Duncan, who shook his head.

"No, trust me." Fortunately, the guise of the no-field was not perfect, and as Teg struggled to think of a likely sounding explanation, the field flickered, and a speckle of sky appeared for an instant before it was quickly covered again.

Duncan saw it, too. "He's right." He gave Teg an awed and questioning glance. "How did you know?"

"The Bashar has Atreides genes, Duncan. You should know by now not to underestimate them," Sheeana said.

As their ship approached, the planetary no-field flickered one more time to give a tantalizing glimpse of an entirely hidden world, a splash of sky, green-brown continents. Teg did not take his eyes from the screen. "A network of satellites generating no-fields would explain it. But the field is either flawed or degenerating."

The no-ship approached the world that wasn't there. Duncan sank back in the command chair. "It is . . . almost inconceivable. The energy requirements would be immense. Those people must have had access to technologies beyond our own."

For years, Chapterhouse itself had been camouflaged by a moat of no-ships, enough to mask the planet from a cursory, distant search, but that shield had been sketchy and imperfect—forcing Duncan to remain aboard the landed no-ship. This world, though, was completely surrounded by an all-encompassing no-field.

As Teg guided the vessel forward, they traversed the unmarked ring of satellites that generated the overlapping no-field. The orbital sensors were blinded for an instant, but the *Ithaca*'s similar masking technology allowed it to pass through.

Behind them, as if their passage had disrupted a delicate balance, the planetary no-field flickered again, winked in and out of existence, and then restored itself.

"Such an expenditure of energy would have bankrupted entire empires," Sheeana said. "No one would do it on a whim. Somebody certainly wanted to stay hidden down there. We must be cautious."

We can learn much from those who came before us. The most valuable legacy our predecessors can leave us is the knowledge of how to avoid the same deadly mistakes.

—REVEREND MOTHER SHEEANA,
Ithaca logs

The powerful civilization that had once thrived on the no-planet was dead now. Everything was dead.

As the *Ithaca* circled the hidden planet in a tight orbit, the bristling quills of scanners picked out silent cities, the distinctive remnants of industry, abandoned agricultural settlements, empty living complexes. Every outside transmission band was utterly still, without so much as the faint static of repeating weather satellites or distress beacons.

"The inhabitants went to great lengths to hide," Teg said. "But it looks as if they were found after all."

Sheeana studied the readings. In light of the mystery, she had summoned several other Sisters to help her study the data and develop conclusions. "The ecosystem seems to be undamaged. The minimal levels of pollutants and residue in the air suggest that this place has been uninhabited for a century or more, depending on its prior level of industrialization. The prairies and forests are untouched. Everything looks perfectly normal, almost pristine."

Garimi's frown etched deep creases around her lips and on her forehead. "In other words, this was not caused in the same manner as the whores turned Rakis into a charred ball."

"No, only the people are gone." Duncan shook his head, studying the information as it flowed across the screens, including city layouts and atmospheric details. "Either they left, or they perished. Do you think they were hiding from the Outside Enemy, so desperate to remain unseen that they covered their entire world in a no-field?"

"It is an Honored Matre world?" Garimi asked.

Sheeana reached a decision. "This place could hold a key to what we are running from. We have to learn what we can. If Honored Matres lived down there, what drove them away, or what killed them?"

Garimi held up one finger. "The whores came to the Bene Gesserit demanding to know how we control our bodies. They were frantic to understand how Reverend Mothers can manipulate our immune functions, cell by cell. Of course!"

"Speak clearly, Garimi. What do you mean?" Teg's voice was abrupt, the hardened battle commander.

She turned a sour look on him. "You are a Mentat. Make a prime projection!"

Teg did not bristle at the scolding. Instead, his eyes became glazed for just a moment, and then his expression returned. "Ahh. If the whores wanted to learn how to control immune responses, then perhaps the Enemy attacked them using a biological agent. The whores did not have the skills or the medical science to make themselves impervious, therefore they wanted to learn the secrets of Bene Gesserit immunity, even if they had to obliterate planets to do so. They were desperate."

"They were terrified of the Enemy's plagues," Sheeana said.

Duncan leaned forward to stare at the peaceful yet ominous image of the tomb world below them. "Are you suggesting that the Enemy discovered this planet even behind the no-field, and seeded it with a disease that killed everyone?"

Sheeana nodded at the large screen. "We must go down there and see for ourselves."

"Unwise," Duncan said. "If a plague killed every single person—"

"As Miles just pointed out, we Reverend Mothers can guard our bodies against the contamination. Garimi can go with me."

"This is foolhardy," Teg said.

"Being safe and careful has bought us little in the past sixteen years," Garimi said. "If we turn our backs on this opportunity to learn about the real Enemy, and the Honored Matres, then we deserve our fate when they come back to haunt us."

GARIMI PILOTED THE small lighter through the time-scoured atmosphere and over the ghostly metropolis. The empty city was ostentatious and impressive, composed primarily of tall towers and massive buildings with a superfluity of angles. Each structure had a thick solidity that expressed a certain *loudness*, as if the builders demanded grandeur and respect. But the buildings were crumbling.

"Showy extravagance," Sheeana commented. "It denotes lack of subtlety, perhaps even insecurity in their power."

Inside her head, the ancient voice of Serena Butler awoke. *In the Time of Titans, the great cymek tyrants built huge monuments to themselves. That was how they reinforced their own belief in their significance.*

Similar things had happened long before that, Sheeana supposed. "As humans, we learn the same lessons over and over and over again. We are doomed to repeat our mistakes."

When she caught the Proctor Superior looking at her oddly, Sheeana realized she had spoken aloud. "This place has the undeniable mark of the Honored Matres. Spectacular yet unnecessary lavishness. Domination and intimidation. The whores bullied those they conquered, but in the end it wasn't enough. Even their incredible expenditure to generate a self-sustaining no-field proved inadequate against the Enemy."

Garimi's lips formed a hard smile. "How it must have galled them to be forced into hiding! Cowering behind invisibility, and still failing."

They set the lighter down in the middle of an empty street. Looking at each other for reassurance and resolve, Sheeana and Garimi opened the airlock hatch and stepped out onto the graveyard world. They each took a cautious breath. Wispy gray clouds scudded across the skies, like memories of industrial smoke.

With their perfect immune-system control, the Sisters could guard every cell in their bodies and fend off any remaining vestiges of a plague. The Honored Matres, however, had forgotten—or never possessed—such skills.

The streets and landing pad were overgrown with tall grasses and hardy weeds that had cracked the armorpave. Wild shrubs grew into writhing shapes, composed mostly of thorns upon which a casually tossed victim could be impaled. Stunted trees resembled racks of swords and spearheads. At one time, Sheeana supposed, the Honored Matres must have considered these plants ornamental. Other knobby growths composed of interlocked lumps rose up like leprous fungi.

The city was not silent, though. A gentle wind blew, moaning a somber song through broken windows and half-collapsed doorways. Flocks of long-feathered birds had taken up residence in the towers and on rooftops. Gardens, probably once tended by slaves, had grown into a wild riot of vegetation. Engorged trees had uprooted flagstones; flowers poked from cracks in buildings like patches of brightly colored hair. A raw wilderness, bursting from its boundaries, had conquered the city. The planet had gleefully reclaimed itself, as if dancing on the graves of millions of Honored Matres.

Sheeana walked forward, on guard. This empty metropolis had an ominous and mysterious feel, though she had satisfied herself that no one remained alive. She trusted her Bene Gesserit senses and reflexes to alert her to danger, but perhaps she should have brought along Hrrm or one of the other Futars, as a guardian.

The two women stood in somber contemplation, absorbing their surroundings. Sheeana gestured to her companion. "We have to find an information center—a library complex or a data core."

She studied the architecture around her. The skyline had a weathered and broken appearance. After a century or more without maintenance, some of the tall towers had collapsed. Poles that must once have held colorful banners were now naked, the fragile fabric had disintegrated with time.

"Use your eyes and what you've been taught," Sheeana said. "Even if the whores did originate from unschooled Reverend Mothers, maybe they were mixed with Fish Speaker refugees. Or maybe they have another origin entirely, but they carry some of our history in their subconscious."

Garimi gave a skeptical snort. "Reverend Mothers would never have forgotten so many basic skills. We know from Murbella that the whores have no access to Other Memory. Nothing in our history explains their sheer violence and unmitigated rage."

Sheeana remained unconvinced. "If they came from the Scattering, the whores have some commonality with human history, provided we go back far enough. In general, architecture is based on standard assumptions. A library or information center has a different look than an administrative complex or private dwelling. In a city such as this, there will be business buildings, receiving centers, and some sort of central information storehouse."

The two walked past the stark thorntrees, studying the structures they saw. The buildings were blocky and fortresslike, as if the populace had feared that at any moment they would need to run inside and protect themselves from a violent external attack.

"This city must have been built before the planetary no-field was put in place," Garimi said. "Note the siege mentality evident in these structures."

"But even the strongest weapons and battlements can't defend against a plague."

By nightfall, after searching in dozens of dark buildings that smelled of animal dens, Sheeana and Garimi discovered a records center that appeared to be less of a public library than a detention center.

Here, surrounded by heavy shielding, some archives had remained intact. The pair dug into the background of this place, activating unusual but oddly familiar shigawire spools and engraved Ridulian crystal sheets.

Garimi returned to the lighter to transmit an update to the no-ship, informing the others of what they had found. By the time her companion came back, Sheeana was sitting gravely beside a portable glowglobe. She held up the crystal sheets. "The plague that struck here is more virulent and terrible than any disease ever recorded. It spread with impossible efficiency and had virtually a one-hundred-percent mortality rate."

"That's unheard of! No disease could possibly be so—"

"This one was. The proof is here." Sheeana shook her head. "Even the horrific plagues from the Butlerian Jihad were not so efficient, and *that* epidemic spread everywhere and nearly brought an end to human civilization."

"But how did the Honored Matres stop the disease once it took root here? Why didn't it infect everyone and kill them all?"

"Encapsulation and quarantine. Utter ruthlessness. We know the whores operate in isolated cells. They fled from their heartland, always moving forward, never backward. There wasn't a cooperative trading network."

Garimi nodded coldly. "And their strict violence probably served them well. They would have allowed no mistakes."

Sheeana selected a shigawire spool and played the recording. An image of a stern Honored Matre flashed orange eyes into the recorder. She appeared to be defiant, holding up her weak chin, baring her teeth. The woman seemed to be on trial, facing a stern tribunal and a growling audience. Female voices howling with anger strayed into the recording from the fringes.

"I am Honored Matre Rikka, an adept of the seventh level. I have assassinated ten to reach my rank, and I demand your respect!" The outcries from the audience showed no respect at all. "Why do you put me here on this stand? You know I am right."

"We're all dying!" another shout came.

"It is your own fault," Rikka snapped back. "We brought this fate on ourselves. We provoked the Enemy of Many Faces."

"We are Honored Matres! We are in control. We take what we wish. The stolen Weapons will make us invincible."

"Really? Look what we reaped from it." Rikka held up her bare arms to show dark lesions covering her skin. "Look well, for you will all experience it soon."

"Execute her!" someone cried. "The Long Death."

Rikka bared her teeth in a feral grin. "To what purpose? You know I will die soon anyway." She showed the lesions on her arms again. "So will all of you."

Instead of responding to the question, an ancient female judge called for a vote, and Rikka was indeed sentenced to the Long Death. Sheeana could only imagine what that meant. Honored Matres were vile enough: What could they conceive of as the worst possible death?

"Why didn't they believe her?" Garimi said. "If the plague was spreading before their eyes, the whores must have known Rikka was right."

Sheeana shook her head sadly. "Honored Matres would never admit weakness or mortality. Better to lash out at a perceived enemy, than to concede that they were all going to die anyway."

"I do not understand these women," the Proctor Superior said. "I am glad we did not stay behind on Chapterhouse."

"We may never know where the whores originally came from," Sheeana said. "But I have no desire to live in their tomb." As far as she could tell, the plague seemed to have burned itself out, devouring every available victim and then leaving nothing else to infect.

"I wish to leave this place as well." Garimi suppressed a shudder, then seemed embarrassed by it. "Even I would not consider this place as a new home for us. The remnants of death will stay in the atmosphere for centuries to come."

Sheeana agreed. Reinforcing their opinions, Teg reported from the no-ship that the satellites generating the planetary field of invisibility were failing. Within a few years, the cloak would fade away entirely. And, since the Enemy had already found and destroyed this world, she and her followers would not be safe and invisible from the hunters here.

Gathering the documentation they had found, Sheeana and Garimi left the detention center and records vault, and hurried back to the lighter in the gathering darkness.

*Information is always available, if one is willing to go to extreme
lengths to obtain it.*

— *The Mentat Handbook*

The Honored Matres wanted everything, and Uxtal feared that
the eight new axlotl tanks in Bandalong would not be enough.
Soon—as ordered by Hellica and Navigator Edrik—he would decant
eight gholas of the Tleilaxu Master Waff, the Masheikh, the Master of
Masters, who had been stored in Hellica's chamber of horrors. Eight
chances to recover the lost knowledge of melange production.

If that didn't work, he would make eight more, and more again, a
constant stream of possible reincarnations, all to obtain one set of
memories, one key to knowledge that Uxtal could not figure out for
himself.

The Matre Superior had given the Lost Tleilaxu researcher everything he needed, and the Navigators had paid her well for his efforts.
But the problem was not so simple. After he removed the identical
Waff copies from those wombs, Uxtal would have to bring them to
maturity, and then break loose their memories and knowledge from
past lives, like a man with a crowbar smashing open a sealed crate.

But that was no easy process, either. Even the twelve-year-old

Baron Harkonnen ghola had still not awakened. Thankfully, that was no longer his problem, since Khrone had decided to perform the task himself on Dan.

Now, on his regular inspection walk among the pasty axlotl tanks, Uxtal felt satisfaction as he surveyed the rounded fleshy bellies, the atrophied limbs, the faces so slack they looked like cauls of skin. Female bodies could be such useful *things*.

Uxtal had already forced reckless speed upon the creation of the Tleilaxu Master gholas. Aware of the constant slippage of time and the growing desperation of the Guild Navigators and Matre Superior Hellica for spice, he decided that speed was more important than perfection. He had used a forbidden, unstable acceleration process, derived from genetic traits associated with a formerly incurable aging disease. As a result, the eight Waffs would be born after only five months in the uterus, and once decanted, they would last two decades at most. They would grow quickly and painfully, and then they would burn out.

Uxtal considered his solution quite innovative. He didn't care about these gholas, or how many he might have to use up before he gained the necessary information. He only needed one to survive, and to awaken.

At any other time, he might have felt important, a vital asset, but neither the Honored Matres nor the Navigator seemed to respect him. Perhaps Uxtal should demand respect and insist on better treatment. He could refuse to do any more work. He could demand his due. . . .

"Stop daydreaming, little man," Ingva snapped.

He nearly jumped out of his skin and looked quickly away. "Yes, Ingva. I am concentrating. Very delicate work." *She can't kill me! She knows it.*

"No mistakes," the sinewy crone warned.

"No mistakes. Perfect work." He was far too frightened to make a mistake.

He shuddered to think of the old Waff copies, brain-dead and strapped to inclined tables. *Sperm factories*. His own situation, while hellish, could have been far worse. Yes, it could have been worse. He tried to summon a hopeful smile, but could not find one within him.

Ingva slithered up behind him and peered down at the axlotl tank that had once been an injured Honored Matre. "You breathe on them too much. Could contaminate them. Frighten the fetuses."

"The tanks require close monitoring." Despite his struggles to contain his fear, his voice came out in a squeak.

She pressed her shriveled body against him, attempting Honored Matre seductive techniques, though her body was like twisted wreckage. "It's such a waste that the Matre Superior has refused to bond you. If Hellica does not want you, then it is time to make you my own toy."

"She—she would not like that, Ingva. I promise you." He felt nauseated.

"Hellica will not be Matre Superior forever. Someone might assassinate her any day now. Meanwhile, I could make you work harder, little man. That would gain me great respect, increase my position of power, no matter what happens."

Fortunately, a commotion and a thick smell cut through the chemical odors in the axlotl labs, distracting Ingva. A dirty man clad in dirty clothes pushed a dirty cart along the sterile hall, his eyes cast down. "Your delivery of slig meat," called the downtrodden farmer. "Freshly slaughtered, still bloody!"

Ingva released Uxtal and stalked off toward the man, turning her ire on him. "We expected you an hour ago. The slaves need time to prepare our feast for tonight." No longer interested in Uxtal, Ingva went to tend to the meat. He shuddered, trying to keep the look of revulsion and relief from his face.

॒

The human mind is not a puzzle to be solved but a treasure chest for us to open. If we cannot pick the lock, then we must smash it apart. Either way, the riches inside will be ours.

—KHRONE,
communiqué to the Face Dancers

A cold rainstorm swept in over the oceans of Caladan. Waves crashed against rugged black rocks far below the restored castle. The local fishermen had brought in their boats and tied them to the docks, then huddled at home with their families. In the dim shadows of cultural memory, their Caladanian ancestors had loved their duke, but they did not hold the same reverence for the strangers who had rebuilt the ancient edifice and moved in.

The castle's plaz windows were sealed against the storm's intensity. Dehumidifiers scoured the ever-present clamminess from the air. Thermal generators operated behind blazing holographic fires, warming the temperature to a comfortable level.

Within a stone-walled chamber lit by fiery artificial light, Khrone laid out the instruments of torture and summoned the Baron ghola. Young Paolo was safe in his own quarters in another village, far from where anyone could find him. Today, though, was Baron Vladimir Harkonnen's day.

The horrifically augmented emissaries from the outside masters stood against one of the stone walls, observing, recording. Their faces were pasty except for scarlet patches of raw flesh and unhealed wounds that held tubes and implants. The machinery made a distracting gurgle and hiss. The observers had been here, always observing Khrone and his pet project, for years. Each day, he expected one of them to break down and fall apart, but the patchwork people remained unchanged, watching, waiting.

He would show them a success today.

Three Face Dancer assistants escorted the haughty young ghola. In the guise of guards, they chose to appear as muscular brutes who could snap a neck with two fingers. Young Vladimir's hair was mussed, as if he had been dragged out of a restless sleep. With a bored expression, he looked around the stone-walled chamber. "I'm hungry."

"Better you don't eat. Less chance of vomiting," Khrone said. "Then again, one additional bodily fluid, more or less, won't make much difference by the end of the day."

Vladimir shrugged off the burly Face Dancer guards. His eyes flicked from side to side, suspicious, confrontational. When he saw the chains, the table, and the torture devices, the ghola smiled in anticipation. Khrone gestured to the equipment. "These are for you."

Vladimir's eyes lit up. "Am I to learn flaying techniques today? Or something less messy?"

"*You* will be the victim."

Before the boy could react, the guards dragged him over to the table. Khrone expected to see a look of panic on the round face. Instead of cursing, howling, or struggling, the young boy snapped, "How am I to trust that you know what you're doing? Or that you won't mess it up?"

Khrone's face formed a gentle, paternal smile. "I am a fast learner."

The patchwork emissaries from Outside exchanged glances, then continued to watch Vladimir, silently absorbing every instant. Khrone expected to put on a good show for their distant masters. The muscular guards strapped the young man's arms securely in place, then manacled his ankles.

"Not so tightly that he can't thrash and writhe," Khrone instructed. "That could be an important part of the process."

Vladimir raised his head and turned toward the smiling Khrone.

"Will you tell me what you intend to do? Or is guessing part of the game?"

"The Face Dancers have decided that it is time to awaken your memories."

"Good. I was growing impatient." This ghola had an uncanny knack for saying the unexpected to disorient anyone who might try to gain the upper hand. His very eagerness might be an obstacle to triggering a sufficient crisis.

"My masters also demand it," Khrone continued for the benefit of the emissaries who stood against the wall. "We created you for one purpose only. You must have your memories, you must be *the Baron* before you can serve that purpose."

Vladimir chuckled. "Why should I bother?"

"It is a task to which you are eminently suited."

"Then how do you know I'll *want* to do it?"

"We will make you want to do it. Have no fear."

Vladimir laughed again as a thicker band was strapped around his chest. Long needle spikes bit into his flesh to encourage the pain, and Khrone cinched it tighter. "I'm not afraid."

"We can change that." Khrone gestured, and his Face Dancer assistants brought forth the Agony Box.

He knew from the old Tleilaxu that pain was a necessary component in restoring a ghola's memories. As a Face Dancer with precise and intimate knowledge of the human body's nervous system and pain centers, Khrone felt he was up to the task.

"Do your worst!" The boy let out a throaty chuckle.

"On the contrary, I will do my best."

The Box was an ancient device used by the Bene Gesserit for provocation and testing. Its flat faces were engraved with incomprehensible symbols, jagged grooves, and complex patterns. "This will force you to explore yourself." Khrone slipped Vladimir's pale, twitching hand into the opening. "It contains agony, in its purest form."

"I can't wait."

Khrone knew that this would be an interesting challenge.

For thousands of years the Tleilaxu had created gholas, and since the time of Muad'Dib they had awakened them through a combination of mental anguish and physical pain that brought the mind and body to a fundamental crisis. Unfortunately, even Khrone didn't know exactly what was required to accomplish this. Maybe he should have brought pathetic Uxtal from Bandalong for the event, though he doubted the Lost Tleilaxu could have helped much.

The Baron ghola was particularly ripe for reawakening. Best to proceed vigorously. Khrone fitted a second Box over Vladimir's other hand. "Here we are. Enjoy the process."

Khrone activated both devices, and the young man's body jerked and twisted. Vladimir's face grew white, his pouting lips pressed together over his teeth, his eyes squeezed shut. Spasms rippled through his face, his chest, his arms. Vladimir tried to withdraw his hands. He must be feeling sheer torment, though Khrone smelled no burning flesh, observed no damaged body parts—that was the beauty of the Box. Nerve induction could evoke unendurable pain, and it need never stop until the victim's mind was overloaded.

"This may take a while," Khrone said, a gentle whisper beside the young man's sweaty brow. He increased the level of pain.

Vladimir shuddered. His lips drew back in a rictus, but he did not cry out. Like water from a high-pressure hose, agony streamed into the ghola's body.

Next, Khrone thrust needles into the ghola's neck, chest, and thighs, siphoning off the adrenaline-laced chemicals that could be used as precursors for the Honored Matres' orange spice substitute. Created with such intensity and purity, Khrone was sure he could sell the product to the Honored Matres on Tleilax. The Matre Superior herself would probably consider it a fine vintage. He could always count on the insatiable needs of Hellica's whores. Under the watchful gaze of the augmented emissaries, Khrone would demonstrate a double efficiency.

After the torture went on for hours, Khrone disconnected the Boxes and looked into the bleary eyes of the sweating young Harkonnen. "We are doing this only to help you."

The ghola looked blankly up at him. No flash of awakened memory in the spider-black eyes. "Not . . . that . . . easy."

So Khrone replaced the Boxes on the ghola's hands. With barely a second thought, he directed that two more be folded around the boy's naked feet. Four unbearable agonies would hit him. The pain was pure and unfiltered, seasoned with adrenaline and garnished with anguish. The torment continued to pound upon the ghola's mind, seeking to free the locked-in memories. Vladimir twisted, cursed, and finally screamed.

But nothing changed.

When it was time for dinner, Khrone invited the patchwork representatives to join him. They left the chamber and sat in the dining hall, listening to the crash of the storm outside. Expecting to celebrate success, Khrone had ordered a long and complicated feast; now they ate each of the fine courses, then returned hours later to the lower chambers. Vladimir continued to squirm, but showed no sign of becoming himself.

"This may take days," Khrone warned the augmented emissaries.

"Then it will take days," they answered.

The Face Dancer began to question his own assumptions, realizing a problem he had not anticipated: Physical pain was not the same as mental pain. The Agony Boxes might not be sufficient.

When he looked down at the thrashing Vladimir, his sweat-drenched clothes, and the defiant grin on his flushed face, the Face Dancer realized another possible problem. The torture might be ineffective for the simple and straightforward fact that this ghola actually *enjoyed* it.

NINETEEN YEARS AFTER

ESCAPE FROM CHAPTERHOUSE

Those who think they see most clearly are often more blind than the rest.

— Bene Gesserit aphorism

Sheeana danced among the worms again as she had done as a child on Rakis. Inside the *Ithaca*'s huge cargo hold, the seven creatures rose around her, twisting and waving their bodies like flexible metronomes. They formed a bizarre audience as Sheeana stamped her bare feet, flailed her arms, and twirled on the crest of the dune.

Among the people of Rakis, the sacred dance had been called Siaynoq. She kicked up dust and sand with her frenzied movements, losing herself. Siaynoq burned away her emotions and her excess restless energy. The intensity was enough to drive doubts from her mind and misery from her heart.

Responding to her dance, the worms pulled themselves high above her and swayed. Sheeana drove herself harder. Sweat droplets flew from her forehead and soaked her matted hair. She had to cleanse her thoughts, to burn this fear and doubt from her mind.

Three years ago, after leaving the dead plague planet of the Honored Matres behind its failing no-shield, Sheeana had felt the dark specter of dismay building in her mind. A world full of dead women, along with their followers and slaves—wiped out by something they could not comprehend, something that had blindsided them.

Sheeana knew that the hated Honored Matres deserved whatever appalling punishment they had brought down upon themselves. But every single person on an entire planet? Surely they had not all deserved to die in such a horrific fashion.

And that was only one world. How many other strongholds had been extinguished by the Enemy's plagues? How many trillions had perished from a disease with a 100 percent mortality rate? And how many more would the Enemy kill, now that the whores had fled like a pack of wild dogs into the vulnerable Old Empire—drawing the incredible foe with their scent?

Sheeana tripped in her dance on the soft sand. Regaining her balance, she did a backflip and continued her gyrations. Despite the exertions, she did not find the inner peace she desperately sought. The endless dance only clarified her troublesome ideas. The melange-heavy breath of the sandworms drifted around her like the mist of an approaching storm.

At the brink of total exhaustion, Sheeana collapsed onto the sand. First she let her knees buckle, then she rolled over, heaving great hot breaths. She lay back, looking up at the high ceiling of the cargo hold. Her muscles ached, her limbs trembled. With her eyes shut, she could feel her heart beating to the rhythm of imagined war drums. She would have to consume a great deal of melange to restore herself.

One of the creatures came close, and she could feel the sand vibrating beneath her. She sat up as the monster glided past, pushing up a dune mound and then stopping. Finding a last scrap of energy within her, Sheeana pulled herself forward and leaned against the worm's hard, curved rings. It was encrusted with dust, and she could feel the solidity of this thing, the power it contained.

She lifted her arm and rested it against the side of the beast, wishing she could just climb up on the ring segments of this worm and ride off to the horizon. But here inside the no-ship, the horizon—the hull—was not far away. "Old Shaitan, I wish I had your knowledge."

Long ago, when she and the simpering Tleilaxu Master Waff and Reverend Mother Odrade had ridden into the desert of Rakis, a sandworm had carried them purposely to the empty remains of old Sietch Tabr. Inside, Odrade had found a hidden message from Leto II. With his incredible prescience, the God Emperor had foreseen that encounter in the far-distant future and had left words specifically for Odrade.

With such prescience, how could the God Emperor not have predicted the destruction of Rakis—or had he? Had the Tyrant made his own plans? How far did the Golden Path extend? Had his supernatural foresight been responsible for Sheeana's rescue of the last worm, so that it could reproduce on a new world, Chapterhouse? Surely, Leto II had not foreseen the Honored Matres or the Enemy of Many Faces.

Sheeana wondered if she still saw too little of the overall picture. Despite their struggles, maybe they were all unwittingly following an even larger plan the God Emperor had laid out for them.

Sheeana felt the pearl of Leto II's awareness in the strong sandworm against her. She doubted that any plan devised by Bene Gesserits or Honored Matres could really be more prescient than the God Emperor himself.

The desert dragons began to churn the sands again. She looked up to the high plaz window and saw two small figures there, looking down at her.

Dirt is something solid you can hold in your hand. Using our science and our passion, we can mold it, shape it, and bring forth life. Could there be a better task for any person?
—PLANETOLOGIST PARDOT KYNES,
petition to Emperor Elrood IX, ancient records

From the high observation gallery above the cargo hold, two boys peered through a dust-smeared plaz window to watch Sheeana and the sandworms.

"She dances," said eight-year-old Stilgar with clear awe in his voice. "And Shai-Hulud dances with her."

"They're only responding to her movements. We could find a rational explanation for it if we studied her long enough." Liet-Kynes was a year older than his companion, who showed amazement at the dance. Kynes couldn't deny that Sheeana did things with the worms that no one else could do. "Don't try to do that yourself, Stilgar."

Even when Sheeana was not inside the hold with the great beasts, the two young friends often came to the observation gallery and pressed their faces against the plaz to stare at the uneven sands. This tiny patch of captive desert beckoned to them. Kynes squinted, letting his vision grow blurry to make the walls of the cargo hold disappear, so that he could imagine a much larger landscape.

During their intensive lessons with Proctor Superior Garimi, Kynes had seen historical images of Arrakis. Dune. With penetrating curiosity, young Kynes had delved deep into the records. The mysterious desert planet seemed to call to him, as if it were an integral part of his genetic memories. His quest for knowledge was insatiable, and he wanted to know more than dry facts about his past life. He wanted to *live* them again. All of his reborn life, the Bene Gesserit had trained him and the other ghola children for that eventuality.

His father Pardot Kynes, the first official Imperial Planetologist sent to Arrakis, had formulated a grand dream of converting the wasteland into a huge garden. Pardot had provided the foundation for a new Eden, recruiting the Fremen to make initial plantings and setting up great sealed caves where plants were grown. Kynes's father had died in an unexpected cave-in.

Ecology is dangerous.

Thanks to work and resources invested by Muad'Dib and his son Leto II, Dune had eventually become lush and green. But as a cruel consequence of so much poisonous moisture, all the sandworms had died. Spice had dwindled to a trickle of a memory. Then, after thirty-five hundred years of the Tyrant's rule, the sandworms returned again from Leto's body, reversing the ecological progress and restoring the vast desert to Arrakis.

The scope of it! No matter how much battering leaders and armies and governments did to Arrakis, the planet would restore itself, given enough time. Dune was stronger than all of them.

Stilgar said, "Just looking at the desert soothes me. I don't exactly *remember*, but I do know that I belong here."

Kynes also felt at peace looking at this swatch of a long-lost planet. Dune was where he belonged, as well. Thanks to the advanced Bene Gesserit training methods, he had already studied as much background as he could get his hands on, learning about ecological processes and the science of planetology. Many of the original and still-classic treatises on the subject had been written by his own father, documented in Imperial archives and preserved for millennia by the Sisterhood.

Stilgar rubbed his palm across the observation window, but the blur of dust was inside the plaz. "I wish we could go in there with Sheeana. A long time ago I knew how to ride the worms."

"Those were different worms. I've compared records. These come from sandtrout spawned by the dissolution of Leto II. They are less territorial, but more dangerous."

"They are still worms," Stilgar said with a shrug.

Down on the sand, Sheeana had stopped her dance and was resting against the side of one worm. She looked up, as if she knew the two ghola boys were in the observation chamber, watching her. As she continued to stare toward them, the largest of the worms also lifted its head, sensing they were there.

"Something's happening," Kynes said. "I've never seen them do that before."

Sheeana dodged lightly away as the seven worms came together and piled one on top of the other, twisting into a single, larger unit that reared up high enough to reach the observation plaz.

Stilgar pulled away, more in reverence than fear.

Sheeana scrambled up the side of the entwined creatures, all the way to the top of the tallest ringed head. While the two ghola boys watched in astonishment, she resumed her gyrations for several minutes, but now she was on top of the worm's head, both a dancer and a rider. When she stopped, the worm tower divided and unraveled into its seven original components, and Sheeana rode one of them back down to the ground.

Neither of the ghola boys spoke for several minutes. They looked at each other with grins of wonder.

Below, an exhausted Sheeana walked with dragging steps toward the lift. Kynes considered making some excuse to rush down and speak with her while she was fresh from the sands, as a good planetologist should do. He wanted to smell the flinty odor of worms on her body. It would be very interesting and potentially informative. He and Stilgar both longed to understand how she could control the creatures, though each boy had a different reason for wanting to know.

Kynes followed her departure with his gaze. "Even after we get our memories back, she's going to be a mystery to us."

Stilgar's nostrils flared. "Shai-Hulud does not devour her. That is enough for me."

I will die four deaths—the death of the flesh, the death of the soul, the death of the myth, and the death of reason. And all of these deaths contain the seeds of resurrection.

> —LETO ATREIDES II,
> Dar-es-Balat recordings

Doria's life had become ridiculous, as Bellonda-within reminded her incessantly.

You're getting fat yourself, said the other Reverend Mother.

"It's your fault!" Doria snapped. Indeed, she had gained weight, and a significant amount, though she'd continued her vigorous training and exercises. Each day she monitored her metabolism with her own inner techniques, but to no avail. Her once lithe and wiry body now showed noticeable signs of bulk. "You weigh like a heavy stone inside me." She heard Bellonda's chuckle clearly in her head.

Grousing to herself as quietly as she could, the former Honored Matre tramped up the face of a small dune, slogging through loose sand. Fifteen other Sisters traipsed along behind her wearing identical singlesuits. They chattered amongst themselves while reading aloud from the instruments and charts they carried. This group actually *liked* doing such miserable work.

These spice-ops recruits took regular spectral and temperature readings on the sand, mapping out the narrow spice veins and limited deposits. The readings were dispatched to the desert research stations, then combined with firsthand observations to determine the best locations for harvesting operations.

As the planet's free moisture diminished dramatically, the growing worms were finally producing more melange—more "product," as the Mother Commander put it. She was anxious to press the New Sisterhood's advantage, to pay for the huge shipments of armaments being assembled on Richese, and to bribe the Guild to facilitate the ongoing war preparations. Murbella spent melange and soostone wealth as fast as it came in, then demanded more, and more.

Behind Doria, two young Valkyrie trainees practiced fighting maneuvers on the soft sand, attacking and defending. The women had to adjust their techniques depending on the steepness of dune slopes, loose dust or packed sand, or the buried hazards of dead trees.

Feeling the hot blood of her Honored Matre past, Doria would rather have been fighting, too. Perhaps she would be allowed to join the final assault on Tleilax, whenever Murbella decided she had gathered enough forces for the great battle. What a victory that would be! Doria could have fought on Buzzell, on Gammu, on any number of the recent battlefields. She would have made an excellent Valkyrie herself—and now she was little more than . . . than an administrator! Why couldn't she be allowed to shed blood for the New Sisterhood? Fighting was her best skill.

Trapped in her position, Doria continued to come out to the desert, but she had grown impatient over the years. *Am I sentenced to babysit this planet forever? Is this my punishment for the single mistake of killing fat old Bellonda?*

Ah, you admit it was a mistake now? prodded the annoying voice within.

Quiet, you bloated old fool.

She could never get away from Bellonda inside her head. The constant taunting reminded Doria of her own shortcomings and even offered unwanted advice in how to fix them. Like Sisyphus, Doria would roll that boulder up a hill for the rest of her life. And now she found her body growing fat as well.

Inside her head, Bellonda actually seemed to be humming. Presently, the internal voice said, *In ancient times on Terra, people had something called a doorbell, which a visitor rang when coming to a door.*

"So what?" Doria said aloud, then quickly turned her face away from the trainees, who looked at her oddly.

So, that is our combined name: Doria-Bellonda. DorBell. Ding-dong, ding-dong, can I come in?

No, damn you. Go away!

Fuming, Doria concentrated on the analytical instruments. Why couldn't the Mother Commander find a dedicated planetologist somewhere out in all the surviving worlds of humanity? On her scanners, she saw merely numbers and electronic diagrams that were of no real interest to her.

Each day for six infuriating years, Doria had gritted her teeth and tried to ignore Bellonda's inner nagging. It was the only way she could go about her tasks. Murbella had told her to subjugate herself to the needs of her Sisters, but like so many Bene Gesserit concepts, "subjugation" worked better in theory than in practical application.

The Mother Commander had been able to mold others into what she wanted, forging the united Sisterhood, even retraining and incorporating some of the captured rebel Honored Matres. Though Doria had insinuated herself into a position of power beside Murbella, she could not completely suppress the natural violence embedded in her nature, the quick and decisive responses that often resulted in bloodshed. It was not in her nature to compromise, but pure survival dictated that she become what the Mother Commander wanted her to be. *Damn her! Has she actually succeeded in making me a Bene Gesserit, after all?*

Bellonda-within chuckled again.

Ultimately, Doria wondered if she would have to face off against Murbella herself. Over the years, many others had challenged the Mother Commander, and all had died in the attempt. Doria did not fear for her life, but she did fear the possibility of making the wrong decision. Yes, Murbella was stern and maddeningly unpredictable, but after almost two decades, it was not so clear that her merger scheme had been wrong.

Suddenly Doria tore her mind from its preoccupation, and she noticed the distant mounds of sand in motion, ripples drawing closer and closer.

The voice of Bellonda harangued her. *Are you blind as well as stupid? You have stirred up the worms with all your stomping around.*

"They are stunted."

That may be, but they are still dangerous. You are as arrogant as ever, thinking you can defeat anything that gets in your way. You refuse to acknowledge a real threat.

"You weren't much of a threat," Doria muttered.

One of the trainees cried out, pointing to the two moving mounds out on the sand. "Sandworms! Traveling together!"

"Over there, too!" another said.

Doria saw that worms were all around them and closing in as if drawn by a common signal. The women scrambled to take readings. "Gods! They're twice the size of the average specimens we recorded two months ago."

Inside Doria's head, Bellonda harped, *Stupid, stupid, stupid!*

"Shut up, damn you, Bell! I need to think."

Think? Can't you see the danger? Do something!

The worms rushed in from several directions; they showed definite signs of cooperative behavior. The shifting lines in the sand reminded Doria of a pack. A *hunting* pack.

"To the 'thopters!" Doria saw that their group had come too far out along the dunes. The flying vehicles were some distance away.

The newly trained Sisters began to panic. Some of them ran, sliding in tumbles of loose sand down the slipface of the dunes. They dropped their instruments and charts on the ground. A Sister sent an urgent commlink message back to Chapterhouse Keep.

See where your stupid plan got you, Bellonda said. *If you had not killed me, I would have been able to keep watch. I would never have let this happen.*

"Shut up!"

Those worms are stalking you now. You stalked me, and now they're stalking you.

One of the Sisters screamed, and then another. More worms rose up from the dunes, homing in on the moving figures. Several Valkyrie trainees stood together, trying to fight against the impossible.

Doria stared, wide-eyed. The creatures were each at least twenty meters long, and moved with astonishing speed. "Begone! Back to your desert!"

You're not Sheeana. The worms will not do as you say.

Crystal teeth flashed as the worms darted forward, scooping up sand and Sisters, swallowing victims into the furnaces of their gullets.

Idiot! Bellonda-within exclaimed. *Now you've killed me twice.*

A fraction of a second later, a worm rose up then dove down, consuming Doria in a single mouthful. At last, the irksome voice went quiet within.

The magic of our God is our only bridge.
　　　　　　　　—from the Sufi-Zensunni scriptures,
　　　　　　　　　Catechism of the Great Belief

D espite the constant bone-grating fear for his life, Uxtal continued his work with the numerous Waff gholas, and he did it well
enough to keep himself alive. The Honored Matres could see his
progress. Three years ago he had decanted the first eight identical gholas of the Tleilaxu Master. Accelerated in their bodily development,
the little gray children seemed more than twice their actual age.

As he watched them at play, Uxtal found them quite appealing
with their disarmingly gnomish appearance, pointed noses, and sharp
teeth. After undergoing rapid educational impression, they had
learned to speak in only a few months, but even so they seemed feral in
a way, tied together in their private world and interacting little with
their prison-keepers.

Uxtal would prod them in any way he felt necessary. The Waff gholas were like small time bombs of vital information, and he had to find
a way to detonate them. He no longer thought, or cared, about the first
two gholas he had created. Khrone had taken them away to Dan long
ago. Good riddance!

These offspring, however, were his to command and control. Waff was one of the heretical old Masters, ripe for reindoctrination. God had certainly taken a circuitous route to show Uxtal his true destiny. Desperate for spice, the Navigators believed Uxtal was their tool, that he was doing their bidding. To him, though, it didn't matter if the Navigators reaped the benefits, or if Matre Superior Hellica hoarded all the profits. Uxtal wouldn't see any of it.

I am performing holy work now, he thought. *That is what matters.*

According to the most sacred writings, the Prophet—long before he reincarnated as the God Emperor—had spent eight days in the wilderness where he received his magnificent revelations. Those days in the wilderness had been a time of trial and tribulation, much like the Lost Tleilaxu race had faced during the Scattering, much like Uxtal's own recent ordeals. In his darkest hour, the Prophet had received the information he needed, and now so had Uxtal. He was on the right path.

Though the little researcher had never formally been declared a Master, he nonetheless considered himself one by default. Who else had a greater position of power now? Who else had more authority, more genetic knowledge? Once he learned the secrets locked in the minds of these Waffs, he would surpass any Elder of the Lost Tleilaxu and any old Master who had ever lived in Bandalong. He would have it all (even if the Navigator and the Honored Matres took it from him).

Uxtal began the process of cracking these eight identical gholas as soon as they could speak and think. If he failed, he could always try with the next eight, which had already been grown. He would hold them—and all subsequent batches—in reserve. *One* of the Waffs would reveal his secrets.

Within only a few years, the rapidly growing bodies of the initial eight would reach physical maturity. Though they might be cute, Uxtal mainly saw the children as meat to be harvested for a specific purpose, like the sligs next door at Gaxhar's farm.

At the moment, the Waff gholas were running around inside an electronic enclosure. The accelerated children wanted to get out, and each one had a brilliant little mind. The Waffs probed the shimmering field with their fingers to see how it worked and how to disable it. Uxtal thought they might just accomplish that, given enough time. They rarely spoke except amongst each other, he knew how fiendishly intelligent they must be.

But Uxtal knew that he was smarter.

Interestingly, he observed dissension and competition, but very little cooperation among the eight children. The Waffs fought over toys and play equipment, over food, over a favorite place to sit, uttering very few words. Were they somehow telepathic? Interesting. Perhaps he should dissect one of them.

Even when they scrambled onto each other's shoulders to see if one of them could leap over the force field, they argued over who got to stand on top. Though the gholas were identical, they didn't trust one another. If he could pit them against each other, Uxtal was sure he could apply the right amount of pressure to wring out the information he needed.

One of the children tumbled off the edge of a slippery ramp and fell onto the hard floor. He began crying and holding his arm, which appeared to be broken, or at least severely sprained. To keep track of them, Uxtal had pressed tiny numerical brands onto their left wrists. This one was Number Five. As the child wailed, his genetic siblings ignored him.

Uxtal told two of his lab assistants to open the force field to let him step through. He was disgusted and impatient with the need to provide unnecessary medical attention; maybe these children would be easier to control if he just strapped them to the tables, like their sperm-donor predecessors.

Old Ingva was there as always, watching, leering, and silently threatening. Uxtal tried to concentrate on his immediate obligations. Kneeling by the injured toddler, he tried to inspect Number Five's arm, to see how badly it was injured. The Waff yanked himself away, refusing to let Uxtal near.

Abruptly, the other seven Waffs formed a circle around the researcher. When they moved closer, he could smell their sour breath. Something was wrong. "Get back!" he barked, trying to sound intimidating. They were on all sides of him, and he had an uneasy feeling that they had tricked him, lured him inside.

The eight Waffs fell upon him with bared sharp teeth, biting and ripping at his skin and clothing. He thrashed and struck back, shouting for his assistants, knocking the small, gnomish gholas away. They were only children, yet they had formed a deadly sort of pack. Were they working together in a hive mentality, like Face Dancers? Even the supposedly injured boy threw himself into the fray, his "broken arm" a sham.

Fortunately, the Waffs were not strong yet, and he sent them skidding across the floor. The anxious lab assistants helped Uxtal keep them at bay while they pulled the shaken researcher back out through the field.

Breathing hard and sweating, he tried to gather his composure and looked around for someone to blame. His injuries were minor, only a few scrapes and bruises, but he was appalled that they had taken him by surprise.

Left in their pen, the identical gholas ran about in a frenzy of frustration. Finally, they all fell silent and went off to different parts of the enclosure to play, as if nothing had happened.

"'Men must do God's work,'" Uxtal reminded himself, from the catechism of the Great Belief. Next time, he would be more careful with these little monsters.

Is it enough just to find a home, or must we create one for our-selves? I am willing to do either, if we would only decide.

—PROCTOR SUPERIOR GARIMI,
personal journals

Another blind jump through foldspace. The *Ithaca* emerged safely, following its random course according to the whims of pre-science. With Duncan at the controls, the no-ship cruised toward a bright, comfortable-looking planet. A new world. He and Teg had con-ferred on the course, on the wisdom of making another journey at all even though the hunters had not found them again—and the two of them had brought the great vessel to this place.

Even from a distance the planet looked promising, and excitement blossomed among the refugees aboard the vessel. At long last, after almost two decades of wandering, three years since the dead no-planet, could this be a place to rest and recuperate? A new home?

"It looks perfect." Sheeana set aside the summary of the scan data, looked at Duncan and Teg. "Your instinct guided us true."

Standing with them on the navigation bridge, anxious Garimi looked at the landmasses, oceans, clouds. "Unless it's another plague world."

Duncan shook his head. "We're already detecting transmissions from small cities, so there's an active populace. Most of the continents are forested and fertile. Temperature is well within habitable norms. Atmospheric content, moisture, vegetation . . . It may be one of the worlds settled in the Scattering, long ago. So many groups were lost, disappearing into the wilderness."

Garimi's eyes gleamed. "We have to investigate. This could be the place to found our new Bene Gesserit core."

Duncan was more practical. "If nothing else, it would be good for us to refresh the ship's supplies of air and water. Our stores and recycling systems can't last forever, and our population is gradually growing."

Garimi blurted, "I will call an all-ship meeting. There is more at stake here than simply replenishing our supplies. What if the inhabitants down there welcome us? What if it is a suitable place for us to settle?" She looked around. "At least for some of us."

"Then we will have an important decision to make."

EVEN WITH EVERY adult onboard in attendance, the *Ithaca*'s huge convocation chamber looked mostly empty. Miles Teg sat back against a low-tier seat, continually repositioning his long legs. Though he would observe the discussion with interest, he expected to make few comments. He had always followed the mandate of the Bene Gesserit, but at the moment he wasn't sure what the mandate was.

A young man took a seat adjacent to Teg, the ghola of Thufir Hawat. The heavy-browed twelve-year-old did not usually go out of his way to be with the Bashar, but Teg knew that Thufir watched him intently, almost to the point of hero worship. In the archives, Thufir often studied details of Miles Teg's military career.

Teg nodded to the young man. This was the loyal weapons master and warrior Mentat who had served the Old Duke Atreides, then Duke Leto, and finally Paul, before being captured by the Harkonnens. Teg felt he had much in common with the battle-seasoned genius; someday, after the Thufir Hawat ghola had his memories again, they would have many things to discuss, commander to commander.

Thufir leaned over, gathered his courage, and whispered, "I have wanted to speak with you, Bashar Teg, about the Cerbol Revolt and the Battle of Ponciard. Your tactics were most unusual. I cannot imagine they would have worked, and yet they did."

Teg smiled with the memory. "They wouldn't have worked for anyone else. As the Bene Gesserit use their Missionaria Protectiva to plant the seeds of religious fervor, so my soldiers created a myth about my abilities. I became larger than life, and my opponents managed to intimidate themselves more than my soldiers or weapons could have done. I really did very little in each battle."

"I disagree, sir. In order for your reputation to become such a potent tool, you first had to earn it."

Teg smiled and kept his voice low, almost wistful as he admitted the truth in his own mythology. "Ah, and earn it I did." He explained to the fascinated young man how he had also averted a massacre on Andioyu, a confrontation against the desperate dregs of a losing army that would surely have resulted in their deaths as well as the slaughter of tens of thousands of civilians. Much had hung in the balance on that day. . . .

"And then you died on Rakis fighting the Honored Matres."

"As a point of fact, I died on Rakis to *provoke* the Honored Matres, as part of the overall Bene Gesserit plan. I played my role so that Duncan Idaho and Sheeana could escape. But after I was killed, the Sisterhood brought me back because they considered my Mentat skills and experiences to be invaluable—like your own. That is why they brought us all back."

Thufir was completely engrossed. "I've read the history of my own life, and I'm convinced that I can learn much from you, Bashar."

With a smile, Teg squeezed the boy's shoulder. Thufir was abashed. "Have I said something amusing, sir?"

"When I look at you, how can I not remember that I myself learned a great deal from studying the famous warrior-Mentat of House Atreides? You and I could be very useful to each other." The boy blushed.

When the debate began, Teg and Thufir turned their attention to the center of the convocation chamber. Sheeana remained seated in the imposing Advocate's Chair, a carryover from when this vessel had been designed for other groups.

Garimi, as usual, was anxious to provoke a change in the status quo.

She strutted forward to the podium and spoke without preamble, loud enough for everyone to hear. "We did not depart on a race or a journey. Our goal was to get away from Chapterhouse before the Honored Matres destroyed everything. Our intent was to preserve the core of the Sisterhood, and we have done so. But where are we going? That question has plagued us for nineteen years."

Duncan stood. "We escaped from the true Enemy who was closing in. They still want us—that hasn't changed."

"Do they want *us*?" Garimi challenged. "Or do they want *you*?"

He shrugged. "Who can say? I am not willing to be captured or destroyed just to have your questions answered. Many of us have special talents on this ship—especially the ghola children—and we need all of our resources."

The Rabbi spoke up. Though he was still fit and healthy, his beard and hair were grayer and longer now; behind spectacles, his bird-bright eyes were surrounded by a mesh of wrinkles. "My people and I did not choose any of this. We asked for rescue from Gammu, and we've been trapped in your folly ever since. When will it end? After forty years in the wilderness? When will you let us go?"

"And where would you like to go, Rabbi?" Sheeana's voice was calm, but Teg thought it sounded somewhat patronizing.

"I would like us to consider—seriously consider—the planet we have just found. I am reluctant to call it Zion, but perhaps it is enough to call it home." The old man looked back at his handful of followers, all of whom wore dark clothes and adhered to their old ways. Though aboard the *Ithaca* they no longer needed to hide their religion, the Jews mostly kept to themselves, unwilling to be assimilated by the other passengers. They had their own children, ten so far, and raised them as they saw fit.

Finally, Teg spoke. "According to our scans, this planet appears to be an excellent place to settle. The population is minimal. Our group of refugees would cause almost no disturbance at all to the local inhabitants. We could even choose an isolated spot and settle far from the natives."

"How advanced is their civilization? Do they have technology?" Sheeana asked.

"At least at pre-Scattering levels," Teg said. "Indications show minor local industries, a few electromagnetic transmissions. No apparent spaceflight capability, no visible spaceports. If they settled here after the Scattering, they haven't done any more traveling to other star systems." In running scans of the new planet, he had enlisted the aid of eager young Liet-Kynes and his friend Stilgar, both of whom had studied more about ecology and planetary dynamics than most of the adult Sisters. All of the readings checked out.

"It could be a new Chapterhouse," Garimi said, as if the discussion were already over.

Duncan's face darkened. "We would be vulnerable if we settled there. The hunters have found us several times already. If we remain too long in one place, we will be ensnared in their net."

"Why would your mysterious hunters have any interest in *my* people?" the Rabbi said. "*We* are free to settle on this world."

"It's clear that we must investigate further," Sheeana said. "We will take a lighter down to the surface on a fact-finding mission. Let's meet these people and learn from them. Then we can all make an informed decision."

Teg turned to the young ghola in the seat beside him and said impulsively, "I intend to go on this expedition, Thufir, and I would like you to accompany me."

In our arrogant assumption of superiority, we believe that our developed senses and abilities are the direct result of evolution. We are convinced that our race has bettered itself through technological advancement. Therefore, we are shamed and embarrassed when something we consider to be "primitive" has senses far superior to our own.

— REVEREND MOTHER SHEEANA,
Ithaca logs

While the mission to the planet was being assembled, the *Ithaca* rode unseen in orbit. Though the no-field limited the ship's sensors, it was a necessary safety factor until they learned more about the inhabitants.

As the de facto captain, Duncan would remain aboard the no-ship, ready in the event of an emergency, since only he could see the mysterious web. Sheeana wanted Miles Teg with her, and the Bashar insisted on bringing the ghola of Thufir Hawat. "Physically he is only twelve years old, but we know Thufir has the potential to become a great warrior-Mentat. We must encourage those skills to blossom if he is to be useful to us." No one argued with his choice.

Concurrent with the fact-finding mission, Duncan made arrangements for a small contingent of workers to go to an uninhabited part of the planet with equipment to gather water, air, and any available food, in order to bolster the no-ship's supplies. Just in case they decided to move on.

As Sheeana was finalizing the details for departure, the Rabbi entered the navigation bridge and stood as if expecting a challenge.

His eyes flashed, and his stance stiffened, though no one had yet argued with him, or even spoken to him. His demand surprised them. "I will go down to the planet with this expedition. My people insist on it. If this is to be a home for us, I will make that decision. You will not stop me from going along. It is my right."

"It is a small group," Sheeana cautioned. "We don't know what we'll encounter down there."

The Rabbi jabbed a finger at Teg. "He plans to bring one of the ghola children. If it is safe enough for a twelve-year-old boy, then it is safe enough for me."

Duncan had known the original Thufir Hawat. Even without his memories restored, he would not consider the ghola a mere child. Nevertheless, he said, "I don't object to you joining the party, if Sheeana will have you."

"Sheeana does not decide my fate!"

She seemed amused by his posturing. "Don't I? It seems to me that all the decisions I make aboard this no-ship have a direct impact on your situation."

Impatient, Teg cut off their bickering. "We have had nineteen years aboard this vessel to argue amongst ourselves. A planet waits for us. Shouldn't we see what we are quarreling about first?"

BEFORE SHE COULD depart for the planet, Sheeana was called to the brig levels by a nervous worker. The Futars let out a great caterwauling, far more restless than usual inside their locked, metal-walled arboretum. They paced, searching for a way out. Whenever they came close to each other, they snapped and snarled, halfheartedly slashing at each other. Then, before more than a few droplets of blood could fly into the air, the beast-men lost interest and continued prowling. One of them emitted a bloodcurdling shriek, a noise perfectly programmed to evoke primal human fear. In all the years aboard the no-ship, the Futars had never exhibited such frantic behavior before.

Sheeana stood at the arboretum doorway, looming like a goddess; against her better judgment, she deactivated the lock field and stepped inside. Only she could soothe the four creatures and communicate with them in a primitive way.

As the largest of the Futars, Hrrm had taken the position of dominance, partly because of his strength and partly because of his connection with Sheeana. He bounded toward her, and she did not move, did not flinch. He bristled, showing his canine teeth, raising his claws.

"You not Handler," he said.

"I am Sheeana. You know me."

"Take us to Handlers."

"I have already promised you. As soon as we find the Handlers, we will deliver you to them."

"Handlers *here!*" Hrrm's next words were unintelligible growls and snarls, then he said, "Home. Home down there." He hurled himself against the wall. The other Futars yowled.

"Home? Handlers?" Sheeana sucked in a quick breath. "This is the home of the Handlers?"

"Our home!" Hrrm came back to her. "Take us home."

She reached out to scratch the sensitive spot on his back. Her decision was obvious. "All right, Hrrm. I will take you home."

The predator rubbed against her. "Not Handler. You Sheeana."

"I am Sheeana. I am your friend. I will take you to the Handlers." She saw that the other three half-human creatures had been standing still, their muscles coiled to pounce if she had given the wrong answer. Their eyes glowed yellow with an inner hunger and a desperate need.

The planet of the Handlers!

If the Bene Gesserits hoped to make a good impression on the inhabitants below, returning four lost Futars might gain them leverage. And it would be good for her to bring them back where they belonged.

"Sheeana promised," Hrrm said. "Sheeana friend. Sheeana not bad lady Honored Matre."

Smiling, she stroked the creature again. "You four will accompany me."

*Even a great tower has its weak point. The accomplished warrior
finds and exploits the smallest flaws to bring about complete ruin.*

—MATRE SUPERIOR HELLICA,
Internal Directive 67B-1138

Now that Matre Superior Hellica had provided the services of her
pet Lost Tleilaxu researcher, Edrik was confident that Uxtal
could re-create one of the old Masters who knew how to manufacture
spice. Had not the Oracle herself told him there was a solution?

But now the Matre Superior demanded something in return. If he
meant to have his manufactured spice, Edrik could not refuse.

Reluctantly, the Navigator accepted the task, knowing full well the
consequences he risked. The witch Murbella would be furious, which was
only part of the reason he took pleasure in what they were about to do.

Five years ago, brash Honored Matres from Gammu had tried to
launch their last few Obliterators against Chapterhouse itself, but that
had been a flawed plan from the start. Even the Navigator aboard that
Heighliner had been unaware of the scope of the threat. By attacking
Chapterhouse, the Honored Matres had meant to wipe out the only
remaining source of melange. Idiocy! The foolish whores had failed,
and Mother Commander Murbella had seized their Obliterators.
Shortly afterward, she had crushed the Honored Matres on Gammu
and destroyed their entire enclave.

This time, though, the objective was different, and Edrik had no qualms about helping Hellica punish Murbella and her greedy witches. The Bene Gesserit would feel the sting, and a billion people would die on Richese in a matter of moments. Edrik did not feel guilty, however. The Spacing Guild had not provoked this crisis. Therefore, the blood would be on Murbella's hands.

The New Sisterhood's draconian spice policies had done little to ensure loyalty or cooperation from the Navigators. The Guild paid exorbitant prices for black-market melange squeezed out of ancient stockpiles, while the Administrator faction happily sought alternative guidance systems that would also make the Navigators obsolete.

Edrik had been forced to seek his own source of spice, relying on the memories locked inside the gholas of Tleilaxu Master Waff. Once those memories were awakened, the Navigators would have their own cheap and secure source of melange.

His Heighliner winked into existence above the industrialized planet. For millennia, Richese had been a sophisticated technological hub. The New Sisterhood had poured fortunes into Richese, and over the past several years the shipyards had grown larger than any of the famed Guild facilities on Junction or elsewhere—the most extensive the human race had ever put together. The Sisterhood claimed their newly manufactured weapons were to be used against the Outside Enemy. Without question, however, Murbella would first turn that might against the Honored Matres on Tleilax.

"Destroy it," said Matre Superior Hellica from her observation lounge below the Navigator's deck. "Destroy it all."

From spaceport complexes below and satellite stations, monitors pinged them with inquiries and communication bursts. Though Richese was a huge manufacturer of armaments, engaged in full-scale preparations for the coming battles, they'd never had any reason to suspect a threat from the Spacing Guild.

"Guild Heighliner, we were not aware of a scheduled arrival."

"Please transmit your manifests. Which docking centers will you utilize?"

"Heighliners, we will prepare our outgoing shipments. Is a CHOAM representative aboard?"

Edrik did not answer. The Matre Superior issued no ultimatum, delivered no warning. She did not even open the channel so that she could gloat.

Guildsmen followed the detailed preparations for deploying the last few Obliterators the rebel Honored Matres had kept on Tleilax. Floating in his sealed tank, Edrik smiled. This would set back the New Sisterhood's military plans by years, if not decades. All those weapons gone, as well as the industrial capability to manufacture more. In a single strike Matre Superior Hellica would remove a keystone from the arch of human civilization.

I do it for spice, Edrik thought. *The Oracle promised us a new source of melange.*

Hatches opened in the Heighliner's belly, disgorging Obliterators that dropped toward the planet like molten cannonballs. Reaching the appropriate atmospheric depths, the weapons fissioned and spread ripples of hot annihilation. The people of Richese could not conceive of what was happening as their whole planet began to catch fire.

Cracks raced across the continents, and flamefronts roared through the atmosphere. The electromagnetic bands were full of desperate cries, screams of terror and pain, and then piercing EMP feedback as the Obliterators completed their work. Across the planet, weapons shops, construction yards, cities, mountain ranges, and whole oceans vanished into ionized vapor. The ground itself turned to a blistering, baking ceramic.

Even Edrik was awed by what he saw. He hoped that Hellica understood what she was doing. This was an aggression Mother Commander Murbella could never ignore, and she would know whom to blame. Tleilax was the only rebel Honored Matre enclave left.

In silence, the Heighliner departed, leaving the now-dead Richese behind.

Rot at the core always spreads outward.

—Sufi proverb

There is a time for violence, and for talking. This is not the time for talking." Murbella had called both Janess and the former Honored Matre Kiria to stand beside her in the highest tower of the Keep. After the annihilation of Richese, her anger grew hot enough to sear even the voices in Other Memory. "We need to cut the head off the monster."

So many vital weapons had been destroyed there, a gigantic and fully armed fleet nearly completed, so much potential for the defense of humanity—all ruined by the bitch queen Hellica! Aside from the armament shipments they had already received, Murbella had nothing but cooling slag to show for her years of payments to Richese.

It was an overcast morning on Chapterhouse, with clouds that owed more to dust storms than to rain. A cold front had swept in. Such were the vagaries of climate in the ecosystem's death throes. On the practice field far below, the Valkyries wore heavy-hooded black robes and gloves against the biting wind, though Reverend Mothers could manipulate their metabolism to endure temperature extremes. Their furious mock combat engagements were breathtaking as they abandoned themselves to violence. They had all heard the news of the destruction of Richese.

"Tleilax is our last and only target," Kiria said. "We should move without delay. Strike now, and without mercy."

Janess was more cautious. "We cannot afford anything but total victory. That is their most powerful remaining stronghold, the one where the whores are most entrenched."

Murbella's expression turned cagey. "That is why we will employ a different tactic. I need the two of you to open the way."

"But we will strike Tleilax?" Kiria was fixated on the idea.

"No, we will *conquer* it." The bitter breeze increased in intensity. "I will kill Matre Superior Hellica myself, and the Valkyries will eradicate the rest of the rebel whores. Once and for all."

Murbella wanted to bravely reassure them that the New Sisterhood would get other weapons, other ships. But from where? And how would they pay for such a massive expenditure when they were already nearly bankrupt, their credit extended beyond any realistic ability to repay?

The necessary steps were clear to her. Increase spice-harvesting efforts in the Chapterhouse desert band and offer more spice to the ravenous Guild, which should convince them to cooperate with the Sisterhood's much larger plan to defend humanity. If she fed their insatiable hunger for melange, the Guild would be happy to help her mount an effective military operation. A small enough price to pay.

"What is your plan, Mother Commander?" Janess asked.

She turned to her grim-faced daughter and the brash Kiria. "You two will take a team down to Tleilax in secret. Dress as Honored Matres and move among them, exposing their weaknesses. I give you three weeks to find ways to bring down our enemies from within their own ranks, and then to implement the scheme. Be ready in time for my full-scale assault."

"You want me to pretend to be one of the whores?" Janess asked.

Kiria sniffed. "It will be simple for us. No Honored Matre could control herself well enough to walk undetected among us, but the converse is not true." She flashed a feral grin at Janess. "I can show you how."

The other young woman was already grasping the possibilities. "By

moving secretly among them, we can plant explosives in key strongholds, sabotage their defenses, and transmit encoded plans with all the
details of how well entrenched they are in Bandalong. We can cause
chaos and disruption at a critical moment—"

Kiria cut her off. "We will open the way for you, Mother Commander." She flexed her clawlike fingers, anxious to let herself become
bloodthirsty again. "I look forward to it."

Murbella stared into the distance. After Tleilax was secured, the
New Sisterhood, the Spacing Guild, and all other allies of humanity
could face the real Enemy. *If we are to be destroyed, let it be at the hands
of our true foe, rather than from a knife in the back.*

"Send for a Guild representative, immediately. I have a proposal to
make."

The Scattering spread us far from the reach of any single threat. It also changed us, making our genetic lines diverge so that never again would "human" mean only one thing.

—MOTHER SUPERIOR ALMA MAVIS TARAZA,
request for analysis and modification
of Bene Gesserit breeding program

Teg circled the no-ship's lighter over a forested area near one of the unusual native settlements. Sheeana noted a parklike city with cylindrical towers interspersed through thick trees, camouflaged to blend in with the forest landscape. The Handlers (if that was who they truly were) distributed their settlements evenly throughout the wooded zones. The people seemed to prefer open spaces to life in a dense, hivelike metropolis. Maybe the Scattering had quenched any desire for crowding.

Though he'd had little opportunity to practice flying, the Bashar obviously remembered his skills from his first life. When they touched down in a flower-spangled meadow, Sheeana barely felt a bump. Young Thufir Hawat sat in the copilot's seat observing everything his mentor did.

The forest city's main buildings were tall cylinders several stories high, made of golden-lacquered lumber like wooden organ pipes for a wilderness cathedral. Guard towers? Defensive structures? Or were these nothing more than observation platforms from which to gain an unblocked view of the serene and rolling woods?

All around them, the thick forest of silver-barked aspen derivatives was beautiful and healthy, as if the natives tended it with loving care. Previously, using the curt descriptions the Futars could give her, Sheeana had done her best to make the no-ship's arboretum reminiscent of the home they remembered. As she looked at the sweeping aspen analogs around them, however, Sheeana saw that she had failed miserably.

Secure in the cargo chamber at the back of the lighter, the four anxious Futars rumbled and yowled, as if they sensed they were home and knew the Handlers were near. When the vessel's side hatch opened and the boarding ramp extended, Sheeana stepped forward first. Teg and Thufir joined her on the soft grass, while the Rabbi hung back in the shelter of the lighter's door.

She drew a breath of bitingly clean air laden with a resinous scent of wood pulp and old leaves, scattered sawdust, and rain. Tiny yellow and white flowers added perfume to the air. The endlessly recycled air aboard the *Ithaca* had never smelled so good, nor had the dry air of Rakis where Sheeana had been a child, nor even Chapterhouse.

Not far away, Sheeana saw figures atop the towers. Other silhouettes appeared behind small windows cut through the lacquered mosaic of flat boards. Lookouts signaled from the circular roofs. Horns blew with a vibrating blat, while strobing light signals flashed to more-distant receivers. Everything looked bucolic, natural, and refreshingly primitive.

When a delegation finally came forward, Sheeana and her companions got their first look at the supposed Handlers. As a race, the people were tall and thin with narrow shoulders and elongated heads. Their long limbs were loose, and bent easily at the joints.

The leader was a comparatively handsome man with bristly silver-white hair. Most striking was the dark band of pigment that ran across his pale face and around his green eyes, like a bandit's mask. All of the natives, males and females, had the same raccoonlike pigmentation, which did not appear to be artificial.

As the group's spokesperson, Sheeana stepped forward. Before she could say a word, she noted an instant spark of suspicion as the natives focused on her, assessing, condemning. Ignoring the Rabbi, the Bashar, and Thufir Hawat, they directed their sharp gazes at her. Only her. She became instantly alert, her mind racing. What had she done wrong?

Then, when Sheeana considered their ambassadorial party—an old man, a young man, and a boy, all of whom accompanied a strong woman who clearly assumed command—she suddenly realized her foolishness. Handlers had bred Futars to hunt down and kill Honored Matres. Therefore, they must consider the whores their mortal enemies. And when they saw her supposedly in charge of these men—

"I am not an Honored Matre," she blurted out before they could draw an erroneous conclusion. "And these males are not my slaves. We have all fought the Honored Matres, and now we flee them."

The Rabbi reacted with surprise, frowning at Sheeana, as if he couldn't understand what she was talking about. "Of course you're not an Honored Matre!" He had not noticed the undercurrent of suspicion.

Teg, though, nodded with quick understanding. "We should have known better." Thufir Hawat also sorted through the information, reaching the same conclusion.

The tallest man with the raccoon eyes considered her words for a moment, glanced at the three men with Sheeana, and then bowed his elongated head. His voice was quiet but resonant, as if it emerged from deep in his chest instead of his throat. "Then we share the same enemies. I am Orak Tho, this district's Chief Handler."

Handlers. It is true, then. Sheeana felt a rush of excitement, and relief.

Orak Tho leaned forward, uncomfortably close to Sheeana. Instead of extending his hand in a more traditional greeting, he drew in a long, loud sniff at the base of her neck. He straightened in surprise. "You have Futars with you. I smell them on your skin and clothing."

"Four of them, rescued from the Honored Matres. They asked us to bring them here."

Teg whispered something to Thufir, and the young man obediently hurried back to the lighter. Showing no fear, he released the four beast-men from the secure compartment. The Futars bounded free, surging happily past the young man with Hrrm in the lead. Taking graceful leaps, he sprang across the soft meadow grass toward the Chief Handler and his companions.

"Home!" Hrrm purred in his throat.

Orak Tho bent his streamlined face closer to Hrrm's. The Handlers' movements also had a hint of the animal about them. Maybe such mannerisms helped the Handlers bond with the Futars, or maybe these two codependent branches of humanity were not so far apart after all.

The freed Futars milled among the Handlers, who touched and sniffed them excitedly. Sheeana smelled the heavy, musky odor of pheromones, released either for communication or control. Hrrm broke away just long enough to turn back toward Sheeana. In the glow of his yellow predator's eyes, she could read immense gratitude.

A ghola's memories can be a treasure trove or a crouching demon waiting to strike. Never unlock a ghola's past without first taking precautions to protect yourself.

—REVEREND MOTHER SCHWANGYU,
report from Gammu Keep

After three years of unsuccessful attempts and different torture techniques to awaken his memories, Vladimir began to fear that Khrone might be losing interest, or losing hope. Trapped in a rut of ineffective methods, the Face Dancer simply didn't know what he was doing. Even so, the fifteen-year-old ghola had come to look forward to their little "sessions of suffering." Having figured out that Khrone would never really hurt him, he had come to revel in the pain.

Today, when the Face Dancer guards told the ghola to lie back on a different table, he didn't bother to suppress his broad grin. Such smiles seemed to make them quite uncomfortable.

Vladimir had no real interest in cooperating just for the sake of pleasing Khrone, but he was very curious to access the thoughts of the historical Baron Harkonnen. He was sure those memories would be full of excellent ideas for amusing himself. Unfortunately, the fact that he wanted to have his memories back, and the perverse pleasure he derived from the pain inflicted upon him, turned out to be a hindrance.

While waiting, he looked around the stone-walled dungeon chamber of the restored castle, envisioning what it might have been like here in ancient times. The Atreides had probably made it sunny and bright, but he wondered if some long-forgotten duke had used this very chamber to torture captive Harkonnens.

Yes, Vladimir could imagine what such devices might have been like. Electronic probes that could be inserted into living bodies, tunneling instruments that could seek and destroy specific organs. Archaic, old-fashioned, and effective . . .

When Khrone entered the chamber, his normally placid face showed tiny marks of tension around the mouth and eyes. "In our last session you were very nearly terminated. Too much cerebral stress. I shall have to gauge your limits better."

"Oh, how awful that must have been for you!" the fifteen-year-old said sarcastically and gave an exaggerated sigh. "If restoring my memories requires so much pain that it kills me, then all your hard work will be for nothing. What to do? What to do?"

The Face Dancer leaned close. "You will see soon enough."

Vladimir heard the sounds of machinery, the noise of something clattering and rolling into the room. It came toward the top of his head, but remained out of his range of vision. The anticipation and ominous fear felt delicious. What would Khrone do differently this time?

The unseen machine sounded like it was directly behind him now, but it did not stop. Vladimir turned his head from side to side and saw a thick-walled cylindrical chamber sliding slowly forward, beginning to engulf him as if he were being swallowed by a whale. The cylinder was like a large pipe or a medical diagnostic unit. Or a coffin.

Vladimir felt a thrill of pleasure as he guessed what this machine must be. A whole-body Agony Box! The Face Dancers must have built it specially for him to create a more intimate experience. The young man grinned, but asked no questions, for fear of spoiling any surprises the Face Dancers might have in store for him. From outside, Khrone watched him with an unreadable expression as the table slid entirely into the chamber. The ugly, patchwork observers were also there, but no one spoke.

The machine's end cap snapped shut and sealed with a hiss. Vladimir's ears popped as the pressure changed. Khrone's voice came over a tinny-sounding speaker system. "You are about to experience a variation on the processes used by old Tleilaxu Masters to develop their Twisted Mentats."

"Ah, I had a Twisted Mentat once." Vladimir laughed with genuine fearlessness. "Are you going to talk about the device, or use it?"

The illumination shut off inside the cylinder, plunging him into complete blackness. Indeed, something different!

"Do you think I'm afraid of the dark?" he shouted, but the walls of the cylinder were coated with a sound-absorbing substance that swallowed even the whisper of an echo. He couldn't see anything.

Surrounded by a faint hum, he felt himself growing weightless. The table dropped away beneath him and he could no longer feel it against his back. Cradled in a suspensor field that held him perfectly balanced and immobile, he could no longer feel anything or see anything. The temperature was perfect inside the chamber, imparting no sensation of heat or cold. Even the faint humming stopped, leaving him in a silence so absolute that he could hear nothing but a slight ringing in his ears, and even that faded.

"This is boring! When is it going to start?"

The darkness remained, and silence, its companion, as well. He felt nothing and could not move.

Vladimir made a rude noise. "This is ridiculous." Khrone clearly did not grasp the nuances of sadism. "You play with my body to get to my mind, and play with my mind to get to my body, twisting, contorting. Is that all you have?"

Ten minutes later—or was it an hour?—he still had no answer. "Khrone?"

Nothing happened. He remained perfectly comfortable, detached from all sensation. "I am ready! Do your worst!"

Khrone didn't answer. No pain came. Nothing. They must be trying to drive his anticipation to a fever pitch. He licked his lips. It would start any second now.

Khrone left him there in dark, weightless isolation for an eternity.

Vladimir tried to clutch at memories of previous sensations, but they kept slipping away, fading from his mind. Struggling to retrieve the thoughts, he followed a mental pathway and felt himself carried on a neural conduit deep into his own brain, a realm of total darkness. The experiences he sought were pinpoints of light ahead, and he swam toward them. But they swam away faster, and farther than he could reach.

Another eternity passed.

Hours? Days?

He could feel nothing, absolutely nothing. Vladimir didn't want to be here. He wanted to swim back out to the light that was his ghola life before this session had begun. But he couldn't. It was a trap!

Eventually, he screamed. At first, it was just to make noise, to disturb the throbbing emptiness. Then he screamed for real, and once he started he could not stop himself.

Even so, the silence remained. He thrashed and struggled, but the field kept him immobile. He couldn't breathe. He couldn't hear. Had the Face Dancers blinded him somehow? Made him deaf?

Vladimir wet himself, and for a few moments the mere sensation was a revelation, but it quickly faded. And he was left alone in empty, silent, darkness. He needed sensation, stimulus, pain, interaction, pleasure. Anything!

Finally, he became aware of a gradual change around him. Nonexistent illumination, sounds, and smells seeped in, gradually filling the stygian universe, converting it to something else. Even the tiniest glimmer was like an explosion. With that catalyst, senses poured into his conscious and unconscious mind, filling every cavity. Pain, a mental pain, made his head feel as if it would explode.

He screamed again. This time, the pain brought no semblance of pleasure whatsoever.

The full life of the Baron Vladimir Harkonnen flooded back into the ghola body with all the subtlety of an avalanche. Every thought and experience came back to him, all the way up to the moment of his first death on Arrakis. He saw the little girl Alia stabbing him with the poisoned needle, the gom jabbar—

The internal universe expanded, and he became aware of voices again. He was outside the chamber now, withdrawn from the large coffinlike device.

The Baron sat up indignantly, pleased and surprised to note his younger body, which was a bit plump from overindulgence but not ravaged by the bloating and debilitating disease the witch Mohiam had inflicted upon him. He looked down at himself, grinned up at the Face Dancers. "Oh ho! The first thing I want is a better wardrobe. And then I want to see that Atreides brat you've been raising for me."

Khrone stepped closer, his expression inquisitive. "You have access to all of your memories, Baron?"

"Of course! Baron Harkonnen is indeed back." He wandered into his thoughts, reassured by the things he had achieved in his original, glorious lifetime. He was delighted to be himself again.

But deep inside his brain, lurking at the back of his mind, he sensed that something was wrong, out of his control. An unwanted presence had joined him inside his mind, hitchhiking on his memories.

Hello, Grandfather, a girl's voice said. She giggled.

The Baron's head jerked. Where was that coming from? He didn't see her.

Did you miss me, Grandfather?

"Where are you?"

Where you won't lose me. I will always be with you now. Just like you were with me, haunting me, appearing in visions, refusing to give me rest. The girl's giggle became more shrill. *Now it's my turn.*

It was the Abomination, Paul's sister. "Alia? No, no!" His mind must be playing tricks on him. He dug his fingers against his temple, but the voice was inside, unreachable. With time, she would go away.

Don't count on it, Grandfather. I am here to stay.

Each civilization, no matter how altruistic it purports to be, has its
means of interrogating and torturing prisoners, as well as an elab-
orate system to justify such actions.

—from a Bene Gesserit report

Though he was genetically identical to the other seven gholas in
the first batch, Waff Number One did not like being so short,
small, and weak. His accelerated body had reached its mature size in
less than four years, but he wanted to be strong enough to escape this
maddening confinement.

As he peered out through the shimmering confinement field, Waff
seethed at Uxtal and the laboratory assistants. His seven counterparts
did the same. The Lost Tleilaxu researcher was like a nervous prison
guard, constantly prodding and herding the eight matching gholas. All
of the Waffs loathed him.

He imagined sinking his teeth into Uxtal's neck and feeling the hot
blood surge into his mouth. The researcher and his assistants were too
cautious now, though. The ghola brothers shouldn't have made their
earlier attack on him, before they were ready to succeed. That had
been a tactical mistake. A year ago they had been so much younger.

Standing safely on the other side of the confinement field, Uxtal
frequently lectured the eight gholas about his Great Belief, implying
that all the original Tleilaxu people had been criminals, heretics. Yet

all of the Waffs could tell that he wanted something from them. Very badly. They were smart enough to realize they were pawns.

The withered Honored Matre Ingva often talked with Uxtal about melange, as if she didn't think—or care—that the Waffs could hear her. She demanded to know when the children would reveal their secrets.

Waff wasn't aware that he had any secrets. He didn't remember any.

"They mirror and mimic each other," Uxtal said to Ingva. "I have heard them speak simultaneously and make the same noises, the same motions. The other ghola groups are growing even faster, it seems."

"When can we get started?" Ingva hovered close to him, making the little researcher squirm. "I am not reluctant to threaten you—or tempt you—with a sexual experience beyond your most incredible fantasies."

Uxtal seemed to shrink into himself and answered in a voice that cracked with fear. "Yes, those eight are as ready as they are ever going to be. No sense in waiting any longer."

"They are expendable," said Ingva.

"Not exactly expendable. The next batch is six months younger, and the others are even more recently removed from the tanks. Twenty-four in all, of varying ages. Even so, if we are forced to kill all eight of these, there will be others soon. We can try again and again and again." He swallowed hard. "We have to expect a certain number of mistakes."

"No, we don't." Ingva released the force field and licked her lips. She and Uxtal entered the protected chamber while the lab assistants stood guard outside. The eight gholas clumped together, backing away. Until now, they had not known that numerous other Waff gholas were being raised elsewhere in the large laboratory building.

Uxtal gave the accelerated ghola children a forced smile of encouragement, which none of the Waffs believed. "Come with us. There's something we have to show you."

"And if we refuse?" demanded Waff Three.

Ingva chuckled. "Then we will drag you—unconscious, if necessary."

Uxtal wheedled, "You will learn why you are here, why we made you, and what you have that we need."

Waff One hesitated, looked at his identical brothers. It was a temptation they could not resist. Though they had received forced educational induction, given inexplicable background to lay a foundation for *something*, the gholas were hungry to understand.

"I will go," Waff One said, and he actually took Uxtal's hand, pretending to be a sweet child. The nervous researcher flinched at the touch, but led the way out of the protected chamber. Waffs Two through Eight followed.

They entered a confined laboratory where Uxtal paraded the gholas in front of a spectacle—several brain-dead Tleilaxu Masters hooked up to tubes and instruments. Drool curled down gray chins. Machines covered their genitalia, pumping, milking, filling translucent bottles. The victims all looked uncomfortably like Waff, only older.

Uxtal waited while the staring children absorbed what they saw. "You used to be that. All of you."

Waff One raised his pointed chin with some measure of pride. "We were Tleilaxu Masters?"

"And now you must *remember* what you were. Along with everything else."

"Line them up!" Ingva ordered. Uxtal handed the Waff roughly to an assistant and waited until all of the accelerated children stood in front of him.

Strutting back and forth in front of the identical copies like a caricature of a commander, Uxtal made explanations and demands. "The old Tleilaxu Masters knew how to manufacture melange using axlotl tanks. *You* have that secret. It is buried within you." He paused, clasped his small hands behind his back.

"We don't have our memories," one of the Waffs said.

"Then find them. If you remember, we will let you live."

"And if we don't?" Waff One asked defiantly.

"We have eight of you here, and others elsewhere. We need only one. The rest of you are completely disposable."

Ingva chuckled. "And if all eight of you fail us, then we will simply turn to the next eight and repeat the process. As many times as necessary."

Uxtal tried to look intimidating. "Now, which of you will reveal what we need to know?"

The matching gholas stood in the line; some fidgeted, some remained defiant. It was a standard ghola-awakening technique, to drive a person to psychological and physical crisis, forcing the buried chemical memories to overcome the barriers inside.

"I don't remember," the Waffs all said in perfect unison.

A commotion interrupted them, and Uxtal turned as Matre Superior Hellica, resplendent in a purple bodysuit and flowing veils and capes, strode into the chamber leading a small Guild delegation and a floating, hissing chamber that held a mutated Navigator. Edrik himself!

"We came to watch the completion of your task, little man. And to reach financially acceptable terms with the Navigators, should you succeed."

Surrounded by plumes of cinnamony-orange gas, Edrik approached a viewing window in his tank. The eight gholas felt the tension in the chamber increase.

Uxtal gathered enough courage to yell at the Waffs, though he seemed almost comical doing so. "Tell us how to make spice in the axlotl tanks! Speak, if you want to live."

The Waffs understood the threat and believed it, but they had no memories to reveal, no stored knowledge. Sweat blossomed on their small gray foreheads.

"You are Tleilaxu Master Tylwyth Waff. All of you. You are everything he was. Before he died on Rakis, he prepared replacement gholas of himself here on Tleilax. We used cells from those"—he jerked his head toward the miserable mindless men on their extraction tables—"to create the eight of you. You hold his memories stored in your minds."

"Obviously, they require more incentive," Matre Superior Hellica said, looking bored. "Ingva, kill one of them. I don't care which."

Like a murderous machine, the old Honored Matre had been waiting to be activated. She could have attacked with a traditional flurry of kicks and blows, but she had come prepared for something more color-ful. She drew a long slaughtering knife she had confiscated from the neighboring slig farmer. With a sideways sweep of the monoblade and a quick flash of blood, Ingva decapitated Waff Four in the middle of the line.

As the head hit the floor, Waff One cried out in sympathetic pain, along with his surviving brothers. The head rolled to a stop at an odd angle, to stare with glazing eyes at the blood pooling out from the neck stump. The gholas all tried to run like panicked mice, but were brutally restrained by the assistants.

Uxtal turned greenish, as if he might either faint or vomit. "The memories are triggered through psychological crisis, Matre Superior! Simply butchering one of them is not sufficient. It must be prolonged, an extended anguish. A mental dilemma—"

Hellica nudged the bloody head with her toe. "The torture wasn't intended for this one, little man, but for the seven others. It's a basic rule: If one inflicts only pain, the subject can cling to hope that the torture will end, that he may somehow survive." A thin smile robbed the Matre Superior's face of all beauty. "Now, however, the others have not the slightest doubt that they will be killed if I say they are to be killed. No bluffing. That certainty of death should provide the correct trigger . . . or they will all die. Now, proceed!"

Ingva left the small body lying there.

"Seven of you remain," Uxtal said, reaching a crisis point of his own. "Which of you will remember first?"

"We don't know the information you request!" Waff Six shouted.

"That is unfortunate. Try harder."

As Hellica and the Navigator watched, Uxtal signaled Ingva. The woman took her time choosing, drawing out the tension, walking slowly up and down the ranks of the young gholas. The Waffs trembled and then shook, as she prowled behind them.

"I don't remember!" Waff Three wailed.

Ingva responded by thrusting the point of her bloody slaughtering knife into his back and out his chest, piercing his heart on the way through. "Then you are of no use to us."

Waff One felt a sharp pain strike his own heart, as if an echo of the blade had stabbed there, too. The clamor in his mind reached a crescendo. He no longer had any thought of defiance or of withholding information. He did not resist the memories or past lives inside him. He squeezed his eyes shut and screamed silently to himself, begging his body to divulge what it knew.

But nothing came to him.

Ingva lifted her long blade, jerking the Waff Three ghola into the air with it, his legs still kicking. Then she let him slide off the tip, and he thudded to the floor. Ingva stepped back, waiting to be called again. She was clearly enjoying this.

"You make this more difficult than it needs to be," Uxtal said. "The rest of you can stay alive—all you have to do is remember. Or does death mean nothing to a ghola?"

With a disappointed sigh, he nodded again, and Ingva killed another one.

"Five left." He looked down at the unpleasant mess, then glanced apologetically to Hellica. "There is a possibility that none of these gholas is acceptable. The next batch will be ready soon, but perhaps we should prepare more axlotl tanks, just in case."

"We're trying!" one of the Waffs cried.

"You are also dying. Time is running out." Uxtal waited for a moment, until his anticipation turned to clear dismay. He was sweating, too; his entire career, such as it was, was hanging on the line.

Ingva killed another one. Half of the Waffs now lay dead on the floor.

Moments later she killed a fifth, stepping up behind him, grabbing his dark hair, and slitting his throat.

Frantic, the remaining three Waffs tore at their own hair and struck themselves in the chests and faces, as if physical blows could dislodge memories. Weaving back and forth with her long knife, Ingva slashed at them, making shallow and playful cuts in their gray skin. Despite their continued frantic protestations, she murdered a sixth ghola.

Only two remained.

Waff One and his last identical sibling—Waff Seven—could feel hidden thoughts and experiences boiling through the turmoil in their minds, like regurgitated food. Waff One watched the agony around him, saw the corpses of his brothers. The memories were locked away, but not by the veils of time; rather, he suspected the old Masters had implanted some sort of internal security system.

"Oh, just kill them all!" Hellica said. "We have wasted your time today, Navigator."

"Wait," Edrik said through a speaker in his tank. "Allow this to play out."

The tension and the panic in the two remaining gholas had reached a peak. By now the pressure of the crisis should have caused a critical meltdown.

Acting on her own, without looking at Uxtal or the Matre Superior, Ingva drew the slaughtering knife across the belly of Waff Seven and eviscerated him. Blood and entrails spilled out, and he doubled over, screaming, trying to hold his intestines inside. He took a long time dying, and his moans filled the room, with Uxtal's repeated demands for information as a counterpoint.

Now the Matre Superior herself strode forward, glaring at Uxtal. "This is a tedious failure, little man. You are worthless." She drew a small, stubby dagger from her waist. Moving up to Waff One, she pressed the point against his temple. "This is the thinnest point in your skull. I'd barely need to press at all to shove my blade into your brain. Maybe that will cut loose your memories?" The knife's tip drew a drop of dark blood. "You have ten seconds."

Waff was giddy with terror, and only distantly aware that both his bowels and his bladder had let loose. Hellica began counting down. Numbers like sledgehammers struck his mind. Numbers . . . formulae, calculations. Sacred mathematical combinations.

"Wait!"

The Matre Superior completed her countdown. The Navigator continued to observe. Uxtal himself trembled in terror, as if convinced she would kill him next.

Waff suddenly started babbling a steady stream of information that he had never learned from the forced-education systems. It flowed out of him like sewage from a burst pipe. Materials, procedures, random quotations from the secret catechism of the Great Belief. He described secret meetings with Honored Matres aboard a no-ship, about how the old Tleilaxu had meant to betray the Bene Gesserit, how he and his fellow Masters did not trust the oddly changed Lost Tleilaxu from the Scattering. Lost Tleilaxu such as Uxtal . . .

"Please withdraw your knife, Matre Superior," the Navigator said.

"He has not yet revealed what we need!" Ingva brandished her own blade, apparently anxious to murder the last ghola, as if she had not yet spilled enough blood for one day.

"He will." Uxtal looked at the terrified, miserable ghola. "This Waff has just been buried by the mudslide of his past life."

"Many lives!" In desperate self-defense, the reawakened Master spewed forth what he could. But his memory was imperfect, and he couldn't get it all. Whole segments of knowledge were corrupted—a side-effect of the forbidden acceleration process.

"Give him time to sort through it all," Uxtal said, sounding pathetically relieved. "Even with what he has said already, I can see the path to new methods that may yield melange." Hellica still pressed her short knife against Waff's head. "Matre Superior! He is too great a resource to waste at this time. We can coax more out of him."

"Or torture it out," Ingva suggested.

Uxtal grabbed the sweaty hand of the last ghola. "I require this one for my work. Otherwise, there will be delays." Without waiting for an answer, he yanked the weak-kneed Waff away from the macabre scene.

"Clean this up," Hellica demanded of Ingva, who in turn ordered the lab assistants to do it.

As Uxtal hurried away with his young charge, he lowered his voice to a threatening whisper. "I lied to save your life. Now give me the rest of the information."

The ghola nearly collapsed. "I remember nothing more. It is all still churning inside me, but I can sense great gaps. Something is wrong—"

Uxtal cuffed him. "You had better come up with something good anyway, or both of us are dead."

As human beings, we have trouble functioning in environments in which we feel threatened. The threat becomes the focus of our existence. But "safety" is one of the great illusions of the universe. Nowhere is it truly safe.

—Bene Gesserit Study on the Human Condition,
BG Archives, Section VZ908

The Handlers welcomed their visitors as friends and allies, wanting to hear more about their struggles with the Honored Matres. The group sat on the roof of one of the wide cylindrical towers. On a flat stone in the middle of the plank floor, a brazier sent a warm, comforting glow into the night.

"We knew you would be coming," Orak Tho said. "When you dropped the no-field to launch your small ships, we detected your great vessel above us. We are aware that you have also sent scavenging teams to uninhabited portions of our world. We were waiting for you to come visit us directly."

Squatting next to Sheeana, Miles Teg was surprised, since these people seemed to have very little technology. "It would take sensitive detectors to spot us."

"Long ago we developed a means to sense the ships flown by Honored Matres, for our own protection. Because those women think they are infallible, it is easier to detect them."

"Hubris is their principal weakness," Thufir Hawat said.

Green eyes flashed from the bandit mask of dark skin. "They have many weaknesses. We've had to learn how to exploit them."

They shared a meal of nuts, fruit, smoked fish, and medallions of a spiced dark meat that apparently came from an arboreal rodent. The Rabbi was more relaxed than Sheeana had ever seen him, though he seemed worried about the origin of the food. She could tell that the old man had already made up his mind: He wanted his people to settle here, if the Handlers would have them.

While they sat together on the open rooftop, listening to the buzz of night insects and watching the swoop of dark birds, Sheeana felt very isolated. According to scan reports, the Handlers' population was relatively large, with mines and industries in other parts of the world. They had apparently developed a quiet and peaceful civilization. "We assume your people originated in the Scattering, long ago after the Tyrant's death. Was this planet the first stop on your wandering?"

The Chief Handler shrugged his bony shoulders. "We have myths about that, but it was more than a thousand years ago."

"Fifteen centuries," Thufir suggested. He was a bright student. Considering his past and his place in history, the Mentat ghola was quite interested in spans of time.

"Our race spread to many nearby worlds. We were not an empire but a . . . political brotherhood. Then out of nowhere the Honored Matres came like a stampede of blind and clumsy animals, as destructive in their ignorance as in their malevolence." Orak Tho bent his elongated face toward the brazier's glow. Orange light washed across his skin.

Other Handlers sat around the upper deck's circular wall, listening and muttering. Their distinctive body smells drifted into the cool air. Their race seemed to have an affinity for scents, as if smell was an important part of their communication abilities.

"Without warning, they came to pillage, destroy, and conquer." Orak Tho's face was as hard as petrified wood, his long jaw set. "Naturally, we had to stop this feral incursion." His lips curved in a faint smile. "So we developed our Futars."

"But how did you do that?" Sheeana asked. If these deceptively simple people could detect orbiting ships and create sophisticated genetic hybrids, their technology must be far more advanced than was evident.

"Some of those who joined us in settling these worlds were orphans of the Tleilaxu race. They showed us how to change our offspring to create what we needed, since God and evolution would be much too slow to provide them for us."

"The Futars," Teg said. "They are most interesting." After their initial reunion, the Handlers had taken the predatory creatures off to holding areas, where they could be with others of their own kin.

"What happened to these Tleilaxu?" The Rabbi looked around. He had never much liked Master Scytale.

"Alas, they are all dead."

"Killed?" Teg asked.

"Extinct. They don't breed the same as others do." He sniffed, as if disinterested in that part of the story. "Our Futars were bred to hunt Honored Matres. Those women came to our planets, confident they would conquer us. But we turned the tables on them. They are fit to serve as food for our Futars, nothing more."

FOR SAFETY, TEG suggested that their group sleep in the lighter with the hatches sealed and defensive fields up, which obviously displeased their hosts. The Chief Handler cast a glance over his shoulder. "Though these forests are well tamed, a few of the old predators still roam the grounds at night. It would be better if you stayed with us, up here in the safe towers."

A flicker of dismay crossed the Rabbi's face. "What old predators?" He didn't want to hear about any flaws with this world.

"The feline beasts that supplied genetic material for creating the Futars." Orak Tho gestured with his loose arms across to another cylindrical wooden tower. "We have a grand show tomorrow. You should be well rested for what you will witness."

"What kind of show?" Hawat sounded eager. At times he seemed no more than the boy he truly was, rather than a potential warrior-Mentat.

With a mysterious smile, the Chief Handler motioned for them to follow him. His green irises now looked like blazing emeralds.

It was full dark outside. Unfamiliar constellations sparkled like a million eyes reflecting firelight. He guided the four visitors across a sturdy plank walkway to a nearby tower, then down a spiraling interior staircase that circled the cylinder twice before reaching the ground level. They walked across the leaf-strewn forest floor to a much shorter tower that looked like a thick, man-made stump.

The stench struck them first. The base of the stout artificial tree had been hollowed out, like a dank lair. Thick vertical bars extended deep into the mulchy ground, blocking off the hollow to form a dirt-floored cell.

Teg raised his eyebrows. "You have prisoners."

The chamber contained five ragged, angry captives. Despite their tattered and beaten appearance, Sheeana could tell they were human. All were females with matted hair, rough hands, and bloodied knuckles. The remnants of torn leotards clung to their pale skin, and their eyes flashed faintly orange.

Honored Matres!

One of the whores saw them approach. Snarling, she lunged toward the wooden bars of her cage, flying sideways to deliver a devastating kick. Her bare foot slammed into the iron-hard wood. The impact produced a faint but hollow crack, and as the Honored Matre limped away, Sheeana realized the crack had been the fracture of bone, not wood. The women had already battered themselves bloody against the barricade.

Orak Tho's face constricted as if a thunderstorm were brewing behind it. "Honored Matres came down in a transport ship three months ago, expecting easy prey. We massacred them, but managed to save some for . . . training purposes." His lips curled back. "It is not the first time they have tried to harass us. They form isolated cells that don't necessarily know what the others are doing. Thus they repeat the same mistakes."

Two Futars prowled around the base of the wooden tower, circling and sniffing. Sheeana recognized one of them as Hrrm; the second beast-man had a black stripe in the wiry hair of its chest.

One of the captive Honored Matres called out in a threatening voice. "Free us, or our Sisters will peel strips of meat from your bones while you still live!"

Hrrm snarled and hurled himself at the cage, backing off only at the last moment. Hot spittle from his mouth splattered the captive Honored Matre. Three of the beaten women came forward to the bars, looking as bestial as the Futars.

"As I said," Orak Tho continued in his calm and confident voice, "Honored Matres are fit for little more than food."

A Handler came with a wooden bowl of red bones to which clung scraps of meat and fatty skin with patches of fur. A second bowl held slick-looking entrails and purplish organs. He dumped the offal through a slot into the cage. The filthy Honored Matres looked at it in disgust.

"Eat, if you wish to have strength for tomorrow's hunt."

"We don't eat garbage!" said one of the Honored Matres.

"Then you starve. It matters not to me."

Sheeana could tell the women were ravenous. After a shaky hesitation, they grabbed for the scraps, tearing off raw pieces and eating until their faces and fingers were smeared with grease and covered with old blood. They looked through the bars at their captors with such hateful expressions that they seemed capable of putrefying flesh.

One of the women glowered at Sheeana. "You don't belong here."

"Neither do you. However, I am outside the cage, while you are behind the bars."

The woman slammed the palm of her hand against the wooden barricade with a loud crack, but it was a halfhearted attempt at an attack. Hrrm pounced beside Sheeana as if to protect her, then prowled in front of the cage, his muscles rippling. He seemed very agitated.

Sheeana found it ironic, knowing what the Honored Matres had done to Hrrm and to his companions. The sexual perversions, the whippings and deprivations. It seemed a strikingly odd turnabout to see the women imprisoned, with the Futars prowling free.

She turned to the Chief Handler. "Honored Matres abuse their captive Futars. Your punishments are appropriate."

"My guests, tomorrow we will put you in our best observation stations, from which you can watch the hunt." Orak Tho reached over to pat both Futars on their heads. "It will be good for this one to run with his brothers, and get in practice again. It is what he was born to do."

With his bestial eyes fixed on the Honored Matres, Hrrm bared his teeth in a menacing smile.

Before they all slept, Teg returned to the lighter to transmit an optimistic report back to the *Ithaca*.

An alliance is often more a work of art than a simple business transaction.

—MOTHER SUPERIOR DARWI ODRADE,
private records, Bene Gesserit Archives

The Guild Navigator finally came to Chapterhouse in response to the Mother Commander's summons. Though she was impatient and frustrated with him, he did not explain where he had been or why he had delayed coming for several days.

In the meantime, Janess, Kiria, and ten other handpicked Valkyries—most of them from the original Honored Matres who had undergone Bene Gesserit training—had already been secretly deposited on Tleilax to begin their underground work. They would be infiltrating the last stronghold of the rebel whores to undermine their defenses, planting the seeds of destruction while setting up for a surprise ambush. A part of Murbella wished she could be with her daughter's team, wearing traditional Honored Matre clothing again, letting the predator half of her dual nature come to the fore.

But she trusted Janess and her companions. For now, Murbella had to arrange the rest of the details and secure Guild cooperation, either through bribery or threat. She had to be the Mother Commander, not just an average fighter.

The mutated Navigator swam in his tank, not looking at all eager or interested, which troubled the Mother Commander. She had hinted that he would be rewarded well for speaking with her, but he did not seem excited by the prospect.

"The gas looks thin in your tank, Navigator," she said.

"It is only a temporary shortage." He did not seem to be bluffing.

"We may be ready to increase your supply of melange, *if* the Guild is ready to cooperate with us and participate in the fight against the oncoming Enemy."

Edrik's metallic voice came through the speakers of his tank. "Your offer comes much too late, Mother Commander. For years you have tried to frighten us with the existence of this shadow Enemy, and you have tantalized us with promises of melange. But your treasure has lost its luster. We have been forced to seek other alternatives, other supply lines."

"There are no other sources of melange." Murbella glided forward to stand close to the curved plaz and peer inside.

"The Spacing Guild is in crisis. The severe shortage of spice—perpetuated by your Sisterhood—has split us into two factions. Many Navigators have already died from withdrawal, while others do not have sufficient melange to perceive safe paths through foldspace. One faction of the Guild led by human Administrators has clandestinely hired the Ixians to develop improved navigation machines. They intend to install them in all Guildships."

"Machines! Ix has been talking about such things for centuries. People in the Scattering used navigational devices, and so did Chapterhouse. They have never been fully acceptable before."

"And after years of intensive research, it seems they may have a viable solution to the ancient impossible problem. I believe they are inferior substitutes, not at all comparable to Navigators. Still, they do work."

The Mother Commander's mind raced ahead, chasing several desirable possibilities she had not previously considered. If the Ixians had developed reliable devices for guiding ships through foldspace, then the New Sisterhood could use them in its own fleet. No longer needing to force the cooperation of the Navigators, they could be independent, not at the mercy of a volatile and unpredictable power base such as the Guild.

If indeed Ix would sell such devices to the Sisterhood. Surely the Guild must have some sort of exclusive contract. . . .

Then she realized that even the short-term solution of using navigation machines for her own battle fleet had its drawbacks. Second- and third-order consequences. Only Chapterhouse had *spice*. With that single substance they could pay and control the Navigators so that no other party could compete. If melange became unnecessary, then the whole worth and strength of the New Sisterhood would diminish.

Only a moment had passed as Murbella considered all of this. "Navigation machines would mean the end of Navigators such as yourself."

"And it would also remove one of the primary customers for *your* melange, Mother Commander. Therefore, my faction seeks a reliable and secure source of spice, so that Navigators can continue to exist. Your New Sisterhood has driven us to this extreme. We cannot depend on you for the spice we need."

"And you have discovered another supplier of melange?" She let a scoffing tone into her voice. "I find that doubtful. We would know about it."

"We have a high level of confidence in our alternative." Edrik drifted away, came back.

Murbella shrugged nonchalantly. "I offer you an immediate increase in spice." With a gesture, she directed three of her assistants to move a small suspensor barrow into the room; it was heaped high with packages of spice, as much as one Navigator could use in the better part of a Standard Year.

The tank's speakers remained silent, but she could see the hunger in Edrik's strange eyes. Murbella feared for a moment that he would turn her down, and all of her carefully thought out tactics would come to naught.

"One can never possess too much spice," the Navigator said after an interminable pause. "We have learned the painful lesson of relying on any single source. It would be better for the Navigators, and for the New Sisterhood, if we could reach some sort of accommodation."

I was right, she thought. "You need our spice, and we need your ships."

"The Guild will listen to your proposal, Mother Commander—

provided it is a discussion rather than a threat. A business proposal between respected partners, not the sting of a bully's lash."

She stared at the tank, surprised by his bold statement. *He might really have another source of spice, or at least the possibility of one. But he seems to harbor doubts and wants to play it safe.*

"I need two Guild ships for transport to Tleilax. One equipped with a no-field and the other a traditional Heighliner."

"Tleilax? For what purpose?"

"We will grind down the only remaining stronghold and eliminate the last viable threat of the Honored Matres, once and for all."

"It will be arranged, within two days. I will take the spice now."

RENEGADE HONORED MATRES. The mysterious Enemy. Face Dancers. Murbella could not avoid them all, but the process of physical exercise—running, sweating, and straining—helped her to think as she planned her final assault on Tleilax.

Dressed in a clinging singlesuit, she sprinted along a stony path toward a hill near the Keep. She pushed herself until each breath slashed her lungs like a razor. Some of the inner voices scolded her for wasting time when there was so much work to be done. Murbella only ran harder.

She wanted to stimulate and provoke those Other Memories, needed them alert. The clamorous sea of past lives was always there, but not always available, and certainly not always helpful. Making sense out of the collective wisdom was a constant challenge, even for the most influential of Sisters.

Upon passing through the Spice Agony, a new Reverend Mother was like a baby thrown into a vast ocean and commanded to swim through the waves of Other Memory to survive. With so many Sisters inside, she could always ask questions, but she also risked getting sucked down into the whirlpool of churning advice.

Other Memory was a tool. It could be a great boon, or a great peril. Sisters who delved too deeply into this reservoir of the past were in danger of going insane. That had been the fate of the Kwisatz Mother,

Lady Anirul Corrino, so long ago during the time of Muad'Dib. It was like reaching for a sword and grabbing the blade instead of the hilt. A matter of balance.

The floating souls viewed Murbella's mind from the inside, and some thought they knew her better than she knew herself. But even though she could see the past Sisters of the Bene Gesserit, her Honored Matre ancestry remained blocked from her by a black wall.

As a little girl Murbella had been captured in one of the Honored Matre sweeps, taken from her family and trained in cruelty and sexual domination. A *whore.* Yes, the Bene Gesserit name was appropriate.

Those terrible women from the Scattering had their dark secrets, their shame, their ignominious crimes. Somewhere in the past they knew their origin, knew what they had done to provoke the Enemy. If only she could find that information inside herself, she would know the truth about the vicious women she was about to face.

Reaching the rustling grasses and flat brown rocks on the hill, she climbed to the boulder-strewn crest and sat on the highest point of rock. From this vantage she could see Chapterhouse Keep to the east and the encroaching dunes to the west. Her heart pounded from the exertion, and perspiration trickled down her forehead and cheeks. Her body had been pushed to a physical edge, and now it was time to do the same with her mind.

She had accomplished much as Mother Commander. Murbella had managed to keep the two poles of the New Sisterhood from tearing each other apart, but the scars still ran deep. She had crushed or consolidated all but one of the enclaves of renegade Honored Matres.

She needed to know more, needed to understand the Face Dancers that had infiltrated the Old Empire, the Enemy . . . and the Honored Matres. *I must have that information before we depart for Tleilax.*

Murbella opened a small pack at her waist and removed three wafers of fresh, concentrated melange shipped up from the deep desert. She held the brownish-red wafers in her hand, feeling the spice tingle slightly as it mixed with the perspiration of her palm. She consumed all three wafers, intending to use the spice as a mental battering ram.

I will go deep this time, she thought. *Guide me, my Sisters, and bring me back out, for I have important information to discover.*

The spice began to work within her. Closing her eyes, she dove inward, following the taste of melange. She could see the sweeping landscape of Bene Gesserit memories extending to an infinite horizon of human history. She seemed to be running down a kaleidoscopic corridor of mirrors, mother to mother to mother. Fear threatened to overwhelm her, but the Sisters within parted and drew her into their midst, absorbing her consciousness.

But Murbella demanded to know about the other half of her existence, to discover what lay behind the black wall that blocked all Honored Matre paths. Yes, the memories were there, but muddled and disorganized, and they seemed to reach a dead end after only a handful of centuries, as if she had sprung from nowhere.

Were the whores descended from lost and corrupted Reverend Mothers, isolated out in the Scattering, as had been postulated? Had they formed their society with surviving Fish Speakers from the God Emperor's private guard, creating a bureaucracy based on violence and sexual domination?

Honored Matres rarely looked to the past, except when they glanced fearfully over their shoulders as the Enemy pursued them.

The spice washed through Murbella, sending her still deeper into her crowded thoughts, slamming her up against the obsidian barrier. In a trance atop the dry rocky hill, Murbella backed through generation after generation. Her breathing constricted, her external vision blurred into blindness; she heard a whimper of pain pass her lips.

Then, like a traveler emerging from a narrow defile, she beheld a mental clearing, in which shadowy ghost-women helped her forward. They showed her where to look. A crack in the wall, a way through. Deeper shadows, cold . . . and then—*I see!* The answer made her reel.

Yes, during the Famine Times, a splinter group of rogue Bene Gesserits, a few untrained wild Reverend Mothers, and fugitive Fish Speakers had indeed escaped in the turmoil after the Tyrant's death. Yet that was only a small part of the answer.

In their flight, those women had also encountered isolated and insular Tleilaxu worlds. For more than ten thousand years, the fanatical Bene Tleilax had used their females only as breeding machines and axlotl tanks. In a closely guarded secret, they kept their women immobilized, comatose, and uneducated, no more than wombs on tables. No Bene Gesserit, no outsider, had ever seen a Tleilaxu female.

When those rogue Bene Gesserits and militant Fish Speakers discovered the horrific truth, their reaction was swift and unforgiving; they left not a single Tleilaxu male alive on those outlying worlds. Liberating the breeding tanks, they took the Tleilaxu females with them on their journey, tending them, trying to bring them back.

A great many of the mindless tanks died, for no medical reason other than that they were unwilling to live, but some Tleilaxu females recovered. When they grew strong, they vowed reprisal for the monstrous crimes the males had committed for a thousand generations. And they never forgot.

The core of the Honored Matres were vengeful Tleilaxu females!

The renegade Reverend Mothers, militaristic Fish Speakers, and recovered Tleilaxu females had united to form the Honored Matres. Lost out in the Scattering for more than a dozen centuries, they had no access to melange, could no longer undergo the Spice Agony, and were unable to find an alternative that would allow them access to Other Memories. Over time, interbreeding with males from populations they encountered, then dominated on other worlds, those women had become something else entirely.

And now Murbella knew why her chain of predecessors ended in dark emptiness. She traveled back, generation to generation, all the way to a Tleilaxu female who had been a comatose breeding tank, a mindless womb.

Gathering her courage and focusing her rage, Murbella pushed harder and *became* the paralyzed tank that Tleilaxu female had once been. She shuddered as the dim and helpless sensations and memories seeped into her. She had been that young girl raised in captivity, understanding little of the world beyond her pitiful confinement, unable to read, barely able to speak. In the month of her first menstruation, she had been dragged away, strapped to a table, and turned into a flesh vat. No longer conscious, the nameless woman had no idea how many offspring her body had produced. Then she had been awakened and liberated.

The Mother Commander understood what it meant to be that

Tleilaxu female and others, and why the Honored Matres became so ferocious. No longer the degraded, despised mothers of Tleilaxu males, they demanded to be revered, to be known from that time forth as "Honored Matres" . . . honored mothers. And through her Bene Gesserit eyes, Murbella recognized their humanity after all.

With understanding came release, and then everything else along the Honored Matre line came to her in a flood. She awoke and found herself sitting on the rock again, but no longer in sunlight. Hours had passed as she journeyed through her other lives. Now a dry night wind chilled her.

Shuddering from the aftereffects of the melange and her devastating journey, Murbella lurched to her feet. She finally had her answers, would share this crucial information with her advisors.

Hearing distant shouts, she looked back toward the Keep. Lights were fanning out from the fortress as searchers came looking for her. She had been a searcher, too, and now she needed to tell the rest of the New Sisterhood what she had found.

The Valkyries would be preparing their assault on Tleilax.

A choice can be as dangerous as a weapon. Refusing to choose is in itself a choice.

—PEARTEN,
ancient Mentat philosopher

Though nearly two hundred people remained aboard, the *Ithaca* felt empty to Duncan. The lighter had landed safely on the new planet, bearing Sheeana, Teg, the old Rabbi, and Thufir Hawat. Recovery teams had discreetly collected water and air, then returned to the no-ship. Everything was calm, on schedule.

The Bashar's recent message had indicated no sign of threat from the Handlers, and Duncan took the opportunity to leave the navigation bridge. Now that he had thought of it, he couldn't get the idea out of his head.

He felt like a prowler, sneaking off to do something forbidden as he stood alone before the sealed nullentropy chamber. He hadn't touched it in years, hadn't even thought about those perfectly preserved items it contained. He moved quietly, making certain the corridors were empty. Though Duncan assured himself he was doing nothing wrong, he did not want to have to explain himself to anyone.

He had fooled himself and many of the people aboard. But still he was not free of the addictive, debilitating hold Murbella had over him. He doubted she even realized the strength of the painful bond; when they had been together, when he had been able to get as much of her as he wanted, Duncan had never felt the weakness.

But in all those years since . . .

The corridor's glowpanels were bright. The breathy white noise of air-recirculation systems was the only sound Duncan could hear except for the pounding of his own heart.

Before he could think too much, forsaking his Mentat ability to project possible consequences, he applied his thumbprint ID and deactivated the nullentropy field. The storage locker opened with a faint exhalation of adjusting atmospheric pressures. And with it came Murbella's smell, like a slap across his face . . . as if she were here, in front of him.

Even after nineteen years, her scent was as fresh as if he had just held her. Her garments and other personal articles carried that unmistakable fragrance that was so essentially *her*. He pulled out the items one by one, a loose tunic, a soft towel, the pair of comfortable leggings she often wore when they engaged in combat practice in the training room. He touched each one with a nervous caution, as if afraid he might find hidden knives there.

Duncan had gathered these items and hidden them in storage very soon after escaping from Chapterhouse. He had not wanted to see traces of Murbella in his personal quarters or in the training rooms. He had sealed them away because he couldn't bear to destroy them. Even then, he had realized the chains she had on him.

Now, he looked at the collar of a rumpled tunic and, as he had hoped, saw a few loose strands of dark amber hair, like fine wires spun from precious metal. And at the end of each strand the pale root. He hoped he had stored these items in time, so many years ago.

Viable cells.

Duncan realized he wasn't breathing. He looked at the strands of loose hair and let his eyes fall closed, intentionally blocking the automatic Mentat trance. The idea was an impossible temptation to him.

It had been years since another ghola baby had been created, though the axlotl tanks remained functional. Sheeana's disturbing vision dream had forced her to call a halt to the project. Nevertheless, they had the capability of growing any ghola they wished. The tanks weren't being used right now. He had every right to consider this, after all he'd done for the people aboard the *Ithaca*.

He picked up one of Murbella's loose tunics, brought it to his nose and inhaled a long breath. What did *he* really want?

Duncan had distracted himself with enough duties and problems that her ghost image had faded back into his subconscious. He had thought he was over her. But his obsessive thinking about Murbella had nearly made him lose the ship to the old man and woman several years ago, and only Teg's quick instincts had saved them.

If I hadn't been distracted, preoccupied . . . obsessed! His mistake had almost cost them their freedom. Murbella was dangerous. He had to let her go. Duncan would not allow his weakness to endanger them again.

But when he'd remembered these items in nullentropy storage, when the idea occurred to him that it was possible—*possible*—to have another Murbella, it was like touching a hot flame to dry tinder.

If he could gather the courage—and ignore his own rational reservations—he could talk to the Tleilaxu Master about the process before Sheeana and the others returned from the planet of the Handlers. He rationalized it to himself, pretending there would be no harm in simply raising the idea to Scytale. It implied no decision on his part.

He threw the articles back into the storage bin. Doing so seemed like swimming upstream against a strong current. The idea had latched itself firmly onto his mind. He slammed the cubicle door shut and sealed it again.

For now.

The only thing I like better than the smell of spice is the smell of fresh blood.

—FORMER HONORED MATRE DORIA,
records of early training sessions

The hunt began at dawn.

The tall, raccoon-faced men used stunner goads to roust the five captive Honored Matres from their stinking cell beneath the wooden tower. Hrrm and the black-striped Futar prowled about; six younger Futars whined and growled anxiously.

With glimmering orange eyes, the women had noticed the *Ithaca's* lighter on the far side of the clearing. Now, two of the Honored Matres burst impulsively out of the noisome cell, delivering swift kicks and blows, knocking aside the stunner goads.

But the Handlers and Futars were well practiced in fending off any resistance. Before the whores could run, the black-striped Futar pounced, driving one of them to the ground. He bared his long teeth at her throat, barely restraining himself from ripping out her larynx and ending the anticipated hunt too soon. She thrashed wildly, but the Futar dug claws into her shoulder, pinning her with his strength and weight.

Hrrm had trapped the second woman, circling her, his muscles coiled. A hungry growl bubbled in his throat. The younger Futars paced nearby, wanting part of the kill.

"Not yet." The Chief Handler allowed a calm smile to flow across his long, streamlined face. Hrrm and Black Stripe froze; the younger ones howled.

Miles Teg had no great love for the Honored Matres, knowing the havoc they had wrought among the Bene Gesserit and how they had tortured him. They had already killed him once, when they devastated Rakis. But as a military commander, the Bashar viewed them as *opponents* against whom he should carry no undue malice. Young Thufir Hawat, seeing the Bashar's intense concentration, imitated him, gathering data as the basis for making further decisions.

The old Rabbi looked squeamish at the very thought of the hunt, even though Honored Matres had hunted his people, too, on Gammu. Sheeana stood by silently, accepting the violence that was sure to take place. She was quite intrigued.

"We will kill you," snarled the Honored Matre whom Hrrm held at bay. She crouched, holding her hands out as weapons, ready to spring. Hrrm was not intimidated by her.

The six young Futars snapped and snarled, eager for their own hunt. Their primal hunger went beyond the desire for mere food. The other three whores emerged from the tree-stump cell. Although they were wary and ready to fight, they decided to wait for a better chance.

"We will kill you," repeated the first trapped Honored Matre.

"You will have the opportunity to try." Orak Tho stood straight, the dark band across his eyes falling into shadow. "Take them into the forest where they can run."

"Why not just execute us here?"

"Because we would not enjoy that as much." Several of the Handlers smiled. They were calm and confident in their superiority.

As she watched, Sheeana tried to formulate a conjecture about these mysterious isolated people, where they had come from and what their true goals might be. She took a step toward the nearest Honored Matre. "Tell us your names, so that I might make a body record when this day is done."

The whore that was still pinned under the black-striped Futar thrashed and yowled. The calmer Honored Matre merely fixed Sheeana with a frozen gaze.

Orak Tho raised his hand lightly, cutting off any further shows of bravado. "Your name will be forgotten by the time your flesh passes through the digestive systems of these Futars. You will end your physical existence as excrement on the forest floor."

The Chief Handler turned his back and strode away with his long-legged, loose-jointed gait. The ravenous Futars closed in to prevent the women from making another escape attempt, herding them along.

"Come, out into the forest." Orak Tho glanced back at the seething Honored Matres. "Out there, you will have your chance to shed blood, or die in the attempt."

ATOP A TALL, open-framed lookout tower constructed of smooth silvery-blond wood, Teg stood on the open platform, grasped a railing, and looked down into the forest. Sheeana was with him. Handlers guarded the base of the tower, their stun-goads ready in case the hunted Honored Matres should come at them like an unexpected ricochet in their flight from the prowling Futars. The guards did not look worried, though they kept Teg and Sheeana safe, high above the killing grounds.

The Chief Handler's guests were allowed to observe from this vantage point, supposedly the best view of the action. Because the range of the hunt itself was unpredictable, the Rabbi and young Thufir Hawat had been sent to a different lookout tower a kilometer away. The old man had made weak protestations, claiming he would rather wait back at the lighter, but the Handlers insisted that they observe the show.

"This will prove we are not your enemies," Orak Tho had said. "Witness what we do to Honored Matres. Certainly you wish to see them suffer, considering the pain they have caused you, too?"

"I would like to observe the hunt and witness your Futars in action," Thufir had said, then glanced meaningfully at Teg. "It is important to see how these women fight, isn't it, Bashar? That way we can prepare, should we run into more of them."

After the four observers were situated in the separate lookout towers, loud vibrating horns blew through the forest. Sheeana and Teg looked down into the maze of enormously tall aspens. The Handler guards at the base of the tower sent out another signal. Somewhere out of sight, the five Honored Matres split up and dashed into the underbrush, scattering dry leaves.

To Teg, it was obvious the Handlers and Futars had done this many times before.

Beneath them, two muscular beast-men bounded along between the aspen trunks, intent on tracking down their quarry. Teg could almost sense the bloodlust from there. The Honored Matres would put up a good fight, but the whores had no real chance. Quickly, the hunting Futars vanished into the labyrinth of trees.

He and Sheeana continued to watch. The great forest that extended out from the tower settlement was an endless maze of autumn gold and silvery bark. Traditional aspen groves were genetically identical, branching off from the same tree as runners rather than being deposited as fertilized seeds. Nature's clones. The tall trunks were surrounded by fallen yellow leaves, like antique solari coins scattered on the ground. From this perspective, the endless straight and rigid trunks looked like the bars of a giant cage.

Slipping into intense Mentat awareness as he waited for the hunt to come closer, Teg analyzed the forest, fitting all the tiny pieces together until he resolved an unexpected pattern cleverly hidden among randomness. At one time, all of the great gray-trunked trees had been laid out in a precise order, carefully staged to present an appearance of "geometrical naturalness."

He studied further. There could be no mistaking it. "This forest was artificially cultivated."

Sheeana looked at him. "A Mentat projection?"

He responded with the barest nod, concerned that listening devices might have been planted in the observation tower. He did not like being separated from Thufir and the Rabbi. Had this hunt been staged to break their party in half so the Handlers could spy on their private conversations?

He made a second-order projection. Obviously, although the original planters of this sweeping forest had strived to create the appearance of wildness, they had not been able to get past their innate sense of order. Had original colonists from the Scattering cultivated this forest in barren ground generations ago? Or had the true natural chaos been so disturbing to them that they razed the existing trees to the ground and designed a new wilderness according to an acceptable blueprint?

From far off came sounds of crashing through the trees, snarling Futars, and female shouts. Abruptly, the disturbance moved toward the observation tower. Sheeana leaned closer to the Bashar, masking her movement with a show of peering down at the hunt below. She spoke in a low whisper, "You have concerns, Miles?" They had just sent a signal to Duncan that everything was safe and under control.

"I have . . . thoughts. This hunt is an example. For instance, we know the Handlers bred their Futars for the specific purpose of killing Honored Matres."

"Considering how dangerous the whores are, it seems a perfectly reasonable thing for the Handlers to create and imprint such predators to protect themselves," Sheeana said. "The Chief Handler's arguments make sense. There's no mistaking that we share a common enemy in the Honored Matres."

"Ask yourself who *else* might wish the Honored Matres to be destroyed, and the alliances become less clear-cut," Teg continued. "Simply because we both hate the Honored Matres does not guarantee that the Handlers have the same goals as we do."

Third-order projection: If the Handlers had learned their specialized genetic knowledge and sophisticated techniques from the Tleilaxu who fled in the Scattering, then what part did the Bene Tleilax play in this overall conflict? Where did their allegiance lie?

He would have to speak frankly with Master Scytale as soon as they returned to the *Ithaca*. Obviously, the last old Master harbored much resentment toward the Lost Tleilaxu who had betrayed his people. Those Tleilaxu stepbrothers had been changed out in the Scattering. Maybe Scytale knew more than he had yet revealed.

His Mentat awareness raced along. He felt his heart pounding, his metabolism speeding up. *We are not the only ones who hate the whores.*

The Honored Matres had somehow enraged the Outside Enemy enough to draw them toward the Old Empire.

Teg gripped the wooden rail more tightly. Sensing his tension, Sheeana gave him a questioning look, but with the faintest shake of his head, he warned her not to speak openly. He tried to think of a way to alert Duncan.

Sheeana grabbed his arm. "Look down there."

One of the five Honored Matres charged through the aspen forest, dodging and weaving around the trunks. Behind her, three Futars surged after their prey, their wiry hair erect and claws extended. The woman ran like the wind, her sinewy muscles and bare feet carrying her through the underbrush as she kicked up leaves like golden clouds of dust.

At the base of the observation tower, two of the bandit-faced watchers held out their stun-goads, but did not interfere. They would let the Futars do the killing.

Though she raced headlong, the Honored Matre could not outrun the beast-men. Her hair was disheveled, her eyes wide, her jaw set with determination, as if she was ready to turn and use her own teeth to rip out her pursuers' throats.

With several swift bounds, the young Futars closed on her, hungry and boisterous. Teg wondered if they had yet been blooded, or if this was their first hunt.

Smelling the hot breath behind her, knowing the Futars were within steps of bringing her down, the Honored Matre leapt into the air, struck the nearest smooth aspen trunk with her bare feet, and rebounded sideways. The nearest Futar tried to turn so swiftly he scuffed up a spray of dirt and twigs.

The woman landed on the ground, then sprang in the opposite direction, arms extended, teeth bared. She crashed into the second oncoming Futar, and the force of her impact was enough to knock the beast-man off balance. She rolled with him, used two fingers like bony spikes to jab out his feral eyes. The blinded creature yowled and thrashed. In a move like liquid lightning, the woman grabbed its muzzle and with a vicious twist snapped the Futar's neck.

Without a moment's pause, barely even panting, she lunged toward the third young Futar, her bloody fingers outstretched. Before the Honored Matre could strike, though, the Futar let out a brutal, shivering shriek, louder and more terrible than anything Teg had ever heard.

The effect of the shriek—no doubt exactly as the Futar and his trainers had intended—was to make the woman freeze. She stumbled as if her muscles had locked involuntarily. *An animal version of Voice?*

Before the Honored Matre could recover, the first Futar struck her down from behind and rolled her onto her back. With a slash of his claws, he tore long, bloody gouges across her face. With his other hand, he dug into her abdomen, ripping through her hardened muscles and reaching in up to his elbow to extract her heart.

The woman twitched in a pool of blood, then lay still. The other Futar sniffed at the body of his dead companion and went over to join the first one as they began to feed on the prey.

Teg watched with fascinated disgust. The Handler guards picked up the body of the slain Futar. The remaining two beast-men paid them no attention as they slashed and tore, wetly devouring the stringy flesh of their victim.

Farther off, from the direction of the tower where Thufir and the Rabbi observed, came the sounds of more horns, more snarling and thrashing. The hunt continued.

To suspect your own mortality is to know the beginning of terror.
To learn irrefutably that you are mortal is to know the end of
terror.

—Bene Gesserit Archives,
Training Manual for Acolytes

Even as her undefeated Valkyries traveled toward Tleilax, the
Mother Commander felt uneasy. Tleilax . . . the Tleilaxu
females . . . the Honored Matres. So much now made sense to
Murbella. The whores' mindless destruction of all Tleilaxu worlds was
no longer entirely incomprehensible.

But understanding did not lead to mercy. The New Sisterhood's
plans would not change. Much hung in the balance here, the culmination of an energy-draining conflict that diverted attention from
preparing for the main struggle. The thwarted attack on Chapterhouse, the obliteration of Richese, the insurgents and Face Dancers on
Gammu. After today, this part would all be over.

The immense Heighliner carried Murbella's troops and equipment
to the last stronghold of the rebel whores. After the Guildship dis-
gorged her obvious fleet of Valkyries in the same warships she had used
to attack both Buzzell and Gammu, the show of force would certainly
be impressive. From what she knew of Matre Superior Hellica, however, Murbella doubted simple intimidation would be enough. The

Valkyries were willing to expend as much violence as might be necessary; in fact, they looked forward to it.

Navigator Edrik insisted on guiding the Heighliner himself. Citing the Spacing Guild's long-standing neutrality, he would not participate in the actual combat, but he clearly wanted to be present during the takeover of Bandalong. Murbella got the sense that the Navigator faction had something to gain here. Was the Guild hiding something on Tleilax? Though the Navigators and human Administrators had vehemently denied any involvement, *some* ship had delivered Hellica's Obliterators to Richese. She had assumed it was an Honored Matre vessel, but it could have been a Guildship . . . like this one.

In a transparent chamber above them, the Navigator swam in fresh spice gas supplied by the Chapterhouse stockpiles. She didn't trust him.

Earlier in the week, an innocuous-seeming Guild supply vessel had sent a coded transmission containing the New Sisterhood's specific plans to Janess, hiding among the Honored Matres. Her team's camouflage was secure, and the intelligence data Janess provided in return had given Murbella much to consider, a wealth of information that allowed her to plan a perfect coup de grace. Along with Kiria and the other ten faux Honored Matres, Janess had made preparations to strike the soft white underbelly of the overconfident whores while they stared up at the skies.

Soon . . .

Emerging from foldspace, the giant vessel went into orbit over Tleilax. Bashar Wikki Aztin already had her orders.

From the Navigator's bridge, Murbella looked down at the planet. The continents still showed great black scars from the original violent takeover by the Honored Matres. The women had unleashed terrible weapons, but stopped short of completely sterilizing the main Tleilaxu world, choosing to crush and conquer the remnants instead of wiping them out. Unconscious revenge on behalf of countless generations of Tleilaxu females. No doubt Matre Superior Hellica did not know her own history, but she knew her hatred well.

In the subsequent decades since the original attack, the draconian women had salvaged what seemed unsalvageable. Now, as Murbella studied the terrain below, her tactical advisors matched details with the intelligence reports Janess and her spies had sent. Though incommunicado, Bashar Aztin would be making a last broad assessment, formulating and finalizing plans for the main, unexpected strike.

The whores down there must certainly have noted the Heighliner's unscheduled arrival. Murbella gave her signal, and more than sixty of the attack ships from Chapterhouse dropped out of the great vessel's hold to hover in neatly organized squadrons, like pilot fish around a large shark. Seeing the military force, the Honored Matres could have no question about the newcomers' intent.

Her communications officer hit the transmit toggle. "Mother Commander Murbella of the New Sisterhood wishes to speak with Hellica."

A woman responded in a defiant tone. "You are referring to the *Matre Superior.* You will show proper respect."

Murbella's voice was infused with confident authority. "As will you. I have come to facilitate your surrender."

The woman sounded indignant and outraged, but moments later another voice took control. "Brash words from an opponent I know is weak. We have annihilated whole worlds. A Heighliner and a handful of ships do not frighten us!"

"Oh? Even if we carry some of the planet-burning weapons you yourself used on Richese?"

"We are not unarmed either," Hellica retorted. "I remain unconvinced of the need to surrender."

Instead of being intimidated, Murbella felt more confident. If Hellica truly possessed such defenses, she would have attacked preemptively instead of issuing a warning.

"Your bravado bores me, Hellica. You know that the rest of the Honored Matre rebels have either joined the New Sisterhood or been annihilated. Your cause is lost. We should try to find another solution. Let us meet, face to face."

The Matre Superior gave a brittle chuckle. "I will meet with you, if only to show you your weakness." Murbella knew full well how the Honored Matres thought: They saw the mere suggestion of negotiation to be a deep flaw in the Bene Gesserit way. Hellica would seize any opening, probably attempt to assassinate her, assuming she could then take control of the Sisterhood. Murbella counted on it.

"Good. I will come down to Bandalong with my escort of sixty ships. Together, we will reach a resolution."

"Come if you dare." The Matre Superior cut off the transmission. Murbella could almost hear the sound of a trap snapping shut.

Earlier, the Mother Commander had pondered the possibility of capturing the pretender queen alive, bringing her into the New Sisterhood as an ally. Niyela from Gammu had killed herself rather than be converted—no great loss. But after the heinous destruction of Richese, Murbella had realized that capturing Hellica would be like bringing an armed time bomb back to Chapterhouse. The Matre Superior needed to be destroyed. Duncan would never have made such a tactically foolish error.

Murbella joined one of the Valkyrie ships and began her descent toward Bandalong. These vessels had been sufficient to conquer Buzzell and Gammu in an impressive show of force, but not overwhelming. The Matre Superior would naturally assume that her followers could defeat them.

If you don't want an opponent to see your hidden dagger, make certain an obvious weapon looks large and deadly.

Her ships approached the waiting Palace.

*Our defenses can become liabilities if they betray our true weak-
nesses to the enemy.*

—BASHAR MILES TEG,
address to troops

From the call to arms and the groups of scurrying Honored Matres
in Bandalong, Uxtal could tell that the newly arrived Heighliner
was not merely another curious delegation from the Navigators. This
was something far more serious.

Since he had already demonstrated his success in reawakening the
Waff ghola's memories, Edrik was satisfied. Why would the Guild be
bothering them now? He was working as fast as he could! Thus far,
Uxtal had succeeded in covering up the significant flaws in the
Tleilaxu Master's knowledge.

To make matters worse, during the sudden emergency he received a
summons to go to the Palace of Bandalong immediately. He hurried off
toward the sickeningly ostentatious building. As he ran the gauntlet of
the colonnaded entry, he ignored the magenta columns and the gar-
ishly dressed statues of Honored Matres arrayed in threatening positions.

A cowed-looking bonded male stood in a bright yellow tuxedo outside the immense door, wearing a dazed expression. Striding up to him,
Uxtal lifted his own chin in a disdainful sniff, since he had never been

sexually twisted by the Honored Matres himself. "I am here to see the Matre Superior."

The man blinked at him and said dully, "She is occupied setting up a trap for the witches. We have been threatened by the New Sisterhood."

Bene Gesserit witches? So that was what all the turmoil was about. Overhead in the sky, a swarm of dark ships was descending like a flock of carrion birds. Uxtal watched nervously, expecting explosives to drop onto the rooftops. Hellica certainly had a way of provoking other people.

The researcher held out the rolled message he had received. "Perhaps the Matre Superior wants me at her side during the emergency. I am her greatest living researcher, the man who will restore melange production from the axlotl tanks. My work may be the key to her negotiations." He crossed his arms over his small chest.

Yes, that must be the real reason. If the witches from Chapterhouse counted on their spice monopoly, then Hellica would want to flaunt Uxtal's success with the Waff ghola. She would offer him as her champion genius! Also, Navigator Edrik would surely never allow harm to come to his work. Uxtal should be safe, no matter what happened.

The tuxedoed man studied the summons, nodded sagely, and then dashed Uxtal's preconceptions. "Ah, now I understand. This is not, in fact, from the Matre Superior. We have prepared a room. Follow me."

"Shouldn't you at least inform her that I am here?"

"No. I was given specific instructions on that account."

Confused and uneasy, the little researcher was escorted down a wide corridor that featured paintings of dead Bene Gesserits in macabre poses. The bonded male indicated for him to pass through an archway and descend a stairway to a large, sunken chamber.

When Uxtal stepped down into the main room, alone, the entire chamber glowed orange as thousands of luminous eyes appeared in the floor. Terrified, he tried to retreat, but the whole staircase melted into the wall, trapping him like an unarmed slave in a combat arena. "Matre Superior? What is it you require of me?" He thought furiously, reminding himself, *They need me, that is why I am still alive. They need me!*

The glowing eyes in the floor went dark, plunging the sunken room into blackness. Through his panic, he became aware of a trickle of noise that entered the chamber like a stream running down the wall. Growing louder, the sound metamorphosed into a woman's grating laughter. "You see? My eyes are always on you, little man."

Burning light filled the room, dazzling him. Peering through his fingers, Uxtal saw Ingva standing before him completely naked. Her aged body was carved from knots of muscle and taut skin; her breasts were too small to sag. "The Matre Superior clearly does not want you. And now while she is preoccupied with the Chapterhouse witches, I will claim you for my own. Then you will really work for me. Hellica need never know, until I decide to make my move."

"But I have done everything requested of me!" His voice cracked. "I have grown gholas, produced your orange spice drug, restored the Tleilaxu Master's memories. Soon I will provide you with all the melange you could possibly—"

"Exactly. And that is why I must control you. Against all of my expectations, you have actually proved yourself to be of value." She moved closer, and he felt like a mouse transfixed by a viper. "From this day forth you will be my slave, which will therefore make *me* indispensable. After my imprinting, no other woman will be sufficient for you—not even another Honored Matre." Her smiling lips looked as ragged as torn paper. "Your service in past years has earned you this reward. Most males do not survive so long among us."

Uxtal didn't dare run, lest he enrage her. This was the lingering threat that he had feared for years. He saw an unquenchable orange fire begin to burn in Ingva's eyes. Sexual bonding, total enslavement—to this hideous crone.

"You are about to discover my pleasures." She caressed his face with a bony, clawed finger. "You're going to enjoy this."

"That is not possible, Honored Matre—"

She cackled. "Little man, I am an adept of the fifth order, a qualified member of the black veil. I can overcome any blockage of desire." She grabbed him by the arm and dragged him to the floor. She was too strong, and he could not fight her off. Smiling as she straddled him, Ingva said, "Now for your reward."

The gnarled woman ripped his clothes away, and Uxtal prayed that he would survive this day. He whimpered. Years ago, at the very beginning, the Face Dancers had tried to protect him before delivering him to Bandalong, but Khrone had not shown himself here for some time. The Face Dancer had discarded the Lost Tleilaxu researcher as soon as he'd provided the Paul Atreides ghola. Khrone had simply left him at the mercy of the Honored Matres. The Face Dancers could do nothing to protect him from Ingva's fury once she discovered what had been done to him.

With sinewy, greedy hands, the crone reached down, gasped, and then hurled him across the floor naked. "*Castrated!* Who did that to you?"

"Th-the Face Dancers. Long ago. I—I needed to concentrate on my work, without the temptation of an Honored Matre's pleasures."

"You disgusting, stupid little man! Do you know what you have denied yourself? What you have denied *me?*"

Uxtal slipped away, scrambling to retrieve the remnants of his clothing before she killed him out of sheer indignation. But Ingva moved like a panther to intercept him. "I have never been pleased with you, little man, and now you have made my job more difficult. Castration, however, does not render you utterly useless as a sexual slave. To an adept with my skill level, even a eunuch is not entirely unreachable. It will require extra effort, but I will imprint you anyway." She pushed him back down to the floor. "You will thank me for this when it's over. I promise you that."

Uxtal argued, whined, and then screamed, but no one heard or cared.

The hunt has been a fundamental part of the natural order since life first emerged. The prey knows this as well as the predator.

—Bene Gesserit dictum

Alone on their breezy observation platform above the giant aspen trees, the ghola of Thufir Hawat tried to absorb everything and see everything, adding details together for a correct summation and analysis. He was not yet a Mentat, but according to historical records, Thufir had the potential to be a great warrior, a strategist, and a human computer.

In his original lifetime, he had served three generations of House Atreides. After the fall of Arrakeen, the Harkonnens had captured him and used a residual poison to coerce him to serve the evil Baron. *How I must have hated that!* Back then, Thufir had been an old veteran, his mind heavy with a lifetime of service and battles . . . somewhat like the old Bashar. Young Thufir very much wanted to live up to those expectations.

Even here, safely high above the ground, he could smell blood in the air from the hunt. Two lanky Handlers stood guard at the base of the wooden tower to protect him and the Rabbi from the dangerous Futars and Honored Matres loose in the forest. Or were the Handlers simply making certain their two visitors didn't go anywhere off-limits and didn't see anything they weren't supposed to see?

The anxious Rabbi paced across the open platform and peered down into the broad grove of silver-barked trees. Thufir had already made enough of an analysis of the old man to predict how he would react in a situation. Hardened by a lifetime of feeling wrongfully down-trodden, the Rabbi fought for his people while trying not to be seen as a victim. Most of all, he feared being indecisive, anything less than a leader.

Now the old man looked sickened and disappointed, as if his dreams of having a perfect new world for his followers were draining away. Would the Jewish refugees ask to stay on this planet, despite the possi-bility of further Honored Matre attacks? Even with the Handlers' odd behavior and their vicious Futars, which the Rabbi found repellent for religious reasons? What would the Rabbi decide as he weighed the advantages and disadvantages?

Thufir was sure he and his fellow young gholas would never come here to live. They belonged on the *Ithaca* with the Bashar and Duncan Idaho, ready to defend against the Outside Enemy. That was why they had been reborn in the first place.

Even if some of the refugees left the no-ship to settle on the planet, Duncan would never allow the *Ithaca* to remain here. *Motionlessness creates vulnerability. Complacency is dangerous.* Regardless of how wel-coming the Handlers might seem, this planet could only be a tempo-rary stopover for most of them. Though his past-life memories had not been restored, Thufir's loyalties remained with the people aboard the ship.

In the forest below, he heard snarling Futars and the sharp cracking of branches. He shaded his eyes, trying to discern details from shadows in the trees as the chase came toward them.

"I do not like this." The Rabbi raised his hands in a warding ges-ture.

"It will take more than a superstitious symbol to block these attack-ers."

"You may think yourself safer, ghola, because you will someday be a warrior, but I fight in a much more important arena. Faith is my weapon—the only one I need."

Below, they saw the cautious predatory movement of two Futars slinking through the trees to set a trap. Thufir realized what was happening: With loud roars in the distance, other beast-men were driving an Honored Matre in this direction, and then the rest of the pack would close in on her.

Using implanted communication devices, the Handler guards at the base of the tower received an update. They turned their bandit-masked eyes up to the observation platform. "Three of the five Honored Matres have been killed," one called. "The hunting ability of our Futars is proven."

But two of the deadly women remained alive, and one was coming toward the observation tower at that very moment.

She ran out of the trees, her face scratched by lashing branches, her left arm mauled and hanging useless, her bare feet torn and bleeding from fleeing across the rough ground. But she showed no signs of slowing.

The Rabbi squirmed and put a hand over his eyes, as if offended. "I will not watch this."

As the woman burst into the clearing, looking over her shoulder, two Futars sprang from their hiding places in the trees and surprised their prey. Another pair of hunting Futars closed in from behind her, running hard. Thufir leaned over the railing to get a better view, while the Rabbi cringed back.

Without pausing in her stride, the Honored Matre bent to snatch up a fallen branch with her good hand. Using amazing strength, she spun and shoved it like a wobbly, off-balance javelin. The splintered end skewered one of the leaping Futars. Mortally wounded, he fell, yelping and thrashing, as she sprang aside.

Another Futar jumped the woman, striking at her wounded side, hoping to latch onto her shoulder and wrench her already-mauled arm out of its socket. Thufir saw instantly that the Honored Matre had merely been feigning the severity of her injury. Her mangled arm darted up and grabbed the Futar by his throat. His jaws snapped only a centimeter from her face. With a loud grunt, the whore pushed the creature away. The Futar staggered backward and crashed into one of the silvery trunks. Stunned, he struggled to his feet.

As the other two Futars closed with her, the Honored Matre looked sideways. Her orange eyes fixed on the two Handlers standing guard by the lookout tower. With a burst of desperate, vengeful speed, she ran directly toward them, leaving the beast-men behind.

Both of the long, lanky men raised their stun-goads, but she out-matched them with a hurricane of movement. Her callused hand knocked the staffs away and she drove in, relishing the brief look of fear behind her first victim's eyes. With a single, powerful blow, she broke the Handler's neck, and he crumpled to the ground.

She lunged toward the second Handler, but the nearest Futar inter-cepted her to protect his master. The other two beast-men came closer, one of them limping. Seeing that she could not fight off the creatures, the Honored Matre grabbed the fallen stun-goad and bounded off into the forest again. Snarling, the Futars ran after her.

Thufir grabbed the Rabbi's arm. "Quickly!" He went to the steep wooden stairs that would take them down to the ground. "Maybe we can help."

The Rabbi hesitated. "But he is already dead, and it is safe up here. We should stay—"

"I am tired of being a spectator!" Thufir descended swiftly, two creaking steps at a time. The Rabbi came after him, grumbling.

When Thufir reached the ground, the remaining Handler guard was bent over his comrade. Thufir expected to hear the lanky man wailing in grief or shouting in anger; instead, he seemed more intent.

Unusual. Curious.

From far off in the forest came a bloodcurdling shriek as the three Futars cornered the Honored Matre again. She hurled obscenities. Thu-fir heard a crashing violence, a crack that sounded like breaking bone, terrible snarls followed by a brief scream . . . and then silence. After a moment's pause, Thufir's sensitive ears caught the unmistakable sounds of feeding.

Huffing great breaths, the Rabbi reached the base of the observa-tion tower, and steadied himself by holding the wooden rail. Thufir hurried toward the Handler and his dead companion. "Is there anything we can do to help?"

Hunched over, the surviving Handler's back suddenly tensed, as if he'd forgotten the two were there. He swiveled his head on a long neck and looked at them. The dark band was a heavy shadow across his eyes.

Then Thufir glimpsed the dead Handler lying on the ground.

The corpse's features had shifted, changed . . . reverted. He was no longer tall and lanky, and his face was not streamlined; he had no black mask around his eyes. Instead, the dead Handler had grayish skin, dark, close-set eyes, and a pug nose.

Thufir recognized it from archival images—a Face Dancer!

The other Handler guard glared at them, then let his face revert to its neutral state. No longer human, but cadaverous . . . and blank.

Thufir's mind spun, and he wished desperately that he had Mentat abilities. The Handlers were Face Dancers? All of them, or just a few? Handlers fought the Honored Matres, a common enemy. The Enemy. Handlers, Face Dancers, Enemy . . .

This planet was not at all as it seemed.

He flashed a glance at the Rabbi. The old man had seen the same thing, and though his horror and surprise had made him freeze for an instant, he seemed to be drawing the same conclusions.

The powerful Handler drew himself up and came toward them with his stun-goad.

"We'd better run," Thufir said.

Even the most delicate plans can be thrown into turmoil by an impetuous action from our supposed masters. Is it not ironic when they claim that Face Dancers are shiftless and changeable?

—KHRONE,
communiqué to Face Dancer myriad

From inside the reconstructed Castle Caladan, Khrone pulled his strings, played his roles, and moved his game pieces. The Face Dancer myriad had manipulated the Ixians, the Guild, CHOAM, and the Honored Matre rebels who still ruled Tleilax. They had already achieved many milestones of success. Khrone had traveled wherever he was needed, wherever he was summoned, but he always came back here to his pair of precious gholas. The Baron and Paolo. The work continued.

On Caladan, year after year, the group of machine-augmented observers sent regular reports to the distant old man and woman. Despite their bodily degeneration, they showed damnable patience, and still they'd found nothing to fault him for. Khrone was always watched by the patchwork observers, but never discovered. Even those hideous spies didn't know everything.

The summons came to him from the castle tower, interrupting his work and concentration. Khrone trudged up the stone staircase to see what the spies wanted. When they invoked the name of their masters, he could not refuse—not yet. He had to keep up appearances for a little while longer, until he could finish this part of his project.

He knew the old man and woman understood the wisdom of his alternative plan. Since their efforts to find the lost no-ship kept failing, it made sense to pursue another route for obtaining their Kwisatz Haderach: the Paolo ghola.

But would the old man and woman allow him the necessary time to awaken the child? Paolo was only six, and it would be several years yet before Khrone could even begin the process of triggering his memories, saturating him with spice, preparing him for his destiny. The distant masters had made their demands and set their schedules. According to sparse reports from the patchwork observers, the old man and woman were ready to launch their vast fleet on a long-anticipated conquest of *everything*, whether the Kwisatz Haderach was ready or not. . . .

Silent and stony, the hideous emissaries awaited him inside the high tower room. Just as Khrone reached the top of the winding stairs, the men turned with stuttering movements to face him. He put his hands on his hips. "You are delaying my work."

One emissary's head twitched from side to side, as if his neurons were firing conflicting impulses that caused his neck and shoulder muscles to spasm. "This message—we cannot deliver—deliver this message—ourselves." He balled his bony hand into a fist. Bubbles gurgled through the tubes. "Deliver a message."

"What is it?" Khrone crossed his arms. "I have work to complete for our masters."

The lead emissary opened his hands wide in a beckoning gesture. The other augmented humans stood motionless, presumably recording his every movement. Khrone stepped into the gallery room while the pale-faced horrors retreated to the wall. He frowned. "What is this—"

Suddenly his vision fuzzed around the edges, and the walls of the tower became indistinct. Reality shifted around him. At first Khrone saw the ethereal grid of the net, strands of connected tachyons completing an infinite chain. Then he found himself in another place, a simulation of a simulation.

He heard the sound of plodding hoofs, smelled manure, and listened to the creaking of rough wheels. Turning to his right, he saw the old man and old woman sitting in a wooden cart drawn by a gray mule. The beast walked along with infinite weariness and patience. No one seemed to be in a hurry.

Khrone had to take a step to follow the cart, which was loaded high with paradan melons, their olive green rinds mottled with splotchy patterns. He looked around, trying to understand the metaphor of their dream world. Far ahead, the road led toward crowded geometric buildings that seemed to move and flow together, an enormous city that looked alive. The perfectly angled structures were like patterns on a circuit board.

In the foreground the old man sat next to the woman on the buckboard, casually holding leather reins. He looked down at Khrone. "We have news. Your time-consuming project is no longer relevant. We have no need for you or your Baron Harkonnen, or for the Paul Atreides ghola you have grown for us."

The old woman chimed in, "In other words, we will not have to wait so many years for your alternate Kwisatz Haderach candidate."

The man lifted the reins and urged the mule to greater speed, but the beast ignored the command. "It is time to be done with all this tinkering."

Khrone walked along beside them. "What do you mean? I am ever so close to—"

"For nineteen years, our sophisticated nets have failed to capture the no-ship, but now we've been fortunate. We have laid a primitive trap, an old-fashioned trick, and very soon the no-ship and all those aboard will be in our control. We will have what we need without resorting to your alternative Kwisatz Haderach. Your plan is obsolete."

Khrone gritted his teeth, trying not to show his alarm. "How did you find the ship after all this time? My Face Dancers—"

"The ship came to our planet of Handlers, and now we have them." The old man smiled, revealing perfect white teeth. "We are about to spring our trap."

On the buckboard, the woman leaned back and said, "When we have the no-ship and its passengers, we will control what the mathematical prophecy says we require. All of our prescient-level projections indicate that the Kwisatz Haderach is aboard. He will stand beside us during Kralizec."

"Our massive fleets are about to launch a full-scale offensive against the worlds of the Old Empire. It will all be over soon. We have waited so long." The old man snapped the reins again, looked smug.

The old woman's wrinkled lips curled upward in an apologetic smile. "Therefore, Khrone, your time-consuming and costly plan simply isn't necessary anymore."

Aghast, the Face Dancer took two more steps beside the cart to maintain his pace. "But you can't do that! I have already awakened the Baron's memories, and the Paolo ghola is perfect, ripe for our purposes."

"Speculation. We no longer need him," the old man repeated. "Once we seize the no-ship, we will have the Kwisatz Haderach."

As if she were giving him a consolation prize, the woman reached into the back of the cart, selected a small paradan melon, and extended it to Khrone. "It was nice to work with you. Here, have a melon."

He took it, confused and disturbed. The illusion around him twinkled and washed out, fading until he found himself back in the tower room. He was empty-handed, his palms cradling a nonexistent paradan melon.

He found himself standing at the very edge of the high tower window, his feet on the brink. The plaz panes were open, and a gusty sea breeze slapped his face. The stomach-lurching drop extended to the rugged rocks at the tide line far below. Another half step, and he would plunge to his death.

Khrone pinwheeled his arms and staggered backward, collapsing to the flagstone floor with an embarrassing lack of grace.

The augmented emissaries regarded him coolly from the side of the tower room. With considerable effort, Khrone maintained his composure. He didn't even speak to the patchwork monstrosities, but stalked out of the tower chamber.

No matter what the old man and old woman said, Khrone would not abandon his plans until *he* was finished with them.

To a seasoned fighter, each battle is a banquet. Victory should be savored like the finest wine or the most extravagant dessert. Defeat is like a rancid chunk of meat.

—teachings of the Swordmasters of Ginaz

The sixty ships descended to the heart of Bandalong, where Hellica would be waiting for them. Murbella was sure that the Matre Superior intended to savor this confrontation, toying with what she saw as an inferior opponent. The pretender queen would expect true Bene Gesserit behavior from the New Sisterhood—discussions and negotiations. It would be a game to her.

Murbella, though, was not entirely Bene Gesserit. She had a surprise for the Honored Matres below. Several, in fact.

Her ships circling over the Palace were far outnumbered by Hellica's forces on the ground. The whores expected civilized behavior from the Mother Commander, diplomatic protocols, ambassadorial courtesies. Murbella had already decided that would be a waste of time. Janess, Kiria, and the other infiltrator Sisters in the city below knew what to do.

Precisely on cue, as Murbella's escort squad prepared to land in the Matre Superior's "trap," seven major buildings in Bandalong erupted into flames. Concussion waves knocked down walls, blasting Honored Matre emplacements into cinders. Moments later, three bombs vaporized dozens of ships on the spaceport landing field.

Before the stunned whores around the Palace could try to shoot down her escort ships, Murbella yelled into the commline: "Valkyries, launch your attack!"

Her escort ships began their bombardment, wiping out the protective forces that encircled the Matre Superior's seat of power. Out of harsh necessity, Murbella had decreed Bandalong expendable. Hellica and her rebels were a dangerous firebrand to be extinguished. Period. The whores below went into a frenzy, rushing about like hornets from a burning nest.

Then, from orbit, Bashar Wikki Aztin launched a second, far more overwhelming wave of New Sisterhood warships. The second, unseen Guildship dropped its no-field beside Edrik's giant Heighliner. Suddenly two hundred more Valkyrie attack ships plunged out of the open hold and streaked down to the battleground.

Up until the date of its untimely obliteration, Richese had made regular deliveries of armaments and specially tailored battleships. Though the largest part of the huge fleet had been turned to slag along with the rest of the weapon shops, Chapterhouse possessed more than enough firepower to render this last Honored Matre stronghold helpless.

Bashar Aztin led waves of ships in performing surgical strikes on the strategic targets and key installations that had been identified in the covert transmissions from the infiltrator team. From her hiding place, Janess activated her own communication lines and coordinated her saboteurs with the swarms of newly landed troops.

While other Sisterhood fighters fanned out across the city and surrounding lands, the Honored Matres scrambled to mount a defense against such a widespread and thorough assault.

The Mother Commander and her Valkyries landed outside the Palace. Murbella positioned military transport vessels to form a complete blockade. Her black-uniformed fighters poured out onto the ground and surrounded the gaudy structure.

Smiling to herself, Murbella went in to kill the Matre Superior. No prisoners. It was the only way this could end.

Accompanied by her entourage of Valkyries, the Mother Commander marched through the main entrance. Honored Matre guards in purple leotards and capes rushed to engage the invader, but the Sister-hood fighters swiftly subdued them.

Inside the Palace, her group passed a bubbling fountain of red liquid that looked and smelled like blood. Statues of Honored Matres thrust swords through frozen Bene Gesserit Sisters; scarlet fluid poured from the victims' wounds into the bowl of the fountain. Murbella pointedly ignored the grotesquerie.

Without a misstep, the Mother Commander found her way to the main throne room and strode in under full guard, as if she owned all of Tleilax. Despite the intrinsic violence of the Honored Matres, the victory of the far-superior Sisters was a foregone conclusion. Murbella had learned, however, from studying the Battle of Junction, where even Bashar Miles Teg had been lured by a triumph that was too easy. She kept her mind and body in the highest state of alert. Honored Matres had a way of twisting defeat into victory.

Preening on her high throne, an unrepentant Hellica awaited them, as if she remained in control of the situation. "So nice of you to come calling, witch." The pretender queen wore a red, yellow, and blue costume that looked more suitable for a circus performer than for the leader of a planet. Her tightly knotted bun of blonde hair was studded with priceless jewels and sharp decorative pins. "You are brave to come here. And foolish."

Boldly, Murbella approached the throne. "It seems to me your city is burning, Hellica. You should have joined us against the coming Enemy. You are going to die anyway. Why not die fighting a real opponent?"

Hellica laughed boisterously. "The Enemy can't be fought! That is why we take what we wish and then move on to fertile ground before the first forces arrive. However, if your witches wish to distract the Enemy with pointless battles, we will welcome the delay, so that we may slip away more easily."

Murbella couldn't understand what Hellica intended to accomplish, why she had rallied her rebels, drawing them all into a debilitating conflict that none of them could win. The enclaves of violent holdouts had caused much damage—Richese was only the worst example—weakening humanity. To what purpose?

"We were nearly ready to depart from Tleilax. Right now, you are in my way." The Matre Superior stood, then dropped into a fighting stance. "On the other hand, if I kill you and take over your New Sisterhood for myself, perhaps we'll stay a while longer."

"At one time, I might have tried to reeducate you. Now I see that the effort would be wasted."

Hellica wanted this conflict. Apparently, she had no illusions about surviving, knowing about the bloody battles occurring all across Bandalong. Her intent must have been to maximize casualties, nothing more. More explosions rang throughout the city.

Staring hard at the beautiful woman, Murbella imagined Hellica dead, slumped at the base of the dais holding her throne. The vision was so clear it seemed like a gift of prescience. A classic Swordmaster technique.

At the edges of her vision, Murbella noticed flickering shadows, bodies moving stealthily around the throne room. Dozens of Honored Matre guards closed in, a surprise ambush. But it would never be enough. Her own Valkyries had been waiting for this trap, the desperate last stand. More than prepared to fight, they turned their superior numbers against them and plunged into the fray. Overhead, Bashar Aztin's clustered attack ships roared across the sky, making the whole Palace shake.

Murbella bounded up the steps to the dais as Hellica vaulted over one of the armrests. The two grappled like asteroids colliding, but Murbella used her balance to throw her weight with a Swordmaster re-orienting technique, and drove Hellica to the floor.

Rolling on the stone tiles in a flurry of deadly blows and blocks, Murbella and the pretender queen tore at each other. The Mother Commander clawed a long gouge down Hellica's cheek, then the other woman smashed her forehead into Murbella's, stunning her just long enough to tear herself free.

Springing to their feet, the opponents faced off, and the Matre Superior demonstrated unorthodox fighting techniques, subtly advanced from anything Murbella remembered in her own Honored Matre training. So, Hellica had learned, or changed.

In response, Murbella altered her timing, sought the opportunity to strike, but the other woman moved with an unexpected flash, more swiftly than Murbella could dodge. A hard, stinging blow bruised her left thigh, but the Mother Commander did not go down. She blocked her nerve receptors, numbed the pain in her leg, and then threw herself back into the fight.

An Honored Matre fought with violent impulsiveness, sheer strength and speed; Murbella possessed those traits herself, combined with the finesse of the long-forgotten Swordmaster art as well as the best Bene Gesserit skills. Once Murbella reset her mind and her approach, the Matre Superior had no chance.

Envisioning an unexpected response of her own, Murbella planned a sequence of moves and countermoves a few seconds into the future. The nonpattern in Hellica's fighting style was really a pattern when viewed from a larger perspective. Murbella didn't need a sword— needed no weapon at all, in fact—just herself.

Despite the Matre Superior's flurry of movement, the parries, punches, and kicks, Murbella saw a straight line of vulnerability—and acted. The instant she envisioned it, her path of attack became no more than an afterthought. The action was over, and successful, as soon as she undertook it.

With the force of a pile driver, her right foot found its way under Hellica's rib cage and smashed straight into the heart. Hellica's eyes opened wide, and she mouthed a curse without getting the words out. She spilled onto the floor at the base of the dais, exactly as Murbella had foreseen her, moments before.

Panting, the Mother Commander turned away and assessed the handful of still-living Honored Matre guards locked in combat with the Valkyries. Many discarded bodies in bright leotards already lay strewn across the tiles, along with far fewer Sisters. "Hold! I am your Matre Superior now!"

"We do not follow witches," one woman snapped indignantly, smearing blood from her mouth and ready to keep fighting. "We are not fools."

With her peripheral vision, Murbella noticed the dead Matre Superior beginning to change. The Mother Commander turned back to her victim and caught the impossible shifting. Hellica's face went slack and grayish white; her eyes sank in, her hair writhed and altered. The thing that had been the pretender queen sprawled in gaudy clothes. Pug nose, tiny mouth, black button eyes.

Murbella's mind raced, and she seized the moment of astonishment and disbelief. "You had no qualms against following a Face Dancer! Now who is the fool? How many more of you are Face Dancers?"

Even as they fought the Valkyries, the remaining Honored Matres glimpsed the blank-faced creature that had been Hellica. More of the whores stuttered to a halt, staring in shock.

"Matre Superior!"

"She is not human!"

"Behold your leader," Murbella ordered, strutting forward. "You obeyed the orders of a Face Dancer planted among you. You were deceived and betrayed!"

Only one of the Honored Matre guards continued to battle furiously. The Valkyries soon dispatched her, and Murbella was not shocked to see the fallen woman transform into a second Face Dancer.

Here, and on Gammu—how far had this insidious infiltration spread? Hellica's provocative actions had somehow served the Face Dancers rather than the whores. Was it a plot spawned by the Lost Tleilaxu, or did it extend even farther than that? Who were the shape-shifters really fighting for? Could they already be a vanguard from the Enemy, sent into the Old Empire to assess and weaken the target?

All those rebel enclaves, the dissent and violence that drained the resources of the New Sisterhood. Could it all have been a plot to weaken humanity's defenses? Setting them against each other, killing viable fighters to make them vulnerable so that the Enemy could wade in and finish the job more easily? With the main fight over in the city, more of her Valkyries streamed into the throne room, consolidating their hold on the gaudy Palace. Throughout Bandalong, Hellica's remaining followers fought to the death, while the Guild Heighliner remained up in stationary orbit, observing the fray from a safe distance.

Her daughter Janess, looking battered but bright-eyed, led them. "Mother Commander, the Palace is ours."

*

*The enemy of your enemy is not necessarily your friend. He may
hate you as much as any other rival.*

—Hawat's Strategic Corollary

With the deadly hunt over and all five Honored Matres dead,
Sheeana and Teg descended the wooden steps of the open-
framed lookout tower. It had been an exhilarating, as well as unsettling, experience. Sheeana sensed that the young Bashar beside her
wrestled with his own questions, extrapolations, and suspicions, but he
could not voice any of them without the guards overhearing.

The Handlers were gathering by their Futars in the leaf-strewn
clearing where the last Honored Matre had been torn to pieces in plain
view. Hrrm and the black-striped Futar had fought over, then jointly
brought down, the last of the terrible whores.

It had been a dizzying fight, with the two Futars circling, lashing
out, and dodging the woman's hands and feet. When she leapt high
with a kick, Hrrm had reached out and caught her ankle with his
claws, like catching a fish on a hook, and slammed her to the forest
floor. Black Stripe had lunged in to tear out her throat. Scarlet droplets
spattered the carpet of golden leaves.

Walking away from the observation platform, Sheeana and Teg
went to stand by the Futars with cold, wary fascination. Recognizing

her, Hrrm gave her a bloody grin, as if expecting Sheeana to come forward and give him a back rub. She sensed his need for acceptance, and for years she had been the only one to give it to him. Though the Handlers—the true masters—were there in the forest now, Sheeana said, "Excellent work, Hrrm. I am proud of you."

A deep purr rumbled in his throat. Then he dug his face into the Honored Matre's pale flesh and ripped out another mouthful of meat. Sheeana had not seen the other three Futars from the no-ship, but knew they must have joined the hunt as well.

Four of the lanky natives, including the Chief Handler, stood watching the grisly scene, apparently satisfied with the creatures' performance. Orak Tho said, "Now you see our true feelings for the Honored Matres."

"We never doubted it," Sheeana said. "But another Enemy is coming—one that those whores provoked. That Enemy is far worse."

"Worse? How do you know this?" the Chief Handler said. "What if there is nothing to fear from this other Enemy? Perhaps you have misunderstood."

Sheeana noticed the other Handlers subtly closing in around them. Teg picked up on it, too, but showed no obvious reaction.

Standing amidst the bloody remnants of the hunt, Orak Tho surprised them by changing the subject. "And now that we have shown our goodwill, I would like to visit your no-ship. I will bring a party of Handlers with me to see it."

Teg gave her a subtle sign of caution.

"That is indeed something we should consider," she said, "but we must first discuss it with our companions. We have much to tell them about your gracious hospitality, and all that you have shown us."

Trying not to reveal his concern, Teg added, "We have only a small lighter. We'll need to arrange transport for your visiting party."

"We have our own ships." The Chief Handler turned, as if the decision had already been made. Teg and Sheeana flashed a look at each other. Their own ships? The Handlers had already talked about having scanners sophisticated enough to detect the *Ithaca* in orbit. This civilization was far more technologically sophisticated than it appeared to be.

The odors of the Handlers, of coppery spilled blood, and of the musky Futars mixed with the forest air in a medley of confusing and disturbing smells. Sheeana also detected a faint, familiar undertone of unwarranted tension. Beside the half-devoured corpse of the Honored Matre, Hrrm and Black Stripe looked up, sensing something amiss. Both Futars growled deep in their throats.

Sheeana interrupted. "Will the Rabbi and Thufir Hawat be rejoining us soon?"

Orak Tho continued as if he had not heard her question. "I will signal my people. I am certain your companions would agree. We will do this as efficiently as possible."

The nearby Handlers stiffened. Their movements were subtle, but she noticed the people slowly coiling into fighting stances, elbows cocked, legs ready to spring. *They are going to attack!*

"Miles!" Sheeana shouted.

The young Bashar lashed out in a strike so swift it was no more than a flicker of movement to the naked eye. Sheeana ducked, thrust her palm into the face of another Handler, and flung herself sideways as the people closed in.

Teg struck one man in the center of the chest with a cracking blow strong enough to freeze his heart—an ancient, but deadly, Bene Gesserit fighting technique. Sheeana grabbed the long forearm of another Handler and, snapping it backward, broke the bone above the elbow. More Handlers loped like predators from the dense aspens.

The natives fought with the clear intent to kill, not even asking Sheeana and Teg to surrender. *But what will the Handlers do when they kill us? How will they get aboard the no-ship, if that's what they want?* Though they were only two people, Sheeana and Teg held their own against the onslaught, but only tenuously.

In a storm of muscles and claws, Hrrm attacked—striking not her or the Bashar, but the Chief Handler. Orak Tho opened his wide mouth in surprise and barked a sharp guttural command, but Hrrm did not stop. The Futar had broken his conditioning. Hrrm drove the Handler to the ground as he snarled her name, "Sheeana!" In unthinking frenzy, he bit down and twisted sideways, snapping Orak Tho's long neck.

Hrrm, knowing nothing of politics or alliances, fought the other beast-man and defended Sheeana against the Handlers. He'd done it for *her.*

Everything happened in seconds. While the Futar stood from his kill, Orak Tho changed. His dead flesh shifted to the inhuman features of a Face Dancer. The other Handler Teg had already killed also shifted. *Face Dancers!*

In the past, Sheeana had always trusted her ability to recognize the shape-shifters by their distinctive pheromones, but the new Face Dancers were far more sophisticated, often undetectable even by the Bene Gesserit. She had known that much before leaving Chapterhouse.

Pieces clicked into place like chits on a counting machine. If these Handlers were new-generation Face Dancers, then they were not allies after all, but enemies. Just because both the Handlers and the Bene Gesserit hated Honored Matres did not necessarily mean that the two shared a common cause.

Roaring, the black-striped Futar leapt into the fight and attacked the traitorous Hrrm. The two growling Futars fought, thrashing and flailing in a tumble of claws and teeth. Sheeana could do nothing to help him, turning to see another threat.

Several of the bandit-masked men also reverted to their Face Dancer shapes, no longer bothering to maintain the disguises. All of the Handlers seemed to be Face Dancers.

Orak Tho had wanted to come aboard the no-ship, and now the reasons were obvious: The Handlers intended to capture the *Ithaca.* For the Enemy! The Enemy had always been after the no-ship. That was why the Chief Handler was so willing to kill the two of them now: Face Dancers could easily take the place of Sheeana and Teg, taking not only their appearance but also memory and personality imprints. Face Dancers could work from within to accomplish what the hunters had not been able to do from afar. She had to warn Duncan!

Sheeana struck at another Handler, driving him back into his comrades. As Teg fought beside her, his Mentat awareness processed the same data, and Sheeana was sure he came to the same conclusions. "They are all connected: the old man and woman, the net, the Handlers, the Face Dancers. Let's go—at least one of us has to live!"

Sheeana knew another sickening truth. "Thufir and the Rabbi are probably dead. That's why the Handlers separated us. Divide and kill."

From the edge of the tall aspens, two more hunting Futars bounded into the fray, instinctively drawn to fight against Hrrm, who had turned on them. It was inconceivable that a Futar had attacked a Handler!

Sheeana didn't see how she and the Bashar could possibly defeat all the opponents arrayed against them. Hrrm continued to fight, though he could not last much longer. He surged up, grasped Black Stripe's neck, and sank his claws into the throat, tearing out the larynx in a stringy, bloody lump. Even as his life's blood gushed out, the striped Futar continued to snap with sharp teeth. Then Hrrm went down under the additional Futars in a snarling mass of claws and torn hairy skin.

In a matter of moments, the Futars would turn on her and Teg. "Miles!" Sheeana struck a Handler full in the face, and he went down.

Beside her, Teg suddenly *blurred*, moving with such speed that she could no longer keep track of him. It was as if a wind rushed through the aspens. All of the Handlers closing in on them dropped to the ground like felled trees. Sheeana barely had time to blink.

Teg reappeared beside her, gasping for breath and looking drained. "Come with me. Back to the lighter. Now!"

Her questions about him could wait. She ran with him. Hrrm had bought enough time for Sheeana to escape, and she wouldn't let his sacrifice be wasted.

Behind them came the noises of more Futars, their hands and feet crackling in the dry leaves and twigs that covered the forest floor. Would the other three from the no-ship help her, as Hrrm had? She could not count on it. She had seen them take down combat-hardened Honored Matres, and she didn't think much of her own chances against so many of them.

No doubt, more Handlers would be waiting at the wooden city-towers. Some had probably surrounded the lighter already. How coordinated was Orak Tho's plan? Were *all* Handlers really Face Dancers, or had they simply been infiltrated?

Sheeana and Teg dashed past the Handlers' main settlement. More raccoon-faced people were emerging from the cylindrical wooden structures, slow to react to the changed situation, all of them closing in.

Ahead in the clearing, the small ship sat waiting for them. As she had feared, two tall Handlers stood in front of the hatch, carrying powerful stun-goads. Sheeana prepared for a life-or-death fight.

In front of her, Teg shifted and blurred again, shooting forward like a bullet, his speed beyond human possibility. The two Handler guards turned, but they were too late. Teg's blows hit them like lightning strikes. The Handlers snapped aside as if thrown by an invisible force.

Sheeana ran to catch up, her lungs on fire. Slowing enough to reappear, the Bashar kicked the stun-goads out of the way. Reeling with exhaustion, he keyed the entry code into the lighter's main hatch controls. The hydraulics hummed, and the heavy door began to slide open.

"Inside, quickly!" He heaved great breaths. "We've got to take off."

Sheeana had never seen a human look so utterly weary. Teg's skin had gone gray, and he seemed to be on the verge of collapse. She grabbed his arm, fearing that he was in no condition to fly the lighter.

I might have to do it myself.

Handlers swarmed out of the towers carrying staffs and stun-goads. With nothing to hide anymore, most of them had reverted to their pug-nosed Face Dancer appearances. Sheeana feared that some might be armed with projectile throwers or long-distance stunners.

With a shout and a frantic rush behind them, two people bolted out of the dense aspen forest, running for all they were worth. Sheeana pushed Teg inside the ship and paused at the hatch, where she saw Thufir Hawat and the Rabbi running pell-mell toward her. More Handlers were hard on their heels, and she heard Futars crashing through the underbrush. Thufir and the Rabbi were both flushed, stumbling forward only seconds ahead of their pursuers. The young man grabbed the Rabbi and hauled him along. She did not think they would reach the lighter in time.

Finally, with selfless resolve, Thufir propelled the old man toward the still-distant lighter while he turned alone to face the Handlers. With balled fists he lunged toward the closest pursuer, surprising him with his turnabout. A sharp rabbit punch to the abdomen of the Handler and a chop to his throat caused the Face Dancer to reel and drop. Through his heroics, Thufir had given the Rabbi time to stagger ahead as fast as he could. Panting but refusing to rest, Thufir then ran after him, catching up to the old man as they closed in on the ship in the meadow.

As the first Futar bounded forward, another beast-man crashed in from the side, slamming into the ship. The pair rolled together, clawing and fighting. A second one of Hrrm's Futars! The delay gained Sheeana and her companions a few more precious seconds.

She grabbed one of the stun-goads from the fallen guards. "Run! *Run!*" Over her shoulder she called into the open lighter, "Miles, start the engines!"

Thufir and the Rabbi ran with last bursts of adrenaline. "Face Dancers," Thufir gasped. "We saw—"

"I know! Get inside the lighter." The ship's engines began to thrum. Somehow, Teg had found enough energy to drag himself to the pilot's seat.

Sheeana planted her feet in the meadow grass and jabbed the stun-goad at the first oncoming Handler, then swung it to smash the side of another's head.

The old Rabbi stumbled aboard, while the twelve-year-old ghola lurched after him. Three more Futars came bounding out of the trees, followed by another group of Handlers. She threw herself through the hatch, scrambling to activate the ramp controls. She dragged her feet out of the way just as the heavy hatch sealed shut. With a crash, the first Futar slammed into the hull.

"Fly, Miles!" She collapsed onto the deck. "Fly!"

Thufir Hawat was already in the copilot's seat. Beside him, the Bashar looked as if he might lose consciousness at any moment, and Thufir reached for the copilot's controls, ready to take charge. But Teg brushed the boy's hands away. "I'll do it."

The lighter rose above the trees, accelerating into the sky. Heart pounding, Sheeana looked at the Rabbi on the floor beside her. His tear-streaked face was flushed with exertion, and she feared he might die of cardiac arrest now that he'd made it to the escape ship.

Then she remembered what Orak Tho had told her: The Handlers had their own spacecraft, and they would no doubt pursue them.

"Hurry." Her voice was no more than a rasping whisper.

Ashen-faced Teg seemed to hear her, though. A burst of vertical acceleration pressed her against the floor.

Radicals are only to be feared when you try to suppress them. You must demonstrate that you will use the best of what they offer.

—LETO ATREIDES II,
the Tyrant

With his mind reeling and his body shuddering, Uxtal could not absorb what Ingva had done to him. Using powers he could neither comprehend nor resist, the old crone had wrung him like a dirty rag, then left him weak and shuddering, barely able to breathe, walk, or think.

It should not have been possible!

Barely even noticing the attack ships closing in on Bandalong, he managed to stumble back to his laboratory. He was more terrified of Ingva than of any falling bombs or raiders. At the same time, he found himself unable to drive the sensations from his mind, the pleasure she had *inflicted* upon him. He felt sick and unclean, at the indelible memory of it.

Uxtal hated this planet, this city, these women—and he couldn't stand feeling so completely out of control. For years, his greatest skill had been as a tightrope walker, constantly worried about what might happen to him if he didn't maintain his balance and alertness. But after his coital ordeal with Ingva, he could barely keep himself from collapsing at a time when he most needed his mental abilities.

Then the massive attack had begun throughout the city, from explosions at strategic centers, to the siege of the Palace, to the sudden appearance of a fleet of Bene Gesserit warships in the skies.

Hidden explosives had already destroyed some walls in his large research complex. Saboteurs and infiltrators must have come here ahead of time, and they had marked his laboratory as an important facility for the Honored Matres.

He staggered back into the main lab and inhaled deeply of the chemicals around the fresh axlotl tanks. He also picked up a caustic cinnamon odor from his initial and unsuccessful experiments that Waff—still terrified—had suggested over the past several days. For now, Uxtal left the half-awakened Tleilaxu Master locked in his chambers.

Uxtal ran for his life. He knew in his heart that, despite the best efforts of Waff, the whole process was flawed. The resurrected old Master did not, in fact, remember enough facts to make spice. His suggested methodology might have been a good beginning, but was not likely to achieve the desired results. Perhaps the two of them might have worked together to rediscover the process. But not with Bandalong under attack.

However, if a Guild Heighliner hovered overhead, maybe Navigator Edrik would rescue him! The Guild would surely want the awakened Waff ghola they had encouraged him to create—and Uxtal, too. The Navigator had to save both of them.

Uxtal heard loud voices and the hum of machinery over the distinct percussive explosions of gunfire and artillery fire. A voice yelled, "We are under attack! Matres and males, defend us!" Further words were drowned out by the sounds of automatic weapons fire, projectile guns, and pulse-stunners. He froze in his tracks, as he heard something else.

Ingva's voice.

His muscles jerked in response, and Uxtal found his legs carrying him involuntarily toward the sound. Sexually bonded by the hideous woman, he felt an irresistible compulsion to defend her, to protect her from the outside threat. But he had no weapons and no training in combat arts. Grabbing a piece of metal pipe from a debris pile near a collapsed wall, he ran toward the sounds of battle, barely able to think straight.

Uxtal saw at least twenty Honored Matres engaged with a larger force of women in black, spiny singlesuits. The invaders fought equally well with bladed weapons, projectile guns, and bare hands. The New Sisterhood's Valkyries! Swinging the pipe, Uxtal scurried into the fray, jumping over the bleeding bodies of Honored Matres. But the black-clad witches threw him aside, as if they didn't consider him worth killing.

With superior fighting skills, the Valkyries easily overwhelmed the Honored Matres. One of the women shouted, "Cease your fighting. Matre Superior is dead!"

Running behind them from the Palace, an appalled Honored Matre cried, "Hellica was a Face Dancer! We have been deceived!"

Uxtal stumbled to his feet, astonished by the assertion. Khrone had forced him to work in Bandalong, but the Lost Tleilaxu researcher had never understood why the Honored Matres would cooperate with eso-teric Face Dancer interests. If the Matre Superior herself had been a shape-shifter in disguise, however—

He nearly tripped over a moaning woman on the ground. She had been stabbed, but even so she clawed at him. "Help me!" Her voice was like a plucked string, controlling him. It was Ingva. Her orange eyes flared with anguish. Her scratchy voice carried an insistent anger over her bubbly pain. "Help me! Now!" Blood oozed from her side, and with each wheezing breath the gash spread open and closed like a gasping mouth.

He pictured her dominating him, raping him with unnatural skills that could draw even a eunuch into her sexual trap. Her grasping hand clung to his leg, but not in a caress. Explosions continued around them in the streets. Ingva tried to curse him, but could articulate no words.

"You are in great pain."

"Yes!" Her agonized glare showed that she thought he was pro-foundly stupid. "Hurry!"

It was all he needed to hear. He could not heal her, but he could stop her pain. He could help her that way. Uxtal was not a warrior, had not been trained in fighting techniques; his body was small and easily cast aside by these violent women. But when he drove his heel down hard, stomping with all his might on the throat of the hated Ingva, he discovered he was perfectly capable of crushing her neck.

With the terrible bond broken, he felt a peculiar giddy sensation in his stomach, and realized he now had a certain degree of freedom. More than he'd had in sixteen years.

The Honored Matres of Tleilax were obviously losing this battle— and badly. Then in the sky he saw two other ships descending toward the laboratory complex, different from the attack vessels brought by the witches. He recognized the Guild cartouche on the sides of the hull. Guildships, surreptitiously landing in the midst of the fray!

They must be coming to rescue him, along with the awakened Waff ghola who remained inside his private chambers. He had to get to where Edrik could find him.

More explosions pummeled the side of the main laboratory build-ing. Then a tower of flames curled upward as an aerial bomb exploded and demolished the warehouse section that held the numerous younger gholas. All of the alternative young candidates went up in a flash of fire and smoke, turned back into smears of cellular material. Uxtal observed the loss with a disappointed frown, then sprinted for shelter. Those extras weren't necessary anyway.

The two Guildships had already landed near the half-destroyed lab-oratory and sent out furtive searchers. But he could not get to them. Another New Sisterhood ship soared low, looking for targets. He saw a group of witches racing through the streets in their search; he could never get past them.

For the time being, he would simply have to hide and let the battle flow past him. The Lost Tleilaxu man did not care which faction won, or if they all destroyed each other. He was on *Tleilax*. He belonged here.

With the attention of the combatants diverted, Uxtal slipped away, crawled under a fence, and raced across a churned muddy field to the nearby slig farm. No one would have the slightest interest in a filthy low-caste farmer like Gaxhar. He could be safe there and demand sanc-tuary from the old man!

Scrambling for shelter, Uxtal reached a section of pens on the other side of the farm, where the farmer kept his fattest sligs. Looking back toward his now-burning laboratory, he saw a group of black-uniformed Valkyries marching swiftly across the field. It was just his bad luck—they would come here soon, he was sure of it. Why would they bother with a man who raised sligs? Other female fighters searched outlying buildings, intent on rooting out Honored Matres who had gone into hiding to lay an ambush. Had they seen him?

Ducking frantically out of sight, Uxtal slid into an empty, muddy pen on the other side of a gate where the fat sligs were kept. A small feed-storage shed was elevated on stone blocks, leaving a small space beneath. Uxtal squirmed into the cramped space where the dominating women—of either faction—would not see him.

Agitated by his presence, the sligs began to slither around in the mud and squeal in peculiar high-pitched tones on the other side of the gate. Uxtal crawled toward the building. The stench and filth made him want to retch.

"It's almost feeding time," a voice said.

Twisting to look through the gap under the shed, Uxtal saw the elderly slig farmer standing at the fence, peering through the slats at him. The slig farmer began tossing bloody scraps of raw meat—more human body parts—into the empty pen. Some of them landed very close to Uxtal. He pushed them away. "Stop, you fool! I'm trying to hide. Don't call attention to me!"

"You have blood on you now," Gaxhar said in a frighteningly casual voice. "That could draw them toward you."

Nonchalantly, the farmer raised the gate and let the hungry sligs through. Five of them: a most inauspicious number. The creatures were great slabs of flesh, their flopping bodies coated with dense mucous, their flat underbellies lined with grinding mouths that could churn any biological matter into digestible mush.

Uxtal scrambled away. "Get me out of here! I command it!"

The largest slig in the pen shoved into the crawl space where the Lost Tleilaxu was trapped, and fell on him. More sligs charged forward, pushing and colliding to reach the fresh meat. The loud grunting sounds easily drowned out the Lost Tleilaxu man's screams.

"I liked it better when all the Masters were dead," Gaxhar muttered.

The slig farmer heard gunfire and explosions in the distance. The city of Bandalong was already a raging inferno, but the battle did not come close to his farm. The lower-caste menial laborers in the nearby hovels were not worthy of notice.

Later, when his sligs had finished feeding, Gaxhar killed the largest and best one, which he had raised with painstaking care. That evening, with the last few sparks of battle rumbling through the city, he invited a few friends from the village to his home for a feast.

"No need to keep such fine meat for unworthy people anymore," he told them. He had fashioned a table and chair from crates and boards. His other guests sat on the floor. In these simple surroundings, the low-caste Tleilaxus ate until their bellies ached, and then they ate even more.

Love is one of the most dangerous forces in the universe. Love weakens, while deceiving us into believing it is a good thing.

—MOTHER SUPERIOR ALMA MAVIS TARAZA

Murbella.

He was supposed to be watching the no-ship. He knew that. But her name, her presence, her scent, her addictive control had grown even stronger since he'd started contemplating the possibility of bringing Murbella back as a ghola. It could be done; he knew it.

For him, the heart call had never entirely stopped in the nineteen years since he had broken from her. It was as if she had caught him in her own net, as deadly as the gossamer mesh cast by the old man and woman. Everything was too quiet during his lonely and tedious shift on the navigation bridge, giving him too many opportunities to think and obsess on her.

Now he intended to do something about it, to solve the problem. He pushed aside his rational assessment that it was a poor solution, a dangerous one, and he forged ahead.

Leaving the navigation bridge unattended again, he gathered up her still-fresh garments from nullentropy storage and went to the quarters of Master Scytale. The grayish Tleilaxu opened his chamber suspiciously, looking at Duncan and his armful of clothing. Behind him, the dimly lit room fuzzed with exotic scents of incense or drugs, and he caught a glimpse of the young Scytale copy. The boy was wide-eyed, both fearful and fascinated to receive a visitor. The Tleilaxu Master rarely let his ghola see or interact with anyone else aboard the ship.

"Duncan Idaho." Scytale looked him up and down, and Duncan had the distinct feeling that he was being assessed. "How may I be of service?"

Did the Tleilaxu still look on him as one of their creations? He and Scytale had been held prisoner together aboard the no-ship on Chapterhouse, but Duncan had never considered Scytale to be a comrade in arms. Now, though, he needed something from him.

"I require your expertise." He extended the rumpled garments, and Scytale flinched in confusion, as if they were weapons. "I preserved these within days of when we left Chapterhouse. I have found loose hairs, and there may be skin cells, other DNA fragments."

Scytale looked at them, frowning. He did not touch the clothing. "For what purpose?"

"To create a ghola."

The Tleilaxu Master already seemed to know the answer. "Of whom?"

"Murbella." He kept finding himself drawn back to the idea as if it were an inescapable black hole and he had already passed the event horizon in his mind. He had dark amber strands of her hair on a pale green towel. "You can grow her again. The axlotl tanks are no longer being used."

The boy Scytale stood close to his elder, who pushed him backward. The older Master appeared intimidated. "The whole program has been halted. Sheeana will not allow any new gholas."

"She will allow this one. I—I will demand it." He lowered his voice, mumbling to himself. "They owe me that much."

Sheeana's possibly prescient dream had forced her to regroup, to reconsider her plans and exercise caution. But now that several years had passed, discussions had already begun about experimenting with another ghola child or two. The fascinating cells from Scytale's nullentropy capsule were just too tempting. . . .

"Duncan Idaho, I do not believe this is wise. Murbella is an Honored Matre—"

"A *former* Honored Matre. And a ghola grown from these cells will . . . will be different." He didn't know if she would come back with her full memories and knowledge of a Reverend Mother, all the changes the Spice Agony had wrought. Regardless, she would be here.

"You would not understand, Scytale. Long ago, she tried to enslave me, to bond me with her sexual powers—and I did the same. We were bound together in a mutual noose, and I cannot break it. My performance and concentration has suffered for years, though I use my strength to resist."

"Why, then, would you wish to bring her back?"

Duncan pushed the rumpled clothes forward. "Because then at least I wouldn't suffer from this endless, destructive withdrawal! It will not go away, so I must find a different solution. I have ignored it for too long."

The fact that he was here at all reinforced his knowledge of the hold that she still had. Even the *thought* of Murbella tied his hands. He should have been on guard, watching from the navigation bridge, waiting to hear the next report from Sheeana or Teg . . . but the idea of resurrecting Murbella had reopened the festering heartache, making her loss seem fresh and painful all over again.

The Tleilaxu Master seemed to understand much more than Duncan wanted him to see. "You yourself know the danger in your suggestion. If you were as confident as you appear to be, you would not have waited until the others were down on the planet. You would not have come here like a thief, whispering your suggestion to me where no one else can hear." Scytale crossed his arms over his chest.

Duncan stared at him in silence, promising himself that he would not plead. "Will you do it? Is it possible to bring her back?"

"It is possible. As to your other question—" He could see Scytale calculating, trying to determine what sort of payment or reciprocal action he could pry out of Duncan.

The alarms startled them both. The danger lights, the warning of an imminent attack, the approaching ships—in so many years, the alert systems had been silent, and now the sounds were both startling and terrifying.

Duncan dropped the garments on the deck and ran for the nearest lift. He should have been on the navigation bridge. He should have been watching, not secretly talking with the Tleilaxu Master.

He would have time for guilt later.

The commsystems at the piloting station buzzed with Sheeana's voice. "Duncan! Duncan, why don't you respond?"

As he threw himself into the chair, he glanced up at the front viewport. A dozen small spacecraft were rising from the planet below, burning streaks through the atmosphere and moving directly toward the no-ship. "I am here," he said. "What's happening? What is your status?" The lighter was coming back at top speed, discarding safety restrictions.

Garimi's voice came over the in-ship channel. "I am already on my way to the receiving bay. Get the ship prepared to receive them. Something has gone terribly wrong down on the planet."

Now Duncan heard a faint emergency message chattering across the commline. Miles Teg, but his voice sounded weak. "Our maneuverability is severely compromised."

Tracer fire came from the other ships that followed close behind. Teg performed evasions with masterful agility, swooping one way and then another, closing in on the orbiting *Ithaca*. With the no-field in place, no one should have been able to see the giant ship's location.

Cursing his distraction and the stranglehold Murbella unwittingly still had on him, Duncan dropped the *Ithaca*'s no-field just long enough to let Teg see where to go. He was already warming up the navigation systems and the Holtzman engines.

Garimi had opened the small landing-bay doors on one of the lower decks, no more than a tiny speck on the hull of the great ship. But the Bashar knew where to go. He aimed directly toward the sanctuary, and the Handler ships closed in. Not designed as a fast military craft, the lighter was losing ground as the much swifter pursuers gained on it. More unidentified ships launched from the planet below. It had seemed to be such a bucolic civilization. . . .

Sheeana was on the commsystem again. "They're Face Dancers, Duncan. The Handlers are Face Dancers!"

Teg added, "And they are in league with the Enemy! We cannot let them have access to this ship. It's what they've wanted all along."

Sheeana joined in, her voice ragged with exhaustion. "The Handlers are not so primitive as they appeared. They have heavy weaponry that could disable the *Ithaca*. It was a trap."

On the screen, weapons fire barely missed the lighter, scoring the broad plane of the *Ithaca*'s hull. Teg did not decelerate, or alter course. On the commsystem, he sounded just like the old Bashar. "Duncan, you know what you have to do. If they come too close, just fold space and get away!"

Teg plunged the lighter into the open docking bay as fast as a bullet, only seconds ahead of the Handler ships. The pursuing craft raced forward, not decelerating, fully prepared to crash headlong into the *Ithaca*. To what purpose? To cripple the vessel so it couldn't leave?

From the landing bay, Garimi yelled, "Now, Duncan! Get us out of here!"

Duncan reactivated the no-field, and as far as the pursuers could see, the *Ithaca* vanished, leaving only a hole in space. The Handler ships could not land, nor did they pull up, apparently willing to do anything to prevent the *Ithaca* from escaping. Six of them continued to accelerate toward where the vessel had been—and plowed into the unseen hull of the no-ship like buckshot hitting a broad wall.

The impacts rocked the immense vessel, and the deck beneath Duncan's feet reeled and tilted. Though damage lights winked on all across the control panels, he saw that the foldspace engines were intact, functional, and ready to go.

The Holtzman engines hummed, and the ship began its move between and around the fabric of the universe. Alone on the navigation bridge, he watched the aurora of colors and bending shapes that surrounded the great vessel.

But something was interfering—a shimmering, multicolored grid of energy threads. The net had found them again! Thanks to the Handlers, the Enemy had somehow known exactly where to look.

The colors and shapes began to roil in reverse, unfolding. Now the next wave of pursuing Handler vessels could fire at the aberration in space, hitting the void and disabling the no-ship without actually seeing it.

Duncan plunged back into Mentat mode, seeking a solution, and a new course finally crystallized in his mind, a random path that would let him slip free of the binding strands. He hammered the engine controls, forced the foldspace equations.

This time the fabric of space wrapped around the *Ithaca*, caressed it, and drew it into the void—away from the planet, away from the Handlers, and away from the Enemy.

No matter how complex human civilization becomes, there are always interludes during which the course of mankind depends upon the actions of a single individual.

—from *The Tleilaxu Godbuk*

At the laboratory complex, during the hand-to-hand fighting between Valkyries and Honored Matres, among the explosions and conflagrations and streaking attack ships, no one noticed a small adolescent escaping through a blast hole in the laboratory wall and running away through the smoke.

Concealing himself, the only surviving Waff ghola hunkered down and wondered what to do. The black-uniformed women from the New Sisterhood marched about the city, mopping up. Bandalong had already fallen. The Matre Superior was dead.

Despite significant gaps in his memories and knowledge, Waff could recall difficulties the Bene Gesserit had given his predecessors. After seeing his seven counterparts slaughtered by Honored Matres, he had no desire to be taken prisoner by either group of women. The knowledge in his mind, though fragmented, was far too valuable for that. The witches and whores were both powindah, outsiders and liars.

He ran furtively into the dangerous streets. Because he had memories of being a Master, Waff was stunned and saddened to see this sacred city burning out of control. Once, Bandalong had been full of holy sites, kept pure and clean from outsiders. No longer. He doubted if Tleilax could ever be restored.

But at the moment, that was not Waff's mission. The Guild would want him. That much was certain. The Navigator who had observed his horrific awakening grasped the importance of having an authentic Tleilaxu Master, rather than that Lost fool Uxtal. He couldn't understand why the Navigators hadn't come to rescue him during the initial attack. Maybe they had tried. There had been so much confusion.

As he kept himself hidden, Waff began to consider the first tantalizing sparks of an idea. The Heighliner must still be up there.

AFTER DARKNESS SET in, the ghola found a small, low-orbital shuttle in a repair yard at the edge of the burning city. The shuttle's engine compartment was open, and tools lay about on the pavement. He saw no one as he cautiously approached.

A door in a dilapidated shed slid open, and a low-caste Tleilaxu emerged, wearing greasy coveralls. "What are you doing, kid? You need something to eat?" He wiped his hands on a cloth, which he stuffed in his pocket.

"I am not a child. I am Master Waff."

"All the Masters are dead." The short man had uncharacteristically blond hair and matching eyebrows. "Did you get hit on the head during the attack?"

"I am a ghola, but I have a Master's memories. Master Tylwyth Waff."

The man gave him a second, less skeptical look. "All right, I'll accept the possibility, for the sake of argument. What do you want?"

"I need a spacecraft. Does that shuttle fly?" Waff pointed at the old vessel.

"Just needs a fuel cartridge. And a pilot."

"I can fly it." He had enough of those memories.

The mechanic smiled. "Somehow I believe you, kid." He trudged over to a pile of components. "I confiscated a pallet of fuel cartridges during the battle. No one will notice, and it doesn't look like the Honored Matres will be around to punish either of us." He put his hands on his hips, regarded the shuttle, then shrugged. "This rig doesn't belong to me anyway, so what do I care?"

Within the hour, Waff flew up to orbit, where the Heighliner waited for the return of the Valkyrie attack force. The immense black vessel, larger than most cities, shimmered with reflected sunlight. Another Guildship, one obviously equipped with a no-field, circled the planet in a lower orbit.

Engaging the shuttle's commline, Waff transmitted a message over the standard Spacing Guild frequency, identifying himself. "I require a meeting with a Guild representative—a Navigator, if possible." He dredged a name from his recent memories, from the bloody day when his seven identical brothers had been slaughtered before his eyes. "Edrik. He knows I have vital information about spice."

Without further argument, a guidance signal locked onto his navigation controls, and Waff found himself drawn toward the Heighliner, directed upward to the elite-level bridges. The craft floated into a small, exclusive landing bay.

A security detail of four Guildsmen in gray uniforms greeted him. Much taller than Waff, the milky-eyed Guildsmen escorted him to the viewing compartment. High overhead, Waff saw a Navigator in his tank, staring down through the plaz with oversized eyes. With his plan to regain the technique of mass-producing melange, Edrik would never inform his Bene Gesserit passengers of Waff's presence on board.

A distorted voice spoke through speakers. "Tell us about spice. Tell us what you remember about axlotl tanks, and we will keep you safe."

Waff stared up at him defiantly. "Promise me sanctuary, and I will share the fruits of my knowledge."

"Even Uxtal did not make such demands."

"Uxtal did not know what I know. And he is probably dead. Now that my memories have awakened, you don't need him anymore." Waff was careful not to reveal his dangerous memory gaps.

The Navigator drifted closer to the wall, his huge eyes filled with eagerness. "Very well. We grant you sanctuary."

Waff had an alternate plan in mind. He remembered every aspect of the Great Belief and his duty to his Prophet.

"I can do better than create artificial, inferior melange using the wombs and chemistry of females. For envisioning safe pathways through space, a Navigator should have *real* melange, pure spice created by the processes of a sandworm."

"Rakis is destroyed, and sandworms are extinct, save for those few on the Bene Gesserit planet." The Navigator stared at him. "How will you bring back the worms?"

Grinning, Waff said, "You have more choices than you realize. Wouldn't you rather have your own sandworms? *Advanced* worms that can create a more potent spice for you Navigators . . . and only for you?"

Edrik swam in his tank, alien, incomprehensible, but unquestionably intrigued. "Continue."

"I am in possession of certain genetic knowledge," Waff said. "Perhaps we can reach a mutually beneficial arrangement."

We all have an innate ability to recognize flaws and weaknesses in others. It takes much greater courage, however, to recognize the same flaws in ourselves.

—DUNCAN IDAHO,
Confessions of More Than a Mentat

After six of the suicidal craft had pierced various parts of the *Ithaca* like spear points, emergency teams and automated systems had rushed to patch the no-ship's hull. Once an atmospheric field was put back into place, Duncan entered the unused bay where one of the Handler ships had crashed through the hull. On five additional decks, other vessels from the planet had also left wreckage and dead pilots.

Probing into the mangled craft, he discovered the burned remnants of a body. A Face Dancer. He looked at the blackened and inhuman corpse, burned beyond recognition. What had they wanted? How were Face Dancers in league with the old man and old woman who tried to capture them?

On his rushed inspection, after receiving reports from other searchers at the five remaining crash sites on different decks, Duncan had found that three of the mangled vessels held a pair of dead Face Dancers in each one, all killed on impact; this craft, however, held only one body, as did two of the other wrecks.

Three empty seats. Was it possible that those ships had each been flown solo? Or that one or more of the Handlers had ejected into space? Or had they somehow survived the crash and slipped away into the *Ithaca*?

After the frantic plunge through foldspace and away from the planet of the Handlers, while teams responded to the emergency, it had taken almost an hour to find each of the crashed ships on six different unoccupied decks.

Duncan was sure that nothing could have survived those crashes. The vessels were destroyed, the Face Dancer bodies trapped within the cockpits. Nothing could have walked away from the wrecks. And yet . . .

Could there now be as many as three Face Dancers secretly hiding in the corridors of the no-ship? Impossible! Even so, his greatest failing would be to underestimate the Enemy. He looked around the bay, sniffing, smelling the hot metal, caustic smoke, and the gritty residue of fire suppressors. An undertone of roasted flesh hung in the air.

He stared at wreckage for a long time, wrestling with his doubts. Finally he said, "Clean this up. Deliver samples for analysis, but above all, be careful. Be extremely careful."

THEIR RECENT ORDEAL was the closest the *Ithaca* had come to being captured since the original escape from Chapterhouse. Miles Teg and Sheeana, recovered now, had joined Duncan on the quiet navigation bridge, where they all waited in brooding silence. Unspoken words hung heavily, making the air nearly unbreathable.

The four members of the exploratory party had survived, even though the Handlers and Futars had tried to kill them. During the escape flight in the lighter, the old Rabbi had used his Suk training to check out the three other escapees, declaring them unharmed except for a few scrapes and bruises. He had not, however, been able to explain Teg's deep cellular exhaustion, and the Bashar had offered no answers.

Sheeana looked at the two men, the two *Mentats*, with her probing Bene Gesserit stare. Duncan knew she wanted explanations—and not just from him. He had suspected that Teg possessed secret, unexplained abilities for many years.

"I intend to understand." Her demand was so sharp and importunate, so impossible to ignore, that Duncan thought she was using Voice. "By hiding things from me, from *us*, both of you put our survival in jeopardy. Of all our enemies, secrets could be the most dangerous."

Teg's face held a wry expression. "An interesting comment for a person in your position to make, Sheeana. As a Mentat Bashar to the Bene Gesserit, I know that secrets are a valuable coin of the Sisterhood." He had eaten ravenously, gulped several melange-laden energy drinks, and then slept for fourteen hours. Even so, he still looked a decade older than he had been.

"That's enough, Miles! I can understand Duncan's burden of the old bonding to Murbella. It's festered in him ever since our escape from Chapterhouse, and I knew he had never succeeded in overcoming his addiction. But *your* behavior poses a true mystery to me. I saw you move down there with a speed that no human could hope to match."

Teg regarded her calmly. "Are you suggesting I am not human? Afraid that I might be a Kwisatz Haderach?" He knew Duncan had seen the same thing on two previous occasions, and the Honored Matres had spread rumors on Gammu about the old Bashar's inexplicable abilities. But Duncan had chosen not to question it. Who was he to accuse the other man?

"Stop these games." Sheeana crossed her arms over her chest. Her hair was in disarray. Using silence like a blunt hammer, she waited . . . and waited.

But Miles Teg also had Bene Gesserit training, and he did not submit to her probe. At last, she asked with a sigh, "Were you somehow altered in the axlotl tank? Did the Tleilaxu betray us after all, modifying you in strange ways?"

He finally broke through his icy wall of reservations. "This was an ability even the old Bashar had. If you must blame someone, point your finger at the Honored Matres and their minions." Teg looked from side to side, still clearly reluctant to reveal his secrets. "Under their torture, I developed certain unusual talents that I can use in times of great need."

"Accelerating your metabolism? Moving at superhuman speeds?"

"That, and other things. I also have the ability to see a no-field, though it remains invisible to all known means of detection."

"Why would you keep this secret from us?" Sheeana was genuinely confused; she looked betrayed.

Teg scowled at her. Even Sheeana didn't see it. "Because ever since Muad'Dib and the Tyrant, you Bene Gesserit have shown little tolerance for males with unusual abilities. Eleven Duncan gholas were killed before this one survived—and you can't blame every one of those assassinations on Tleilaxu intrigues. The Sisterhood had plenty of complicity, both passive and active."

He glanced at Duncan, who nodded coolly.

"Sheeana, you have an unusual talent, to control the sandworms. Duncan also has special skills. In addition to his ability to see the Enemy's net, he is genetically designed to be a sexual imprinter more powerful than the Bene Gesserit or the Honored Matres—which is how he ensnared Murbella long ago. That was why the whores were so desperate to kill him." Teg lifted a finger to emphasize a point. "And as the rest of our ghola children grow older and regain memories of their past lives, I suspect that some, if not all, will exhibit their own valuable skills, which will help us to survive. You will have to accept, and embrace, their anomalous skills, or else their very existence is moot."

Duncan heaved a deep breath. "I agree, Sheeana. Don't censure Miles for hiding his gifts. He saved us, and more than once. My own mistakes, on the other hand, nearly cost us everything." He pondered other times when his obsession with Murbella had distracted him, slowing his reactions during an unexpected crisis. "I can no more break free of Murbella than you or any other Reverend Mother could simply stop using spice. It is an addiction, and admittedly a destructive one. It's been nineteen years since I've seen her or touched her, and the wound still has not healed. Her powers of seduction, and mine, along with my perfect Mentat memories, prevent me from escaping her. Here on the *Ithaca* there are reminders everywhere."

Sheeana spoke, her voice quiet and cool, without compassion. "If Murbella felt the same way back on Chapterhouse, the whores would have sensed her weakness long ago and killed her. If she is dead—"

"I hope she is alive." Duncan rose to his feet from the pilot's chair, searching for strength. "But the need I still feel for her affects my ability to function, and I must find a way to break free. Our survival depends on it."

"And how will you accomplish that, if you haven't succeeded in all these years?" Teg asked.

"I thought I had a way. I suggested it to Master Scytale. But I know it was wrong. A delusion. Chasing that illusion took me away from the navigation bridge when I was most needed. I could not have known ahead of time, but even so, my obsession almost cost us everything. Again."

Closing his eyes, Duncan went into a Mentat trance, and forced himself back through his memories, digging deep into his sequential lifetimes. He searched for some personal handhold to grasp, and at last he found it: *Loyalty.*

Loyalty had always been the defining trait of his character. It was at the core of Duncan Idaho's being. Loyalty to House Atreides—to the Old Duke who had made possible his escape from the Harkonnens, to the son Duke Leto, and to the grandson Paul Atreides, for whom Duncan had sacrificed his first life. And loyalty to the great grandson Leto II, first a smart and endearing young boy and then the God Emperor who resurrected Duncan again and again.

But he found it harder to give his loyalty now. Maybe that was why he had lost his way.

"The Tleilaxu wired a ticking time bomb into you, Duncan. You were to ensnare and destroy Bene Gesserit imprinters," Sheeana said. "I was the real target, but Murbella triggered you first, and both of you found yourselves caught in the snare."

Duncan wondered if that innate Tleilaxu programming was at the root of his inability to break free of his obsession. Did they make him that way intentionally? *Damn the gods, I am stronger than this!*

When he looked over at her, Duncan saw that Sheeana wore a strange, determined expression. "I can help you break those chains, Duncan. Will you trust me?"

"Trust you? An unusual thing for you to ask."

Without answering, she turned and left the navigation bridge. Duncan could only wonder what she had in mind.

INSTANTLY ALERT, HE awoke in the darkness of his quarters. He heard the familiar faint tones of the no-ship's security door code activating in his chamber. No one knew that code but him! It was sealed within the memory banks of the vessel.

Duncan slid off the bed, moving like quicksilver, his senses on guard, his eyes absorbing details. Light spilled through the doorway from the corridor, outlining a figure there . . . female.

"I have come for you, Duncan." Sheeana's voice was soft and husky.

He took a step back. "Why are you here?"

"You know why, and you know I must."

She sealed the door behind her. The glowtabs in the room increased the illumination to just above the darkness threshold. Duncan saw tantalizing shadows, and her silhouette bathed in a soft orange glow. Sheeana wore next to nothing, a wispy gown that swirled around her like windblown spice silk revealing her entire figure.

His Mentat machinery whirled and suggested the obvious answer. "I did not ask—"

"Yes, you did!" *Using Voice on me?* "This was your demand of me, and it is your obligation. You know we were meant for each other. It is there inside you, down to your very chromosomes." She let the filmy garment fall, and stood before him, her body all curves and shadows with the highlights of her breasts and the honey-warmth of her skin enhanced by the faint illumination.

"I refuse." He stood straight and ready to fight. "Your imprinting will not work on me. I know the tools and techniques as well as you do."

"Yes, that is why we can use our mutual knowledge to break this hold Murbella has on you, shattering it once and for all."

"And make me just as addicted to you? I will fight it."

Her teeth shone in the shadows. "And I will fight back. In some species, that's an important part of the mating dance."

Duncan resisted, afraid to face his own weakness. "I can do this myself. I don't need—"

"Yes, you do. For the sake of us all."

She came forward with a languid yet unsettling speed. He reached out to stop her, and she grasped his hand, using it as an anchor to pull herself toward him. She made a humming noise deep in her throat, one of the priming tones that played on a subconscious mind, activating an atavistic nervous system.

Duncan felt himself responding, becoming aroused. It had been so long. . . . But he pushed her away. "The Tleilaxu wanted me to do this to you. They designed it in me so that I could destroy you. It's too dangerous."

"You were meant to destroy an untrained waif from Rakis, one who had no defenses against you. And you were meant to topple a Bene Gesserit Breeding Mistress, far less experienced than I am. Now, if anyone in the universe can stand up against the great Duncan Idaho, it is me."

"You have the vanity of an Honored Matre."

As if lashing out in anger, Sheeana grasped the back of his head, dug her fingers into the wiry black hair, and pulled his face to hers. She kissed him savagely, pressing her soft breasts against his bare chest. Her fingers touched nerve clusters in his neck and back, triggering programmed responses. Duncan froze for an instant, paralyzed. Her desperate, hungry kiss became more gentle. Helplessly, Duncan responded—perhaps more than Sheeana had bargained for.

He remembered how all this had been triggered in him the first time the Honored Matre Murbella had attempted to enslave him. He had turned the tables on her using his own sexual abilities. That noose had strangled him for so many years. He couldn't let it happen again!

Sensing her danger now, Sheeana tried to push him away. Her hand struck his shoulder a sharp blow, but he caught it and knocked her backward. They both tumbled onto the already rumpled sheets of his bed, fighting, embracing. Their duel turned into aggressive lovemaking. Neither had any hint of a choice once those floodwaters were unleashed.

In numerous clinical training sessions on Chapterhouse, Duncan had instructed Sheeana in these selfsame methods, and she in turn had helped to polish uncounted Bene Gesserit males who were turned loose as sexual land mines against the Honored Matres. The havoc those men wrought had sent the whores into an even greater frenzy.

Duncan found himself using all of his powers to break her, just as she tried to break him. The two professional imprinters collided, using their mutual abilities in a tug-of-war. He fought back in the only way he knew how. A moan escaped his throat, and it formed a word, a name. "Murbella . . ."

Sheeana's spice-blue eyes flew open, burning into him even in the dimness. "Not Murbella. Murbella did not love you. You know this."

"Neither . . . do . . . you." He wrenched the words out as a counterpoint to his rhythm.

Sheeana caught at him, and he nearly lost himself in the powerful wave of her sexuality. He felt like a drowning man. Even his Mentat focus had faded to a blinding distraction. "If not love, Duncan, then duty. I am saving you. *Saving* you."

Afterward they lay together, panting and sweating, as exhausted as Miles Teg must have been after he put his body through its incredible acceleration. Duncan sensed that the razor thread within him had finally broken. His connection to Murbella, as tight and deadly as a strand of shigawire, no longer held his heart. He felt different now, a sensation that was both giddy freedom and lost drifting. Like two enormous Guild Heighliners caroming off of each other, he and Sheeana had intersected with inexorable force, and now they moved away from each other on separate courses.

He lay holding Sheeana, and she didn't speak. She didn't have to. Duncan knew that at last he was drained, and stunned . . . and cured.

We create history for ourselves, and we have a fondness for partic-
ipating in grand epics.

—Bene Gesserit basic instruction,
Training Manual for Acolytes

They were magnificent ships, thousands upon thousands of them
lined up across a wine-dark sea. Overhead, a heavy grayness in
the sky set an appropriate mood with brooding clouds of war. The
tableau represented a fleet such as had never been gathered in all of
history.

"Awe-inspiring, is it not, Daniel?" Smiling, the old woman stood on
the weathered boards of the dock and looked across the imaginary
waters at the antique-design vessels, sharp-prowed Greek war galleys
with angry eyes painted on their prows. The triremes bristled with long
oars to be pulled by hordes of slaves.

The old man was not so impressed, however. "I find your preten-
tious symbols tiresome, my Martyr. As I always have. Are you suggesting *you* have a face worthy of launching a thousand ships?"

The woman let out a dry chuckle. "I don't consider myself classi-
cally beautiful or handsome—or even particularly male or female, for
that matter. But surely you can see how these events now are similar to
the start of the epic Trojan War. Let us paint the appropriate picture to
commemorate the event."

Of continuing concern to them, the one target they desperately sought—the wandering no-ship—had escaped yet again from the seeming certainty of a carefully laid trap. They still did not have the one thing the predictions said they needed.

With impatience and arrogance—decidedly human traits, though the old man would never admit that—he had decided to launch his great fleet anyway. It would take time to crush all the inhabited worlds of the Scattering and every planet of the Old Empire. By the time Kralizec neared its end, he was confident he would have what he needed. There was no logical reason to delay the expanded campaign.

The old man looked at the symbolic wooden war galleys crowding the faux ocean all the way to the horizon. With their sails furled, the boats rocked and creaked in the gentle swells. "Our fleet is thousands of times greater than the handful of boats used in that old war. And our real battleships are infinitely superior to this primitive technology. We are conquering a universe, not a minor country on a planet that most people have now forgotten."

Transfixed by the spectacle she had created, the old woman bent her bony legs to sit on the dock. "You have always been so maddeningly literal that metaphors are entirely beyond you. The Trojan War stands as one of the defining conflicts in human history. It is still remembered even now, tens of thousands of years later."

"Primarily because *I* preserved the records," said the old man with a huff. "This is to be Kralizec, not a skirmish between barbarian armies."

A stone appeared in the old woman's hand, and she tossed it into the water with a clear, loud splash. The spreading ripples vanished quickly in the stirring waves. "Even you want to cement your place in history, don't you? Paint yourself as a great conqueror. For that, you must pay particular attention to details."

The man stood rigidly beside her, eschewing the informality of sitting on the dock. "After my victory, I shall write all the history I like."

The old woman made an additional mental effort, and the illusory war galleys crystallized to the point that tiny figures appeared on their top decks, acting as crew. "I wish the Handlers had succeeded in capturing the no-ship."

"The Handlers have been punished for their failure," said the old man. "And my confidence remains unshaken. Our recent . . . discussions with Khrone should have helped clarify his priorities."

"It's a good thing you didn't kill him and scuttle his plans with the Paul Atreides ghola. I have warned you about impetuosity. One shouldn't throw away a possibility until all is said and done."

"You and your inane platitudes."

"Once more unto the breach," the old woman said.

"Why do you bother studying these humans so much if our goal is to destroy them?"

"Not destroy them. *Perfect* them."

The old man shook his head. "And you say that *I* embrace impossible tasks."

"It's time to launch."

"At last we agree on something."

She made a slight gesture with her pointed chin. The bare-chested commanders aboard the prows of the triremes shouted orders. Heavy war drums began thumping a resonant beat, completely synchronized across the thousands of Greek war galleys. Three rows of oars stacked on each side of the vessels lifted from the water in unison, dipped down, and pulled.

Behind them, where the edges of the imaginary ocean faded and reality began, the sharp lines of a tall and complex city resisted the softening effects of sea mists. The great living metropolis had spread across the entire planet, and similarly on numerous other worlds.

As the war galleys moved out, each one an icon symbolizing a space battle group, the images shifted. The sea became a black and infinite ocean of stars.

The old man nodded with satisfaction. "The incursion will proceed with greater vigor now. Once we begin to engage in direct battles, I will not allow you to waste time, energy, or imagination on such stage shows."

The old woman flicked her fingers as if to knock away an insect. "My amusements cost little, and I have never lost sight of our overall goal. Everything we see and do contains an element of illusion, in one form or another. We simply choose which layers to unveil." She shrugged. "But if you continue to nag me about it, I would be happy for us to revert to our original forms whenever you like."

In a blink, all of the realistic images were gone and the two found themselves standing in the midst of the immense kaleidoscopic metropolis.

"We have waited fifteen thousand years for this," the old man said.

"Yes, we have. But that isn't really very long for us, is it?"

Seeing is not knowing, and knowing is not preventing. Certainty can be as much of a curse as uncertainty. Without knowing the future, one has more options in forming a reaction.

—PAUL MUAD'DIB,
The Golden Chains of Prescience

The Oracle of Time kept herself aloof. She had existed since before the formation of the Spacing Guild, and in the subsequent millennia she had watched the human race grow and change. She witnessed their various struggles and dreams, their commercial ventures, the building of empires and the wars that tore them back down again.

Within her mind, within her artificial chamber, the Oracle had seen the broad canvas of the infinite universe. The wider her temporal horizons grew, the less significant were individual events or people. Some threats, however, were simply too momentous to ignore.

On her tireless search, the Oracle of Time left her Navigator children behind so that she could continue her solitary mission, while other parts of her vast brain considered possible defenses and methods of attack against the great ancient Enemy.

She plunged intentionally into the twisted alternate universe where she had found and rescued the no-ship years ago. In this strange quagmire of physical laws and inside-out sensory input, the Oracle sailed along, though she already knew Duncan Idaho would never have returned here. The no-ship was not inside this universe.

With a thought, she emerged again to normal space. There, she found the incorporeal traceries stitched through the void, a lacework of extended lines and conduits the Enemy had laid down. The strands of the tachyon net branched out farther and farther, questing like the root tendrils of an insidious weed. For centuries now, she had followed the extensions of the tachyon net in their random windings.

She shot along one such strand from intersection point to intersection point. If the Oracle followed them long enough and far enough, she would eventually reach the nexus from which they all emanated, but the pieces were not yet in position, and the timing was not right for that battle. Following the tachyon net farther would not serve the Oracle's purposes, nor would it take her to Duncan Idaho and the no-ship. If the net had found the lost vessel, the Enemy would have seized it already; therefore, logically, she needed to look beyond the net.

Soaring at the speed of thought, the Oracle remained amazed by the vessel's uncanny ability to elude her, yet she knew very well the power personified in a Kwisatz Haderach. And this particular one, by his very destiny, was more powerful than any previous one. The prophecies said so. Future history, when looked at from a broad enough perspective, was indeed predetermined.

Trillions of humans over tens of thousands of years had exhibited a latent racial prescient ability. In myths and legends, the same prediction kept cropping up—the End Times, titanic battles that signaled epic changes in history and society. The Butlerian Jihad had been one such battle. She had been there, too, fighting against the terrific antagonist that threatened to obliterate humanity.

Now, that ancient Enemy was returning, an all-powerful foe that the Oracle of Time had sworn to destroy back when she was a mere human named Norma Cenva.

She continued her search across the universe.

The future is not for us to see as passive observers, but for us to create.

—the recorded speeches of Muad'Dib,
edited by the Paul Atreides ghola

With Chani's help, Paul easily broke into the no-ship's spice stockpiles. Because of their personal connection and their burgeoning young romance, he and the Fremen girl frequently went off by themselves. The proctors no longer saw their behavior as unusual. Paul didn't doubt that the no-ship had surveillance imagers monitoring them, that some Bene Gesserits were assigned to watch over the children. But maybe—just maybe—he and Chani could get away with what they needed to do, if they moved quickly enough.

Paul did not falsify his affections for Chani in order to divert attention, however. Though neither of them possessed their previous life's memories, he truly cared for this girl, and he knew it would grow into something much more. He could rely on her when he did not dare trust anyone else, not even Duncan Idaho.

After pondering the question for weeks—especially after the *Ithaca's* near capture at the planet of the Handlers—Paul concluded that he had to consume the spice. The ghola children had been created for a specific purpose, and the danger remained close. If he was ever to help the people aboard the no-ship, he had to know what was really inside him.

He had to become the real Paul Atreides again.

The melange storage chamber was not heavily guarded. Since axlotl tanks now produced more than enough spice, the substance was no longer so rare as to warrant drastic protective measures. The spice was kept in metal cabinets protected only by simple locking mechanisms.

Always wary, like a true Fremen, Chani checked the doorway behind them to make sure no one had been alerted to their presence. Her gaze was intense and concerned, but she harbored no doubts about Paul.

The seals delayed him only for a few seconds. When he swung aside the metal door of the locker, a rich smell swept across him, redolent with the lure of potential memories. In preparation for their later obligations, all the ghola children received melange in carefully measured doses in their food. They were familiar with the flavor, but never consumed enough to experience any of the effects. Paul was well aware of how dangerous it could be. And how powerful.

Touching the neatly stacked spice, Paul knew it was all chemically identical, regardless of the manufacturing processes. Still, he searched among the wafers and selected several specific ones. He didn't know why, but in his heart he could feel it was right.

"Why those, Usul? Are the others poisoned?"

Then he understood. "Most of this spice came from axlotl tanks. But not these—" He showed her his chosen wafers, though they all looked the same. "This spice was made by *worms*. Sheeana harvested it from the sands in the hold. The closest thing to spice from Rakis itself." He took out several wafers of the compressed spice, much more than he had ever before consumed.

Chani's eyes grew wide. "Usul, that is too much!"

"It is what I need." He touched her cheeks. "Chani, spice is the key. I am Paul Atreides. Melange opened me to my potential before. Melange made me into what I became. I'm going to explode inside unless I find a way to unlock myself." He closed the storage cabinet again. "I am the oldest of the ghola children. This could be the answer for all of us."

When Chani set her jaw, the muscles in her lean, elfin face stood out. "As you say, Usul. Let us hurry."

They ran through the no-ship corridors, using private passages where few surveillance imagers would be, and opened one of the thousands of empty, unused cabins. They slipped inside together. What would the Sisterhood's watchers think of that?

"I should lie down before I start." He sat on the narrow bed. She brought him water from the wall dispenser, and he drank gratefully. "Watch over me, Chani."

"I will, Usul."

He sniffed the wafers of spice, merely guessing but pretending that he knew how much he had to consume. The smell was maddening, mouthwatering, terrifying.

"Be careful, my beloved." Chani kissed him on the cheek, then hesitantly on the lips, and stood back.

He ate the entire wafer, swallowing the burning melange before he could lose his nerve, then grabbed some more and ate it as well. Finally, feeling as if he had stepped off a cliff, he lay back and closed his eyes. A tingling numbness was already creeping in from his extremities. His body began breaking down the chemicals inside him, and he could feel the liberated energy surging through once-familiar pathways in this Atreides body.

And he fell into a pit of Time.

As everything grew dark and he dropped deeper into a trance, lost and searching for the road within him, Paul beheld flashes, familiar faces: his father Duke Leto, Gurney Halleck, and the icily beautiful Princess Irulan. At this level, his thoughts were unfocused. He couldn't tell if these were real flickers of memory or just stored data points boiling to the surface from accounts he had read in the Archives. He heard his mother, Jessica, reading words to him, the verse of a ribald song Gurney sang as he played his baliset, Irulan's unsuccessful attempts at seduction. But that was not enough, not what he sought.

Paul dug deeper. The spice sharpened the images until the details were too intense, too difficult to discern. The fragments suddenly coalesced, and he saw a true vision, like a snapshot of reality exploding inside his mind: He felt himself lying on a cold floor. He was bleeding, a knife wound deep within him. He felt warm blood pouring onto the floor. His own blood. With each pulse of his slowing heart, more and more redness drained away.

It was a mortal wound; he knew it as surely as any animal that crawls away to die. Paul's mind spun. He tried to look beyond himself to see where he was, to see who was with him. He was going to fade away and die there. . . .

Who had killed him? Where was this place?

At first he thought he was the ancient blind Preacher dying among crowds before the Temple of Alia in hot Arrakeen . . . but this wasn't Dune. There was no mob, no hot desert sunshine. Paul could discern the outlines of an ornate ceiling above him, a strange fountain nearby. He was in a palace somewhere, a great domed and colonnaded structure. Perhaps it was the Palace of Emperor Muad'Dib, like the model the ghola children had built in the recreation room. He could not tell.

Then he remembered an event from his library research. Count Fenring had stabbed him . . . an assassination attempt that would have placed the daughter of Feyd-Rautha and Lady Fenring on the new throne. Paul had very nearly died then.

Was he seeing a flashback of that crucial moment in the first years of his reign, during the bloodiest time of his jihad? It was so vivid!

But why, of all the memories that might be locked within him, would this particular one come to the front of his mind? What was its significance?

Something else didn't seem right. This memory felt uncrystallized and impermanent. Maybe the melange hadn't triggered his ghola memories at all. What if it had instead activated the famed Atreides *prescience*? Perhaps this was a vision of something deadly that was yet to occur.

As he lay writhing on his bed, deep in the spice-induced vision, Paul felt the pain of the wound as if it were unbearably real. *How can I prevent this from happening? Is this a true future I am seeing, a new vision of how my ghola body will die?*

The scene blurred before him. The dying Paul continued to bleed on the floor, his hands covered with red. Looking up, Paul was shocked to see *himself*, a young face very much like the one he routinely saw in a mirror. But this version of his face was pure evil, with mocking eyes and the laughter of gloating triumph.

"You knew I would kill you!" his other self shouted. "You could just as well have driven in the dagger with your own hands." Then he greedily consumed more spice, like a victor taking his spoils.

Paul saw himself laughing, and he felt his own life fading. . . .

PAUL WAS BEING shaken out of the blackness. His muscles and joints ached terribly, but this was nothing like the searing pain of the deep knife wound.

"He's coming around." Sheeana's voice, grim, almost scolding.

"Usul—Usul! Can you feel me?" Someone was clasping his hand. *Chani.*

"I don't dare risk another stimulant." It was one of the Bene Gesserit Suk doctors. Paul knew them all, since they had been so maddeningly efficient at checking the gholas for any possible physical flaw.

His eyes flickered open, but his vision was veiled with a blue spice haze. He saw Chani now, looking worried. Her young face was so beautiful, and such a stark contrast to that evil, laughing image of himself.

"Paul Atreides, what have you done?" Sheeana demanded, looming over him. "What were you hoping to accomplish? This was damned foolish."

His voice was dry, barely a croak. "I was . . . dying. Stabbed. I saw it."

This both alarmed and excited Sheeana. "You remember your first life? Stabbed? As an old blind man in Arrakeen?"

"No. Different." He searched in his mind, realized the truth. He'd had a vision, but had not triggered the full return of his memories.

Chani gave him water, which he gulped. The Suk doctor hovered over him, still trying to help, but she could accomplish little.

Coming out of the spice haze, he said, "It was prescience, I think. But I still don't remember my real life."

Sheeana gave the other Bene Gesserit Sister a sharp, startled look.

"Prescience," he repeated, with more conviction this time.

If he had meant to allay Sheeana's worries, Paul had not succeeded.

The flesh surrenders itself. Eternity takes back its own. Our bodies
stirred these waters briefly, danced with a certain intoxication
before the love of life and self, dealt with a few strange ideas, then
submitted to the instruments of Time. What can we say of this? I
occurred. I am not . . . yet, I occurred.

— PAUL ATREIDES,
Memories of Muad'Dib

Now that he was himself again, Baron Vladimir Harkonnen found
that his days on Caladan were always full, though not in a way
he would have preferred. Since his awakening, he had worked to
understand the new situation and how descendants of the Atreides had
mucked up the universe since he'd been gone.

Once, House Harkonnen had been among the wealthiest in the
Landsraad. Now the great noble house didn't even exist, except in his
memory. The Baron had plenty of work to do.

Intellectually and emotionally, he should have been pleased to lord
it over the homeworld of his mortal enemies, but Caladan didn't compare to his beloved Giedi Prime. He shuddered to think what that
place looked like now, and he longed to return there and restore it to
its former glory. But he had no Piter de Vries, no Feyd-Rautha, not
even his cloddish but useful nephew Rabban.

Khrone had, however, promised him everything—provided that he
helped the Face Dancers with their scheme.

Now that the Baron's ghola memories were back, he was allowed
some diversions. In the dungeons of the castle, the Baron had certain

playthings. Humming to himself, he skittered down the stairways to the lowest levels, where he paused to listen to the enchanting whispers and moans. The moment he entered the main chamber, however, everything fell silent.

His toys were arranged all around, according to his precise instructions: Torture racks with settings for pulling, squeezing, and cutting body parts. Masks on the walls with internal electronics that drove the wearers mad, could even wipe their brains if the Baron so desired. Chairs with electrocution connections and barbs to be installed in intriguing places. It was all so much better than anything Khrone had used.

Two handsome boys—slightly younger than himself—hung from the walls, secured by chains. Eyes filled with terror and a profound sadness watched his every move. Their clothes were ripped where he had torn them away for his own enjoyment.

"Hello, my beauties." They did not respond in words, but he saw them flinch. "Did you know that both of you have Atreides blood flowing through your veins? I have the genetic records to prove it."

Whimpering, the pair denied the assertion, though in truth they had no way of knowing. The bloodline had become so watered down after all this time, who could tell without a full genetic workup? Well, it was the sentiment that really mattered, wasn't it?

"You can't blame us for the sins of centuries ago!" one cried pitifully. "We will do whatever you say. We will be your loyal servants."

"My loyal servants? Oh-ho, but you already are." He moved close to the one who had pleaded, caressed his golden hair. The boy trembled and looked away.

The Baron felt aroused. This one was so lovely, his cheeks smooth with only a thin fuzz of undeveloped beard, his features almost feminine. Touching the soft skin of the face, he closed his eyes, and smiled.

When he opened them again, he was shocked to see that the victim's features had changed. Now the beautiful boy was a young woman with dark hair, an oval face, and the deep blue eyes of spice addiction. She was laughing at him. The Baron backed up. "I'm not seeing this!"

"Oh, but you are, Grandfather! Didn't I grow up to be beautiful?" The lips of the chained woman moved, but the voice came from inside his mind. *I let you think you got rid of me, but that was just my little game. You like games, don't you?*

Muttering nervously, the Baron retreated from the torture chamber and scuttled down the dank hall, but Alia stayed with him. *I'm your permanent companion, your lifetime playmate!* She laughed, and laughed some more.

When he reached the main floor of the castle, the Baron anxiously scanned the weapons hanging on the walls and in display cases. He would dig Alia out of his brain, even if that required killing himself. Khrone could always bring him back as a ghola. She was like a noxious weed, spreading toxins through his body.

"Why are you here?" he shouted aloud into the ringing silence of the stone-walled banquet room. "How?"

It seemed an impossibility to him. Harkonnen and Atreides bloodlines had crossed in centuries past, and the Atreides were known for their Abominations, their strange prescience, their peculiar way of thinking. But how had this infernal taint of Alia infested *his* mind? Damn the Atreides!

He marched toward the main entrance, past several bland Face Dancers who looked at him inquisitively. *Must not act up in front of them.* He smiled at one, then another.

Isn't it fun to relive old glories and vengeance? asked the Alia-within.

"Shut up, shut up!" he hissed under his breath.

Before he could reach a pair of tall wooden doors, they swung open on massive hinges, and Khrone entered the castle accompanied by an entourage of Face Dancers and a young dark-haired boy with oddly familiar features. He was six or seven years old.

The voice of Alia-inside was filled with delight. *Go welcome my brother, Grandfather!*

Khrone pushed the boy forward, and the Baron's generous lips curved in a hungry smile. "Ah Paolo, at last! You think I do not know Paul Atreides?"

"He will be your ward, your student." Khrone's voice was stern. "He is the reason we have nurtured you, Baron. You are our tool, and he is our treasure."

The Baron's spider-black eyes lit up. He went straight to the child, and studied him closely. Paolo glared back at him, which caused the teenage Baron to chuckle in delight.

"And what, exactly, am I allowed to do with him? What is it you want?"

"Prepare him. Raise him. See that he is primed for his destiny. There is a certain need he must fulfill."

"And what is that?"

"It will be explained to you in due course, when the time is right."

Ah, Paul Atreides in my grasp, so I can ensure that he is raised properly this time. Just like my nephew Feyd-Rautha, a lovely boy in his own original lifetime. This will make up for a great many historical wrongs.

"You now have your memories, Baron, so you can understand the true complexities and consequences. If he is harmed, we will find a very special way to see that you regret it." The Face Dancer leader was quite convincing.

The Baron dismissively waved a pudgy hand. "Of course, of course. I was always sorry that I disconnected his axlotl tank back on Tleilax. That was foolish and impulsive of me. I didn't know any better. I have learned restraint since then."

A burst of pain lanced through his head, making him wince. *I can help you with your restraint, Grandfather,* Alia said inside his skull. He wanted to scream at her.

With a colossal mental push, the Baron drove her away, then chuckled as he bent toward the young ghola. "I've been waiting a long time for this, lovely boy. I have so many plans for the two of us."

Command must always look confident. Respect all that faith riding on your shoulders while you sit in the critical seat, even though you must never show that you feel the burden.

—DUKE LETO ATREIDES,
notes for his son, recorded in Arrakeen

Tleilax had been conquered, and the rebel Honored Matres were no longer a threat. The Valkyries had flawlessly accomplished their most important mission, and the Mother Commander could not suppress her feelings of pride, both in her daughter and in the whole New Sisterhood.

At last, we can move on.

Under the domed rotunda of the Chapterhouse library, Murbella had little time to rejoice or reflect on the recent victories. She glanced out a small window toward the skeletal orchards and the ravenous desert beyond. The sun was setting on the horizon, outlining the craggy rock escarpments as an artist might. Each time she looked, the desert seemed to loom larger and closer. It never stopped advancing.

Like the Enemy . . . except that the Bene Gesserit had intentionally put the sands in motion, sacrificing everything else to produce one substance—melange—for the ultimate victory they hoped to achieve. The war against the Honored Matres had cost humanity dearly for the past several decades, inflicting great harm and destroying many planets. And the whores were by far the lesser threat.

Accadia, the old Archives Mother, stood in the center of the projection field in silent reverence, with a hundred of the New Sisterhood's most intelligent followers. "This shows what you need to know, and the scope of the threat we now face. I've drawn heavily on candid testimonies provided by our former Honored Matres, tracking their initial expansion into unexplored territories . . . and their recent abrupt withdrawal back into the Old Empire."

Now that Murbella had broken through the black wall in her Other Memories, she understood exactly what the Enemy was and what the Honored Matres had done to provoke them. She knew more about the nature of the Outside Enemy than Odrade, Taraza, or any previous Bene Gesserit leader had ever guessed.

She had lived those lives.

In particular she saw herself as a harsh, ambitious, and successful commander, driving her squadron of ships outward, ever outward. *Lenise. That was my name.* In those days she'd had spiky black hair, obsidian eyes, and an array of metal adornments protruding from her cheeks and brow—battle trophies, one for each rival she had killed in her rise to power. But after failing in a bid to assassinate a higher rank, she had taken her loyal squadrons and plunged farther out into uncharted territory. Not as an act of cowardice, Lenise had assured herself. Not to flee. But to conquer new territory of her own.

In their rapacious expansion, she and her Honored Matres had blundered into the fringe of a vast and growing empire—a nonhuman empire—the existence of which had not been previously suspected. Unknown to them, this dangerous Enemy had its genesis more than fifteen thousand years ago, in the last days of the Butlerian Jihad.

The Honored Matres had encountered a strange manufacturing outpost, a bustling interconnected metropolis inhabited entirely by machines. Thinking machines. The significance of this had been lost on Lenise and her women; they had asked few questions about the origin of what they'd found.

The self-perpetuating, evolving computer evermind had taken root again, building and spreading a vastly networked landscape of machine intelligences. Lenise had not understood, nor had she cared.

She had issued the order—lost in the vision of history now, Murbella mouthed the words again—and the Honored Matres had done what they did best: attacking without provocation, expecting to conquer and dominate.

Never guessing the scale or strength of what she had found, Lenise and her Honored Matres had surprised the machines, stolen shiploads of powerful and exotic weapons, destroyed the outpost . . . and then left. She had added several metal adornments to her face to celebrate the victory. And then returned to reconquer the other Honored Matres who had initially defeated her.

The machines' response had been swift and terrible. They launched a massive retaliation that swept forward into the settled worlds of the Scattering, exterminating whole Honored Matre planets with deadly new viruses. The Enemy continued to hound them, hunting down and destroying the whores in their hiding places.

Murbella saw various generations in different memories. Never terribly subtle, the Honored Matres began their panicked flight, stampeding across star systems, plundering them before moving on. Setting bonfires and burning bridges behind them. What an embarrassment to them . . . how resoundingly they had been defeated by their foe!

All the while, they led the Enemy toward the Old Empire.

Murbella knew it all. She saw it vividly in her past, in her history, in her memories. She needed to Share those experiences with other Sisters who had not yet unlocked their generational secrets. *The Enemy is Omnius. The Enemy is coming.*

Now, under the domed rotunda with the audience hushed, Accadia worked the display with gnarled fingers. A holoprojection of the Known Universe materialized over their heads in the great vaulted room, highlighting key star systems in the Old Empire as well as planets described by those who had returned from the Scattering. A variety of independent federations had formed out there—clustered governments, trade alliances, and isolated religious colonies, all tied together by a thin common thread of humanity.

The Tyrant spoke of this in his Golden Path, Murbella thought. *Or is our understanding imperfect, as usual?*

The old librarian's voice crackled. "Here are the planets the whores already charred, using the terrible Obliterator weapons they stole from the Enemy."

A spangle of red spattered like blood across the star chart. Too much red! So many Bene Gesserit planets, even Rakis, all of the Tleilaxu worlds, and any other planet that happened to be in the way. Lampadas, Qalloway, Andosia, the low-gravity fairyland cities on Oalar . . . Now graveyards, all of them.

How could she not have seen this blatant horror when she called herself an Honored Matre? *We never looked behind us except to find out how close the Enemy was. We knew we had provoked something ferocious, but we still barged into the Old Empire like a hound into a chicken house, wreaking havoc in our attempt to flee.*

When the Enemy got here, the stirred-up planets would fight instinctively, and they would be annihilated. The Honored Matres used that as a stalling tactic, throwing obstructions in the path of the oncoming opponent.

"The whores did all that?" breathed Reverend Mother Laera, one of Murbella's administrative advisors.

Accadia seemed intrinsically fascinated by what she could show. "Look—this is far more frightening."

Another swath of the perimeter systems turned a dull, sickly blue. The star charts displayed some as blurry points, indicating unverified coordinates. The number of affected worlds was far greater than the red wound of Honored Matre destruction.

"These are the planets we know have already been destroyed by the Enemy out in the Scattering. Honored Matre worlds wiped out primarily through devastating plagues."

Studying the huge, complex projection, Murbella didn't need a Mentat to draw the obvious conclusions from the patterns she saw. Her Bene Gesserit and Honored Matre advisors muttered uneasily. They had never before seen the outside threat so plainly displayed.

Murbella could truly sense the nearness of "Arafel," the cloud-darkness at the end of the universe. With so many dark legends pointing in the same direction, she smelled her human mortality.

Even Chapterhouse, marked on the three-dimensional holoprojection as a pristine white ball far from the Guild's main shipping lanes, would become the target of those relentless hunters.

The unified Sisters now had the Spacing Guild to assist them, though Murbella did not fully trust the Navigators or the less-mutated Administrators. She harbored no illusions about a lasting alliance with the Guild or CHOAM, if the war went badly. The Navigator Edrik dealt with her only because she'd bribed him with spice, and he would cease to cooperate if he ever found an alternative source of melange. If the Guild's administrative faction chose to rely on Ixian mathematical compilers, then she had very little hold over them.

"The Enemy does not seem to be in a particular hurry," Janess said.

"Why should they be?" Kiria said. "They are coming, and nothing seems able to slow them."

Searching, Murbella noted the general mark—a locus in space, poorly defined by only anecdotal coordinates—of the first encounter with the Enemy, where a long-dead Honored Matre named Lenise had stumbled upon the fringe outpost.

And now we are left to clean up the mess.

Maybe her beloved Duncan Idaho would survive far out there. She felt a pang for him in her heart. What if, at the end of fabled Kralizec, the only remnants of humanity were those few with Duncan and Sheeana aboard the no-ship? A life raft in the cosmos. She scanned the grand projection that filled the library. She had no idea where the vessel might be.

Each life is the sum total of its moments.

—DUNCAN IDAHO,
Memories of More Than a Mentat

D uncan looked in on the ghola children as they engaged in a role-playing game inside one of the activity chambers. They had grown old enough now to show distinct personalities, to think and interact not only with each other but with the crew members. They understood their prior relationships and tried to deal with the oddities of their existence.

Genetically a grandmother to little Leto II, Jessica had bonded closely with him, but she acted more like his big sister. Stilgar and Liet-Kynes were close, as usual; Yueh tried to be friends with them, but he remained a perpetual outsider, though Garimi studied him very closely. Thufir Hawat seemed to have changed, matured, since his experiences on the planet of the Handlers; soon, Duncan expected the young warrior-Mentat to be very useful to their planning. Paul and Chani always stayed close to each other, though she seemed a veritable stranger to Liet, her "father."

So many living reminders of Duncan's pasts.

In her last assessment the Proctor Superior had offered her analysis that the Bene Gesserits should begin to awaken their memories. At least some of the ghola children were ready. Duncan felt a twinge of anxiety and anticipation.

As he turned to walk away, he saw Sheeana standing in the empty corridor, watching him with an enigmatic smile. He felt an involuntary flush of desire, followed by embarrassment. She had bonded him, broken him . . . saved him. But he would not let himself become trapped by her the way he had been bound to Murbella. He forced out the words. "It is best if we keep our distance from each other. At least for now."

"We're on the same ship, Duncan. We can't just hide."

"But we can be careful." He felt burned by the sexual cauterization that had cured him of Murbella, but knew it had been necessary. His own weakness had made it necessary. He dared not let it happen again, and Sheeana had the power to ensnare him—if he let her. "Love is too dangerous to play with, Sheeana. It is not a tool to be used."

ONE LAST THING remained for him to do, and he couldn't avoid it any longer. Duncan had retrieved all of Murbella's belongings. Master Scytale had carefully picked over them after Duncan had unceremoniously dropped them on the deck when the alarms rang. Duncan had demanded them back, then turned a deaf ear as the Tleilaxu Master insisted that most of the cells were too old, too long out of nullentropy storage, but the possibility of usable DNA fragments—

Duncan had cut him off, walked away with the garments. He didn't want to hear any more, didn't want to know about the possibilities. All such possibilities were unwise ones.

He had tried to fool himself that he could just ignore the idea, make up his mind not to think about her anymore. Sheeana had freed him of his chains to Murbella . . . but, oh, the temptation! He felt like an alcoholic staring at an open bottle.

Enough. Duncan himself had to do the last of it.

He stared at the rumpled garments, the keepsakes, the few stray strands of amber hair. When he gathered everything in his arms, it was as if he held her—at least the essence of her, without the weight of her body. His eyes misted over.

Murbella hadn't left much of herself behind. Despite all the time she'd spent on the no-ship with Duncan, she'd kept only a few temporary possessions here, never really calling it her home.

Remove the threat. Remove the temptation. Remove the possibility. Only then could he finally be free.

Marching down the corridors with intense concentration, he made his way to one of the small maintenance airlocks. Years ago, this was how they had ejected the mummified remains of Bene Gesserit Sisters into space during the memorial service. Now Duncan would perform another sort of funeral service.

He dumped the paraphernalia into the airlock booth and considered the rumpled debris of a past life. It seemed like so little, but with such great portent. He stepped back and reached for the controls.

From the corner of his eye, he noticed a strand of hair still clinging to his sleeve. One of Murbella's hairs had come loose from her garments, a single amber strand . . . as if she still wanted to cling to Duncan.

He plucked the hair with his fingertips, looked at it for a long, painful moment, and finally let it drift down among the other items. He sealed the airlock door and, before he could think, cycled the systems. The last breaths of air were evacuated, and the material was swept out into space. Irretrievable.

He stared out into the emptiness, where the objects quickly disappeared from view. He felt immeasurably lighter . . . or perhaps that was just emptiness.

From now on, Duncan Idaho would rise above any temptations that were thrust in front of him. He would be his own man, no longer a piece to be moved around on someone else's game board.

⚬⚬

At last, after our long journey, we have reached the beginning.
—ancient Mentat conundrum

The Enemy ships cruised toward the Old Empire, thousands upon thousands of enormous vessels, each carrying weapons sufficient to sterilize a planet, plagues that could eradicate entire populations. Everything was going extremely well after so many millennia of planning.

Back on the central machine world, the old man had dropped his illusions. No more games or façades, only rigid preparations for the final conflict foretold both by human prophecy and extensive machine calculations: *Kralizec.*

"I assume you're quite pleased that you have already destroyed sixteen additional human planets on your march to victory." The old woman had not yet dispensed with her guise.

"So far," said the booming old man's voice that echoed from all buildings and all screens everywhere.

The structures in the endless machine city were alive and moving like an immense engine, tall towers and spires of flowmetal, enormous blocky constructions built to house substations and command nodes.

With each new conquest, cities just like Synchrony would be built on planet after planet.

The old woman looked at her hands, brushed the front of her dress. "Even these forms seem primitive to me, but I have grown rather fond of them. Perhaps *accustomed* is a more precise word." At last, her voice faded, changed, and settled on an old familiar timbre. In her place stood the independent robot Erasmus, intellectual foil and counterpoint to Omnius. He had retained his platinum, flowmetal body, draped in the plush robes to which he had grown accustomed so long ago.

Having discarded his physical form, Omnius spoke through millions of speakers in the great city. "Our forces have pushed to the fringes of the human Scattering. Nothing can stop us." The computer evermind always had such grandiose dreams and aspirations.

Erasmus had hoped that by constraining the evermind within the guise of an old man, Omnius might begin to understand humans and learn to steer clear of these extreme gestures. That had worked for a few thousand years, but when the violent Honored Matres careened into the carefully reconstituted Synchronized Empire, Omnius had been forced to respond. In truth, the anxious evermind had simply been looking for an excuse.

Now he said, "We will prove that the Butlerian Jihad was merely a setback, not a defeat."

Erasmus stood in the middle of the vast, vaulted chamber of the central machine cathedral. All around them, the buildings themselves stepped back, shifting aside like sycophants. "This is an event we should commemorate. Behold!"

Though the evermind thought he controlled everything himself, Erasmus made a gesture, and the floor of the chamber cooperated. The smooth metal plates spread apart, pulling away to reveal a crystal-lined gullet, a wide pit whose floor rose up, lifting a preserved object.

A small and innocuous-looking probe.

"Even seemingly insignificant things have great import. As this device proves."

Centuries before the Battle of Corrin, the last great defeat of the thinking machines, one of the evermind copies had dispatched probes out to the unexplored reaches of the galaxy with the intent of setting up receiving stations, planting seeds for the later expansion of the machine empire. Most of the probes had been lost or destroyed, never reaching a solid world.

Erasmus looked down at the small device, marvelously engineered, pitted and discolored from its many centuries of unguided flight. This probe had found a distant planet, landed, and begun its work, waiting . . . and listening.

"During the Battle of Corrin, fanatical humans almost—*almost*—annihilated the last Omnius," the robot said. "That evermind contained a complete and isolated copy of me inside itself, a data packet from the time when you once tried to destroy me. You showed great foresight."

"I always had secondary plans for survival," the voice boomed. Watcheyes came closer, flitting over the probe like curious tourists.

"Come now, Omnius, you never imagined such a dramatic defeat," Erasmus said, not scolding but merely stating a fact. "You transmitted a complete copy of yourself off into nothingness. A last-gasp attempt at survival. A desperate hope—something a human might feel."

"Do not insult me."

That transmission had traveled for thousands of years, degrading along the way, deteriorating into something else. Erasmus had no memory of that endless, silent journey at the speed of light. After their incalculable trek through static and interstellar waste, the Omnius signal had encountered one of the long-dispatched probes and seized upon it as a beachhead. Far, far from any taint of human civilization, the restored Omnius began to re-create itself. Over millennia it had regenerated, building a new Synchronized Empire—and Omnius had begun making plans to return, this time with a far superior machine force.

"Nothing can match the patience of machines," the evermind said.

Fully restored from his backup copy while the new civilization built itself, Erasmus had pondered the fate of humans, a species he had studied in painstaking detail. The creatures had always been infuriating, yet intriguing. He was curious as to how they would fare without the guidance of efficient machines.

He looked down at the small probe on its altarlike stand. If that receiver hadn't been in the right place, the Omnius signal might still be drifting, attenuating. Quite an ignominious end . . .

Meanwhile, believing themselves victorious, the human race had gone through their own struggles. They continued to push their boundaries; they clashed with each other. Ten thousand years after the Battle of Corrin, a Tleilaxu Master named Hidar Fen Ajidica improved and dispatched a new breed of Face Dancers as colonists bound for far-flung wastelands.

As his empire regrew, Omnius had intercepted those first Face Dancer ambassadors—beings based on humans but with some attributes of the best machines. Erasmus, fascinated with the possibilities, had quickly converted them to appropriate goals, then bred more of the shape-shifters.

In fact, the independent robot still had some of those first Face Dancer specimens preserved in long-term storage. Occasionally he took them out for inspection, just to remind himself of how far he had come. Long ago on Corrin, Erasmus had dabbled with similar biomechanics, trying to create biological machines that could mimic the flowmetal capabilities of his own face and body. His new breed of Face Dancers did that, and more.

Erasmus could replay all of the memories in his head. He wished he had a few more of those Face Dancers here, to experiment on because they were so fascinating, but he had already sent them back into the human-settled star systems, to pave the way for the great machine conquest. He had already absorbed the lives and experiences of thousands of these Face Dancer "ambassadors." Or were they better called spies? Erasmus had so many of them ringing through his head that he was no longer entirely himself.

Knowing the strength and capabilities of human civilization and understanding the extent of his enemy's capabilities, Omnius had reassembled his forces. Large asteroids were broken down and converted into raw materials. Construction robots assembled weapons and battleships; new designs were tested, improved, tested again, and then produced in great numbers. The buildup lasted for thousands of years.

The result was indisputable. Kralizec.

When he could tell that Omnius was not impressed with history or nostalgia, Erasmus caused the floor to swallow the enshrined probe again and fill the crystal-walled gullet.

Leaving the vaulted cathedral, the robot strode through the streets of the synchronized city. The structures moved around him, pumping and sliding smoothly, always leaving openings for him. He pondered the buildings, all of which were mere manifestations of the evermind's spreading body. He and Omnius had both evolved greatly over fifteen millennia, but their goals remained the same. Soon every planet would be exactly like this one.

"No more games or illusions," said the booming voice of Omnius. "We must focus on the greater battle. We are what we are." As he listened, Erasmus wondered why the evermind liked to hear himself talk so much. "We have gathered our strength, measured our enemy, and improved our odds of success."

"Remember, we still need the Kwisatz Haderach, according to our mathematical projections," Erasmus cautioned.

Omnius sounded miffed. "If we get a human superman, so much the better. But even if we do not, the conclusion of this conflict is still clear."

The independent robot linked himself to the computer evermind, accessing everything that Omnius could see and experience. A part of the extravagant computer was aboard each one of the numerous machine war vessels. Through the connection Erasmus could see the vessel swarms plunging ahead, spreading plagues, launching waves of destruction. They were expanding the boundaries of the machine empire, and soon they would swallow all human territories.

Efficiency required it. Omnius required it. The great battleships moved onward.

BRIEF TIMELINE OF THE DUNE UNIVERSE

Approx 1287 B.G. (Before Guild)

Time of Titans begins, led by Agamemnon and "Twenty Titans," all of whom eventually convert to cymeks, "machines with human minds."

1182 B.G.

The overly independent and aggressive computer network of the Titan Xerxes seizes control over several planets. Naming itself Omnius, the "evermind" takes over all Titan-ruled planets in a short time and establishes the Synchronized Worlds. The surviving Titans are made servants of Omnius. Unconquered human planets form the "League of Nobles" to stand against the spreading Synchronized Empire.

203 B.G.

Tio Holtzman, taking work from his assistant Norma Cenva, develops his scrambler shield and lays the basis for his famed equations.

201 B.G.

Beginning of Butlerian Jihad, after centuries of thinking-machine oppression. The independent robot Erasmus kills the baby of Serena Butler, inadvertently triggering a widespread revolt.

200 B.G.

Using atomics, the League of Nobles wipes out the thinking machines of Earth.

108 B.G.

End of Butlerian Jihad. Massive and widespread atomic strikes led by Vorian Atreides and Abulurd Harkonnen destroy all thinking machine infestations except for one last stronghold on Corrin.

88 B.G.

The Battle of Corrin destroys the last evermind, Omnius. Abulurd Harkonnen banished for cowardice, beginning the age-long rift between House Atreides and House Harkonnen.

Later, formation of Bene Gesserit, Suk doctors, Mentats, Swordmasters.

1 A.G. (approx A.D. 13,000)

Foldspace Shipping Company takes the name Spacing Guild and monopolizes space commerce, transport, and interplanetary banking.

After the horrors of the Butlerian Jihad, the Great Convention forbids all further use of atomics or biological agents against human populations.

Council of Ecumenical Translators releases the Orange Catholic Bible, meant to quell all religious divisions.

10,175 A.G.

Birth of Paul Atreides

10,191 A.G.

House Atreides leaves Caladan to take over spice operations on Arrakis, triggering the chain of events that leads to Muad'Dib becoming emperor.

10,207 A.G.

Birth of twins Leto II and Ghanima

10,217 A.G.

Leto II begins symbiosis with sandtrout, overthrows Alia, begins his 3,500-year reign as God Emperor of Dune.

13,725 A.G.

Assassination of God Emperor by Duncan Idaho. Sandworms return to Rakis.

Later, Famine Times
    The Scattering

14,929 A.G.

Birth of Miles Teg, who will become the great Bashar, a military hero for the Bene Gesserit.

15,213 A.G.

The twelfth (current) Duncan Idaho ghola of the Bene Gesserit project is born.

Honored Matres begin to return from the Scattering, wreaking havoc and destroying anyone in their way. They are apparently fleeing from something even worse, a mysterious Outside Enemy.

15,229 A.G.

Honored Matres destroy Rakis with devastating weapons stolen from the Enemy. Only one sandworm survives, brought to Chapterhouse by Sheeana.

15,240 A.G.

Battle of Junction destroys most Honored Matre leadership, beginning of great unification of Bene Gesserits and Honored Matres under Murbella. Duncan Idaho, Sheeana, and others flee in no-ship to escape the Enemy and avoid the dangers of unification.

(compiled with the assistance of Dr. Attila Torkos)